The WHITE RUSSIAN

ALSO BY VANORA BENNETT

The WHITE RUSSIAN

VANORA BENNETT

Thomas Dunne Books
St. Martin's Press
New York

THOMAS DUNNE BOOKS.
An imprint of St. Martin's Press.

THE WHITE RUSSIAN. Copyright © 2014 by Vanora Bennett. All rights reserved. Printed in the United States of America. For information, address St. Martin's Press, 175 Fifth Avenue, New York, N.Y. 10010.

www.thomasdunnebooks.com
www.stmartins.com

The Library of Congress Cataloging-in-Publication Data is available upon request.

ISBN 978-1-250-07941-1 (hardcover)
ISBN 978-1-4668-9214-9 (e-book)

Our books may be purchased in bulk for promotional, educational, or business use. Please contact your local bookseller or the Macmillan Corporate and Premium Sales Department at 1-800-221-7945, extension 5442, or by e-mail at MacmillanSpecialMarkets@macmillan.com.

First published in Great Britain by Century

First U.S. Edition: February 2017

10 9 8 7 6 5 4 3 2 1

A NOTE ON NAMES AND RUSSIAN WORDS

Even though Russian is written pretty much phonetically, the transliteration of Cyrillic Russian into Roman-alphabet English is a notoriously chaotic business. There are several competing systems of romanization, some preferred by academics, others by scientists, others by journalists, and anyone who tries to stick to one prescribed system inevitably comes up against someone else's long-established usage, which is at odds with their own particular convention. The surname that I would spell Dostoyevsky in English, as it is pronounced, can also be found with alternate transliterations ranging from Dostoevsky to Dostoevskii or Dostoevskyi to Dostoevskij.

If you add to that uncertainty the extra puzzlement caused when a Russian leaving his country makes his first foreign home outside the English-speaking world, acquiring a new Latin-letter name pre-transliterated in, say, the German or French style, before moving on to the Anglosphere with a first name that, while now fixed with the spelling 'Jascha' or 'Iacha' is pronounced as 'Yasha', it is easy to understand why foreigners have come to think

Russian is an impossibly complicated language. Thus I have 'Troubetskoi' as the family name of one Russian prince who settled in France, sharing the aristocratic estate of Clamart with his poorer fellow countrymen, because it is so well known from its transliteration into French – though it would be more English to write his name as 'Trubetskoy'.

In yet another layer of enigma within a conundrum within a mystery, the way Russian is transliterated has also changed over time. Early in the twentieth century it used to be widespread for Russian surnames ending in '–ов' (the Cyrillic letters '–ov', which, however, are usually pronounced '–of' at the end of a word) to be transliterated by using the Roman letters '–off'. Nowadays, the accepted transliteration is '–ov', regardless of the pronunciation. It's one rather charming way of telling the Soviet or post-Soviet Russians (the Smirnovs) from the older Tsarist émigrés (the Smirnoffs). But it isn't easy.

I've used several Russian names and other words in my text. However, I've tried to keep things simple, so I've transliterated them in the style used by Reuters, the BBC and British and American newspapers (technically, a simplified form of a system called BGN/PCGN) because it is the most intuitive for English speakers to pronounce.

This means writing things as they will be said. So the single Russian letter 'e' – which is pronounced either 'ye' or 'yo' – is written in English here with the double letters 'ye' or 'yo'. I believe this gives the non-Russian the best chance of saying the word correctly. The same rule applies to other Russian soft vowels (all those that sound as though they start with a 'y' sound) so that the single Russian letter 'я' is rendered with the double letters 'ya' and 'ю' becomes 'yu'. In this system, too, endings that would be fully transliterated from Russian by the complex clusters '–iy' and '–yy' in Russian are simplified to the less alien-looking '–y'. Apostrophes used in other systems for 'ъ' (a silent Russian letter) and 'ь' (a 'half-y' sound softening the consonant it comes after) can be omitted for ease (though personally I prefer to keep them).

I hope readers will not be confused by words they may have seen elsewhere with different spellings: the name Yevgeny, as I have given it, can also sometimes be written as Evgeny, Kovalyovsky as Kovalevsky, Kutyopov as Kutepov. I hope, too, that they won't be afraid to try pronouncing these words the way they're written here.

For reference, the stresses on the main characters' names fall as follows.

NADÉZHDA PLEVÍTSKAYA:
   Na-**DYEZH**-da (**NA**-dya, **NA**-dyen-ka)
   Ple-**VEET**-ska-ya

YEVGÉNY MÍLLER:
   Yev-**GHE**-nee
   MEE-lyer

NIKOLÁI SKÓBLIN:
   Nee-ko-**LAI** (rhymes with 'pie'),
   (**KO**-lya, Nee-ko-**LA**-sha)
   SKO-blin

PART ONE

The American Girl

1

September 1937

The Le Havre boat train to Paris was crowded with other young Americans.

Some were staring out at the green fields and red roofs of northern France trundling backwards in the hot afternoon sun. Others were whispering, then suddenly laughing too loudly, so that they embarrassed themselves, before hastily turning their laughs into coughs, and blushing.

They were mostly young men in baggy tweed jackets, and many had notebooks in hand, as if planning on writing their great novels before even reaching Paris.

They were so hopeful that I couldn't help liking them. I'd talked briefly to some of them on the boat, whenever I couldn't shut myself away behind a book. In other circumstances, I might even have flirted with one or two. But now I unfolded my copy of *Le Figaro* across my lap and hid myself and my slightly wrinkled flowery dress behind it, not really reading it but just letting the stories about the aftermath of the Blum government's collapse and whether Charles Lindbergh was going to move his family to France dance before my eyes. I wasn't part of their crowd. I wasn't about to write a modern novel, or become an artist, or go on south to fight fascism in Spain, or to Berlin to interview Mr Hitler.

It wasn't that I thought their dreams mundane. Not at all. I was with them all the way, inside my head. What 21-year-old wouldn't be? But I'd spent eighty dollars for my own one-way steerage ticket on the *Normandie*, that rolling old rust-bucket we'd all just escaped from, in pursuit of an ambition so much more miniature and domestic than any of theirs that I couldn't help thinking that all those young heroes would find *my* plan dull.

I was going to Paris because I wanted to meet my grandmother.

2

I didn't know my grandmother. Or I hadn't thought I did until, when I was about to turn eighteen and was just back from boarding school, a letter to my mother came from her in Paris, out of the blue, offering to pay for me to go to college, to Bryn Mawr. The letter put my mother in bed for a month.

I was at what people call the tongue-tied stage, though in my case it was just how I'd always been. So for days, weeks maybe, at the start of that summer of 1934, I let the tearful whispered discussions go on between Mother and Hughie. (To be strictly accurate, the tearful, whispering part of the conversation was all from her. His contribution was, as usual, soothing murmurs, flowers and Martinis.) I must have figured there was no point in getting involved or expressing a preference of my own, even though, as soon as I'd heard the offer, I'd started quietly hoping they'd eventually accept it. I imagined myself sitting in a huge dream library with a book in my hands, turning the pages and smiling. Zelda was going, after all, and Louise. In fact, all of my friends were going to college. I was the only one staying home after graduation, and not because we couldn't afford school, either – the Depression hadn't touched Hughie's business, and Father had left Mother well provided for – but because Mother was old-fashioned and thought it right for an unmarried girl to stay in the bosom of her family.

I had no idea either what my future would be like once we got back home to New York and our town house on the Upper East Side in the fall. Our summer in the big family house on Shelter Island, where we were the first arrivals of a crowd of cousins who would turn up through July and August, was limbo time, before the detail was worked out. But I already felt listless at the vista opening up in my mind of an infinity of chintz, and of helping Mother arrange parties and flowers, and of hopeful introductions to smooth-faced young men like youthful Hughies. Maybe Hughie couldn't see the point of a grown-up girl hanging indefinitely around the house, because he didn't seem to be taking this college offer half so badly as Mother. But, even though I could guess that he might think it a good idea, and be minded to say yes, I knew it was important for me not to think too much about what was only a possibility. Nothing ever happened in our house unless Mother wanted it. The thing was just to sit tight until the matter was resolved, and accept the outcome. It was outside my control.

But I did pick up the photo left on the breakfast table with the abandoned letter that first morning, among the cold pieces of toast and the empty coffee cups Hughie and Mother had left. She'd let the letter fall and said, in tragic tones, '*Now* she wants to *send my child away* . . .' and, blinking back a tear, trailed to the door. There, with both of us staring, she'd paused and added, 'To "broaden her mind", or *so she says*.' And then she'd headed upstairs, followed by Hughie, who was already sighing and murmuring, 'But, sweetheart . . .'

My first idea, left alone, was to read the letter and find out exactly what the fuss was all about. But I never got that far, because my unknown grandmother had also enclosed a picture of herself, half smiling into the camera, and that was what came out of the envelope first: an unremarkable woman in her late sixties, with a fullish face, thick grey-black hair, and just the hint of an amused smile on her lips. She was thin: the kind of slim that would maybe have just recently become scrawny. She was wearing a tweed jacket and skirt and a white blouse and spectacles. The spectacles had a thick dark frame across her eyebrows. Underneath that, eyes enormously magnified by the lenses looked out. She seemed a little nervous, shy maybe, but nice too. I could see she'd be fun. She looked ready to laugh.

I looked at that photo for a long time. That worn, slightly baggy face seemed so familiar. It had nothing of Mother's blonder, rounder, more prettily girlish looks. But there was something in it not unlike my own thinner face and long scrawny limbs (even if my own hair was fair and cocked up in two widow's peaks on either side of my forehead, like Mother's). I couldn't put my finger on exactly what drew me to it. It was just a pleasure to look at it, and daydream. And the more I looked, the more warmly I felt towards the woman in tweed.

I took her away. I put her up in my own bedroom, propped against my lamp, and went on looking.

And, very slowly, a kind of memory of my own began coming to the surface, though I couldn't be sure it wasn't just my imagination. I did have an over-active imagination, from too much reading. I knew that. Mother was always saying so.

But, in my head, when I looked, I could hear a sort of gentle background music of 'peekaboo', repeated, like a bird's call, in the soft singsong tones you talk to children in. I could see her laughing at me and me grinning back into those big eyes through the glasses. Maybe I was sitting on her knee. Certainly I was very small, and very close, and very happy. All of her was big compared with me, and the skin on her cheek was soft and wrinkled, with cords on her neck that I knew, with quiet regret for her, to be ugly. I could feel my little-girl fingers smearing those big glasses, pulling them aside, then hear myself laughing in puzzled astonishment that whenever those eyes didn't have that thick glass in front of them, they were ordinary-sized.

I could imagine my fingers, too, pulling at a rope of enormous rough golden beads until the skin on her neck puckered and I let go. I must be making at least that part up, I thought, because, in the picture, there was no jewellery visible at all. But I could almost feel those beads, warm to the touch and so big my hand could hardly cup the bottom one. Strung together with brown thread.

Peekaboo!

Silly, of course. I knew that. A story I was inventing for myself. After what seemed a very long time, I sighed and hid the picture inside a book.

Mother never mentioned that the photo was gone. Perhaps she hadn't noticed it? Her migraine – the drapes-closed, weak-voiced, oh-please-just-a-little-dry-toast-and-water variety – stayed with her, on and off, for days more.

I don't remember the sequence of the days that followed the letter's coming very exactly; just that it was the kind of tense time when you want to spend a lot of the day in your room, on your own, reading. I didn't mind. Even though I was still so young that I didn't much notice the world outside my own small world – the bigger world that contained the Depression – I already didn't want to go to the half-empty beach on my own that summer. There was something so sad about the boarded-up holiday cottages, and all the remembered people who weren't there any more. It was the evenings that kept going wrong. Dinner would start all right, with carefully bright questions between the three of us about Hughie's day and Mother's symptoms and who'd be going to the island when and what had been in the newspapers. We'd be sitting among the silver and flowered plates and cut glass, waiting till Florence entered, blinking back steam as she planted the tureen on the table. But our conversations kept fizzling out once the maid had gone, and soon afterwards the meal would end too, with Mother hastily leaving the room, blinking back more tears. Once the details of the offer from my grandmother had become clearer, though not the reason for Mother's reaction, I do remember asking, cautiously, 'I was wondering . . . why is she even interested in me and in my schooling? When I didn't know she even knew I existed?'

I could see at once that I hadn't requested this information nearly carefully enough. The question was enough for my mother to turn her beautiful, brimming, accusing eyes on me. My heart contracted. I'd given offence. With what I could muster in the way of defiance (because what was wrong about my question, after all? *Why* couldn't I ask?)

9

I looked back at her, keeping the innocence of my enquiry clearly displayed on my face, like a shield.

There was a long, dizzy-making silence, broken only by the clink of a single spoon, when Hughie, after a brief glance, went back to his tomato soup, as if nothing important were happening. Mother made sure I was aware of her looking at me, then she gathered herself, dropped her napkin on the table, and rushed off again with a stifled sob. She didn't shut the door. We could hear her footsteps rushing up the stairs. I wasn't yet far enough removed from our family life to be able to judge this manoeuvre in the way I did later: to feel exasperated by the melodrama of her distress, or at any rate to know whether I felt exasperated, or what I felt at all. This was just what things were like. So I sat looking down into my soup, making myself small, crumbling my bread with my fingers, crushed by knowing I'd made things worse with my thoughtless question, wondering why we couldn't be more like the cheerful, robust families that I was always reading about in books, and wishing most of all, wishing like hell, that I'd just kept quiet.

Hughie was already by the door, going to her, when he looked around and noticed me.

He's a kind man, my stepfather. He's big and good-natured, with his gut bulging smoothly over his waistband and his round cheeks pink and unlined. When he's not at the office, which mostly he is, he's fond of his golf and tennis and the big shots of bourbon any man would need to keep up with Mother's demanding crises. He's always calm. And perhaps I looked extra downcast. He smiled at me.

'Your mother's a very sensitive woman,' he said, looking for the blandest way of calming the situation. 'And you know she's always had a hard time with your grandmother. She's only upset because she loves you . . . and wants to protect you.' He nodded, as if convincing himself. 'It's nothing to worry about.'

I pressed my lips together. 'Oh, I'm not *worried*,' I said, as defiantly as I could. 'I just don't understand. I don't know my grandmother. She doesn't know me.'

It was more than 'didn't know her'. My grandmother was a part of the past we didn't ever discuss. Mother's life before me, as far as I could piece together from her accounts of it, had consisted only of family vacations with her cousins during school breaks, along with shopping, piano playing, and her brief romance and marriage with Father before he went to the war in Europe.

Father had been a hero, often invoked, painted in unreal bright colours: a distant cousin, invited up here from DC by Aunt Mildred when Mother was eighteen, because choosing your own kind is best; a brilliant advocate for the Preparedness Movement, a rising star in the War Department until he'd volunteered for active service himself because he was a crack shot. Yet his fighting prowess had been tragically wasted. He'd died of influenza when I was two on his way to the Argonne Forest. By the time I was three, the year after the war had ended, Mother had married Hughie, a calm, stolid, moneyed older man, who'd been Father's boss at the War Department but was now in the defence business for himself. She'd known him four years by then. He'd been the best man at her wedding to Father.

I knew, in an abstract way, that Mother's own father had died young, just like mine, even though her father had been a diplomat and not a soldier like mine. Her father had been blown up, along with several others, by a terrorist bomb in Imperial Russia on his first foreign posting. It was easy enough to see why *he* didn't figure, because Mother, born in 1896 after his death, hadn't even known him, but it was where her mother had got to in the story that was more mysterious. If ever I dared ask Mother about her mother, she'd just kind of wilt. I'd tried once or twice, while watching her brush out her pale hair at the end of the day, preparing for evening, concentrating on the smooth strokes. But as soon as I mentioned my grandmother, Mother would do a slow unhappy thing with her eyebrows, while I cringed, in a quiet agony of contrition. Then, after an eternity of silence, she'd sigh. 'Some things in life are just . . . difficult. It's best not to dwell on them . . . Just be thankful for your own happy upbringing,' she'd say, and I'd have to leave it at that. All I knew was that my grandmother was called Constance and lived far, far away, in Paris, France, and never came home.

'You did know your grandma,' Hughie added eventually, as if he'd been weighing whether to say even this. 'But maybe you won't recall. You were very small.' He measured the air with his big pink hand, bending slightly to get it down to beside his knee. Toddler height.

This surprised me, all right. But I didn't want him to suddenly remember they'd decided not to talk about it in front of me. So I turned the alert flicker I felt pass across my face into a look of half-remembering politeness – a kind of visual 'Uh-huh? Oh, how *interesting*.' It was the sort of thing I'd got good at, at home with Mother, with her dangerous sensitivity to slight: staying buttoned up; not doing very much.

It was working, too, I thought. Hughie's face lightened as he started to reminisce.

'It was the only time I ever saw her, either, come to think of it. She showed up from the south of France to stay here with us, a couple of months after your mother married me – right here on Shelter Island. Just after *she'd* married, too – her Russian count. She brought him with her. I don't expect your mother could have stopped her. It's your whole family's holiday house, after all.' His lips twitched. Keeping my mind blank yet receptive, I smiled and widened my eyes encouragingly. 'You don't remember him either, I guess? The Russian count? Well, he was a real piece of work. Tall, stood like a soldier, impressive to look at, at least till you got close enough to know what you were seeing. And then, well . . . to my mind he had too much grease on his hair, collars all gone, even if he did bow all the time and kiss ladies' hands and wear white gloves – grubby ones – at breakfast. Too darn knickerbocker for me. Couldn't stop telling us all the usual stories: about how grand he'd been before the Revolution . . . and how tragic his life had become since . . . how he'd walked for days across a lake of ice to get to safety . . . about the priceless jewels sewn into his dead first wife's corset, you know the kind of thing?'

Despite myself, I felt my smile get more uncertain. It was good talking to Hughie, even if he never told Mother to stop when, for weeks at a stretch, something upset her and the whole rhythm of our life got messed up. We weren't close, exactly, and I sometimes worried that he'd maybe have preferred it if I weren't there and he could enjoy life with his beautiful, emotional wife without the quiet child who'd come attached to her. But I liked his slow way of

13

talking. As he was saying all this, I told myself that I'd figure it out later, when I was alone: put the pieces of this unfamiliar story together in my mind. But what I couldn't understand, right now, in this strange conversational byway we'd somehow gone down, was this: how could any of those wild, romantic stories possibly be called 'usual'?

Hughie's grin broadened. 'You won't have come across many of *them* yet, either: Russians? Well, you soon will. The world's full of lost Russians these days, all waiting for someone to buy them a drink and a meal. Just go to the Russian Tea Room any day: you'll see crowds of 'em, and every one with a title and a tall tale, getting taller every time they tell it. Not that I blame them. That's revolution for you. There's nothing to stop them exaggerating, now that the place they came from has disappeared. None of them has two dimes to rub together, mind, but they all have plenty to say for themselves. The con man, that's what I called Constance's count.'

He chuckled. I did too.

'So, *he* spent the summer drinking his way through my wine, which I'd been hoping to impress my new wife with, though nothing I'd brought could impress him; he'd always drunk far better with the Tsar or a grand duke, back in his glory days; and bending anyone's ear who'd listen about how he was going into town in the fall to sell Marie Antoinette's earrings to Mrs Hussey Degen, and make enough money to keep Constance – your grandma, that is – in luxury for the rest of her days.

'To do her justice, Constance didn't have a moment to spare for his émigré talk. She just laughed whenever she heard him start on about the past, and left it to me to listen

14

– though she did it with charm; she's quite a woman. *She* was more interested in the future. And I don't just mean reading out improving texts from *The Delineator*, either, about New Women playing golf and driving automobiles, because it was 1919.'

He raised an eyebrow, enjoying drawing me into his story. '*She* spent that summer campaigning for female emancipation.'

I couldn't help the quiver of astonishment that went through me at that.

'Well, you can imagine how that went down with your mother,' he added.

I shook my head. Even then, years and years after the Nineteenth Amendment, Mother, unlike almost every other female I knew, still had no time for women working, or voting, or taking an interest in social improvements, or in fact leaving the home much at all. Mother, when she wasn't upset, was kittenish, or maybe butterflyish. She thought women were for fluttering.

'Do you mean giving out pamphlets?' I asked weakly.

He laughed out loud. 'Oh, worse than that. Far worse. She was a whirlwind: committees, readings, meetings, you name it . . .'

He paused. I waited. 'But her really big idea was the parade,' Hughie continued. 'She'd read about one like it in *The Delineator*, and she was hell bent on copying it here. She was organizing getting on for a hundred women to go stand outside Prospect House in yellow sashes, holding yellow parasols.'

I thought of those yellow amber beads I'd remembered.

'And this is where it all went so wrong. You see, she

asked Jeannie to head the parade, dressed as the Statue of Liberty.'

I felt my eyes widen. In fact, I was so shocked I hardly knew how to make my body take in air.

'She was quite insistent. And when Jeannie refused, and had me promise to take her right back to town on the weekend of the parade – I made it all right, you know; told Constance there was a dinner we couldn't get out of – well, Constance just came right back and asked, very briskly, if she couldn't "borrow" you instead? Put you in your best white dress up at the front instead – as the woman voter of the future?' He caught my eye and nodded. 'She was very keen on you, you know. She spent a lot of time playing with you.'

I was having trouble breathing again. '. . . And . . . did she?' I eventually managed to ask, gulping a bit. 'Did I?

He smiled regretfully. 'Your mother would never have allowed it. You know that.'

I nodded. Of course.

'We took you back to town with us. Just in case, Jeannie said. She didn't want Constance getting ideas.' He looked more serious now. 'And once we were home, Jeannie wrote Constance a letter, the kind of letter that's probably more about all the things that have happened between people in the past than about whatever's got on their nerves today, I'd say . . .'

Hughie looked away from me, but even so I could see how carefully he was picking his words. I was guessing he'd decided not to interfere when this letter was being written.

'A terrible letter,' I hazarded. 'The sort that says, "Never darken my door again." '

Mother wasn't a forgiver. When Mother fell out with a person, that person fell utterly from grace, suddenly turning out to have committed many, many earlier misdemeanours, stretching back through time, all detailed in faint, hurt tones to anyone who'd listen. Any such person stayed away from beach and card parties ever after.

'It was about you,' Hughie continued. 'On the face of things, anyway. Jeannie told Constance never to think of trying to influence you to be like her, and a whole lot more besides. And that she could stay on the island until after the damn parade, but that she had to be gone by the end of the week, when we'd be coming back. And that was that.'

He spread helpless hands.

I ran through a mental list of things I should say: 'Poor Grandmother' or 'Poor Mother' or maybe something about having seen the photo Grandmother had sent. Or how I'd remembered those yellow beads, and were they connected with the yellow of the parade?

Instead, into my mouth came other words. 'I would like to go to Bryn Mawr,' I heard myself saying.

Whatever could have gotten into me? I'd broken my number-one rule for avoiding trouble: never say what you want, or it will be too disappointing when you don't get it. But when I finally dared look up, when the silence had gone on too long not to, I saw that Hughie was looking back at me with a faintly surprised smile, and nodding.

'Well, then,' he said calmly. 'Let's see if we can make that happen.' And although I didn't yet know the way he'd find to 'make it all right', which this time he would achieve by telling Mother I should be allowed to go away, but that

17

he should pick up the bill instead of Grandmother, I could already see in his eyes that everything was all settled.

I would go to college. To Bryn Mawr.

3

Going away changed everything for me. First, there were the books we were all studying and arguing over – endless discussions about novels that transported us into revolutions in Asia and left us tussling with agonizing existential choices, or took us down the mean streets with Sam Spade, or to the house at Tortilla Flat in which Danny and his jobless friends became wino Knights of the Round Table. And then there were the people: an intoxicating rainbow of real people, whose lives had till now been so completely other from mine that finding out about them felt almost more exciting than the ideas of the humanities course, until I realized that, in all the important things, they were just like me. We all wanted to live, breathe, eat, dance, laugh, argue about FDR's fireside chats and whether he, along with Hitler and Stalin and Mussolini, were really, as the *Chicago Tribune* had it, the Four Horsemen of the Apocalypse. Then there was the possibility of war in Europe and the rights and wrongs of Spain and fascism and anarchy and communism, along with questions about hunger and the dustbowl and whether poverty bred degeneracy and what about birth control and what would come of the union disputes. Anyway, in all that, happening at a rate so fast you could hardly keep up except at a breathless gabble, I soon stopped being tongue-tied. There was just no time for shyness.

But I did have one secret I never shared with anyone.

The first letter I received on campus was a small parcel from a bookshop in Paris called Shakespeare and Co. I didn't know anyone in Paris; there was only my grandmother, who'd wanted me to study here. I had her picture, still folded into a book, somewhere in my still-unpacked box. I kept that little package in my bag all day, hugging the knowledge of it to myself, full of expectation. I didn't open it until I got back to the privacy of my room in the evening, pleased that my new roommate was out. But there were no revelations inside. It contained no note, nothing, just a book: a small, plain, cloth-covered Everyman edition of a Russian novel in translation. *Anna Karenina*, I read on the spine. Leo Tolstoy. I opened it, a little disappointed, and looked at the first line. 'Happy families are all alike,' I read; 'every unhappy family is unhappy in its own way.'

Was it a kind of oblique message? I looked for a return address. Could I at least write and thank her? But there was nothing.

Well, Mother had told my grandmother not to try to influence me any more. I guessed she was trying to obey that order, while showing she wished me well. I couldn't see what to do except read the book she'd sent, and move her photo into it, and keep it on my shelf, and treasure her kind thought.

I made a point of reading my Tolstoy in a Russian café downtown, a dusty little place hung with dingy lace drapes. It was run by a grey-haired woman called Madame Brodyanskaya. She was tall and upright with thick lips and wore a flowered shawl round her shoulders. She spoke terrible English, but made good pancakes that she called *blinchiki* with sour cream, thicker sour cream, and sugar. You could see from her eloquent eyes that she had a big personality. She was a poet, she said, the one time we talked, after she'd noticed I was reading *Anna Karenina*.

At the back of the café, behind the samovar and near the icon corner, was a bookshelf of Russian poetry. People brought in the dog-eared books they'd finished and took others out. Sometimes they sat half the day reading, over tea in a glass in a filigree holder. They weren't young, yet they had good faces and thoughtful eyes. Madame Brodyanskaya said they were, or had been, writers. They didn't smile much, these Russians. But sometimes when a new sombre person came in, brushing the rain off his hat, someone sitting quietly in a corner would look up, and they'd suddenly start laughing big bear laughs and hugging big bear hugs, with as much joy as if they'd cheated death to be reunited. I never dared start talking to them – I never heard them speak English – and of course I couldn't understand what they said to each other. But I didn't think these people were boasting about lost estates or jewels, as Hughie had suggested all Russians did. Probably they were really just talking about something mundane most of the time: the price of gas, or where to get potatoes. But I liked to imagine them philosophically meditating, like Levin in my novel, about the right way to live. And I imagined Grandmother sitting among them, nodding.

The following September, another little parcel from

Paris was waiting for me on my return to campus. It was another translated Russian novel, this time *Fathers and Sons* by Turgenev, which I was now sophisticated enough to characterize quite quickly as a wistful story about generation gaps. I was proud of being able to see more easily now what my mysterious correspondent was getting at. And the gentleness of her move made me feel warmly towards her. I wished, again, that there was some way I could respond. But, again, there was no return address.

The third and last parcel arrived just as I was packing up to go home for good. It contained a different kind of book: a paperback of French surrealist poetry, wrapped in newspaper. I spoke French, by then; we'd had to read the poetry of Baudelaire and Victor Hugo and Mallarmé, but this dancing, dreamy, modern stuff – the first page I opened described a dear old priest lifting up his cassock and flying away across the lake, then wondering why his hem was wet – was quite different.

Unlike the other gifts from Paris, too, I saw that this little book was used. There was nothing written in it, but the spine was bent in a couple of places. And there was a thin slip of paper inserted at a page-long verse called 'Poem to the Mysterious Woman'. I pulled out the bookmark. Nothing there. So I read the poem.

> I have dreamed so much of you that you're losing your
>   reality.
> Is there still time to reach for your living, breathing
>   body
> and kiss on that mouth the birthplace
> of the voice I cherish?

The White Russian

I have dreamed so much of you
    that my arms, accustomed
while embracing your shadow to cross themselves over
   my chest would maybe
not fold around the contours of your body.
    And that, faced with the actual appearance of
   what has haunted and
governed me for days and years,
It might be I who became a shadow.
O sentimental scales.

I have dreamed so much of you
that I might never wake up again.
I sleep standing up, with my body exposed
to all the appearances of life
and of love and you, the only person
who counts for me today –
I could less touch your forehead and your lips
than the first lips and the first forehead that
   happen by.

I have dreamed so much of you,
walked and talked and slept with your ghost so much,
that maybe all there is left for me to do
is to be a ghost
among the ghosts, and a shadow
a hundred times more shadowy than the one strolling
and ready to go on eagerly strolling
over the sundial of your life.

The yearning tenderness of those verses tugged at my

heart. I put it down on the bed, still open at that page. It was a poem to a lost lover, I could see, rather than to a child, and yet . . .

And yet, how I wished I knew the person who'd sent me that poem.

I flipped over the wrappings. The book wasn't from a store this time. It had been folded first in a layer of old newspaper and then in brown paper and string.

I flattened out the newspaper first, a torn-out part-page with a blurry mix of tail-ends of stories about Leon Blum and ads for corsets around the edges. In the middle was a bigger ad for a Russian singer's show at a Paris restaurant. 'Retour de La Tsiganka!' was what I saw first, in big cheery letters, above a photo of a stout, heavily made-up, soulful-looking middle-aged woman, in a patterned shawl like Madame Brodyanskaya's. Underneath, in smaller letters, I read, 'Une soirée inoubliable . . . Nadezhda Plevitskaya de retour Chez Raspoutine, rue de la Néva,' along with details and a date a couple of months before.

It was only when I also smoothed out the brown paper that I saw that there was a return address this time: Mme la Comtesse Sabline, 29 rue du Colisée, 8ᵉ.

I got out a sheet of writing paper straight away.

But when I sat down at the desk it looked too white, too empty.

After a long time staring at that page, biting the handle of the pen in my hand, dipping it in the ink, wiping the ink against the side of the bottle, and wondering what I'd say, I put the pen back in the holder.

No . . . I'd need to gather my thoughts first, I thought, getting up; I'd wait till I was home.

4

I'd been nervous for months about the approaching end of college. Put simply, I didn't want to go home for good.

Mother, who seemed more frail among her orchids and gardenias these days than I'd remembered her being before, only drooped extra wearily if, while on vacation, I ever actually answered her question about what it was I'd been doing while away. I'd keep my answers brief, and Hughie would nod tolerantly until I fell silent, then pass me the drink he'd been concentrating on mixing as I spoke – always a Manhattan, the first night back – after which he'd make the same jovial toast, 'To homecoming!' And then, with very visible tact, he'd start asking about the brothers and families of my new friends, raising his eyebrow only just enough to make me uncomfortable when it turned out they weren't at all what he would call marriageable. They weren't, I could see that. My friends all wanted to be writers and painters and photographers and editors. They weren't ladylike in the least – nothing like the delicate flowers Hughie would have liked me to be friends with, the husband-hunters my friends and I laughed at so much for just marking time till their weddings. Thank God he didn't realize, at least, quite how shockingly different to his our political ideas were! Or even to think, in those early months of 1937, that girls might have any valid opinions at all! As soon as the ceremony of welcoming me back for a vacation was done, he and Mother would resume their complaining about the New Deal and pro-convention campaigning dinners and Republican comeback soirées and Hoover one-liners. 'Blessed are the young,' as Hughie liked to say, nodding sententiously at me after his second drink, 'for they shall inherit the national debt.'

So I did what I could to not offend, when at home. I tried to keep in check the critical faculty that college was developing in me, and to quell the suspicion I'd begun to find coming into my head whenever Mother was having one of her querulous fits that she might not feel ill at all, but just be play-acting, for attention, so that we'd all jump, as we always did, and whisper and tiptoe and look after her. But as my college time went on, a kind of sourness seemed to creep into our relationship all the same.

There'd been a lot of talk, for instance, during my last college Christmas, about the shape my twenty-first birthday celebrations should take at Easter. It started on the evening of the day I'd seen the lawyer and been pleasantly surprised at how big my settlement from Father was going to be once I turned twenty-one; my first idea had been to throw a party and invite my college friends. But no one in the family had responded to my suggestion.

A family dinner at a restaurant with some of the cousins was what was decided on; but what to wear? When, before Easter, my mother took me shopping for a dress, the saleswoman took one look at me and put me straight into heels and a shocking-pink halter-neck evening gown in some new industrial silky stuff, and gasped when I stepped out in it, feeling six feet tall and swaying like a movie star.

My mother gasped too, but less approvingly. 'Haven't you got something . . . prettier?' she asked.

We left ten minutes later with a flowery, flouncy, chiffon thing in light blues and greens, in what felt an oppressive silence. My mother looked pained for hours; I felt obscurely guilty.

We spent the rest of our day together in various stores while she tried on gown after gown and listened fretfully to the praise of sales clerk after sales clerk. When we were alone, I dreamed up little stories about the cousins or the movies to tell her, and asked nervous questions about her friends and committees, all to earn her forgiveness. It was evening, and we were home and dressed for dinner, waiting for Hughie, before she relented, and the look of suffering finally left her face. She ruffled my hair, and smiled her beautiful smile, and, to my tremendous relief, said tenderly, 'My baby, and such a pretty girl . . . we need to sort out your hair.'

I didn't want anything done to my hair. Why bother? I was happy with my hair falling over my shoulders and held to one side by a clip; and there was no need for extra curling, as it was naturally wavy. But Mother, who had always favoured complicated chignons and Grecian tendrils of hair falling past her ears, cheered up at this new thought.

Leaning conspiratorially towards me, she murmured, with a soft voice and a loving look, 'I've talked to my hairdresser about you, and she says she would *love* to style the hair of the most important person of the birthday party.

Would you let me take you? She is a *wonderful* artist. I would *love* to introduce you . . .'

And so I said yes, of course, though with a slightly sinking heart at what kind of freakish coxcomb the mystery hairdresser might give me to match that flouncy dress, and the appointment was made. Off we went together, in the back of another cab, on the morning of the dinner a week or so later. Mother was smiling and chirping away, brighter and more energetic than I'd seen her for weeks, so that I was happy, mostly, to have given in.

'You'll *love* Colette,' Mother said more than once, playfully smoothing down the fur on her lap with her gloved hand. 'And she's *so* excited to be doing the hair of the most important person of the evening . . .'

It was only once we were actually on Fifth Avenue, and had passed through the red doors Mother pointed to and into a padded interior place where sleek young women were converging on Mother, who knew them all, that I began to realize this wasn't going to be the kind of two-girls-together grooming morning I'd envisaged. A much older, stouter female, clearly the terror of the establishment, emerged from behind a door, and the young bird-females scattered to a respectful, watchful distance.

'Madame,' the new arrival said in Gallic tones. She deftly swept up Mother's mink. 'What a pleasure! 'Ow excited I am to be creating ze coiffure of ze most important person at your party . . . you will be ze belle of ze ball.'

They gazed into each other's eyes for a long moment, in a silent duet of mutual appreciation. Then Mother's faint social laugh tinkled out and she gestured at me. 'My daughter, Evie . . .' Colette nodded and her mouth turned up without her eyes leaving Mother's face. And then, with another little laugh, one that sounded more definitely false this time, Mother added: 'I wondered, dear Colette, whether you might also have time to do my daughter's hair?' Now Colette swivelled her eyes towards me, as if seeing me for the first time, to give me the full benefit of her disapproving glare. 'She hoped you might fit her in too,' Mother added.

Colette turned her face towards me, though her smiling eyes didn't quite meet mine. 'But . . . no time! No stylist! We are a very famous salon! So busy . . .!' she growled, and the bird-girls twittered.

I was hot and cold with mortification; sinking into the floor with it. Was there no appointment for me? Had I completely misunderstood the purpose of the trip? In my panic, I couldn't even remember whether Mother had ever specified that it was *my* hair that was to be cut, or even whether I *was* the most important person of the evening at all: had I simply been so arrogant as to make that assumption for myself? 'It's really not a problem,' I said, eyeing the door. 'I think there must have been a misunder—'

But the terror of the establishment was already rising to the occasion. ''Owever, for *you*, madame,' she said, and as she turned back to Mother her face sugared up again, 'we can always find a way. Nadine,' she barked at the youngest of the girls, '*you* will take zis young lady. And I will be wiz ze most important person of ze evening for ze next two hours.'

My head went on spinning throughout the long silent period of washing and heat and snippings that followed. I still hadn't got my thoughts together or my voice back even by the time we came out on to Fifth Avenue together, my hair only a bit shorter and puffier than before I'd gone in, but Mother's in full stiff-curled golden splendour, and got into the cab home. The only thing I had in my mind, the closest I could get to a strategy, was not to react, especially when I felt so light and hot and stifled. You didn't quarrel with Mother. She was delicate.

I was aware of her looking at me, sideways, beady-eyed.

'Your hair looks beautiful,' I said, to avoid giving offence.

'Colette is an artist,' she answered, pleased, and her hand wandered hairwards. And then, as she patted, she added, 'Didn't you think her *charming*?'

Avoid conflict. I kept the half-smile on my face and looked out of the window.

After a while, she said, rather accusingly, 'You seem angry.'

'Angry?' I said, wonderingly, in my most innocent voice. Outright denial seemed the best strategy. 'Oh no, Mother. Why would I be?'

'Well, you're not saying anything.'

'Ahh . . . well, maybe I'm a little nervous,' I said, making my smile wider and my voice warmer. 'It's a big thing, after all, turning twenty-one. My big day.'

I wondered whether I'd put too much stress on the word *my*. But it was too late to unsay. I smiled more. Mother pursed her lips. She didn't answer. She began fiddling with the clasp of her big crocodile-skin purse. We were nearly home.

Aunt Mildred was my mother's aunt, and my great-aunt, and the matriarch of our family. In mountainous black taffeta, she was stirring her coffee and looking approvingly down the restaurant table at her army of descendants. Everyone but me and Mother (who with Hughie was safely at the other end) had the same very dark hair, the girls' curled and crimped above their flowery, floaty, A-line pastel dresses, the boys' all neatly smoothed down from side partings. It was a neat, correct group, with barely a concession to modernity. In the car on the way here, Mother, in flirty high spirits, had been singing the praises of my various male cousins: Cousin Ned, rising star at Bethlehem Steel and her favourite relative of my generation, and Cousin Theo, already doing so very well at J. P. Morgan . . .

'How we've all changed. I can't believe Sophie and Chloe used to be so naughty,' I said as she stirred. My cousins were meek as milk now, halfway down the table, in identical pink and blue. They were Aunt Mildred's favourite grandchildren. She glanced at them and grunted happily.

'Do you remember?' I continued, suddenly knowing what I wanted to know and how to get round to the subject. It might not have occurred to me to ask, if it hadn't been for the hairdresser's visit earlier. Neither of us had referred to it again, just as Mother didn't seem to have noticed that, on returning home, I'd gone to my room, brushed out my salon hairdo and changed the style. 'What teases they were when they were small? Dancing round me at the beach and shouting, "Evie's got a crazy grandma"?'

Aunt Mildred snuffled at that, and raised the coffee cup to her lips with her strangely small, delicate hand.

'I've often wondered, since,' I added casually as she sipped. '*Is* she crazy? Is that why we never see her?'

31

Aunt Mildred's little dark eyes darted down the table, fixed on Mother safely in animated conversation with Cousin Theo, and then returned to meet mine. She put the cup down and leaned closer. 'Crazy', she said carefully, 'would be putting it too strongly. But what my sister Constance has always been . . .' and here she paused and narrowed her eyes in the search for the *mot juste*, '. . . is unconventional.'

I was none the wiser. I'd always understood Aunt Mildred to hold that unconventional and crazy were pretty closely related anyway.

'Not raving in the street, exactly . . .?' I pursued tentatively. 'But . . .?'

'Art.' Aunt Mildred disapproved of art, and all that went with it. Her lips shut tight as a trap on that 't'.

I raised an eyebrow. I knew there'd be more if I waited. Aunt Mildred had had two glasses of wine. Her cheeks were pink.

'She was always a great one for ideas. She read too much, you see; too clever for her own good. When poor Eddie – your grandfather – was killed in Russia, of course we brought Constance back to have the baby – your mother – in our home. We did everything we could for her: we knew it wouldn't be an easy time for her, and she was family. We even sent her to a sanatorium for her nerves, because she was so thin and sad that she couldn't feed Jeannie. More fool us. We thought a summer of Switzerland and mountain air would do her good. And of course I said we'd look after Jeannie until she came back. I had three of my own by then, and there was room in the nursery. But no one could have expected Constance to head for Paris, and take up with . . . *artists* . . . and *intellectuals* . . . and want to stay there indefinitely.'

I shook my head. 'It was stifling at home,' Aunt Mildred added forbiddingly. 'Or so she said.'

'What about Mother?' Had Grandmother just abandoned her child? Or had she been pushed out? 'Didn't she want *her*?'

'*Well*.' Aunt Mildred glared down at her cup. 'She did write. She wanted me to let Jeannie go to Paris and live with her there, can you believe?'

I made my smile more encouraging and waited for more.

'Of course I said no. Highly unsuitable. Opium, lunatics, bordellos and men cutting their own ears off: not at all the environment one would want one's niece growing up in.'

Despite myself, I smiled inside. I could just hear Aunt Mildred saying those words. 'Didn't *that* change her mind?'

Aunt Mildred's jowls quivered as she shook her head. 'Though she did leave Paris for a while,' she conceded. 'She came home and tried to argue with us. But Herbert and I stood firm, and we had the family behind us. We told Constance she could still spend the summers with Jeannie, if we could be confident that it would be done in seemly fashion – here, or near – but she'd proved she couldn't raise her on her own. So she went off to live with a colony of *lady artists*' – Aunt Mildred's voice quivered with disgust at these last words – 'in New Mexico, over the winter, though she did turn up the next summer, as promised. But by then it was up to Jeannie to choose. And *she* didn't want to go. She wanted to spend her summers with us.'

Sadness stole through me. I could imagine how outraged Aunt Mildred would have felt, how sincere she'd have been, and what she'd have said . . . I could imagine, too, how a small child hearing what her family was saying would have feared the idea of a summer alone with her shockingly improper and invisible parent . . . At the same time, I thought I also had an inkling of why a bookish, well-travelled young woman like my grandmother, so recently a widow, and then, while still in grief, a mother, might have felt stifled by her return home. I could imagine her falling in with what she thought they wanted, at first, and going to Europe – and then being bewildered when she found they'd locked her out forever, and she'd lost her daughter.

'And that was that,' Aunt Mildred finished, not without satisfaction. She eyed me.

'She went back overseas . . .?' I prompted.

'Yes, off she went, and from then on she seemed to be positively going out of her way to be outrageous. There was another painters' colony in a fishing village in Italy; Rapallo, I think she called it, because she did write, sometimes. She said it was peaceful. And then ambulance driving in France in the Great War, which she said was her duty – which was quite absurd: it was clearly no job for a woman . . . or at least a lady. We couldn't even find her to ask her to poor Jeannie's wedding . . .' At this, Aunt Mildred picked up her coffee cup and stared fiercely at the grounds, in a way that suggested she hadn't tried very hard. 'But we always kept the door open, in case she'd changed. And, sure enough, she did pitch up again, after the war – and even though she brought some shady new Russian husband of her own to meet me, she made a very affecting speech, about how sad she was not to have known your father, and how much she wanted to meet Hughie, and could she spend a few weeks on the island with the family?'

Aunt Mildred put down the coffee cup. 'So I put aside my doubts and did the decent thing. I said she could go to you all in July, before my children and I got there, when the top floor was free. I suppose I was impressed that she'd come to ask my permission. And that she was still trying at all. Maybe I even felt sorry for her . . . But it was a terrible mistake. I realized that afterwards. I blame myself. She hadn't changed at all.'

'You mean', I said, making myself small, making my voice very innocent, wondering if I'd be giving away too much knowledge, or too much interest, by finishing my question, 'because of the women's parade?'

A great snort travelled through Aunt Mildred's tightly encased frame. '*That!*' she rumbled dismissively. 'No, long before *that*. Your mother said it was clear from their first day there. She said that Constance was *teaching you the Charleston* whenever her back was turned, and *reading Dostoyevsky*. She had to go.'

I bit my lip. Excommunicated, then . . . I supposed it was only to be expected that Mother would get her revenge, in the end, for having been abandoned as a child. And suddenly, despite the sadness of this tale of inevitable estrangement, Aunt Mildred's emphatic horror at those two particular crimes made me want to laugh. As did the guilty question that came fleetingly into my head: what would Aunt Mildred, or Mother, think if they knew I also had *The Brothers Karamazov* in my trunk, packed ready for my departure in the morning?

'And now?' I asked quickly.

'Oh . . . Paris. Artists, no doubt. Maybe more Russians. It does no good to know too much. The point is, she was always too clever for her own good, my big sister. But, in the end, all her ideas did her no good at all. They just left her on her own.' Aunt Mildred stretched out her black sheeny arm towards me, setting her taffeta-encased flesh swinging. The improbably small finger that touched me felt improbably hard. 'That's something for *you* to think about, too, my girl,' she added with the glint in her eye that I'd always found amusing, 'now you're nearly through with your college education: the danger of ideas. Don't get your head too full of them to know what really matters. It's family that counts.'

I felt much more warmly towards Mother by the time we set out for home, now that I could picture her as a lost, worried, golden-curled child, looking along the beach for a lost mother and crying too much over every grazed knee or lost toy.

I even half imagined, half hoped, we might somehow talk together about Aunt Mildred's revelations. But of course this didn't happen. She chattered happily to Hughie all the way home in the car, as if we had all had a pleasant evening together. But her eyes passed blackly through me as she kissed me goodnight.

It was only once I was alone in my room, in my bed, going over in my head the events and discoveries of what was perhaps my first day as an adult, but full of an unsettled, unnameable sadness, too – perhaps it was loneliness, I thought – that I finally said, though only to myself, 'Poor Grandmother.'

5

My friend Eliza's brothers came in a rattling jalopy to empty our college room after graduation that summer and bring both of us roommates back to New York forever.

Mother didn't come to the phone when I called to ask whether I could travel home with Eliza. It had been a while since I'd managed to speak to her, and recently I only seemed to get Florence, our maid, when I called home. Your mother's asleep, she'd say; or, your mother asked not to be disturbed. Try again tomorrow, Miss E. I'll send her your love. This time I got Hughie, who said Mother wouldn't mind my travelling with Eliza; she was a little indisposed and needed to rest up for a few days.

It was a bad line, but his voice sounded distant in every way. It made me uneasy. Guilty, too, without knowing quite what I should be feeling guilty about. But by the time we set out in our convoy of three packed cars on another hot morning, full of the fresh greenness of early summer, all talking nineteen to the dozen about our plans, I had forgotten my unease about that possible coolness in Hughie's voice. My friend Dorothy was going to stay with her married sister over the summer while she pestered a magazine in the city for editing work. Her brother and his friend were talking, in snatches of breeze, about going to Spain and fighting fascism. Eliza's brothers, one a painter, one a photographer, had found a partially furnished temporary apartment above a pastry shop on the corner of Bleecker and Barrow, where Eliza was going to camp for the summer, too, and write her novel.

It was easy for all of them, I found myself thinking with a twinge of envy that seemed so ungracious I tried to stifle it. Eliza's German philosopher father and Dorothy's intellectual doctoring family didn't mind at all what their daughters did. I could bet their fathers never fretted aloud about the national debt, either. You were so much freer to ride around with the wind in your hair, talking about philosophy or whatever else came into your head, if your family were not-rich immigrants with big ideas and kind hearts from somewhere in Europe. How lucky my friends were not to come from money.

'What great swells,' Mother said the next evening, leaning out of the bedroom window of our house. 'Where are you all off to tonight?'

The sun was setting, the light golden, the temperature still sticky hot. My friends were on the sidewalk, drinking the cocktails that one of the men was mixing al fresco – Florence had put glasses and a shaker and bottles just inside the front door – while we waited for the stragglers to arrive for the evening.

We looked like a snapshot of youthful happiness; I could see that. Everyone talking plans again, loudly and happily. Eliza's brothers were scuffling – arm-wrestling and

laughing, with Winthrop, the older one, calling '¡*No pasarán!*'
and playfully barring Bill's way. Freddy the doorman from
the apartment building down the road was watching with
silent disapproval. Mother, too, from her window, with her
hair arranged in a gold cascade on her head and her white
bedjacket ribbons fluttering. There were maybe a dozen of
us down below: the girls, like me, in thin dresses and heels,
the men in white ducks ranging from clean to careless, but
all with touches of colour that I knew would make Mother
wince. Winthrop was in a Burma pink jacket with a green
silk cummerbund, brushing back too-long blond hair
from his sunburned face. The other one, the painter, was
in grubby shorts and a sleeveless undershirt, but then he
wasn't coming out with us. I was aware of Mother's eyes
stopping on him. He looked far too unconventional for her.

No one answered her question. Instead they turned their
faces up to her like flowers to the sun, and smiled, shading
their eyes, waiting for me to answer. 'Oh, we haven't really
decided,' I called, trying to sound casual. 'The Stork Club
. . . Twenty-One . . . who knows?'

'Well,' she said, emanating sadness, 'you enjoy yourselves.'

Eliza's raggedy brother raised his glass as if to toast that,
but Mother had already turned away and disappeared
back inside.

In case he felt snubbed, I said quickly, 'Bill, doesn't that
glass need freshening?'

But he was still grinning with his face turned up to the
window, a little drunk. 'Pretty, your mom,' was all he said.
He hadn't noticed.

Perhaps I was being over-sensitive. But it had been a
very long first day home and, oh, I was so excited to see

them all again, with their carefree talk and brown faces, and so relieved, too.

I was already wishing I'd made a plan of my own. Two days ago, back in my college room, I'd still been telling myself it would all wait. There was plenty of time. I wasn't in any hurry to decide what to do next with my life. I could take the summer off, maybe get a job in a bookstore (through her Gurdjieff-obsessed brother, Eliza knew of a woman who'd got hold of some of the dead Sunwise Bookstore's stock, from years back – radical books wrapped in exotic-coloured paper covers, tattered textiles and unwanted paintings – and was looking for unpaid assistants to help her set up a little store of her own, paint it orange, and sell them off). What would be good about that, I'd thought, would be that it would mean I wouldn't have to go away with my family to Shelter Island for a month or more this summer. I'd much prefer to enjoy my new crowd of grown-up friends milling around the city before deciding on a longer-term future. I was also wondering if I should ask Eliza if I could move into that space they'd found over the bakery, right now. I hadn't realized, until I got back here, how unhomelike my old home might seem.

There was something new and threatening here. Hughie had mixed me his familiar Manhattan yesterday evening, and toasted homecoming as usual, but despite his practised joviality I'd felt a restraint I didn't understand. Mother hadn't got up at all, even for dinner, and hadn't felt well enough to see me; he'd taken her a tray, saying he wouldn't be a minute, then spent an hour away. I waited in the dining room, watching my soup congeal, wondering whether it would be rude to start, until Florence, taking pity on me, said, 'You go on and eat, Miss Evie.'

'Is Mother ill?' I asked Hughie when he came back. He shook his head, but in a way that didn't necessarily mean no, just that he felt sad for her.

'One of her headaches,' he said. 'You know she doesn't find the heat easy.'

She didn't appear at breakfast, either. 'Go to her, Miss E.,' Florence urged kindly. 'You haven't seen her since Easter. She'll want to hear your news.'

'What is it, Mother?' I whispered as I came into her room holding the breakfast tray Florence had given me. But she shook her head, and turned away from me.

'Well, can I bring you a cool drink, at least?' I asked. Silence.

At noon, still worried, I went out to meet Eliza. Her idea had been to hunt down the bookstore woman she'd been trying to locate. We walked to her door and knocked. Even though there was no answer, it was a relief to be out with the sun on my back, laughing with a friend who laughed back.

'Let's go look at those photos Dorothy was talking about, then,' Eliza said cheerfully after we'd given up knocking. 'I think the woman who takes them lives somewhere just close by.'

'I've got to get home,' I said, and the laughter went right out of me. 'My mother's not feeling well.' I stopped before reaching home and bought a big bouquet of white roses and ferns.

'Look, Mother,' I whispered from the door, trying to sound excited and not just nervous, peering into the gloom of drawn drapes, 'aren't they beautiful?'

Slowly, she turned her head and, when she saw the

flowers, and maybe the worry in my face, she let her tight, sick expression loosen just a bit, and nodded weakly before turning back towards the wall.

'I'll put them here, on the chest by your bed, shall I?' I babbled, hoping against hope that this was the beginning of something better. 'Look, do you see, I'll move the water glass over here, and these photos on to the window . . . then you'll be able to see them easily.'

I moved the photos in their silver frames, very carefully. Mother in white lace, with Aunt Mildred and Uncle Herbert. One of a young Mother, looking beautiful in pearls and very carefully made up, with a small, howling, red-faced, newborn me. Mother and Hughie, waving from a yacht . . . a family shot of all the cousins, grinning at the camera, on the island . . . Hughie and Mother, in Venice, waving from a gondola . . . there were so many of them.

It was only when I lifted the big vase on to the chest that I noticed something was lying on the mahogany top, among all that metallic display. It was a small sepia photograph in an oval card frame that I hadn't ever noticed before among these stiff public mementoes. It didn't have a frame. It must have got stuck at the back of something else, I thought, picking it up. It showed two young people in long-ago fashion, side by side, hand in hand, a young, timid-looking girl in white lace mutton-chop sleeves, with her black hair pinned up in a bun, looking very seriously at the camera, and a thin young black-haired man, maybe her cousin or brother – they were very alike – in a stiff jacket, waistcoat and high collar, looking just as serious.

When I turned it over, a little furtively, I saw the words 'Constance and Eddie, 1893' in faded ink and old-fashioned loopy copperplate. I held my breath. That must be my very young grandparents, in the year they married and set off for Imperial Russia together. I'd had no idea that any such picture existed. I wanted to stop and stare, or even ask . . . Touched that my mother had secretly kept it all these years, tucked away behind the display of her happy family, I put it carefully down with the others on the shelf.

And then I caught sight of another faded picture, which had slipped down somehow behind the chest and was stuck between its back and the wall. I nudged it out, not wanting to tear it.

It was the same picture as the one I'd kept for the past few years, which was now tucked into that book of French poems, with the wrapping next to it: Grandmother in her sixties, looking straight at the camera, with that hint of a smile, half-amused, but a little bit nervous too, on her face. No frame or anything. How strange, I thought, straightening it out, unable not to stare. It even had a fold in the bottom right-hand corner, where the photographic paper had cracked, in the same place as my one.

Had she been receiving more letters from Grandmother then? I turned to her, almost ready to ask, before my nerve failed me, and I pushed the picture under the other one, face down, on the window ledge. 'What a lot of pictures you have here . . .' I half whispered, but Mother didn't seem to notice. She didn't say any more, either, but when I tiptoed out a moment later, murmuring, 'You have a little sleep, now,' I was easier in my mind, because, although she was still wan and wild-haired, she would, at least, have those flowers to look at and smell when she turned around: a reminder that I'd been there, and that I'd tried.

*

We didn't make it to the Stork Club or Twenty-One that night, as it turned out. There was a flyer up outside the Russian Tea Room for a singer. 'The return of Nadezhda Plevitskaya!' it read. 'La Tsiganka! The Tsar's Nightingale!' and when I looked closer I saw the same stout, heavily rouged face that had been gazing out of Grandmother's newspaper.

'I've heard of her,' I called, startled by the coincidence. 'Let's go listen.' And the group wavered and coalesced around me in the hot dark and good-naturedly headed for the doorway.

I don't think any of the others were really in a listening mood. Winthrop and Bill got caught up in a discussion with the moustachioed waiter about whether a vodka Martini had any place in Russian life. The girls squeezed in next to them on the red banquette, laughing.

So I went and sat down on an empty chair near the singer by myself. This place didn't have the wistful charm of Madame Brodyanskaya's. I couldn't tell whether it really was full of escaped princesses and down-on-their-luck counts, as Hughie had once told me. My impression was that it wasn't that full at all. Apart from my friends at the banquette table nearest the door, all I could really see was smoke and silhouettes, the occasional flash of glass and, in front of me, in the most interior corner, a large woman in a tight burgundy dress and a loose flowered shawl with jet beads, already well into her programme.

The pictures had been flattering. The reality was older and blowsier and at least thirty pounds heavier. But she had a good pair of lungs on her, and a big, deep, swoopy voice. She sobbed her way through songs that you didn't need to understand the words of to know they were about heartbreak, and Cossacks, and wolves in the snow, and the tremble of greyish vines against the dacha window, and war, and partings . . .

They were shamelessly sentimental, those songs, just like the candelabra at that last table lighting the singer and the balalaika player in the shadows by her side, but they brought a lump to my throat all the same.

There was only a thin scatter of applause when she stopped and bowed. My friends didn't stop their noisy talk, even for a moment.

Blinking a little, the singer sat down at the candelabra table with her accompanist.

I got up too. Perhaps it was just the gallantry of that shawl draped over her quivering arms. I wanted to pay my respects.

Close up, I saw that Plevitskaya's face was damp under the kohl-lined black eyes, and her grey-streaked black curls were gleaming. A huge Orthodox cross was dancing up and down against her heaving décolletage. Even against the lurid red and green décor you could see that she was sweating heavily.

I'd thought she looked disconsolate, but as soon as she saw someone approaching she was suddenly radiant again. It didn't matter that there were flashes of gold in her mouth. The smiles she was now giving her accompanist, who was also so lit up by the appearance of audience that he started kissing her hand, said, in the simplest and most joyous way imaginable, 'Here I am. Here you are. Let me make music for you. Let me give you pleasure.'

I liked them both at once. '*Prekrasno . . . prosto divno . . .*' he was saying, to her, but also watching me out of the corner of his eye, before adding, in English: 'You are *won*-derrrful.'

'Wonderful,' I echoed, feeling something new opening up and my own tentative smile grow to radiantly joyful proportions as well. '*Wonderful.*'

'But I already knew you would be,' I added, with a heady flash of boldness, 'before I heard you, because I think my grandmother has seen you in Paris. Countess Sabline . . .'

I couldn't have been more surprised at her reaction. Her eyes opened wider in a great melodrama of astonishment.

'*Constance!*' she cried, as if overcome. She reached for my hand, and held it very tenderly, and gazed into my eyes. 'Can it be possible! You – my dearrr Constance's grand-daughter! Of course – your eyes! Everything! I see! My God! Sit, sit! Please!'

Overwhelmed, I sat. 'You mean . . . you *know* her?' I whispered.

But it took only a moment more, as my shock receded, to see that she wasn't going to ask difficult questions. She wasn't going to ask anything, in fact. She was going to talk.

'Dear Constance,' she said throatily, and I thought she might weep from pleasure. 'Of course! My God. An *angel*. My benefactor.'

She looked mistily down at the empty table. The balalaika player too. Why, oh why, I wondered, once the possible cause of these looks dawned on me, hadn't I asked the barman to send them drinks before approaching? I hadn't got at all used to having my father's allowance – a hundred dollars a month! A fortune! – at my disposal.

But, before I could risk breaking the mood by looking for a waiter, she sighed and went soulfully on: 'My sponsorrr.

A wonderful, generous woman. An arrrtist at hearrrt. *She* appreciates a voice once admired by the Tsar of all the Rrrussias . . . our Little Father . . . the Tsar's Nightingale, they called me once . . .' Her voice died away. She dropped my hand and crossed herself; then she resumed, with much more bite and boastfulness: 'She is having Magnetophon recording made of my voice. For posterity, you understand.'

My head was spinning. Still half looking for a waiter while wondering what I might ask about her voice recording, I hardly noticed the tapping at my shoulder.

'Dearrr Constance speaks often of you,' Plevitskaya went on, superbly.

'She does?' I said eagerly, feeling a shimmering happiness spread through me. Again I disregarded the tapping on my bare upper arm.

'She has told me *so much* . . .'

It was Plevitskaya who became aware of the extra presence in our midst first. Her big dark eyes widened as they shifted to somewhere above my left side; her smile became flirtatious again.

I followed her gaze. There was Winthrop, in his peacock pinks and shimmering greens, brushing hair out of his eyes, laughing back down at her, enjoying the scene but coming to take me away. 'They're all ready to go, Evie,' he murmured, turning to me. 'We've heard there's a man at a place up the street right now who can tell Bill and me about Spain. He knows the cheapest way to get to Europe – some ship they practically pay you to take passage on – and everything else, too. We want to catch him.'

I nodded, feeling disappointed that we'd been interrupted, but also obscurely relieved. Of course, I told myself, I hadn't really believed, not for a moment, that Plevitskaya would have heard stories about me from Grandmother. She'd just been telling me what I wanted to hear. It was best to go now, and keep this moment magical.

Plevitskaya was looking at Winthrop with frank admiration. Well, he *was* good looking. 'Young girrrls. Things just *khappen* to them. *Won*derful,' she purred, almost licking her lips. He grinned back. He liked being admired. And he had nice manners.

'May we', he said, with perhaps a quicker understanding than mine, 'leave you with a glass of champagne? We all loved your singing . . .'

While they happily cooed and billed, and I got to my feet, he gestured for a waiter.

'Will you', I asked Plevitskaya as Winthrop, having ordered their drinks, put his arm through mine, ready to go, 'be singing here again?' Even if I didn't believe her, I couldn't quite bear to just let her go, all the same. Just in case. I might regret it tomorrow.

I thought there was regret in her eyes too as she shook her head. But the words she replied with were all grandeur: 'Tonight is the end of my Amerrrican tourrr. But come to Paris. Come, please! I am performing there verrry often.'

'How would I find you?' I persisted. 'Before you leave town?'

Her eyes flickered. 'Ritz-Carrrlton Khotel,' she said splendidly, but I could tell right off that she wasn't really staying there. It was just a boast.

'Well, please,' I said, feeling deflated, 'if we don't meet, give my best to . . .'

But what was the point? Winthrop was applying gentle pressure to my arm to get me to start moving towards the door. The others were waiting.

She inclined her head and eyed the sparkling glass in front of her. 'Of courrrse.'

6

I could tell it was late as soon as I opened my eyes. There was mid-morning sunshine streaming in through the window, and Florence was in the doorway, only her skirt and ankles visible under that big pile of laundry I'd left yesterday.

'Ten o'clock, Miss E.,' she said. Then, kindly, 'Thought you should sleep through.'

I sat up guiltily. 'How's Mother today?' I asked.

'Got a visitor.'

By the time I'd dressed and run a comb through my hair and got to Mother's room, Aunt Mildred was getting wheezily to her feet, ready to go.

She eyed me with disfavour. 'Up late, I see,' was all she said. Mother, sitting up against her pillows, sighed.

'Let me see you out, Aunt Mildred,' I said hastily, eager to make amends. I leaned over and kissed Mother's cheek, miserably aware of her faint movement away from me.

Aunt Mildred sailed down the corridor in her summer grey, ominous as a battleship. I hastened after her, bobbing in her wake. We were at the door, and I was fussing around finding the parasol she said she'd come in with but which neither of us could see, before she cleared her throat and said, 'I'm assuming you do know that your mother has been feeling unwell?'

I straightened up and stepped out of the closet, full of sudden dread. 'Yes,' I said, and I could hear my voice sounded thin.

She shook her head. 'Well, I think she would have appreciated just a little concern and care,' she said grimly.

'But . . .' I stammered with a last flicker of self-defence, 'I have . . .'

My proof: hadn't she and Mother been sitting together in the healing rose fragrance that my white flowers, so lustrously fresh and perfect, were sending out into the room?

'She's hardly seen you, she says.'

I hung my head. The rest of what she said washed over me: the 'children can be so unthinking's, and the 'of course their own lives seem so much more interesting's.

'It doesn't do a girl's reputation any good, you know,' Aunt Mildred added, more severely still, and the force of whatever else she and Mother had also been discussing made it sound as though every word she said were capitalized, 'What You've Been Doing.'

Whatever That Is, I told myself with inner defiance, though 'going out till all hours drinking cocktails', 'keeping company with disreputable young men' and 'letting communists disturb the neighbourhood' possibly had something to do with it.

'My parasol is there,' she added in a different voice.

Wordlessly, I passed it out.

She gave me a challenging stare. 'I don't need to say any more, do I?' she finished.

I shook my head.

'I can only say it's a good thing you're all coming to the island from tomorrow,' she added, opening the door herself. 'We'll have some good behaviour *there*, at least.'

The door clicked shut.

In my room, where the bright sunshine through the windows now seemed to be mocking me, I looked at the books still in the bottom of my trunk. They didn't seem to be in quite the same places I remembered. I couldn't see the French poetry book with the bundle of extra bits of paper, including the torn-out ad for Plevitskaya, the so-called Nightingale, whom I'd met last night, and the photo of Grandmother, folded inside the cover. I turned the whole box out. It wasn't anywhere.

I went to the kitchen. There were noises from the washroom behind.

'Are we really going to the island tomorrow?' I asked Florence.

Florence, half-submerged in a sudsy tub, looked up at me sympathetically.

'That's why I'm washing everything today,' she said carefully. 'Though how all this will ever get dry in time God only knows.'

Then she scrunched up her face in that sympathetic, I-know-more-than-I'm-admitting way she had, and added, 'Nothing for it but to say yes, Miss E. Just like I do.'

'But for how long?' I asked, ignoring her advice. 'Did she say?'

She shook her head.

I turned away. 'Did you move any of my books?' I asked, half out of the door. 'The ones in the trunk? While you were getting the washing?'

She shook her head again. I could see the kindness in her eyes. And of course I'd known the answer already.

I didn't knock on the way into Mother's room. She was lying in bed, reading the paper.

'A little better,' she murmured, turning her eyes to the wall. 'Aunt Mildred . . . so kind . . .'

I stood by her bed, looking down at her. She shifted her shoulder a little further towards the wall.

Looking round, I saw that one of the big pots of orchids from the window was on her bedside chest this morning – its blooms white and smooth. Unnatural-looking, parasitic things, I thought, suddenly disgusted by them: half-flower, half-fungus.

'That's a pretty orchid,' I said brightly. 'Did Aunt Mildred bring it?'

A tiny frown appeared on her face, as if pain might be returning. 'No, it's always been there . . .'

'Well, yesterday, for instance, there were some white roses there. I bought them for you myself, and put them in a vase right here,' I said, keeping my voice as steady and reasonable as I could. 'I had to move all the pictures on to the window to fit the vase on to the chest. Don't you remember?'

Yet the pictures were in their usual place now – the whole shiny array, dusted, in tidy rows around the orchid pot. For a yawning moment, looking at them, I wondered whether I hadn't just imagined, dreamed, the white roses . . .

And then Mother's eyes flickered. 'Oh,' she said, looking down at her hands, 'those. They died.'

'Uh-huh,' I said.

In the silence that followed, a whirring, chattering, pounding-red interior monologue began inside me.

What time had she had to get up this morning, that voice was asking, to make sure my flowers were disposed of and the orchids in place instead and the pictures dusted and arranged, all before Aunt Mildred's early call? Had she known, beforehand, that she'd want my roses gone so she could complain about my selfishness more freely? And, if she was so sick, where had she found the strength to heave that heavy orchid pot into place?

'But, oh look,' I went on, with bright, false concern, 'I think you must have dropped one or two of the pictures you had here yesterday?'

Mother put one hand to her forehead, and shook her head.

'Both the ones of Grandmother . . .?' I went on, pronouncing the taboo word with the greatest possible precision. 'Because they've gone.'

Her frown deepened. 'I don't know what you're talking about,' she said.

'Grandmother,' I repeated sweetly. 'Yesterday you had her wedding picture here, and also that recent one she sent from Paris. The one from my poetry book. Would you like me to look and see if they've fallen under your bed?'

Silence.

'Your mother,' I prompted, after a moment, but I could already feel that brief flush of heat and anger fading inside me. 'Constance.'

She closed her eyes. 'Inconstancy, more like,' she whispered.

'Grandmother then,' I prodded. 'Shall I look for the photographs?' I moved towards her bed.

'I don't know what you mean about pictures,' Mother

suddenly snapped in a much stronger voice. 'There are no pictures of her here.'

I straightened, smiling down at the floor. 'Ah, well, perhaps I imagined them,' I said with what insouciance I could still manage. With the last vestiges of my brave anger, I told myself: So she's put the pictures somewhere else, that's all *that* means.

'I need to rest,' she said.

I got almost all the way to the door before she whispered at my back, 'Did Aunt Mildred tell you she's asked us all to the island from tomorrow evening?'

I turned, submissively. The darkness had gone from her face. She was almost smiling.

'I've asked Florence to get your clothes ready.'

I nodded again. I so wanted to trust that hint of warmth. My mind was leaping ahead, showing me wishful-thinking pictures of sunlight on the water, and us all laughing together – but such pictures, I knew even as I imagined them, were only illusions.

As soon as I'd left her room I went straight to the telephone in the hall.

'Eliza?' I whispered, when she came to the phone. 'What was the name of the ship to Europe the man was talking about last night?'

PART TWO

An Apartment in Paris

7

September 1937

'Two o'clock already,' General Miller sighed as soon as he'd finished the lunchtime *plat*, showing none of his usual interest in the cheese. 'I must go . . . *Davno pora.*'

Constance glanced around, a bit surprised by his change of language. He didn't always talk Russian with her. His English wasn't bad at all, even if, after all these years here, his French was still lousy. Her Russian was good enough, but she still preferred to speak English with him. But it only took a moment to see why he'd reverted to his native tongue. The housekeeper was in the doorway, ready to take away the plates.

Constance smiled up at him. Our secret, his eyes flashed back. As usual there was both laughter in them and a mute appeal. It was fine, they were telling her, for Marie-Thérèse to be aware that he sometimes came up from his office on the ground floor for lunch with his old friend one floor up. But anything else was not a housekeeper's business.

As it happened, there'd been nothing at all private in the conversation they'd been having. In fact, Constance had spent the meal quietly agonizing over *not* having found a way to broach the big subject on her mind.

Instead they'd just had their usual disagreement about art. It was almost a ritual, this bantering argument, in this big rented apartment, whose fussy pastel-flowered walls and Louis Quinze furniture she'd by now pretty much covered with all her purchases of wildly colourful avant-garde art. He'd shake his head at the latest item, whatever it might be – today a rather magical exquisite-corpse sketch done collectively, one foot or breast or mouth at each fold of the paper, by the wonderfully dishevelled Surrealists she'd fed last night. He'd say, clearly enjoying his mock despair, 'My God! Another daub! A scrrrible! terrrible!' while she laughed back and said, 'Ah, what have you ever understood about art?' ('All our exchanges about art are conducted in an atmosphere of controlled mutual contempt,' she'd once told him wryly, and liked his unabashed reply, 'Ah, but there is warmth in it, at least, and that is the important thing.')

But the ordinariness of what they'd been talking about wasn't the point, she thought tenderly. It didn't matter whether there was really anything that needed keeping from Marie-Thérèse. It was enough that he felt vulnerable enough to want the protection of secrecy. Russians did, these days. She would, too, if she, like him, were running a White organization whose previous leader had been kidnapped in broad daylight right here on a Parisian street seven years ago, and never been seen again, and the one before that poisoned. She knew that was why there were all those burly young secretaries at the office of his military outfit, which was what the White Army had become after being driven out of Soviet Russia fifteen years ago. They didn't like him to go about the streets on his own. It was also why she'd taken this grimly conventional apartment in the staid, cheerless 8th arrondissement, when, frankly, she'd rather have been in chic Montparnasse with the art crowd: because the apartment one flight up was the only place he could easily get away to.

If he also wanted to pretend to her housekeeper that he never came back at night, after Marie-Thérèse was safely tucked away upstairs in her *chambre de bonne*, well, that was fine by her, too – even though, for God's sake, Marie-Thérèse was an unshockable Parisian, who'd surely seen it all. Her housekeeper was also the last person Constance could imagine reporting to Soviet Moscow, if that was the unlikely way his mind was turning (though she rather enjoyed the absurd notion of Marie-Thérèse mumbling into a secret radio with her coat collar turned up). She watched him sometimes, in the morning, eyes scouring the bedroom for any forgotten trace of himself before he left. Maybe he just thought the housekeeper would gossip, and somehow word that he had a mistress would pass through the Paris concierges' bush telegraph, and reach his son. But Constance never asked – and to be honest she didn't really care – why he pounced so energetically on stray socks and shaving brushes, tucking them away in his briefcase with that furtive glance her way, as if worried she'd notice. He should know, she thought, that he was safe enough here. But if being so terribly cloak-and-dagger made him happy, what did any of it matter? She could humour him.

All Constance wanted was for him to feel comfortable whenever he could get away to her here.

As he took her hand now, formally, and kissed it with the absurd old-world courtliness she laughed at in him, but privately adored, Constance felt the familiar stab of a sweetness that was almost pain, both at the beautiful straightness of his back and the vulnerable-looking silver of that head of hair, which she remembered once so strong and wavy and golden. Well, we're none of us getting any younger, she thought wistfully.

It was three years since she'd run into him again, here in Paris. She hadn't been able to believe her luck that first day. She still remembered the tremor in her voice when the face of the sternly staring man hunched over the chessboard in the park had, somehow, resolved itself into that unformed young face from long ago; when she'd whispered, '. . . Miller?' and those altered features had relaxed into a joy that looked so *exactly* like what she'd already started feeling inside, too . . . She still couldn't always believe her luck.

And now she was overwhelmed by her good fortune at simply being here with this man, in this moment, after all those other less happy years – here, and gratefully watching time draw its lines on him. On both of them. She'd never expected so much of life.

'*Dorogoye serdtse*,' she murmured, entering his game of secrets by speaking Russian. ('Dear heart.') Then, leaping up, she completed the sentence in English. 'I'll see you out.'

Leaving Marie-Thérèse with the ruins of the rack of lamb – all those little bones sticking up, never Constance's favourite meal, though in this hot weather the scent of thyme and rosemary and garlic reminded her happily of the Midi – she walked behind him down the corridor.

Just before he reached for the catch on the front door –
no need for him to stop for coat or hat for he'd slipped up
here as he was, in shirtsleeves and waistcoat, leaving his
jacket on the back of his chair – the music started again.
It was so sudden, and so loud, that they both jumped and
turned to stare at the closed door of the study they'd just
passed.

A deep woman's voice belted out the word 'LOOOOOVE'
from behind it. Then there was a skidding plastic noise,
and a whir. Then the same phrase began again.

Constance sighed. She must have heard it a hundred
times this morning, since Marie-Thérèse had let in the
engineers who'd come with their big machine to sit in the
study going through the tapes they'd recorded, playing
them over and over to find the best versions. She could
have done without this, today of all days. There were too
many other things for her to think about.

He sneezed. He had a cold. He'd been sneezing all
through lunch. Grumpily he said, 'I can hear it from
downstairs, too, you know. What a torment.'

Constance looked at him with slight worry as the peace of
a moment ago faded. She knew he was happy, in principle,
that she'd offered to pay for the Magnetophon recording of
the voice that all his Russians downstairs loved so much.
But she also knew he'd been less happy to discover that she
had agreed the editing could be done at her home. To be
honest, she never would have done if she'd realized how
noisy it would be, or how long it would take.

'Too awful,' she replied pacifically, 'darling. But it'll be
done by the end of the week.'

She didn't regret her generosity, not really. You had

to share your luck. And poor Plevitskaya – time hadn't been kind to *her*. That once lovely, coarsened face danced before Constance's eyes, with its thick kohl and rouge, that disconsolate look. Constance had been touched by the hope that had come into the singer's mournful eyes when she'd first suggested this; a hope she'd seen growing and growing as she talked persuasively on, through 'You have to keep up with the times', to 'You're only as old as you feel', and 'Who knows? Wouldn't it be a hoot if the recording was a hit? You still have armies of fans . . .'

Constance had been thrilled to be of help when Miller's deputy downstairs, General Skoblin, had first shown her the German newspaper clip of the miraculous recording machine that had been displayed at the Berlin Radio Show. It used magnetized tape to catch the human voice. Skoblin wanted to buy one, and even knew someone who could bring one back from Berlin. But he didn't have quite enough money right now . . .

Constance didn't really like General Skoblin, with his thin black comb-over, little moustache, comically short eyebrows – an inch of black over the middle of his eyes – and impassive face. In her head she called him the Goblin. She liked most of the other White Russian officers downstairs, who she was on chatting-on-the-stairs terms with. They loved her knowledge of Russian and her ability to reminisce with them about their long-ago glory days in St Petersburg. Yet she'd never managed to look at the poor Goblin with anything like affection.

All the same, she'd wanted to help, because the Goblin was Plevitskaya's husband. And he'd wanted the machine to make a recording of his wife's voice. And that was only right and proper, because Plevitskaya, anyone could see, wasn't taking the slow fading of her singing career well. As her husband had only half explained, out of a delicacy that Constance rather admired, the great benefit of this new recording technique with tape was that you didn't have to sing perfectly all the way through a song any more. (And poor Plevitskaya didn't, always, any more; there were, all too often, strange fades, and swoops, and hoarse shouts, and notes that were so off-key you had to bite your lip to avoid a smile.) The beauty of tape was that you could sing your thing over and over until you had a good version of every line, separately, then cut out all the bad bits and just stick together the good ones – and end up with a magically perfect version of whatever you'd sung. Constance liked the sound of that editing and improving on reality, the auditory equivalent, she thought, of the half-knowing way she ignored her wrinkles when she looked in the glass. We could all do with a bit more imaginary perfection as we get older, she thought kindly.

'I LOOOOOVED HIM,' the amplified voice bellowed, again.

The door was almost vibrating. Constance looked anxiously at it. She knew her modish art enthusiasms often tested Miller's patience. Was this one odd project too many?

'You were too soft with our Nightingale,' he said, but to her relief his exasperation had gone and his voice was gentle again. 'You should have told her this part must happen in *her* home.'

'But I couldn't, *chubchik*,' Constance said. 'You know she lives out in the sticks. And I expect the engineers are German, like the machine. Foreigners would never have found their way out there without a car. Anyway, she steamrollered me. You know no one can resist Plevitskaya.'

She looked pleadingly at him. As he moved towards her in the dusk behind the front door, she was suddenly aware of his bulk and pompous tie and waistcoat and old-world whiskers, so unlike her wavy thinness and boyish, straight, progressive bob, which her artists always said she was right to stick with, whatever the latest fashion for waves, because she was expressing her inner essence. No wonder her adorably skinny and starving young geniuses didn't even seem to *see* Miller, let alone speak to him, any more than he had shown any interest in them, on the very few occasions she'd been unable to prevent them briefly crossing paths. They were just too different. She thought, and it was a bittersweet notion: What unlikely lovers we would seem, if anyone ever *did* see us together . . .

. . . but then he was pulling her to him, and she stopped thinking. He'd once told her that Cossacks greeted each other with one-armed hugs like this, pulling up their horses side by side and embracing from the saddle. She breathed in his cologne. She could hear his heartbeat and feel the rumble of his laugh. And, with the knowledge that brought, that he was as happy as she was, peace returned. 'Different though we are,' he was whispering. 'Different though we became before finding each other now, we are one.'

'There's something we should talk over together,' she whispered back, at last forcing herself to raise the question that had been on her mind all day. She couldn't let him go without even mentioning it. That would be too cowardly. And it was already nearly too late. 'I wondered . . . maybe you'd come back on your way out, later?'

There. She'd said it, or started to. They were really going to have to talk about what was on her mind, and very soon, too.

But he was shaking his head. 'I regret,' he said, though with such tenderness that she knew he really did regret it. 'Tonight I have a meeting downstairs. A long and important meeting. And later, a family commitment . . .'

Constance knew better than to look downcast. He did, sometimes, have family commitments. He had a wife, a helpless invalid, wandering in her mind. And a grown-up son, who wrote, and also, like so many Russians here, drove a taxi; a good-looking young man who kept the entire family financially afloat with his night job, she knew. Of course sometimes Miller had to be with them. These were things you had to take with grace. But tomorrow would be too late.

'Maybe a quick cocktail before you go home?' she persisted.

He shook his head. 'Tomorrow, I hope,' he said. He kissed her hand and stepped out.

Feeling deflated that she'd have to think out the next step on her own, Constance watched him descend the apartment-block stairs. He already had the thoughtful look that suggested he was far away, preparing himself for that meeting. She still found it hard to imagine why the Reds of Moscow would be remotely interested in pursuing these ageing, defenceless class enemies. She had no picture of what all those dear, courtly gentlemen – clinging on tight to their memories, refusing to let their children go to French school (at least Miller hadn't been that much of a fool) and still dreaming of some impossible, glorious reconquest of the land they'd lost – did all day down in their office. But she couldn't believe that meeting today would really be about something very earth-shattering. All the poor officers seemed to talk about was setting up night schools to teach Russian literature to veterans and their children, finding charitable funding for more Russian old people's homes, and poring over the Soviet newspapers for possible signs of weakness in the enemy. Constance had long ago decided she wouldn't try to know too much.

As she shut the door, a new phrase began. 'LOOOOVE IS STILL PERHAAAAPS . . .'

Squeezing back against the corridor wall, she made way for Marie-Thérèse, that stubby monument to Gallic disapproval in her brown serge and apron, who was bearing down on her, weighed down by her tray and her rage against the music.

'*Encore . . . !*' Marie-Thérèse muttered in long-suffering tones as she passed, just loud enough for Constance to hear. '*Mais j'en ai marre de cette musique!*'

Constance bit her own lip to stop herself smiling. It was no secret to her that her housekeeper disliked all immigrants, but loathed the many Russians living in Paris most of all. And now this music . . . Marie-Thérèse pushed open the kitchen door with an energetic, angry swing of the hips and passed through into her domestic domain, and Constance grinned as she heard her cross voice again, much louder, from the other side of the door: '*Sacrés Russes!*' ('Darn Russians!')

Eventually Constance settled down in her bedroom. It was a little quieter there. She fished in her bag for the wire she'd got before lunch from Le Havre. She put on her spectacles.

'HOPE YOU GOT LETTER STOP ARRIVING EVENING TRAIN STOP EVIE', it still said. (She'd been half thinking, all through lunch, that when she looked again it might turn out to say something quite different.)

She'd had no inkling, until it appeared, that this was about to happen. Evie's letter, presumably sent many days ago, before the ship set sail, had not arrived.

Just as it had this morning, the sight of that telegram form set Constance's stomach churning. It was one thing to put out tentative feelers in the hope that something might come of them and that maybe someday . . . and quite another for it to just *happen* like this, with no time for mental preparation. *Altogether* different. Altogether hellish.

Constance wasn't a strategist by nature. As she was always telling her artists, spontaneity was more her thing. But the idea of improvising *this* visit, with all its complications, was making her feel sick. '*Mon Dieu,*' she said wanly, out loud. Then, perhaps still influenced by Miller's change of languages earlier, she added, '*Bozhe moi,*' and watched her reflection in the dressing-table glass shake its dark head and put hand to brow. For all her worry, she was – just a little – impressed by the elegance of the reflection's gesture. She put back on the chic modern black-and-white geometric bangle she'd taken off when Miller was due. Somehow, that made her feel better.

What did she even look like now, that excitable little girl? Constance tried to picture her stretched and straightened and twenty-one, but her imagination failed her.

There would be so much to catch up with. So much to find out . . . but also (don't get distracted, she warned

69

herself) so much to tell. That was the part she needed to think out – what to say to the child; how to explain herself; and what was she going to say to Miller? And when?

Explanations, so unimaginable . . . But she mustn't let it all crowd in at once. One thing at a time.

The important thing was not to panic. She started to try to picture herself relaxed and calm, speaking to this unknown Evie . . . an adult Evie who behaved like a friend, who wasn't full of the stuffy, huffy spite of the rest of the family, who'd learned to read and think independently while away at school and was easy to talk to, a girl who loved pictures and ideas as much as she did.

'I always wanted to know you and be close to the family. But it seemed too difficult, for a long time,' she told her reflection in the glass tentatively. 'Then, three years ago, quite by chance, I met someone I'd known when I was young in Russia, playing chess right here in the Jardin du Luxembourg, under the lilacs. And, even though our lives had each taken such different paths since those young days, we fell in love. And that inspired me to try again. To write to your mother. To offer you an education. To send you books . . .'

There were so many other things they'd move on to, later, once they'd got to know each other. But that would do, wouldn't it? For a start . . .?

And maybe she'd show Evie that picture?

It was hidden away in a small cardboard box of trinkets packed in tissue paper that she'd pushed under her bed when she'd moved in. The trinkets were those long-ago lover's gifts you never quite want to throw away: mineral monstrosities, jewelled troikas poised on marble ostrich

eggs and the like. Oh, how she'd treasured them when she'd first been given them. But now it was only the photograph she could bear to look at. There she was, all sepia and faded, young and pretty in a white lace blouse, sitting in a boat – a picnic, she remembered. A summer's day near St Petersburg, a river bank, a meadow of wild flowers. Maybe thirty people, Americans and Russians both. The picture showed two or three people on the bank – arms and backs, anyway – and one other person in the boat with her, a very tall, thin young man buttoned up to the neck in a military tunic despite the heat, with thick wavy fair hair and wide-set eyes, holding the oars. (Preobrazhensky Regiment, First Brigade, she remembered him telling her, and his blue eyes smiling, though had that been here, in this boat?) In the picture, her young self, looking over at her boatman, was the one smiling.

Constance put it up against the glass above the fireplace.

That first step felt like an achievement.

She went over to the ugly little lap desk that was part of the apartment's overdone clutter and opened it. There was no writing paper inside. She'd forgotten to order it again. There weren't even any discarded envelopes in the wastepaper basket (curse Marie-Thérèse for her impeccable housekeeping). There was just blotting paper.

Sitting down on the bed, she wrote 'Now' down the left-hand side of the blotting paper, and 'Later' down the right.

After a while, she added a question mark to each side. She put down the pen, and sighed.

She still had no idea what else to tell her granddaughter, who was probably already on the train here. Or when.

But she was, at least, relieved when the music stopped, and footsteps came out of the study. They'd done for the day, then. Thank God. Two very deep male voices in the corridor rumbled polite goodbyes at the silent presence that must be Marie-Thérèse. She was a little surprised to hear these engineers speak the Russian-accented French of so many shabbily dressed people here in Paris. (Heavens, why had she thought they'd be German?)

Shamed by Marie-Thérèse's surly silence, she called out, warmly, *'Do zavtra, gospoda.'* ('See you tomorrow, gentlemen.')

When the door had shut quietly behind the men, she asked Marie-Thérèse to bring her apéritif to the now-empty study.

You got the sunset from the study.

She pulled up a chair to the French window in there and, lighting a cigarette, looked out at the honeyed evening scene before her: trees fuzzy with leaves and pale-gold house fronts. She liked the stillness of this time on a hot day. This is where she'd bring Evie, for the first discussion she'd imagined . . . Slowly, she felt a fragile sort of quiet return. This was what she'd wanted, after all, wasn't it, even if it was now coming more suddenly than she'd have liked? If all the reversals Constance had survived had taught her anything, it was that life was, almost always, more of a comedy than a tragedy. And this, too, would almost certainly all come out all right in the end.

When Marie-Thérèse came in with her glass of champagne, Constance asked, in a voice she had to make as calm as possible, trying to believe this was the most normal request in the world, 'Would you make up the spare room before you go? And also ask Gaston if he'd meet the Le Havre evening train later on? My grand-daughter's coming to stay.'

To her astonishment, Marie-Thérèse's reply of '*Oui, madame*' was only slightly grumpy.

Taking a sip of champagne, she moved away from the window to the big table she used as a desk.

The men had left their equipment out.

The machine – a big futuristic-looking thing, with two spools of magnetic tape wound round the front, and knobs and buttons everywhere – was standing right in the middle of the table. There was a pile of tape sweepings on the floor, with a broom beside it.

Absurdly, considering how she'd hated hearing the music playing all day, Constance now wanted to see how the machine worked. Maybe it would amuse Evie, later.

She plugged it in at the wall and it whirred into life. Lights flashed. But she couldn't see which was the 'on' button that would make the reels move, or how you would operate it.

Still . . . imagining herself further into this game, she picked up the heavy headphones the men had left on the back of the chair, sat down, and fitted them on her ears.

What would you hear, with these on?

It took her a moment or two just to get used to the feel of them covering her ears, like a pair of hands. It seemed a very long while before she realized that – even though the recording machine wasn't moving – she was hearing something through them.

At first all she could make out was static, like a badly tuned radio station.

73

But then voices came muttering through the storm, loud, then quiet, then loud again: men's voices, speaking Russian.

Why, she thought, astonished, surely the engineers haven't just been sitting in here recording themselves?

It took a moment or two more to be able to make out what the voices were saying.

MAN ONE: 'I may have the news we've been waiting for by tomorrow.'

MAN TWO: 'What, really? My dear colleague, do you really mean it? At last?'

The second voice, fuzzy and hard to hear though it was, was so endearingly full of hope that Constance warmed to it even as she tried to puzzle out what was going on. Was there a radio receiver built into this equipment, perhaps? she wondered, still hoping that a sensible explanation would come to her. Could one of the engineers maybe have been listening while the other edited?

But who would transmit Russian radio here in Paris? Miller's people certainly didn't have a radio station. She didn't think even those other Russians – the ones at the Soviet diplomatic mission – did . . .

'I can hardly believe it,' the second voice went on emotionally. How familiar its cadences seemed through the crackle and fuzz in her ears. And then there was a sneeze.

Of course she knew who it was. Miller. He'd had a cold for two days. Which meant this wasn't a recording, or a radio. It was reality. Somehow, and Constance didn't like to imagine how, she was listening to Miller quietly talking to someone downstairs.

'Well, let's just see tomorrow,' the first man was saying, through the thump of her heart. 'But it is looking pretty good.'

Constance began twitching for a cigarette. She needed to think, but she had a pain in her chest.

Hurriedly she let the headphones drop, pushed the chair back and ran out of the room, stumbling against bits of furniture, clattering on the parquet.

'Marie-Thérèse!' she called hoarsely, hoping the house-keeper hadn't already finished making up the bed in the spare room for Evie and gone upstairs. 'Marie-Thérèse! I need you. Now!'

8

Marie-Thérèse couldn't help noticing that the two muscly Russians were sitting outside at the café again when she let the doctor in at dusk. As usual, they were muttering at each other and ignoring the chessboard they were supposed to be looking at.

They'd been there every day for a month, those two men, with their cheap suits, bad skins and pudding-bowl haircuts. They looked . . . well, wrong, in a way she couldn't place.

She was too preoccupied this evening, what with the doctor, Madame's *crise* and the bit of whalebone that had strayed out of her corseting and was prodding into her flesh, to give her full attention to resenting these *sacrés Russes* in the wholehearted way she usually did – thousands of them, wherever you went, feckless vodka-swilling drunks, taking jobs from good French workers, always kicking up a stink about their papers and their tragedies, cooking cabbage, assassinating and kidnapping people, as had happened downstairs a few years back, which had meant police prying everywhere for months. There goes the neighbourhood.

From her earlier observation of this little conspiracy of Russian café visitors – and every gathering of Russians *was* a conspiracy, she was sure of it – she knew that, any minute now, they would be joined by their more recent friend. This more definitely lower-class man might even – she recoiled almost physically at this thought – be a market trader, if his apron stinking of crab was anything to go by. Marie-Thérèse knew from past experience that this person, wildly unsuitable for a café in the serious, respectable rue du Colisée, wouldn't be playing chess any more than his cronies did. They'd all just sit there all evening, ignoring the game and muttering away together.

If only Madame wasn't so taken up with Russians, she thought, and her regret was tinged with shame and anger that, as a result of her mistress's poor social judgement, she too was, at one remove, also implicated in Russian goings-on. Not that the courteous, old-fashioned officers were bad neighbours, exactly, but those dirty artists who were always round here, staying up all night, eating Madame out of house and home, draining the wine cellar and stubbing their cigarettes out in the flower vases; not to mention the fact that a decent young Frenchman like her nephew Pierre couldn't get work in the car factories at Billancourt these days, because he couldn't understand what was being said around him if he didn't speak Russian . . . *ça alors!*

She shut the door on the scene with feeling, and followed the doctor up the stairs towards Madame's bedroom.

It didn't take General Skoblin long to spot his wife through the clouds of murky steam that the trains were blowing back along the platform.

Plevitskaya always stood out. Ignoring tonight's heat, she was wearing a wide-brimmed dark felt hat festooned with ostrich feathers. Her lips were a crimson pout, and she had gold hoops in her ears. In that clinging burgundy dress, walking with a slight waddle caused by new shoes he could see were too high and small for comfort, she was sweating but magnificent.

Watching her approach, amid the stares and turning heads of the other boat-train passengers, her husband quietly folded up his newspaper. In the half-hour he'd been waiting under the great glassed-in roof of the gare Saint-Lazare, no one in the crowds of porters and pigeons and passengers pushing one way or the other had spared *him* a second glance. But then he was an inconspicuous man in late middle age, with neat grey-black hair, a moustache and a suit of about the same colour as the dark metal stanchion he'd been standing by. He didn't stand out. He was used to playing second fiddle.

Even though he could see her eyes searching the crowd for him now, he didn't do any of the flamboyant things people might expect the husband of such a woman to do: run forward, sweep her up in his arms, press passionate lips to hers, or even wave. He wasn't given to melodrama. He just stood there, thinking, and sighing a bit at the mountains of luggage bobbing along behind her equally mountainous form. He didn't like to think of the shopping she must have done in New York, whatever she'd promised him before leaving. At least she'd travelled second class this time, so hopefully there'd be fewer new debts. Thank God, in so many ways, for the second job, and his good news.

'Darrrling!' she erupted with her best throaty vibrato when she finally sighted him from ten feet away. She speeded up to a curvaceous totter, rushing to his arms.

He stepped dutifully forward and embraced her back. He could smell at once that she'd been replenishing her supplies of Chanel No. 5, and at American prices too. As she and the porters and observers all clearly expected, he raised her hand to his lips and kissed it. She curved her big mouth up into a satisfied smile, then, before he'd had a chance to say a word, opened it again and started volubly talking. 'My golden treasure! My little sun!' Her lips caressed each endearment, showing off for the watchers she was pretending to ignore, giving them a performance as she always did. Her great stone-studded gold cross flapped energetically up and down between her breasts. Her black-rimmed eyes widened theatrically. The train – *dreadfully* crowded. The ship – a tossing, turning, heaving nightmare full of God knows who; the *indignity*. The *unworthiness* of the restaurants she'd been booked to sing in in New York. And the hotel waiters – all Chinamen in pigtails . . .

Silently he nodded and smiled. He distributed francs among the porters (she didn't even look – she was too busy talking). He shepherded them all along towards the waiting car. She'd shut up sooner or later. Then he'd get a chance to speak.

Her monologues never needed answers. So at least there was a kind of peace to be found in them. He used it to recall that there'd been a time – so long ago he could barely remember – when the sight and sound of her hadn't made him sigh.

Back in the Crimea . . . and for a moment General Skoblin could once again smell the thyme and sea in the glittering air of his youth – and call to mind, too, the hasty packings of tents, the listing of rifles and ammunition (fewer every time) and the terrifying creepings and rustlings of the night. The last thing he'd needed, on top of his part in the fading hopes of that campaign, was a consignment of Red prisoners sent down from Kursk to deal with. Until he'd seen *her* among them, and heard the indrawn breaths and whistles: the Nightingale! She'd gone to the Red lines, it turned out – joined the enemy. She'd been caught singing to keep the Bolsheviks' spirits up. That's how she'd got herself tangled up in that impossibly churned-up war world. But before that, and even before she'd been the Tsar's favourite musician, given jewels and asked to perform at Tsarskoye Selo and the Winter Palace; before both her previous husbands, in some impossibly remote, lost dream-era when there still was no Revolution, and no war, he'd seen her sing at the Yar restaurant, back when she was still just a country girl who'd run away from a provincial convent choir and wore a red sarafan: a dark slip of a girl with a magical voice and a liquid-eyed way of looking at you . . .

And suddenly there she was, his prisoner. He'd married her two years later, in a refugee camp in Turkey. By then no one remembered she'd briefly been the Red Nightingale. By then, the Civil War had been lost, and everyone just wanted to forget.

And of course it had been a blessing, in some ways, their marriage. While most of the other White officers he'd fought and lost with had been completely down on their luck – stuck for years in those transit camps, some of them – she'd whisked him off on the new touring life she soon began, turning herself effortlessly back into the Tsar's Nightingale and lucratively singing the sad songs of exile to any nostalgic émigré Whites who'd managed to make it as far as Germany, Yugoslavia, Romania, Bulgaria . . .

They climbed into the Cadillac. (His little weakness, this; sometimes he explained it by saying he needed a grand car to drive his wife around in; sometimes, more churlishly, he told himself that surely he too was allowed a gesture of flamboyance every now and then?) Out of the corner of his eye, he watched his wife dump her handbag carelessly on the creaking pale-leather back seat. He was pleased when, apparently only now realizing it had landed on a newspaper whose front-page article was illustrated by a solemn picture of Yezhov, the new head of Soviet intelligence, she carefully moved the bag to the floor, giving him a furtive look.

He nodded grimly. She liked to show off in public. All right. But he was the man. It was right that she should respect him and his work. Alone together, they both knew who the boss was.

It was only when they were on the road out of Paris, and she'd stopped complaining about the indignity of second class, that Skoblin lit a cigarette and said, exhaling a cloud of smoke, 'Tomorrow, to celebrate your return, we're going to go back into town and buy' – he paused for emphasis – *'crab in the market.'*

He preferred talking in the car. There weren't so many cats here as in their little house in Ozoir.

'Oh!' she said weakly, sounding as shocked as if she'd never expected to hear the phrase.

'Yes,' he continued, level-voiced. 'The crab salesman is here.'

He wasn't displeased with the nervous way she shifted in her seat.

9

As the dusk thickened, and the train began passing through thicker clumps of villages, then mean outer-city districts of factories and poky housing with lights beginning to come on as workers came home for the night, I found myself getting so nervous that, in the clammy evening heat, my hands felt hot and damp and, I saw, were covered in newsprint smears.

I put the paper down in my lap, thinking uneasily that I hadn't had a reply to my letter; well, there hadn't been time for a reply. I'd sailed the night after I'd bought the ticket, without telling Mother. I'd been trying, all the way over, not to think of the one-line note I'd left on my pillow at home, before heading off to spend the in-between time at Eliza's. My note had said no more than that I was going to Paris for the summer. Every time I did remember it, I got a sick knot in my stomach. I hadn't thought about it much on board ship either. It was only once I'd sent Grandmother a follow-up wire from Le Havre, before getting on this train, that the vagueness of my arrangements had really struck me. I couldn't be sure anyone was expecting me. What if there was no one to meet me at the station? Would I just take a taxi and go to Grandmother's address? What if she was away?

I was almost relieved when a very tall young man, weighed down by a big backpack and a guitar suspended across his front by a string, shimmied down the jerking length of the open carriage, only just avoiding all the bags and feet that might have tripped him up, to sit down next to me.

'Best to be at the front of the train when you're getting off,' he said cheerfully by way of explanation, perching on the front of his seat (he couldn't lean back, with that backpack) and flicking dark-blond curls off his handsome face. And then, looking properly at my face: 'I remember *you*.'

It was a relief, at that uneasy moment, to be recognized; and, besides, I remembered him too. We'd talked a bit on the boat. He was Dutch, I thought; and I half remembered that his mother had been an actress and his father maybe a theatre manager, but he'd come to America as soon as he'd left school; I thought he'd maybe been hanging around Hollywood for the past few years, like so many of the boys on the boat: doing little jobs, hoping for a break. But I definitely remembered that he'd recently been in Spain, taking pictures. He'd told me he'd been slightly wounded. He'd even rolled up his pants leg to show me the scar across his calf where the shrapnel had been picked out. He'd gone to New York to heal up and tout for work from American papers for his return to Spain. The Yanks paid better, he'd said cheerfully – only he'd said 'de Yanks'. The Dutch had no cash. Nor did the French.

He grinned at me. 'You got somewhere to stay in Paris?' he asked casually.

His smile was so infectious that I grinned back, despite myself, and nodded. 'I think so,' I said cautiously, and then pointed at his guitar. 'Do you play?'

Well, of course he does, if he's carrying around a guitar, I reproved myself. What kind of stupid question is that?

But he only nodded and grinned wider and lovingly patted the body of his instrument. '*Ja*, I started learning last year in Andalucía from the gypsies. The last thing you'd expect in a war, *ja*? But, you know how it is, things just turn out the way they do. And I met some people, and they taught me a bit. And we got along so well, me and my gypsy friends, that they even ended up by giving me a gypsy name: Arai, which means something like "not of our blood, but one of us anyway".' He put his fingers gently on the strings: long, thin, elegant fingers, I noticed. The strings vibrated softly under his touch. 'Did you ever hear flamenco music?'

Perhaps it was just that by then I was so rattled by the prospect of finding myself alone on a strange continent, on my quite likely futile mission, but I half wanted him to start playing, right there in the carriage, while he talked about Spain and gypsies. But when I looked round, the train was already pulling in under a grimy glass awning. I could feel it ominously slowing.

He looked around as if surprised, too, to have reached journey's end so fast. Then he shrugged in that carefree way he had, leaped up and, picking up my bag, too, as if we'd decided to go travelling together, said, 'Come on. Let's beat the crowd.'

I let myself be drawn along in his wake at the front of the crowd leaving the train, half running to keep up, laughing a little, as much out of surprised pleasure at this chance taste of friendship and freedom as from my nerves. Perhaps, after all, I'd got to a place where everyone *was* as spontaneous and happy as Eliza and Dorothy and their amusing brothers and chatty European fathers? Even if there was no one waiting for me at the station or at Grandmother's home, how bad could it be? I'd just go and find myself a hotel and some new friends. Maybe this was the start of it all?

Even when we got to the ticket barrier, and there was, after all, a fat, red-faced man in a peaked cap holding up a cardboard sign which I saw, with a thrill of recognition, said, 'Mme la Comtesse Sabline', I was (just a bit) sorry to say goodbye to the first new young friend I'd made.

Arai the Flamenco Dutchman surrendered my bag to the chauffeur willingly enough. Then he nodded farewell at me, looking a little sad too.

'Look me up,' he said with another flashing smile, 'if you want. I'll be putting up at La Ruche for a bit. A blanket on the floor, I expect – no creature comforts – but it's always fun.' Before I'd even got out the words, 'But what is La Ruche?' he was already off at high speed, whistling. But he turned one more time and called back through the crowd that had by now caught up with us, and the pigeons flapping in the ironwork, 'Oh, ask anyone! Everyone knows La Ruche!' and waved before he vanished.

And then I was alone with the chauffeur.

He was called Gaston. I knew that because, with my bag in one hand, walking towards the automobile he'd parked outside the station, he used his free hand to thump at his own chest and said, speaking loudly and enunciating very carefully, as if I wouldn't understand a word and was deaf into the bargain: 'Gaston.'

'Evelyn,' I replied, with my best social smile and brightest tone, 'Evie. *Enchantée!*' He just grunted. I could see he'd got it in his head I wouldn't understand French, because he ignored all my subsequent polite attempts to chat: about the weather, about the crowds, about the pigeons . . . After a few minutes of scratchy struggling, I stopped trying to converse with him and just concentrated on getting inside the motor car.

Because, really, who cared about a surly driver? I was here! And, as I settled myself in the back seat, my mind was already leaping ahead – out of sheer relief, probably, at knowing I did, after all, have a journey's end after that unsettling last hour of worrying in the train. And, now I was here, I'd befriend Grandmother. Of course I would. And maybe there'd be an afterwards, too, once I'd filled that gap in my family's past and answered the questions in my head, once I'd found a family member who wouldn't automatically disapprove of all the things my friends wanted to do with their lives. And, if she'd liked that Russian singer (funnily enough, I'd actually seen her again, on the ship, though only from far away; she'd been sitting on a deck chair behind the railing separating me from the second-class deck of the boat, looking windswept and glum and dumpy under a shawl, staring out to sea; I'd even waved, but she hadn't seen *me*) . . . well, maybe I'd discover that Grandmother would enjoy the idea of wandering musicians as much as I'd liked that brief brush with the handsome young Dutchman. And (since she obviously liked romance and adventure and travel too – two husbands! And all those artists' colonies all over the world!) she might even think it a good idea for me to go off to Spain, to see what it was all about. And even if she *was* against that idea, for better reasons than any I'd have heard from Aunt Mildred or Mother, well, no harm done. Because maybe I could just stay on in Paris for longer, and learn to paint or write my own novel . . .

'. . . *mademoiselle*,' Gaston was saying, turning round and taking one hand alarmingly off the wheel. I realized he'd been trying to get my attention for several moments.

I nodded and put an intently listening look on my face. I could see he'd need encouraging out of his *idée fixe* that all young Americans in Paris were complete, uncomprehending idiots. I leaned forward.

But it didn't matter what look I put on my face, or how I arranged my body. He just looked a mixture of agonized and patient and impatient all at once, and went on in the kind of pidgin French he must think easier for me to understand: '*Madame – malade. Madame – malade, comprenez?*'

After a moment's panicky thought, I said weakly, '*Oh là là*,' as if I really were the half-wit he took me for, then instantly cursed myself for feebleness. He only shook his head and sighed eloquently (proof!); then – and this, at least, was a relief – he turned his eyes back to the road and accelerated off, making the automobile growl. By the time I got my wits together enough to add, '*Qu'est-ce qu'elle a, la pauvre?*' ('Poor thing, what's the matter?') he was concentrating on his driving, and the car was probably making too much noise for him to have heard. At any rate, he didn't reply.

I think what I imagined was a touch of flu, or just a headache. My euphoria at having reached Paris was so intense that it never crossed my mind that there might be anything really wrong. Why would it? I'd never seen any illness but Mother's turns.

Perhaps I should stop for flowers? I thought vaguely, while also letting my eyes drink in the great squares as they rose up before us, and the bridges, the boulevards, the trees, the statues, but as I didn't have the faintest idea of how you'd buy flowers here and wasn't about to tangle further with Gaston to try and find out, and it was pretty much night-time anyway, I didn't take the idea that seriously. Anyway, I already had a gift. I'd brought Grandmother the new novel everyone was talking about back home about two landless men looking for work in California – a grand little novel, despite its melodrama, the *New York Times* had called it, and it had struck me, midway through, that those two characters, George and Lennie, wandering the dry heat of the West with their bundles on sticks, were a bit like me and my own quixotic, uncertain journey here. It would be enough for her to read that in bed as she recovered, I decided. So I let my mind form vague pictures of myself taking her cups of smoky China tea in a vast Empire bed, and the gratitude of her smile as she looked up from the book. And I stared around me.

When we finally stopped, it was in front of a large, handsome building in blond stone with elaborate chasing, lit by several equally elaborately leaved-and-flowered wrought-iron lamp-posts. From what I could see, the entire street was built to the same level of grandeur. I got out, feeling impressed by the stateliness of it, though also

slightly puzzled, as this didn't seem exactly the picturesque *vie de Bohème* I'd expected of someone who'd earned so much family disapproval by devoting her life to art.

As I stood on the sidewalk, breathing in the hot night air and gazing round while Gaston thumped his slow way around the automobile and, grunting, pulled my bag out of the trunk, I saw half a dozen men come out of the front door. They were solemn-looking, straight-backed, elderly men, all wearing what struck me as thrillingly foreign, Ruritanian-style military uniform – the kind that's all gold frogging and epaulettes and medals. I strained to hear what they were saying, because I figured every word of real French I could soak up would only help get my French sounding more authentic, but I soon realized they must be speaking some other language. I couldn't make out a word.

The one who was clearly the boss – I could see that because everyone else was deferring to him as they bowed goodbye – was a dignified type with a pot belly and big old-fashioned side-whiskers. He had twin widow's peaks in the light-grey hair on either side of his forehead, just as I did, I noticed (though his hair didn't have grips holding it off his face, as mine did, so the two kinks at the sides were pushing up in defiance of a very fierce recent damp combing-down). For a moment I wondered idly if his hair annoyed him as much as mine often did me.

He waved at the taxi parked just in front of Grandmother's car. Then he headed across the wide sidewalk towards its passenger door. But, before he reached the car, a tall dark young man with startling blue eyes leaped out of the driver's seat and hurried to intercept him. For a moment I saw their eyes meet, and the quiet smile that passed between them as the young man opened the door for him and put a solicitous hand under his elbow to help him in. I was only a few feet away, and I couldn't help admiring that dashing foreign warmth, and thinking: Why, you'd never get a New York taxi driver behaving like that. I thought I was admiring it unobtrusively – at least until, as the young driver shut the door behind his client and straightened up, still half smiling, my eyes accidentally met his. Feeling the blood rush to my face, I realized I must have been gawping straight at them.

The young taxi driver didn't react in any of the ways I might have expected. He didn't drop his eyes, or grin flirtatiously, or ask pugnaciously what I thought I was staring at, lady. Instead he completely stopped moving – froze immobile – and stared right back at me out of pale, pale eyes. For a strange moment, I actually thought he was scared.

'*Mademoiselle*,' Gaston said from behind me. He had my small bag in his hand.

At that, the taxi man glanced over at Gaston; then he scowled at me, for all the world as if he were furious at having been, briefly, terrified. He had extremely handsome, noble-looking features for a taxi driver – a straight nose, good cheekbones, black waves of hair – but his scowl was so fierce and aggressive that it turned his two eyebrows into one lowering black line across his face, and made me wonder if he wasn't going to leap forward and intercept me.

All he actually did, though, was to shake his head and turn on his heel, go back to his car, slam the door shut behind him, start his vehicle up and roar off into the night with his passenger.

'*Sacrés Russes,*' I heard Gaston mutter. (Ah, so *that's* what they were!) Then, louder and slower, nodding to me and then to the door to indicate where I should go, Gaston – who no longer seemed half as tricky a proposition, compared with this other Parisian driver; was suddenly looking kind, even – added: '*Mademoiselle.*'

Keeping his face averted and his nose high in the air, Gaston swept past the remaining Russians without acknowledging them, and entered the building.

10

The frail shape in the bed was so thin, the hair so dull and tousled on the pillow, that I couldn't help my gasp of shock.

There was just one faint lamp glowing on a table in the corner of the room, and a plump woman who must be the housekeeper – Gaston's wife, too, I guessed, because he went straight to her – stirred in an armchair beside the bed, as if the sound of our entrance had disturbed her from a doze. There was a tray on the floor beside her, I could see, but nothing had been eaten.

Nodding to the housekeeper as she rose clumsily to her feet, I stood near the enormous feather bolster under Grandmother's head, looking down. Gaston and his wife were at the other end of the bolster, side by side, looking expectantly at me. I realized they were waiting for directions. They were only servants, and I was family – the only family there was, too. It hit me right in the gut. I'd have to take charge.

The left side of Grandmother's face had sagged. She wasn't asleep – she raised anxious prisoner's eyes to me, and a trembling right arm, though her left side did no more than twitch. I took both the raised right hand and the stiff left one in mine, and pressed them very warmly in mine. Hers were frail and papery, blue-veined and brown-spotted, and cool. But the right hand, at least, gripped mine with bony urgency. 'MMMM,' she mumbled, out of one side of her mouth. Her voice was shockingly loud.

I didn't know how to respond. 'Dearest Grandmother,' I started in a whisper, gazing back into her mute, imploring face with a mixture of tenderness and pity and fear. I hadn't expected to be in a situation where I was so very out of my depth. 'I'm here. I'm so happy to see you,' I stumbled on, relieved to find I had the presence of mind, after another moment's wordless panic, to at least add, 'but I'm so sorry to find you unwell.'

Even like this, I'd known her as soon as I'd seen her. I could now picture us together, long ago, on the island. It was a very precise memory: the two of us laughing together. I could clearly picture the charisma and glamour Grandmother had had back then. We'd been dancing . . . yes, that was it, to Russian violin music that kept getting faster and faster. And then Mother had walked in. I could remember the moment she did as if it were now: my arms outstretched and my head raised rapturously, spinning around with my slender, breathlessly smiling giant of a partner.

Now that same face, though diminished, was lying before me, in a pitiful halo of thin, too-black hair. Her mouth opened, and there was a frantic message in her eyes. But the only sound that came out was another strangled 'Mmm . . .'

It wrung my heart, and it frightened me a bit, too, that the person I remembered so alive had become this spittle-stained, moaning ruin. I tried to concentrate on the fact that there was so clearly something this new version of Grandmother wanted to tell me, and couldn't. 'What is it, darling?' I asked, trying to keep my voice soft and appealing because I could see she needed me; trying not to remember myself asking the same anxious question of Mother so very recently. But still no words came, just more gurglings.

It was a relief when the housekeeper diverted me by nodding towards something on the bed that showed Grandmother had been trying to communicate in writing.

It was a lap desk – one of those awkward boxes you fold out to make a sloping writing surface. There was writing all over the blotting paper on top of it. The housekeeper – who must have set the thing out on the bed – was nodding at the paper.

I picked it up, but I couldn't make out the words, which looked like a drunk spider-in-the-inkwell scrawl. There were lines and question marks and words all over the page. What caught my attention was something that I thought looked a bit like the letter M, repeated several times in enormous letters, like a child's first attempt with a pen. There were many other less dramatic squiggles, too, in smaller but still jagged script that, in the dim light, I couldn't make head or tail of either. I took it over to the lamp. Written sideways from the worst of the nonsense were some relatively legible words, in a clump dotted with ink soaks and splodges.

'Pictures', I eventually thought I saw. 'Jewels'. 'Evie'. And then a shape I couldn't read, which reminded me of 'Xxxx'. This last shape was the most neatly written of the lot, though what was Xxxx? Try as I might, I couldn't make sense of that word. Then another moment of clarity, when, further down, amidst a lot of spiky nonsense going in a different direction, right off the page, I saw, in wildish letters, 'Evie' . . . 'Xxxx' . . . 'Protect' . . . 'Make amends'.

Did it mean something? Doubtfully, I came back towards the bed with the box still in my hand. The housekeeper nodded encouragingly at me. I thought she wanted me to tell Grandmother I'd understood her message. As soon as I looked at Grandmother, dribbling out of the corner of her mouth, with that alarmed look still on her face, I realized I couldn't let her see I hadn't understood. It would be too cruel.

From here, I could see grey roots at the top of Grand-mother's pitifully rumpled black hair. In the heavy silence broken only by our four different sets of breath, each clearly audible, I thought: Maybe I shouldn't worry if I can't under-stand what she's written; maybe it's some memory from long ago that's troubling her? After all, what could be so frightening other than what's happening to her?

'Grandmother, don't worry; everything's going to be all right,' I said as reassuringly as I could. But my voice came out scared and small. I knew I should put the lap desk down, take her hands in mine and reassure her. But I couldn't. I didn't admire myself, but I didn't feel grown-up enough.

After a few minutes, her eyelids started to droop, and she slipped into a snuffly sleep.

The housekeeper nodded. Taking our cue from her, we tiptoed out.

Gaston and his wife, the housekeeper Marie-Thérèse, lived in a little maid's room at the top of the house, so they didn't mind staying late at work, in these circumstances, they told me.

I'd come out of the bedroom ashamed that I hadn't known better how to deal with my sick relative. Now it was a relief to see, from the sympathetic glances they were giving me, and the warmth of their voices, that they didn't seem to think any the worse of me. We were sitting in the kitchen and, in fact, they seemed to be mothering me. I brushed aside their wish for me to take dinner *comme il faut* in the dining room, where the table had been set hours ago, now so sadly, for two. Instead, I ate the chicken stew that had been waiting on the stove for me at the scrubbed-pine kitchen work table with them, while the housekeeper talked.

'*Avec les trains, on ne sait jamais,*' she began darkly ('You never can tell with trains'), I thought explaining the dinner she was ladling out, which was far too hot and hearty for this weather. '*Il vaut mieux avoir quelque chose qui mijote.*' ('Best to have something you can simmer.')

I didn't think I'd be able to eat it, but I was so relieved to discover that Marie-Thérèse didn't seem to have any of her husband's fear of talking normally with foreigners that I decided to make an effort. I took a polite forkful, and it tasted delicious. So did the glass of white wine that Gaston poured from an already opened bottle standing next to a dish of little cheeses covered with a wire-mesh dome – pulling out the cork with an expert pop and placing the glass on the table beside me with the care of a waiter. I was surprised at how hungry I was, and I was childishly pleased when Marie-Thérèse and her husband, both on their feet hovering around me – they wouldn't sit – raised their eyebrows and said appreciatively to each other, '*Elle avait faim, la petite, dis donc!*' and '*Elle apprécie la cuisine française, celle-ci!*' ('Hungry!' 'And likes French cooking too!') as I finished my serving.

The doctor would be back in the morning, Marie-Thérèse said as she put the cheese in front of me, while Gaston chopped more bread and dropped it into the basket on the table. Madame had had a stroke, but it wasn't one that would kill her. She'd recover, in time, even though she might never be as good as she'd been before. It would take her a good while to learn to walk again, probably, and talk, too, though people often did make a good recovery.

I nodded, encouraged. 'Well, I'll be here,' I said, so restored after all that food that I felt better able to believe I'd be confidently running things by tomorrow. 'So I can—'

'But what you have to watch out for is the next one, the doctor said,' Marie-Thérèse swept on, cutting across me with gloomy gusto. 'Because there might be another stroke at any moment, he said. It happens a lot. A shock, a door slamming, anything might bring it on; or it might just happen anyway. And *that* one could be the end of her.'

The way she smacked her lips at that, the way Gaston shook his head . . . Suddenly I wasn't quite so sure we were all going to get along as well as I'd been hoping.

I felt a lump in my throat. I couldn't eat the cheese. I didn't want them to think me a complete fool, though, so instead of sitting there like a dejected child, or worse, I looked fiercely round, found my bag, dug in it for the bit of blotting paper with all the scrawls on it that I'd brought out of the sickroom with me, and held it out.

'Can you read this?' I asked. 'What does it say?'

Marie-Thérèse took it. Gaston came and stood behind her shoulder. They both stared at where I'd pointed. 'But it's English, isn't it?' Marie-Thérèse said doubtfully after a long examination.

'Not that word,' I replied, pointing again at the mystery 'Xxxx' word. 'The other words are "Evie" – that's me – and "Pictures" and "Jewels". It's over there again, too, look: "Evie "– "Xxxx" – "Protect" – "Make amends". It's just that one word I can't read. I can't make out the letters; but then I don't know her handwriting . . . I thought maybe you would?'

They stared hungrily at it again. I could see they were disappointed not to be able to uncover a secret, and reluctant to admit they were none the wiser than me.

'Maybe it's a Russian word,' Marie-Thérèse said, after another long pause.

It mobilized them, that new thought, but not in a good way. As soon as I saw Marie-Thérèse's face darken, I remembered the way her husband had hissed *'sacrés Russes'* as he'd swept past the men outside.

'Because I'm afraid Madame has a weakness for a lot of the tramps and ne'er-do-wells who like to make out they're artists so they can come and fill up our city,' Marie-Thérèse said crossly. 'The Russian ones, too, who let me tell you are worse than all the rest put together. It's because she speaks their language, you see. It makes her a soft touch. They all turn up, with their hard-luck stories, weeping and asking her to save them. It's unbelievable how they prey on her. She buys all their rubbish – pictures, she says, but, my God! I could do better myself. This place is full of the things; you'll see; and the dusting I have to do . . . And they're always here, her vagrants, dropping in by the dozen and eating and drinking and smoking and God knows what else till all hours. Very noisy they are, too: they wake the whole building up, sometimes, shrieking and roaring into the night.'

I'd loved the idea of all things Russian for so long that this seemed very strange. But then my idea of Russians was based on the highly civilized gentry in the novels I'd read, or my thoughtful café companions. Yet the two faces going red in front of me showed that an altogether more hostile view was possible. Gaston was puffing himself up like a bullfrog. Marie-Thérèse had her hands on her hips. 'If we can't read it, and it's Russian, all I can say is that there'll be no problem finding people in *this* town who can.'

And off they both went, nodding at each other, capping each other's phrases, gesticulating and grimacing as their voices rose and rose until they got dangerously close to shouting.

Russians were cheats. Russians were thieves. The only way to please the supervisors at the Peugeot factory and the Citroën factory was to speak Russian, because all the supervisors were Russians. They crept in through every nook and cranny . . . All the waiters' jobs had gone to Russians, too. There were probably Russian waiters who'd once been grand dukes spitting in your soup in every restaurant in town! And as for the taxi drivers, reading Russian novels in their fancy white gloves, and the balalaika orchestras you couldn't get away from in every public place . . . And the worst of it was that these people came all this way to get to civilization, and yet brought their violent ways with them and still went around kidnapping each other and bumping each other off! A Russian with a gun had even shot and killed the President of France!

'They said he was crazy,' Gaston cried, looking a little crazy himself. 'The man who shot President Doumer, I mean. They said he was a Red. They said he was a White, too. But what I say is, they're all crazy. And They Should Send Them All Back Where They Came From.'

The words 'But they can't' trembled on my lips, because of course I knew that Red and White Russians didn't mix, and that if you sent the White refugees back to Soviet Moscow now, twenty years after the Russian Revolution and the long civil war that had followed, which the Whites had lost, they'd all be shot by the Red Soviets.

But I didn't want to argue with these two. In the end I raised a warning hand – a signal to stop.

They stared at me, baffled, with their angry eyes.

'Thank you for dinner,' I said. 'But I'm tired. Would you show me my room?'

It was only when they took me to my room that I realized the extent of Grandmother's art habit. There were pictures against every wall, along the corridor, and propped against every one of my new room's walls, half a dozen deep: rough canvases in every imaginable size and shape, but also bits of paper, things stuck to other things, and things sticking out of things. Some were luridly coloured. Some were faded and brownish. There was thick oil and there were spindly pencil lines. There was nonsense. There were doodles around the edges of poems I couldn't make sense of. There were imprints of leaves in primary colours. There were broken bits of glass from which the imprints of leaves in primary colors had been made. The artworks covered everything.

It was late. I was too tired to care. I stripped off my clothes and fell into the bed. But when I woke up the next morning, I found myself unable to look peacefully at the great rectangle of hot blue sky through the window, and gather my thoughts for another day, because it made me so uneasy being stared at from every side by large naked ladies, roughly drawn in thick blue paint, all of them fleeing and panic-stricken, with sketchy draperies streaming behind – and a misshapen bull, too. So I turned some of the more dreadfully dramatic pictures towards the wall.

I dressed and went to the dining room. (More pictures! This time with an odd kind of romance in them, mostly men in suits clutching at naked women, all floating in rudimentary treetops, sometimes with goats and violinists.) Today, mercifully, the table was only set for one. It was so hot outside that when I glanced through the window I could see wavy lines in the air. There were birds in liquid song outside, between the honkings of car horns. There was a tree outside the open window, partially covering the blue of the sky with soft dappled green. It was the kind of weather that couldn't help but make you feel happy and hopeful. I sat down, glanced at the newspaper set by my place but didn't unfold it, drank down some warm milky coffee and ate a couple of mouthfuls of very fresh bread and damson jam.

The morning was – almost – glorious enough to make me able to conquer the dread I felt at the idea of going into Grandmother's room.

But I still felt a little ill at the prospect. I had to force myself. It was only after I'd run out of things to do – after I'd poured more coffee, prepared a little more bread on the same plate, and picked up the newspaper – that I went next door to sit with the invalid.

I'd been imagining that I might give her a sip of coffee . . . read the news to her, maybe. But any thought that she might have recovered enough to take food from me, sit weakly up, even begin to talk – well, any of those fantasies went as soon as I entered the close darkness of the sickroom. Here there was no summer joy. The drapes were still drawn, though the windows behind them were open and there was a bunch of peonies in a vase on the dressing table. The lamp was still on. The air, warm and sour, smelled of illness.

I was rather relieved to see that Marie-Thérèse had been here, and recently, too, because Grandmother was in a new white cotton nightgown, which still looked impeccably laundered, with sharp creases at the edges of its thin pintucked sleeves. There was a fresh water jug on the tray by the bed, and a half-full bowl of chocolate, and the torn-up remains of a croissant, and a cloth that she must have used to wipe Grandmother's mouth after popping in little morsels of the soft bread dipped in chocolate. By the door stood a bigger bowl, too, of warm soapy water, with the flannel Marie-Thérèse must have sponged her down with still sodden in it, and yesterday's rolled-up nightgown beside it, and another, covered pot. The housekeeper was good at her job, I could see: attentive and kind-hearted, however much she disliked Russians. And she was clearly a far more expert and experienced nurse than I'd have been. But, for all the housekeeper's care, the woman lying with closed eyes in front of me, breathing shallowly through that dragging, sideways mouth, was far away, lost in a dream I couldn't follow.

Quietly I sat down in the chair at the side of the bed, and put down my bread and coffee. I'd thought I might read the paper while I watched her, but now that seemed

uncaring. As I listened to the distant sounds of outside, and watched the dust motes dance in a stripe of sunlight falling across the neatly remade bed, I realized, again, that I didn't know what to do. Grandmother's good right hand crept out across the sheet, pushing it down. Perhaps she was hot. Feeling brave, I leaned forward and stroked that hand. But there was no response.

I was just leaning back and, trying to suppress the thought that I might get bored, sitting here alone with a sleeping invalid for hours, and wondering whether, after all, I shouldn't try to read the paper and drink that coffee, when the doorbell rang.

I heard heavy, hurried footsteps come out of the kitchen and go to answer it.

Then I heard men's voices at the door – rumbling deeply in French so gutturally accented that, at first, I couldn't understand it – and Marie-Thérèse's tart answer: '*Mais Madame est malade. Vous allez donc revenir demain, vous n'allez quand même pas la déranger aujourd'hui avec vos histoires de musique . . .*' ('Madame is sick, so you'd better come back tomorrow; I'm not letting you in to annoy her with your music today.')

What's all that about? I wondered, rather shocked at the housekeeper's frankly rude tone of voice. In front of me, still with her eyes shut, Grandmother began uneasily stirring. Putting my hand on hers again, I listened for the door to click shut on the snubbed guests. But instead I heard a brief discussion in an unknown foreign language, after which the men came pushing in anyway, I sensed right past the reluctant Marie-Thérèse, saying with great certainty in their bad French, with heavily rolled Rs,

'*Notrrre trrravail ici – fini*' ('Our work here – finished') and '*il faut prrrendre le . . . la . . . apparrraturrra . . . avec*' ('We've got to pick up our . . . our . . . *apparatura*'). Then I heard the creak of a door, and the male footsteps going determinedly into another room, followed by Marie-Thérèse, who'd started squealing, very fast and outraged, through the thumping, banging sounds of machinery being gathered up that ensued. '*Mais je suis persuadée que l'appareil est à Madame, pas à vous! Vous n'allez pas la lui prendre comme ça sans sa permission, dites donc!*' ('But I'm sure that's Madame's machine, not yours! You're not going to just take it like that, without her say-so!')

On the pillow in front of me, Grandmother's eyes suddenly opened. For a moment, she looked straight at me: an urgent gaze that seemed to take me in, and know me. For a moment, I thought she might be about to come to. But my hope disappeared when she screwed up her wrinkled sideways face in a grimace of utter horror, and started waving her good hand helplessly in the air, and opening and shutting her mouth, and nearly shouting those frantic sounds she'd been making last night, 'MMM . . . MMMM . . . MMM!'

I didn't lean forward and try to hear what she wanted to say. I didn't do anything. She might be having another attack. She looked so frightening. For a long, long moment I just hovered, feeling helpless. I needed Marie-Thérèse, I told myself, leaving the room and going into the corridor. She'd know what to do.

Behind me, Grandmother was tossing to and fro, plucking at the air with that frighteningly waving hand. 'Mmm . . . mmm!' she was calling. I turned my back on her. In front of me, Marie-Thérèse was looking very put out, and shutting the door to a room I hadn't yet been in. '*Sacrés Russes*,' she muttered, turning to me with outraged eyes. 'You see?'

'She's woken up,' I said urgently. 'I don't think she's well. Please come.'

Marie-Thérèse's face changed, and she came into Grandmother's room with me. But by the time we'd got back to her bedside, there was no movement from it at all.

There was an hour or so more of panic-stricken endgame: the hopeless attempts at resuscitation; the calls to the doctor and the concierge; the injections; the strangely friendly eye-meets and muttered reassurances that created a brief semblance of normality between each new person's intervention. It was almost lunchtime by the time a kind of dull flatness settled on us all, and the concierge was sent out to fetch an undertaker. But I'd known, from that first moment when I turned my eyes back to the sudden stillness on that bed, that the shape in it, so familiar and unfamiliar all at once, still with the lines of cheekbone and nose and chin and shoulder that I recognized, the source of so many memories that I was only just beginning to regain, had stopped being Grandmother.

And mixed up with my sadness was a numbing sense of inadequacy. Not only had I not got to know her, I hadn't even been brave enough to sit with her at the last. I'd left her on her own, as surely as all the rest of my family had, long ago.

11

'I've been thinking,' Marie-Thérèse said, 'about Madame's note.'

It was mid-afternoon. Two men from the undertaker's had taken the still shape that had been Grandmother away. When they'd shifted her off the bed on to their trolley as roughly as if she'd been a side of meat and an arm had come swinging out from the side of the sheet, horribly, and I'd glimpsed that fragile blotched hand before one of the men had grunted and shoved it back against the body and flapped the sheet over it again – well, I suppose Marie-Thérèse must have seen my face, because she'd bustled me into the kitchen with a determined look. 'I think we all need a dose of medicine ourselves,' she'd said. 'Leave them to it.'

Gaston seemed as shocked as me. He was pale under the red spider-veins in his cheeks. He kept saying, 'I can't believe she's gone,' and, 'Just like that,' and, 'She was right as rain this time yesterday.'

We both gathered around Marie-Thérèse as she poured out three stiff slugs of brandy. We did our best not to listen to the men in the corridor grunting and groaning and banging into things as they manoeuvred their burden to the front door, and the stairs. And when the door had shut, and we were the only ones left, we raised our glasses, met each other's eyes, and drained the brandy.

I could feel the comforting burn of it in my throat.

'I called Madame's lawyer. I said she'd passed away. He'll drop in at four,' Marie-Thérèse said, pouring more brandy. 'He needs to discuss arrangements with you.' She set the bottle down on the table. 'Which is why I've been thinking about the note,' she went on.

She had an idea, I could see. I felt as though I were seeing everything at a great distance, very small and quiet. I didn't understand anything quite enough.

'What note?' I said.

'The one you showed me,' she said patiently. 'The one on the blotting paper.'

Those jottings hadn't been a note when I'd last thought of them, just random words. And they had no more certainty or positive meaning than anything else, especially now that I was facing the prospect of having to go creeping home to Mother and Aunt Mildred, like a dog with my tail between my legs. Now that I'd failed.

But Marie-Thérèse's eyes were gleaming. 'It seems to me', she said, 'that Madame must have had a premonition of what was in store for her . . . and she must have been writing that note for you, mademoiselle, so you would know she wanted you to have her pictures and jewels. That note was like a will – her last wishes.'

'Oh,' I said dully. What difference did a few bits of old jewellery make?

But Gaston, who was beginning to look a bit more his usual self after that brandy – after draining his second shot, his cheeks had gone back to their usual red colour – had a hungry look in his eye. 'What jewels?' he asked.

Marie-Thérèse wasn't wasting her story on him. Keeping her gaze fixed on me, she said: 'Do you want to see them?' Then, without waiting for me to respond, she was on her feet and out of the room.

As soon as the door shut behind his wife, Gaston poured himself a third brandy.

'It's always Russians, isn't it,' he said, reflectively, as he put down the glass.

Puzzled, I looked up. His cheeks were sheeny with sweat.

'Those men this morning,' he explained. 'I wouldn't be surprised if the way they stormed in and grabbed that machine – the *noise* they made – wasn't what set Madame off.'

'Who *were* they?' I asked.

'Engineers,' he said truculently. 'Russians. They've been making our lives a misery for days. Madame had them here to work on a music recording – some singer who's scraped her acquaintance. She said they'd be here all week. A godawful racket it made, too – that singer's voice really set your teeth on edge.'

I remembered now that the Russian singer in New York had been talking about Grandmother and a recording. I might have said I'd met the singer, but Gaston rushed on: 'We're pretty sure that Madame bought the machine. But they'll have been thinking, if the old lady's ill, no one's going to ask any awkward questions; we'll help ourselves and be off. That's Russians for you.' He shrugged, eloquently.

Feeling overwhelmed, I shook my head. But Gaston went quiet as soon as Marie-Thérèse came rushing back in a moment later, looking excited. Excited, too, he drew closer as she put the hatbox in her hands down on the table.

'Look, mademoiselle,' she breathed.

Inside was a big messy bundle of letters, tied together with a faded ribbon. They were on their sides, stashed between some little packages balled in newspaper.

My hand went straight to the letters. For a moment, I felt a new flicker of hope that, even if Grandmother had gone, the letters might tell me something about her.

'Open the packets, mademoiselle,' Marie-Thérèse whispered raptly.

I hesitated, with my hand on the bundle of letters.

'Oh, those. You won't understand *those*,' she went on a little impatiently. I picked up the bundle. Sure enough, even though they were written in what I could see was an elegant, old-fashioned, copperplate hand, I couldn't make out a word. 'You see? Foreign,' I heard.

(But how had Marie-Thérèse known? I asked myself, though it was clear by now that she must have taken a peep herself at some point. I could hear Aunt Mildred's resigned voice in my head, saying, 'Servants always know everything.')

So I put the letters aside – I wasn't giving up hope on them, but I'd have to come back to them later – and picked up one of the little newspaper bundles instead.

The newspaper wrapping was French, and only a few years old – yellowed, but not brittle. The contents must have been rolled up in it during a relatively recent move – but then Grandmother had moved around a lot in her lifetime.

As I pulled it off, Gaston's and Marie-Thérèse's heads came eagerly closer, almost obscuring my view. Inside the newspaper was a medium-sized jeweller's box. When I opened that, I saw a very finely made cigarette case in lilac enamel, with gold vines chased over its surface and gold fastenings.

Marie-Thérèse gasped in loud awe. Even though she was clearly acting, and wasn't looking at the cigarette case for the first time, her awe was real enough. She didn't even notice Gaston pour himself another inch of cognac.

We soon had six ornaments on the table in front of us. They were fussy little things, and not at all to my taste, but I could see that each one was more finely finished than the last and they'd certainly all been expensive. The second package we opened contained a scent bottle. Then came a hip flask, and a bracelet with a sapphire clasp. There was a monstrously vulgar miniature bulldog carved out of reddish semi-precious stone, with a tiny gold-and-jewelled collar, and a still more ornate and awful jewelled miniature troika on a marble egg. Finally, there was a pendant on a chain – a malachite-and-silver egg that opened up to reveal two spaces for portraits.

'Look at the box, mademoiselle,' Marie-Thérèse breathed. The jeweller's name was inside the last box. Half the letters were nonsense, but the other half were clearly enough printed, in French. They read: 'Carl Fabergé & Cie, St.-Pétersbourg, Moscou, Londres.'

I drew a sharp breath too at that. I didn't know much about jewels, but everyone had heard of Fabergé. The Tsar's favourite jeweller, the man who'd created the ornaments that Russians everywhere, even today, were still said to be trying to sell to finance themselves in exile. Hadn't Hughie told me that, years ago now?

So these are the jewels she meant, I told myself, as the words Grandmother had written on the blotter shimmered and became, in my memory, something much more like the will Marie-Thérèse was suggesting. A faint but delicious warmth spread through me. Maybe it was just the brandy, but I so wanted to believe that Grandmother had been thinking of me – writing to me – from her sickbed, and leaving me a message. And those scribbles were, after all, quite likely to be her last wishes, weren't they?

I'd come here thinking I would find the one person in my family who wasn't bound hand and foot by convention. I'd thought of Grandmother as brave and original, someone who might be more like me than the more familiar relatives I'd grown up with. I'd hoped she would show me how to be an adventurer. And then I'd disappointed myself, shamed myself, and spoiled everything by running away. But maybe everything wasn't completely lost, after all? Because if I could only understand the words on the blotting paper, interpret the last wishes they must represent, and carry them out . . . it might be that I had a reason to spin out my time here, and not just to slink back to New York in defeat. Because how could I rush off home if I had a mission to complete for Grandmother in Paris?

I looked up at Marie-Thérèse with the beginning of excitement on my own face.

'Why I'm showing you now, mademoiselle, is because you wouldn't want the taxman to know about *these*,' said Marie-Thérèse, licking her lips. 'They'll be worth something. So when the lawyer comes, I think you shouldn't mention them to him either.'

For a moment I was a little repelled by the bright greed

in her eyes. But then I thought: No wonder she's so excited. She wasn't rich, and these ornaments must look like a wonderful treasure trove to her. I told myself I should be grateful for her honesty; admire it, even. She could so easily just quietly have pocketed them, and I'd never have known. If Gaston, by now looking rather fuddled at her side, had been the one to find the little things, I doubted I'd ever have seen them. But Marie-Thérèse had made sure I'd got them. She was looking after me.

How motherly she was feeling towards me became clearer still when she added, 'And you ought to find out what that other word Madame wrote meant, too. Because – you never know – it might be something else; some other memento for you.'

'It's a person's name,' I said, with growing certainty. The idea was developing in my mind, too. 'I'm almost sure it is, because of the place where she wrote "Evie protect make amends" with that word next to it. She must have wanted me to go and find someone, do something to help them and look after them; maybe someone she'd fallen out with. Perhaps she wanted me to share her pictures and jewels with them.'

I'd gladly carry out that wish, I thought. In fact, I'd give them all the jewels. I didn't even much like jewellery, especially not this ostentatious stuff. I'd far rather have those wild daubs of pictures as my memento of the woman who'd danced with me to Russian violin music, getting faster and faster, whirling me round till I laughed with joy . . . They'd be a better reminder of her.

Marie-Thérèse and Gaston looked doubtful.

'She had a Russian husband once,' I said, wishing I

knew more. 'If those things are Russian, they must be old gifts that he gave her, and his letters, too, I suppose. And maybe some of his family is here – and that word is the name of some relative of his whom I should find. After all, in a family, there's always someone to make amends to . . .'

It sounded a promising line of inquiry.

But Marie-Thérèse decisively shook her head. 'Oh, no, mademoiselle,' she said firmly. 'That's not it. Madame and that husband were only together for a year before Madame moved back to Paris. And she once told me that he'd been a shameless fortune-hunter, who'd only married her in the belief she was rich and would support him in style, and who started threatening to leave her as soon as her family cut off her allowance. She met him because she used to give money to the Russian orphanage that his sister – another vulture – ran out in the suburbs here. She said he'd spent all his own money long before he latched on to her. That was no surprise to me, of course; in my experience, Russians usually take more than they give. He had very nice manners, she said: he could charm birds down from trees. But it was a blessing in disguise that he died when he did.'

Yes, I'd known about him, hadn't I? Hughie had said something similar. But what struck me most about Marie-Thérèse's last remark was the reference it contained to Grandmother's family having cut off her allowance. I'd never heard anything about that from the family. This casual mention of it filled me with a searing pity for Grandmother, and anger against the rest of my family, who, I hotly told myself, had so spectacularly failed her – Mother in particular, but even affable, no-nonsense

Hughie. He administered the family trusts, after all. He must have let Mother's spite affect his judgement. He'd just cut her loose! If Marie-Thérèse was right, and it had happened while Grandmother had been briefly married to her Russian count, he must have done it after that time she'd stayed with us, when I was small. They must have been punishing her for that, when what had poor Grandmother actually done on that visit that was so terrible, except dance with me and organize a harmless procession in favour of women's emancipation? Without her allowance, I knew, she'd have been left with nothing more to live on than her small widow's pension from the diplomatic service. Was this why she'd stayed in Paris all these years, where life was so famously cheap, and not come home again? Was *that* why I'd never had a chance to get to know her?

This was when my resolve formed. I was going to do what someone who's needed does, I told myself. No one at home even knew Grandmother was dead (and even if they did, I thought hotly, would they care?), so it would be up to me to clear up the remnants of her life here, and while I did so I was also going to make it my business to find out what Grandmother had been trying to tell me. By the time I was done, I'd know everything that had been in her heart, and I'd take that knowledge home with me. They'd tried to write her out of their story, but I was going to be her historian. I was going to write her back in.

'Well, at least I should go and visit that sister at the orphanage. Maybe, if it is a Russian name, she'll be able to tell me more,' I said carefully.

Marie-Thérèse nodded unenthusiastically. 'But be sure

to ask all of them – all her Russians,' she added cannily. 'Not just that one woman. You'll have to phone them all at some point, anyway, to say she's died and tell them about the funeral. Remember, you can't trust Russians. Every one of them will probably tell you that the word is their name. Make sure you double-check.'

By that night, I knew a few more things.

The first was that Grandmother had left me her money. The lawyer (thin and faintly disapproving and dressed in hot black, regardless of the weather, like all lawyers everywhere) had shown me her will, written seventeen years before. Below an official declaration that she had no other family – I guessed, from this disavowal, that the will must have been her angry response to my mother and stepfather and her own sister's decision to cut her out of our family finances – she'd written that I was to be her sole beneficiary.

'*Mais, mademoiselle,*' he'd added cautiously, nibbling at his pen and raising an eyebrow, 'it is my impression that there isn't much to leave. The apartment is rented – it's paid for until the end of the year. She had an American official widow's pension which dies with her. There are personal effects, of course: clothes, furs, jewels, which I don't think are worth enough for you to worry about their incurring tax. But there is nothing else.'

Remembering Marie-Thérèse's warning not to let the taxman know about the Fabergé trinkets, I'd kept quiet about the box. But I'd gestured around at the pictures – the ones in the salon were mostly curling-up pages of yellowed paper pinned to the wall, with jagged lines and cut-out bits of violin curve stuck on to them, and asked, timidly, what about these? The lawyer had just smiled.

My second discovery was that both afternoon and evening were bad times to telephone Parisians, whether French, Russian or American. I hadn't managed to strike up a chatty friendship with a single White Russian, trustworthy or otherwise. Every number I was put through to was answered by a haughty-sounding maid saying, '*Madame revient prochaînement,*' or '*Monsieur dîne à l'extérieur,*' and offering, with no great grace, to take a message. There hadn't been many gracious expressions of condolence, either, when the message I'd dictated had been an invitation for Monsieur or Madame to attend a funeral the day after tomorrow.

One person I'd thought I might show the paper to, and ask what the mystery word meant, was the singer I'd met in New York – Plevitskaya, the so-called Russian Nightingale. Briefly, I'd been pleased at the idea of our paths crossing again. Here, among strangers, even someone I knew as little as Plevitskaya felt like a dear old friend. But, when I'd looked in the book, I hadn't seen anything that looked like the singer's long last name. (Or had I just remembered it wrong?)

Nor was there an entry I could recognize as being the orphanage woman's number. I'd just have to wait to talk to the people who came to the funeral to find out more, I saw.

Grandmother's Russian artist friends didn't even have a telephone number. There was just an address: 'Surrealists – chez Père Boucher, passage Dantzig, rue Dantzig, 15e. Or try Café Dantzig (NB beware drunk butchers)'.

So, when I'd given up on the telephone, I'd got Gaston

to take me there, through a district of slaughterhouses, foul smells and screaming cattle. Sighing deeply, he'd dropped me at a half-ruined octagonal building I'd felt a little scared to enter. The plot it was built on was full of other, smaller, more definitely ruined temporary buildings, like exhibition pavilions long gone to seed, with a garage at the end. It was very noisy. There were people banging at metal and wood on all sides. Most of the windows were broken. There were makeshift stovepipes sticking out of several squares with no glass. A man dressed as a cowboy was howling from a tiny balcony near the top, '*Moi génie! Moi génie!*' But no one was listening.

Everywhere I looked I saw depressed-looking people in rags dragging themselves about or muttering together. No wonder they looked so miserable. It smelled of herring and filth, cabbage and turpentine. I could feel the rats. I was about to leave without daring to speak to a soul when I saw an old Frenchman wearing a military ribbon in his buttonhole, wandering with a donkey on a halter through a litter-strewn garden dotted with sculptures (or so I thought – though they were so odd that I also thought they might just be bits of buildings that had come down). When I explained my errand, his eyes filled with sympathetic tears and he took me straight into a not-so-bad apartment on the ground floor. As he murmured, '*Ah, la pauvre Constance,*' a crowd of other lost souls followed us in, all of them emaciated and paint-damaged but suddenly bright-eyed too.

'My bees,' the old man explained vaguely, and the way they were buzzing around him was rather like bees; was this, then, the beehive – La Ruche – that the Dutchman

I'd talked to on the train, a lifetime ago – yesterday – had been heading for?

'Are you making tea, Papi?' one of the young people asked in guttural French; Russians, I thought, and my hunch was confirmed when he turned to me and explained, with a joyful flash of a smile, 'Tea is the centre of all our nostalgias.' Then, turning on the skeletal youth behind him, the speaker added, quickly: 'Because if you are, I happen to know Kostya has a bottle of vodka in his pocket. So if you have bread and maybe a bit of sausage for a *zakuska*, too, we could all treat this lovely young lady.'

And so it had been maybe an hour before I'd got away – an hour during which several more people had crammed in to see me, many of whom had said warmly that Grandmother had been their dearest friend and patron, most of whom had asked me to their studios to see their work, and all of whom had said, very eagerly, that they'd be sure to come to the funeral. It had felt encouraging to be among people who'd known Grandmother and wanted to tell me how much they'd enjoyed her company and support, and who might at any moment let slip some inconsequential story that would perhaps let me feel closer to her. I yearned to hear her spoken of in a way that would illuminate her. So I'd sat very quietly, smiling at everyone and letting them pour more drink and talk, being patient when they broke into the language I couldn't make head or tail of but now knew to be Russian. And it was only when I'd been getting up to go, with my head swimming from the vodka my new friends had been making me gulp down, neat, from a tin mug, followed by a tiny bite of herringy bread, followed by roars of applause, that I'd remembered my blotting paper.

'Женя!' they'd all sung out, on seeing the mystery scribble. 'It says "Zhenya"!' And I'd gazed back, soft with euphoria and hard liquor, loving them all, before I'd realized that this didn't really solve anything for me, since I didn't know what it meant. It was a name, of course, they said. The short pet name for Yevgeny – a Russian man's name.

'Well, are any of *you* called Yevgeny?' I asked, hoping against hope that Grandmother would turn out to have one favourite among this lot. But the tousled heads shook, one by one. When they'd finished cheerily calling out all their first names, which went from Khaim to Konstantin but didn't include anything like the one on my paper, I'd swallowed my disappointment, thanked them and left. Why did you even think it would be that easy? I'd told myself sternly. All the same, I blinked, very hard, all the way back to the car.

It had taken me the entire drive home to see things more optimistically.

It was only as I got into bed that I finally could. The third and most important thing I found out today, I told myself, as I switched off the lamp, is that I'm looking for a man called Yevgeny.

PART THREE

White Russians

12

On the ground floor below Constance's apartment, a stout elderly man in a suit was sitting at his desk, bathed in strong morning sun, not looking at the one letter on its vast empty surface. He wasn't looking out of the window, either, at the crowd of peculiar-looking people in the street, all watching a coffin being loaded into a hearse. Not really. Not any more than he was really looking at the two ponies strapped to the hearse, or at the tall, attractive, well-dressed young woman in black, a stranger to him – but, he thought, with a moment's approval, a lady, at least, unlike all those other ragamuffins – as she got into the car parked behind. Even though he wanted to look. Even though there were tears in his light eyes.

What General Miller of the Russian General Military Union – discreetly identified on this apartment's doorplate only by his international-sounding surname and its Russian initials, ROVS, transliterated into Roman letters – was doing, instead, as Constance's odd cortège assembled on the street, was staying very still, and trying to keep those tears from rolling down his cheeks.

He was remembering how he'd brushed Constance off

at lunch three days ago, when she'd wanted him to come back to her apartment later on, and talk something over with her. Self-important fool that he was, he'd told her he was going to be too busy.

And now it was too late.

Constance had been the one taste of freedom in his life. He might not have liked all those terrible degenerate young men painting dreadful pictures whom she'd taken to cossetting. (He could half see several of them outside now.) But he'd admired her free spirit in choosing them, all the same. She wasn't a person to let herself be tied down by other people's expectations. She'd always done what she wanted. An extraordinary woman . . . To someone as defined as he was by the great struggle that had dominated his life for so long, that freedom of manoeuvre of hers had been something to appreciate. When he'd been with her, during those snatched moments together upstairs, he'd sometimes, briefly, also felt free. She'd had the knack of making it seem as though everything might, after all, be possible. She'd had hope. She'd had joy.

But now she was gone. How trapped he felt.

The door had just shut behind Jean, who'd taken one look at him while putting down a cup of breakfast-time coffee (still steaming, unnoticed, on the table by the sofa) and said, immediately, with concern in his voice, 'Pap, you shouldn't stay up all night working like this. Does you no good. The Soviets will wait another day to be conquered. You don't look well. Come home with me now. Get some sleep, eh?'

Of course he hadn't agreed. But that was nothing to do with the faint scepticism about his mission in life that he'd heard in Jean's remark either. Jean was a good boy, whose hard work in his unworthy calling as a driver kept them all financially afloat. Jean was entitled to his opinion. He had no right to argue with Jean.

There was a good practical reason for refusing to go home. This respectable office was in an apartment that had been a legacy to ROVS from an elderly Russian émigré, who'd had the good fortune to pass away while he still had something left to leave. The apartment still had a faded dignity about it: high ceilings (though with flaking paint) and space to breathe and spread out maps. But the dingy little place in the sticks that he and Jean called home only had one bedroom, and that was for Katya, his wife, with the old nurse who lived with them in a cot at the side of the room. Where he slept, at night, was on the sofa in the other room. Jean slept on it during the day, after his nights out scouring Paris for fares. They were both big men. They couldn't exactly share the sofa for a day's sleep, could they?

And anyway, he wanted to be here, watching Constance's funeral cortège set out.

What he'd really have liked, if he'd been another person with another life, would have been to go to the funeral himself. But he wasn't allowed out by himself. He was too important to the White cause. His colleagues didn't want any more leaders of what was left of the White Russian army – the man on whom they pinned all their hopes of a return, one day, to the lost motherland – to fall victim to any more Soviet plots. It might just have been a rumour that the strange, sudden TB that had taken off Vrangel', his predecessor but one, had really been caused by a dose of Soviet poison. But there'd been no doubt when Kutyopov had been clubbed and chloroformed and shoved inside a car seven years ago – right here on the street, in the middle of Paris, in the middle of the morning – by men dressed as French police. The hand of the Kremlin's secret agents was clearly visible. No one knew exactly what had become of that White military leader, but the likelihood was that poor Kutyopov had been spirited off by ship to Russia and ended up in the Lubyanka. At any rate, he'd never been seen again. So, since General Miller had taken over the job, he'd been watched, day and night, not only by Jean – who ended every night's driving work by picking him up from home in the taxi and bringing him here, then started every new night by coming back to pick him up – but also by all those young men in the outer office: the secretaries, always buzzing around, checking on him, bringing him things . . . like flies.

If he tried to slip out of the building now, they'd ask questions. They'd try to come too.

And he didn't want that. Some things were best kept private.

He didn't even dare get up and go and stare out of the window, memorizing the details of Constance's last departure. He was too aware of Jean's habits not to know that, after leaving him here in the mornings – or, on this particular morning, just dropping in to check he was all right – Jean always sat out there in the driver's seat for a few more minutes, rolling a cigarette to smoke before heading home to sleep. (A filthy habit, General Miller sometimes remonstrated; but Jean was tired by the morning, yawning and red-eyed, and would answer without anger that he needed that cigarette to get his strength up to get to his bed.) So General Miller had no intention of going near the window until he heard the chug of Jean's motor heading away. He wouldn't want to be seen gawping out at the many strange persons gathered out there – strays from all the old Russian empire's subordinate nationalities – in their weird clothes, dirt and disarray.

He couldn't stay still. He got up. But instead of going to the window he walked to the fireplace and picked up the small framed photo on it. It showed a thin young fair-haired man in military uniform, rowing a boat, with a dark-haired young woman in the mutton-chop-sleeve fashion of two generations ago smiling tremulously at him. He held it to his heart, remembering how young they'd both once been, and obscurely comforted by its still being here. Constance's smile had always had that power over him.

Whatever he'd told her, after their last lunch, about being too busy, he'd half meant to change his mind and slip upstairs for that cocktail anyway. He really had. She was always in his thoughts. But then, by the end of the afternoon, his head had been too full of the marvellous news Skoblin had brought him – that letter from Wilhelm Canaris's office, still lying there on the desk now, with its black, black Gothic lettering and its long German words. The letter held out the possibility of the alliance they'd been dreaming of for all these years: Germany's military might thrown behind their increasingly futile struggle to unseat the Reds from Russia (futile because they were none of them getting any younger, and because so many of the young had, like Jean, given up hope of ever going home – but how different everything would look, if they could lean on Berlin) . . . He'd been so full of pride in his security chief – Skoblin, the quiet man no one had trusted, whom he'd insisted on appointing; his faith in his subordinate now triumphantly vindicated – and in the future opening up for them all that he hadn't been able to think of anything else. He hadn't slipped upstairs, as he'd intended, not even for a moment. He'd just let Jean take him back to his own apartment instead.

If only he'd fobbed Jean off, said he had to work late, as he sometimes did, told him to come back hours later or not at all, that he'd sleep on the office sofa, anything. If only he'd forgotten about duty and the war against the Soviets for once. If only he'd said, as a normal man might have, to hell with the cause, I want to see my lover.

He tightened his hold on the picture, as if she were somehow still in it and reachable, touchable, addressing his excuses to her. The thing was that, at that moment, on that afternoon three days ago, he hadn't been able to think of anything but the Germans, who, as the letter said, were already on their way to Paris for that long-awaited secret meeting. In his mind, he'd been sketching out what they might look like, where the meeting would be, and what he'd say to persuade them. He couldn't have said anything about any of that to Constance, of course, and he wouldn't have been able to explain his elation . . . and (incredible as this now seemed, in the darkness enveloping him this morning) he'd so wanted to celebrate. He couldn't, not with anyone else, because only Skoblin knew, and Skoblin had had to go back to his own little hovel in the sticks, and his wife. So, tiptoeing around so as not to disturb Katya, who was asleep in her sickroom, he'd sat out on the balcony at home and got a little happily drunk, all on his own, gazing out through the night air at the stars and allowing himself to wonder if there might, after all, be any chance that one day before he died he'd again look up at this sky – but a bigger, more luminous, old-country version of it – from that beloved shabby spreading house from the past, with its fluttering curtains, its smell of Pears soap and Dusya's apple cake, its little river beach, and its peace, surrounded by the pine forest where, in summer, he'd once raced between trees on a bicycle . . .

And the next morning – could it really be only the day before yesterday? – with a muzzy head but still full of his private joy, he'd helped the nurse wheel the wordless Katya, dribbling and twitching in her invalid chair, out on to the balcony to enjoy the sunlight. He'd stood there beside the poor wreck of a woman his wife had become, not feeling sad for her for once because he was so lit up with his excitement. He'd waited for the sight of Jean's taxi in the street below, not even listening to the traffic noise because he was lost in the peace and beauty of that other place, the estate, the blossom, the lime-tree promenade. He'd let little wisps of expectant half-thought run through his head – when would he arrange for Katya to move home, *if* . . .? And, Katya would have the care she needed, back home, *if* . . . And, more privately still, would Constance come with him to a place that would be so alien to her, *if* . . .? But all those were questions for later. He didn't let his racing mind stop on any of them. As soon as he'd seen Jean he'd drunk his coffee in a gulp and rushed to work, eager as a child.

'You're in a good mood today,' he remembered Jean saying wearily.

'Developments,' he'd replied, importantly, feeling the letter in his pocket with his hand. 'Developments, dear boy.'

Now the memory of that secret pride he'd been bursting with made him want to howl and smash his fist through something. How could he not have known – after all the reverses he'd suffered in his long life – that you should never take such hubristic pleasure in the advances of a single day? They could all be wiped out the next. They usually were.

This time, his joy had been wiped out as soon as they'd reached this office building. He'd noticed people on the stairs – more to-ing and fro-ing than usual in the lobby. He hadn't thought much of it. But perhaps he'd had a raised eyebrow, or an enquiring look on his face. At any rate, the secretary who'd answered their door had explained the fuss without even being asked, saying, with gloomy pleasure, 'A death in the building, your excellency; the American lady upstairs.'

The silence that followed seemed to go on forever. The universe, flipping over, the stars changing their course . . .

Then he remembered that he'd said – snapped: 'I don't want to hear gossip. I have work to do. I don't want to be disturbed today,' and rushed into his room, leaving the secretary, and Jean, staring round-mouthed behind him.

He'd been here ever since. He'd phoned Skoblin and said he wanted to be left alone for a day or two to work out how best to approach Canaris's men. That had got rid of *him*. When Jean came to pick him up, in the evening, he'd sent the boy away too. Pressure of work, he'd said. Last night, too. Now the sofa was a frowsty mess of blankets. He hadn't changed his shirt. His hair was sticking up.

He knew they were all waiting outside, all his colleagues,

expecting ideas and initiatives from him. But he hadn't looked at the letter. Not once.

He was a man like any other. He just wanted to be left alone to mourn; to cover the mirror up decently with a cloth as the old superstition demanded; and to go to Constance's funeral and bury his love. And he couldn't.

Although, he suddenly thought with a wild little leap of the heart, if he were to try, just once, slipping out of the back door, the cook's door, not just for a smoke in the courtyard, but to get to the alley at the back of it, and out past the dustbins . . . now, that might work . . . especially now, around midday, when the secretaries who worked here during the morning were all busy taking off their dignified suits and uniforms, putting on workmen's overalls instead and heading off to the labouring jobs that they needed to keep them in bread and wine and rent money in this alien land they'd somehow fetched up in; while the others – the afternoon secretaries – were still straggling here, in ragged workers' clothes, from their early shift in some unmentionable car-factory suburb, ready to resume their real dress, their real language, and their real, Russian way of life, only once they walked in through this front door . . .

For a moment, he could almost imagine himself walking, free and unaccompanied, down the street, between the roaring of traffic, with the breeze ruffling his hair.

It was what Constance would have done: paid no heed to the world, just followed her heart.

But heart-following wasn't his destiny. He shook his head (carefully, realizing as he did that he shouldn't have toasted Constance's passing in vodka in the middle of last night, without so much as a *zakuska* to help the alcohol down;

it wasn't good for his heart). No, no, he was a man with responsibilities. He'd better look at that letter, and start making plans. He started making his way heavily towards the desk, hating the juxtaposition of mahogany slab, white paper rectangle and jacket neatly hung on the chair, dreading sitting at it again and closing down his heart.

He was still walking across the room when he heard the taxi outside pull away.

He stopped. He changed direction.

What he'd imagined he would do now was to go to the window.

But instead he went to the door, opened it – no one there – and slipped out in his shirtsleeves. They'd never know he'd gone, he told himself, opening the door at the back of the courtyard, as long as they could see his jacket on the back of his chair.

13

The bright crowd in ragged motley came clattering into the little church, looking about them and whispering in many different languages. Some of them I recognized from the artists' refuge the day before yesterday; one of them, a large woman ostentatiously kissing people through a mass of attention-seeking black feathers, I was almost certain was the Russian singer I'd met in New York. Marie-Thérèse and Gaston, beside me in the front pew, near the coffin, were rigid with disapproval. But I didn't mind. Even if no one except me had bothered to send flowers, there was no disrespect intended in their too-loud chatter. The door shut behind us.

Then, just as the priest approached the altar to begin the service, the door opened again. A sombre-looking elderly man of a quite different sort, in shirtsleeves and correct, if worn, cavalry twill trousers, stuck his head in. He didn't look the type to go out without a jacket. His hair had just been damped and combed over his big head, and he had a neat grey imperial beard and side-whiskers. He was composing himself, but he was still out of breath. He looked as though he must have been running.

He blinked once or twice as his eyes got used to the interior twilight. For a long moment, he looked around. I saw his eyes fix on the waving black feathers above that woman's splendid shelf of a bosom. I couldn't help smiling to myself at the horror on his face as he took in the appearance of the crowd.

Then he retreated. The door shut, very quietly, as the first word of prayer began.

I forgot about the unknown worshipper for the next few hours. Marie-Thérèse had set out wine and canapés for the guests back at the apartment, and until the middle of the afternoon the artists were there, talking, mostly incomprehensibly in languages I couldn't understand, and gesticulating, and drinking, and eating. Hardly anyone bothered to come and tell me the stories about Grandmother that I'd been so hoping to hear. They were too busy knocking back food and drink. I asked everyone I did speak to if, by any chance, their name was Yevgeny, but I just got headshakes in reply. Increasingly disappointed, I resolved that, once we'd got rid of them all, I would go and visit the sister of Grandmother's dead husband – the one Marie-Thérèse had told me ran an orphanage in the suburbs somewhere. I'd got her name, Maria Sabline, from the art-colony man with the donkey. He couldn't remember her address, but he told me it would be in the phone book. He'd laughed rather sadly at the thought of her, and added, not very distinctly, 'It'sh been a long time shince it was an orphanage there. Children grow up; they all grow up . . .' before grabbing at some cheese slices being passed around by Gaston and forgetting about me. It had occurred to me that the orphanage woman's

brother – Grandmother's dead husband – might have been called Yevgeny.

Only the singer – Plevitskaya *was* her name, I now knew for sure – came waddling over to offer condolences, but even she was soft with brandy before she remembered me. 'It is good to see you again,' she slurred, pushing back strands of black feathers that kept slipping down from her enormous hat. Her breath was pure Rémy Martin, but she clearly remembered meeting me before. 'And here in Paris. But so sad, so sad, that we are at funeral of my dear old friend.' She was clutching at my shoulders, hugging me to a too-warm, too-padded breast. Some of the artists came up and said something kind but discouraging to her, in Russian, but she shrugged them off in exclamatory English. 'No! This is grand-daughter of my dear Constance! We are acquainted! Like grandmother, this beautiful young lady came to hear me sing in New York – then came to Paris to find Russians. Grandmother too – dear, dear Constance. Years ago, she hear me in New York – love Russian music so much – followed me to Paris. Same story. One Russian voice, and they are enchanted.' Her eyes filled with tears.

'*Da ladno,*' one of the young men said tenderly, gently detaching her from me and taking her away to rest on the sofa. 'I ask forgiveness!' she said, looking at me in glistening alarm. 'But I have another question!' It came out as 'kves-shon!' I smiled uncertainly, but I didn't go and join her on the sofa. She was too drunk, and too unmanageable. I could barely remember why I'd wanted to show her the paper with Grandmother's writing on, the other day. There'd be someone easier to ask, I now felt sure. I didn't really believe Grandmother had come to Paris as a result of hearing her sing, any more than I'd come because of that, but I felt sorry for her tears, all the same. The others didn't. They just winked and grinned at me, as if sharing a joke, and moved on.

Plevitskaya wasn't the only one who seemed overwhelmed by the plentiful refreshments. The sofas were filling up fast with shouting, weeping people. 'It's unbelievable, what they're getting through,' I heard Marie-Thérèse mutter as she came rushing out of the kitchen with another tray of food. 'Gaston says they're drinking the cellar dry.'

I smiled and spread my hands in resignation, signalling: Oh, let them gorge themselves. They don't look as though they eat enough, usually. It was my guess Grandmother would have wanted a cheerful send-off.

But after a while – once I'd seen Plevitskaya consult her watch, then totter out in a not completely straight line – I slipped away too and left the rest of them to it and went back to the churchyard. I thought I'd sit by Grandmother's grave and clear my head, and Gaston could see off the stragglers and clear up.

To my surprise, there was someone else at the graveyard already, under the old yew tree spreading shade next to that morning's mound of upturned earth, with its flowers. He was sitting with dignity on a stump, straight-backed, not seeming to notice how uncomfortable it must be. And he was gazing into the distance, cradling something square in his arms. His eyes were reddened and his face looked rough, as if he hadn't slept. But his expression was calm. It was the same elderly man I'd seen in church: the one in crumpled shirtsleeves, with the beard and whiskers. There was something familiar about him, I thought now. Perhaps I'd seen him around here somewhere before or perhaps it was just I could now see that his silvered hair, no longer neatly combed down but blowing all over the place in the breeze, was, rather like mine, prone to rising up irrepressibly in two places at the temples. His, unrestrained by the grips that held mine, had started to look a little comical as it fluttered in the wind. Between the two wiry kinks that had escaped their moorings and were pushing out and up, the softer hair from the middle part of his forehead had blown forward to hang limply over his eyes, which must be why, every now and then, he was unconsciously shaking his head, like a horse flicking its mane about to rid itself of flies. Looking at him made me smile, even as it reminded me, sympathetically, of my own struggles with my disobedient hair.

I stopped at the gate. I couldn't know if it were Grandmother's grave that had drawn him there, or if he were just sitting there by chance. He hadn't stayed in church for her funeral, after all, but I didn't like to disturb him, all the same. I could sense the depth of sadness in him.

There was so much sadness in this city, I was just beginning to see; so many people hugging secret sorrows to their hearts. There was so much I didn't yet understand.

I was already walking away by the time I realized there'd been something else about that scene. I'd been expecting to see just my bunch of flowers on the grave. But someone had brought more since I'd left the churchyard. There'd been a whole scatter of loose red and white carnations, just now, blowing over Grandmother's grave.

14

The feathers kept getting in Plevitskaya's eyes as she walked. In spite of the havoc being wrought on her feet by these excruciating New York high heels, she'd chosen to walk all the way to the 17th arrondissement, rather than hail a cab, because she could tell she'd somehow got a bit tiddly at the wake and wanted to sober up before she met her husband and the others for the early dinner they'd planned. This meeting might change both their lives. She couldn't let him down.

Irritably, she brushed the tickly black fringe out of her face. If only the sun weren't so hot, and her dress so tight. She wasn't the type to drink, she told herself; it was just the once, because she was sad, and that was understandable enough . . .

As soon as she'd peeped round the door of Constance's office, at the start of the wake, she'd seen that the equipment for her voice recording, which had been lying everywhere just the other day, beeping and gleaming, had all gone. Vanished. She'd meant to ask the girl what had happened to it, but sadness had overwhelmed her, and the girl had been too busy to concentrate. It was clear that the recording would never be made now. She'd pinned so much faith on it. She'd so hoped that being on phonograph, especially this superior type, which would show her at her best advantage, was going to revive her career. She'd been dreaming about it non-stop ever since her husband had come home, looking pleased, and said he'd put the question of paying for it to Constance so subtly that she'd almost ended up thinking it was all her own idea. Her husband, despite his pursed lips and moodiness, did, often, still think of wonderful ways of pleasing her. It wasn't his fault this one hadn't worked. But it was a reverse, a considerable reverse. No wonder she'd poured out the cognac with a more generous hand than usual today. The frustration was enough to make a saint weep.

Pausing at the bottom of the rue Daru, clutching at a lamp-post and shifting around for a minute to ease the pain in her feet, she looked around in distaste at all the tatty Russian restaurants running up one side of the Alexander Nevsky cathedral, the heart of Little Russia. The waiters and waitresses moved from one restaurant to another, here or elsewhere in their adopted city. Sometimes they became proprietors themselves, drinking champagne on the opening night and putting out announcements in the Russian papers:

Pyotr Vasilyevich Sidorov has the honour of informing his dear friends and clientele that he has opened his own restaurant, Tsarskaya Okhota, in such-and-such a street. Head chef: Valery Ivanovich Karpov. Large selection of hors d'oeuvres. *Plat du jour* – today *rasstegai*; tomorrow, suckling pig in sour cream.

Substantial artistic programme. Daily performances
by the public's darling, Nadezhda Plevitskaya, the
Tsar's Nightingale.

She could hardly bear to call to mind the magnificent
chandeliered halls in which she'd once sung, back home,
so unlike these nasty little dumps. She didn't have to
look, or go in, to know the meagre size of the restaurant
interiors, the steel-and-glass flowers on the table, the little
lamps with shades, and the squashed space they offered
at the back for a single singer to cram herself onstage and
do her best to entertain their drunken, unappreciative,
cheapskate audiences. As for the fees – she grimaced. The
only dates in her diary, these days, were in these unworthy
venues. Without that recording, which might have done
so much for her, it really was possible that she was all
washed up.

Shaking her head, as if to get rid of the bad thoughts,
Plevitskaya straightened up, thrust her feet back into the
agonizing shoes, and walked on.

Of course, today, they weren't going to meet their secret
guests in this central zone of gossipy Little Russia where
everyone knew everyone. No, her husband had chosen a
more private meeting place on the other side of the rue
du Faubourg Saint-Honoré, in one of the cafés behind
the art deco concert hall. It was only five minutes' walk
away, but it might as well have been a different country,
for those cafés were inhabited by an entirely different tribe:
impecunious music lovers, skinny young things spinning
out single glasses of wine for hours with their noses stuck
into scores and librettos. None of them would notice a few

stray Russians sitting in a corner. No one would understand
a word they said.

So Plevitskaya walked away from the rue Daru, and the
cathedral, and the rue de la Néva and the rue Pierre-le-
Grand, turning her broad back decisively on the triangle
of streets that constituted Russia abroad and on her career
worries. Now wasn't the moment to think about that, she
admonished herself, feeling quite sober by now. She had
to concentrate on the important business meeting with
the crab salesman, and the benefits it might bring to her
husband.

Her husband needed a boost in life, she reflected. He'd
lived with disappointment for so long. Before Kutyopov had
been kidnapped, her husband had thought *he*'d be named
the next head of ROVS. It was the job he'd always wanted.
But then, as the result of the unhelpful rumour that had got
about that he'd had a hand in the kidnapping himself, he'd
been passed over, and General Miller appointed instead.
She had to imagine how disappointed he must have been
– perhaps almost as intensely disappointed as she now
felt at the disappearance of her recording – because he'd
never complained. He'd taken the number-two job instead,
without a murmur. He'd never said a bad word against that
fat old fool Miller, in all these seven years, even if he'd got
more grumpy and disagreeable at home. It was time he got
his chance to shine now. A bit of real success might make
him less irritable, and less penny-pinching, too. It might
turn him back into the pleasant consort he'd once been.

Her husband and the two guests – one in a cheap Moscow
suit and the other in a market-trader's apron smelling of
crab – were already at a table on the *terrasse* by the time

she found the back-street café. Her husband was looking irritably at his watch. That made her nervous. And feeling nervous made her act flamboyant. Breaking into their quiet conversation about cargo – she heard a few words about when the freight carrier *Maria Ulyanova* should stop at Le Havre to pick the cargo up for dispatch to Leningrad – she kissed, and exclaimed, and smiled, all the while trying not to stare too openly at the crab salesman, who she knew was the boss, despite his workman's clothes.

She could feel her husband's disapproving eyes on her. 'We've ordered,' he said. 'You were late.' Then he added, 'I've ordered water for you. The wine's for the men. You just need food.'

She subsided into a seat, still flashing smiles around the table and wishing she could have a glass of wine to calm her nerves. Not looking at her husband, she told the hovering waiter she wanted the lobster. Well, she knew this was a meal that would go on somebody's expenses, probably Moscow's, and if everything went according to plan their money worries would soon be a thing of the past, anyway. She could afford to treat herself.

If there'd been just the two of them there, she thought, her small extravagance would definitely have made her husband furious. But the crab salesman just nodded expressionlessly, and the waiter went away.

The crab salesman, Plevitskaya thought, sneaking a proper look at him as she reached for the bread basket, must be in his late thirties. There was nothing remarkable about his appearance. Under his beret was dirty-blond hair and a flat, wide face, the ordinary Russian kind with a short nose and wide mouth. His hands were big and calloused.

It was only his stillness, and those ice-blue eyes, that made him a little frightening.

Suddenly he smiled directly at her. 'A magnificent choice,' he said in a nasal Moscow voice. The smile made him look quite handsome. But Plevitskaya started feeling clammy, all the same. (Perhaps it was the brandy.) 'And a magnificent woman is just what we are going to need.' Plevitskaya nodded, quiet as an obedient child.

'Your job, on the day,' he went on, 'will be to provide Skoblin here with an alibi.' He turned and smiled at Plevitskaya's husband, who, like Plevitskaya, remained silent and round-eyed. 'It will be a simple task for a magnificent woman like you. We're going to send you out shopping at Monsieur Epstein's boutique.'

Monsieur Epstein's boutique! Feeling suddenly happier, Plevitskaya sucked in her tummy, sat up straighter, and carried on nodding as she listened to the rest of the plan.

It was only when the crab salesman had finished speaking, and everyone started saying how clever and foolproof the plan was, that Plevitskaya felt her husband stir. She glanced at him. She could see from the eager way he was smiling that, although he was scared of saying the wrong thing, he was also desperate enough to impress the Muscovites – especially the crab salesman – to venture a remark of his own.

'The old man doesn't suspect a thing, you know,' her husband said. 'He read the letter twenty times in front of me. He was practically jumping for joy. And he's been shut up alone in his office with it ever since, thinking out his strategy for his secret meeting.' Leaning forward, he put a tentative, tender hand on the crab salesman's arm. 'So your

German must be up to snuff!' he finished, then exploded into what Plevitskaya thought was probably unintentionally loud laughter.

The crab salesman didn't even crack a smile in return. Plevitskaya felt almost sorry for her husband as he put a napkin to his red face, turned his laugh into a cough, and, still gasping for breath, spluttered, 'Crumb in my throat . . . sorry,' into the silence.

'Have some water,' the crab salesman said. Quietly, she passed him her glass.

15

Jean

The first thing I noticed, after getting the taxi out of the garage as evening drew on and driving to Father's office to see if I could get him home tonight before I started work, was that a lot of drunk chancers were weaving out of his building on the rue du Colisée. Many of them, I could see at once, were some sort of Russian – some blue-eyed Slavs, others skinny lads with the dark look of Romanians or Jews – and they were all looking as pleased with themselves as dogs who've stolen the chicken. I could guess what had brought them in such numbers, of course; they must have been filling their bellies at the funeral of the American woman who'd died upstairs, the one with the Russian name left her by a stray husband long ago – the woman who'd liked to patronize artists. Well, God be with her, I thought (not that I actually believe in any deity), and felt sorry that she had no one better to mourn her passing than these scroungers.

The second thing I noticed – on my way out, once Father had told me, irritably, that he wasn't ready to go home; hadn't got his work for the day done yet; what was I bothering him for so early, and more in the same uncharacteristic, tetchy, red-eyed vein that made me think he must be sickening for something – was the girl.

She was waiting at the taxi rank as I got back into my parked cab – tall and very slender, and wearing a grey dress and pearls. She was standing in a beam of sunlight. But, under all those exuberant blond curls, her face was pensive.

I remembered her arriving here the other evening, driven by the American woman's chauffeur. The memory contained a touch of shame, because, just for a moment, seeing a new face among the familiars of our street, I'd wondered whether this wasn't *it* – the attack on Father that we spent so much effort trying to prevent: the bomb, the stabbing, the injection of poison, whatever. Once I'd properly taken in which car she'd come in, and the quality of her foreign clothes, I'd recognized the stupidity of the thought. But it had taken a moment or two to relax out of my combat-readiness, and a part of me still felt apologetic that, for a moment, I'd been ready to attack this innocent passer-by.

She'd had an uncertain, watchful look on her face then, too. But it had been transient, I'd thought; the effect of arriving in a new place, or of not understanding the fierce look I'd perhaps directed at her. I'd easily been able to imagine her with the shadow gone – turning back into just one more of the mass of identical sleek, contented, smugly established young people of her class, to whom everything came so easily. That hadn't happened, though. There was no ease on her face. If anything, the shadow looked deeper now.

Well, no wonder. She must have been staying with the old

lady when she'd died. Perhaps she was family? Even if she wasn't wearing proper mourning, she was probably dressed as sombrely as a holiday wardrobe allowed. And she must have spent this afternoon fending off the scroungers, too. Both things would be enough to make anyone sigh.

I gave her a sympathetic look as I drove up to the rank.

But there was no answering echo. She didn't recognize me. In point of fact, she didn't even look at me as she leaned in through the open window, smelling faintly of something elusive, not quite the innocent flower fragrances of young girls or the powerful musk-and-caustic of prostitutes (I'd left the windows open to get rid of that).

I'd been a taxi driver long enough to know a lot about prostitutes and their clients. I came across them every night, and they always spoke to me as though I were one of them. 'We do the same kind of work, you and us,' they liked to say. When the sun was rising, on my way to the garage after finishing work, I often gave these women lifts – they'd be heading home after a night's work too – and they'd always offer me payment in kind. I usually had them sit in the back of the car and not beside me, as they were all drenched in their strong cheap perfume, and their proximity gave me a nauseating taste in my mouth. They'd go, but the smell lingered on. I'd shut my nostrils.

Unlike now. I took a cautious breath in, enjoying the mysterious otherness of this girl's scent, and the pure white skin of her cheek.

The moment's pleasure didn't last. She broke the spell by rattling off an all-too-familiar address, which I recognized at once as that of the Russian old people's home run by Madame Sabline out in the suburbs. (Wasn't that also the borrowed name of the American woman? I thought, unable to resist curiosity. Had the Russian she was said to have once married been some connection of Madame Sabline's?) Then, with lowered eyes, the girl folded herself in back of the car and looked away, waiting for me to drive.

Now, there's nothing unusual about avoiding a taxi driver's eyes. Parisians do it all the time. But, to a taxi driver, it's a bad sign, a sign of a person who feels no restraining influences – someone who's thinking: What does it matter what this driver thinks of me if I will never see him again and he has no way of telling my friends about it? Because, by absurd chance, I'd been obliged to adopt this job as my calling in life, I saw my chance clients as they were in reality and not as they wished to appear, and my contact with them had shown them in a very bad light on almost every occasion.

Abruptly, I pulled away. I regretted my momentary sympathy for the girl now. Her indifference brought rushing into my head all the usual mixture of irritation and regret that such comfortless and pointless experiences should be my lot. Rage, too: when I looked down at my hands on the wheel, I saw that there were white points on my knuckles.

I accelerated round a corner, sharply, not looking behind to see whether my passenger was shaken by the sudden speed, barely hearing the angry cacophony of car horns that resulted. I was remembering the man I'd given a lift to at dawn, who had five suitcases and whom I'd driven to the avenue Victor-Hugo. He'd got out of the car and said, as if it were the most natural thing in the world, 'Now take these suitcases up to the fifth floor.' There wasn't any doubt in his voice. He didn't even bother to say 'please'.

'Listen, *mon vieux*,' I said, and he turned round at my familiar tone, looking as shocked as if I'd hit him. 'Your arms aren't paralysed, are they?'

'No, why?'

'I just don't see why I should suddenly start carrying your suitcases up to the fifth floor, or any other floor. If I had to change a wheel, I wouldn't turn to you and ask you to do it for me, would I?'

He looked at me. Then he asked, 'Are you a foreigner?'

'No,' I replied, provocatively. 'My father is a butcher at 42 rue de Belleville.'

He'd complained to the police, of course. But, as always happens when these misunderstandings arise, everything was sorted out as soon as I handed over my nonsense passport to the police, and they saw I was a Russian. After all, I hadn't committed a crime. I'd just offended a wealthy man's sense of the relationships that should prevail between different categories of citizen in France.

I turned another corner, with a judder. I was secretly pleased to see, in the mirror, the girl's hands closing quickly on the strap in the side of the door to hold herself steady.

In this dark state of mind, which often came upon me, I felt that everything good in the world had been closed off from me. I was alone, locked out, and desperate not to be caught up forever in the endless human vileness with which my work brought me into nightly contact. By this I didn't just mean the women on the streets, the men destroying their livers in the cafés, or the night people who inundated the city in a state of sexual frenzy – for, if you were a Paris taxi driver working at night, even the Russian Civil War could not compare with the absence of virtue of the streets I'd ended up in. No, what depressed me even more than all that was this strange separation of people into estates, and orders, as remote from each other as Eskimos and Australians, and the stultifying way no one ventured into acquaintanceships or even geographical areas not allocated to people of their sort, or even spoke much to anyone who wasn't precisely the same as himself, or indeed herself. That Paris was made up of fixed zones for the different orders I learned, first, from the elderly worker next to me in a paper factory off the boulevard de la Gare. It was one of the first places I worked after getting here. He told me that during the entire forty years he had lived in Paris he had never been to the Champs-Élysées because, as he explained, he had never worked there. He couldn't imagine any other reason for someone like him to see the centre of the city.

I'd hardly been able to believe that. But experience confirmed it over and over again afterwards. Although working people at least all talked to me as if I were one of them – there was no side to them – the poor were even more limited in their outlook than their rich oppressors. They had absolutely no idea that there might be ways out of their misery. For instance, I could never get it across to my fellow factory workers, back in those days, that I was going to night school. 'What are you going to study?' they'd ask, baffled. I'd tell them. 'You do know it's hard. You'll need to know a lot of special words,' they'd reply, shaking their heads doubtfully. A woman worker advised me to give up all of this useless stuff. It wasn't for working people like us, she said, and tried to persuade me not to take the risk but to stay there, where, as she put it, in ten years' time I

might become a foreman or the head of a team of workers. 'Ten years!' I said. 'I'd die ten times over in that time.'

'You'll come to a bad end,' she said, finally.

When I was on my way home, in the mornings, at five or six o'clock, driving through the unrecognizably empty and sleepy streets, I'd often pass through Les Halles. I'll never forget how struck I was when I first saw workers in the vegetable market harnessed to those small carts on which they carry their cabbages and carrots. I still remember looking at their weather-beaten faces and strange eyes, which seemed to be covered with a transparent and impenetrable film, typical of people unused to thinking – most prostitutes have the same sort of eyes – and reflecting that Chinese coolies and Roman slaves probably had the same eternally veiled look and pretty similar conditions of existence, too. The entire history of human culture had never existed for people like these. All those names – Galileo, Da Vinci, Michelangelo, Mozart, Tolstoy, Bach, Balzac – all the hundreds and thousands of years of human civilization meant nothing here. There was just dawn, and the harness, and the same old slave hauling his cart.

Whenever this savage mood was upon me, I'd try to reason with myself. I'd tell myself that I'd never have learned all this if I hadn't become a Paris taxi driver. I'd tell myself (feeling it to be a lie) that all experience was good. I'd tell myself that my experiences would, in some way, enrich the writing I was one day going to do, if ever I got any free time between driving, sleeping and the needs of my father and the poor sick creature whom, out of politeness, I called my mother. I'd say . . .

Well, what does it matter what I told myself? It never

worked, telling myself all that uplifting rubbish. So this evening, still intensely aware of that girl sitting on the back seat looking out of the window – aware of the lovely line of her neck and shoulder and of her casual disrespect, I tried something simpler. I emptied my mind and let the hypnotic movement of the streets all around calm me.

One after another, round street lamps appeared then disappeared in the darkening air.

The same streets, always the same streets rearing up around me: but sometimes, if I forced myself to take notice of them, the beauty of those luminous night lines, the conjunction with a black avenue here or a rustling park there, did have a soothing effect.

Drawing away from the centre of town, I found this happening now. Remembering the wild eyes of other wealthy clients when I'd answered their unthinking rudeness with spirit, saying things like, 'If you're not happy, get out and take another cab,' I did wonder how this girl would have responded if I'd challenged her. But, by then, as we headed off down a quiet suburban avenue, my anger had pretty much dissipated. And when I looked in the mirror and saw the pinched look on her face, I thought better of it.

She was so obviously not happy.

Anyway, I thought, finally able to enjoy the breeze moving the great lime trees that lined this avenue, had she really done anything so wrong? She hadn't talked, true. But had I, so quick to take offence, actually even tried to talk with her either?

I'd have been utterly corrupted by Paris if I too became unable to converse with people outside my station, I

realized. The thought gave me courage and a little surge of warmth that was perhaps what hope, that feeling I hadn't experienced for so long, might be like.

I half turned, trying to catch her eye. 'So what takes you to this outpost of Little Russia?' I asked.

My voice startled her. My question too. She looked straight at me. 'You know there are Russians there?'

Her French was good, I noticed, with hardly any accent. Her voice was low and pleasant.

I was so delighted that she'd answered, and looked properly at me, that I rushed into an uncharacteristically long and detailed reply. I started telling her all the usual things people said about the estate we were heading for: that it was a big mansion with spacious grounds, and had once belonged to a Russian nobleman; that, after the Revolution in Russia, he'd turned it into a charity so that all the impecunious gentlefolk who'd escaped and ended up here in France had somewhere seemly to visit, walk in the grounds or go to classes or meetings in the former drawing rooms. There'd even been an orphanage, for a while, until all the Civil War orphans grew up. Now they were taking old folk in instead. 'The old folk feel right at home,' I said, and I felt my smile twist into something dangerously like a sneer, because it felt so hard to explain with anything like sympathy the joylessness of their exiled existence, 'because there are samovars everywhere, and every franc can be mournfully sub-divided into kopeks . . .'

I thought she might laugh at that. People sometimes had, when I'd said it before.

I also thought she might ask, 'Are *you* Russian?' If she does, I was already thinking, realizing I was sitting up straighter than usual, I'll tell her. There'll be no stories about Belleville butchers today.

But she didn't laugh, or ask me any questions. She just looked at me without moving, so that, in the dusk, I couldn't tell if she was even taking in what I was saying.

At last she nodded. But all she said, in a small, blank voice, was, 'Well, I don't have any old relatives. Just business.'

And then she turned her eyes down and started looking at her hands.

There was nothing rude about it. She just didn't want to talk. If anything, she looked vulnerable. There was even, I thought, a faint possibility that there'd been tears springing up in her eyes.

Well, there was nothing I could do about it. I couldn't force her to talk to me or, come to that, dry her tears. I was no one to her . . . just a taxi driver. Feeling, this time, sad more than angry, I turned back to face the road, and drove on.

But of course I listened to what her private business was. I stood out in the drive, by the car, breathing in evening air and smoke as I waited to bring her back into Paris, while she sat in the ground-floor office just a few feet away and with the window wide open and the curtains not drawn, talking with that old charlatan Madame Sabline.

I didn't dare stare in. I thought she might feel my eyes on her. I kept my gaze fixed on the end of my cigarette glowing in the dark. But I eavesdropped shamelessly.

One of nature's great money-sniffers, Madame Sabline trumped all the girl's questions about the American woman

– who, it turned out, had been the girl's grandmother, as well as Madame Sabline's sister-in-law – with her own brutally self-interested questions about the will, the estate, who'd inherited what, what there'd been to leave. And then, when it turned out that the answer to these questions was 'not much', and there was no bequest to Madame Sabline or the home she ran, she broke the conversation off, quite abruptly, with the words, 'Well, it's nearly the dinner bell; time's pressing; I'd better be getting on.' I hadn't heard her offer a word of condolence.

'But . . . well, of course,' I heard the girl reply, sounding crestfallen if polite. 'Only there is one thing. Please can you look at this, and tell me what it says?'

There was a rustle of paper. ' "Zhenya",' Madame Sabline pronounced indifferently after a moment. I heard her chair scrape.

'My grandmother wrote that when she got ill, you see. So I'm wondering, is there a Zhenya you know of who knew my grandmother?' the girl persisted. 'Someone she might have been thinking of at the last?'

Madame Sabline came over to the window. Without looking, I could see her silhouette. She could probably see mine too, standing by the taxi. I kept my eyes down. It was probably rude of me not to nod a greeting, but she was one of the Russians I didn't like to associate with: the kind whose mind was full of the most banal lament imaginable for all the unimportant material things lost years ago when she left home behind: an inventory of missing silver spoons and chandeliers and bracelets. She started fiddling with the curtains. I'd been to enough evening classes in philosophy and writers' get-togethers at that place myself, over the years, to know that its administrator wouldn't actually draw those curtains shut in the presence of a guest – they were in shreds. Looking out and twitching at the great ruined folds of dark-red damask so that the rings jingled against the rail was just her way of showing impatience.

'It wouldn't have been her husband – your brother?' I heard from farther back in the room.

'No. God rest his soul, he was Pavel Pavlovich.'

'And he didn't have any children from his first marriage?'

'No.'

'And my grandmother didn't take an interest in any of your orphans called Yevgeny?'

Madame Sabline shook her head, leaning out of the window, taking in a deep breath of night air and my cigarette smoke. 'Not particularly, no,' she said. 'Anyway, the orphanage closed down years ago. We're none of us getting any younger.'

She perched herself on the window ledge, twisting back towards her guest. 'Mademoiselle, it could be anyone, or everyone,' she said with the brutality people sometimes call being cruel to be kind. 'There's no way you'll ever know who was on her mind. It's a common enough name. Every fifth Russian man is called Yevgeny. There are probably thousands of Yevgenys in Paris.' Her harsh voice cracked into something approaching a laugh. 'Why, even your taxi driver's called Yevgeny.'

16

'I didn't realize you were Russian,' the girl said to me.

It was fully dark now. I was concentrating on a round-about. I couldn't look behind but, feeling warm, I moved my shoulder in a kind of nodding shrug to show I was listening.

'Madame Sabline in there says your father runs the White Russian military in Europe?'

I nodded. I had such mixed feelings about Father's work that I couldn't feel proud, exactly. But I liked the respectful way she pronounced the words.

I turned off the roundabout, deep in the usual argument with myself that always began when I thought of Father. That dear old man, tap-tapping around with his cane and his belly, was almost cultured, and not without humour. But I'd never been able to grasp why a man with so little killer instinct would first have chosen to devote his youth to fighting, and then to have gone on and on with what he doggedly went on believing to be his calling despite the crushing defeat of the Civil War. They just weren't cut out for the savagery of fighting in the twentieth century, he and all the other genteel ex-generals of ROVS. It was agonizing to watch someone so unsuited to strategic thinking still vainly trying to plot the overthrow of Communism, like listening to a person with absolutely no ear for music trying to be a violinist. His past career contained nothing but monstrously irreparable mistakes, which were as obvious as they could possibly have been, yet it made no difference. He went on trying. He was so proud to be running ROVS in that apartment full of maps stuck through with coloured pins, even though there was nothing real about any of it. Even the journal he edited, which so many of his former associates from that long-dead army wrote for or subscribed to – for there were still tens of thousands of army men like my father, all over Europe; he claimed a membership of a hundred thousand – even the journal made me sad.

I was so absorbed in these painful thoughts that I was surprised when the girl spoke again.

'And that your name is Yevgeny? Zhenya?'

I did turn round now. I could hear the irritation come unbidden into my voice as I snapped, 'No! It's Jean.' But why bite her head off? None of the things that angered me were her fault. I added, eyes back on the road, hastily trying to sound less sour, 'Though I *was* called Zhenya, Yevgeny, once, a long time ago, in Russia . . . But I live in France now. I go by a French name. I've been here for twelve years – pretty much half my life – so I reckon I'm pretty much a Frenchman, even if I do have Russian blood and a nonsense stateless passport. There are too many Russians who reject reality: people who'd rather just pretend they've never left Russia and are living in some sort of imaginary Saint-Pétersbourg-sur-Seine. That bores me. I keep out of the way of Russians. I don't like all their spite and squabbles, plots, counter-plots, the endless talk about lost splendours. All I want is to earn my crust; live my life in peace. What's the point of living in the past?'

I'd still sounded more bitter than I'd meant to, I thought miserably. That wasn't a well-put, worldly, amused explanation. It was a rant. I'd spoiled the moment. There'd be no more talk now.

But she did speak again, after a moment's pause. She said, 'And I'm Evie.' Her voice was soft and, I thought, sympathetic. '*Enchantée, Jean.*'

I snatched a glance at her in the mirror. I could see she was smiling, because the moon was out.

For a while we drove in that moonlit quiet down the leafy suburban roads, heading for the porte d'Orléans.

I kept my eyes on the faintly shiny, gently moving clouds of foliage all around, but my mind was full of the girl behind me. I wanted to hear Evie's voice again. I wanted, more than anything I'd wanted for a long while, to ask her questions. But I couldn't find a way to frame the questions I wanted to ask. Why had she come all the way across the world to visit a family member, yet knew so little about the grandmother who'd died that she'd been reduced to driving around Paris at night, asking strangers questions about names scribbled on bits of paper? She'd told Madame Sabline that there was no money to leave, so she couldn't have been asking for the obvious reason – because of something in the American woman's will.

That old brute Madame Sabline had been rude, but she hadn't been wrong. Unless this girl – Evie – already had some inkling who this Zhenya she was looking for was, she'd never find him now the old woman was dead.

'No one lives in the past in America,' I heard suddenly. She sounded tentative – almost, I thought, as if she'd also been trying to come up with the right way to carry on. I couldn't help a quick private smile – she couldn't see my face, after all, in the driver's seat – as I realized that she wanted to talk to me. 'Maybe you'll think this is funny, but I actually came here because I *wanted* to find out more about the past . . .'

And then she was off, telling me about the Paris grandmother no one in her family talked about, who'd once been married to a diplomat who'd died in Russia, long ago, and then been cut out of the family and forced to leave her child behind because she had artistic yearnings (which, I thought cynically to myself, was probably just a respectable family's code name for too many of the wrong kind of love affairs) and, finally, when the girl went to college, had started sending her gifts. About deciding she'd come over to Europe as soon as college was over, and get to know this grandmother for herself. About buying a ticket and just setting off, alone – 'I wanted an adventure!' she said, rather shakily – and making it all the way here, only for the old woman to die before they'd had a chance to talk. About how, before the old Countess Sabline had died, she'd written the name Zhenya down in a last note on a bit of blotting paper, and how Evie now wanted to find this Zhenya, because she thought he was someone her grandmother wanted to look after.

I nodded and nodded, finding solace in the possibility of relationship and the music of her voice.

I could hear many things in her story: not just the obvious fact that she had enough money to cross the world on a whim, but also the cold wind that must blow through her family to have made her travel so far to seek love. I appreciated her good French and careful choice of words, too, which spoke of intelligence and a trained mind . . . And yet I also heard a contradictory note of naivety in what she was saying. She was talking about that piece of paper in her hand with what seemed to me too much of the wrong kind of hope, as though it were a clue in a detective story; as though it would actually take her to a living person, who'd give her vital information that would reveal the dead woman to her.

That was something I could sympathize with, and not just because I felt so drawn to her. I understood that yearning of hers to find something that was, in reality, irretrievably lost. The piece of paper was all she had left of the dead woman.

Gently, I said, 'Shall I give you a piece of advice from Tolstoy?' Then, before even bothering to look in the mirror at the puzzlement that would inevitably be on her foreign face, I added, 'Who was a great Russian writer . . . He believed history was like a great clock moving unstoppably forward . . . and his advice to ordinary people, the helpless cogs in that clock's machinery, was just to live in the present moment, as well as possible. He said: "If you want to be happy, be."'

'Ah,' I heard. She didn't sound downcast. In fact, I heard a bright pleasure in her voice. 'Yes, Tolstoy. But he also said, "Everything comes in time to him who knows how to wait," didn't he; and, "The strongest of all warriors are these two, Time and Patience." And I've got time, and patience . . . so I hope I'll find out what I need to know.'

Thank God there was a red light, because I took my eyes right off the road to turn around and stare. 'You know Tolstoy?' I said. She was looking – just a bit – mischievous, pleased with herself at having risen to that challenge and capped my quote, I thought.

She smiled wider at my frank astonishment. 'The quote's from *War and Peace*, I think,' she added with satisfaction. Then, 'Do you know the light's green . . .?' I turned round, smiling myself, and put my foot down. We glided on.

'It's not every young American girl who knows Tolstoy,' I said over my shoulder.

'I love Tolstoy,' she responded. 'My grandmother sent me *Anna Karenina* when I started college. I've read lots more since.' A pause. 'It's not every taxi driver who's read Tolstoy, either . . .'

I almost laughed at that generalization, which, while it might be true of most Parisian drivers, certainly wasn't of us Russians, many of whom had been professors once.

But I wanted to avoid sounding bitter, so I told her about some of the writers I was occasionally invited to spend evenings with, so I could listen to them talking about literature or reading bits of whatever they were working on. They'd started to let me come, as an acolyte, because they knew I wanted to write, too, one day. Someone had seen promise, somewhere, in some dark comment I'd made a year or two before and introduced me; these writers' evenings were the chink of light in my life. The writers were all grindingly poor by any normal measure, but at least they were in a position to give some of their mind to the work of the mind that they'd been intended for. As I described them now, I dwelled in particular on my

Russian writer hero Sirin's wry descriptions of the bizarre job his lover had taken to get them at least a taste of food – trimming poodles at a barber for rich pets – and of his own apartment, so tiny he had to write in the bathroom with an ironing board across the bidet for a desk. I even found myself trying to explain to the American girl his pun about our pennilessness in Paris: *'pas riche'* in a city we knew, in Russian, by the same two syllables: *'Pa-rizh'.*

I was gratified when I heard, behind me, her laughter in the dark.

'So gallant, the Russians you talk about; how I admire that spirit . . .' She sighed, then, 'You'll be a writer too,' as if she were beginning to understand more. 'Won't you? One day? Maybe you write already?'

I wriggled in my seat, and knew there was bashfulness in my laugh. 'Maybe a little . . .'

'It must be strange driving a taxi,' she said hesitantly, 'if you weren't born to it . . .? I mean, as an educated man . . .'

'Why?' I said, keeping my voice neutral. 'It's just realistic. There's no point standing on one's dignity when there's no Russian dignity left. My father would do anything – has been fighting for years – to go home to where he was born. That's his calling. And it doesn't matter whether, left to my own devices, I'd just forget the past. I have to respect his dream. But someone has to pay the rent, too. Someone has to exist in the real world of Paris in 1937. So I go out and drive.'

'Maybe it's not so strange,' she said, pushing back her golden hair. 'I know so little, that's all. But maybe you're a bit like a man I met in the train, who was off to Spain to fight for the rights of the poor – perhaps, for you, it's all a matter of principle.'

Principle?

I opened my mouth, trying to stop her say something so catastrophically naive that it would lose her my respect forever, but before I could say anything she'd gone artlessly on, 'Because . . . after all, how good it must be to live and work among simple, honest people.'

I shook my head on a rising tide of silent fury directed both at the futility of my own existence and at her unforgiveable callowness. What made this rich young girl think being poor was good, or made you honest? Who did I know who was either simple or honest, however poor? The former foreign minister of a Balkan state, whom I met every now and then, still telling his worn diplomatic anecdotes from twenty years before? The other once influential people I sometimes had a cheap dinner with in a Russian restaurant, who were now labourers or drivers? Or might she mean the people I met in my other life: the Russian scroungers, the French vagrants, the prostitutes, the pimps?

'Simple, honest people?' I said, and my rage was all mixed up with unbearable disappointment that this girl and I would not, after all, have anything more to talk about. 'I don't know any of those. Though I do know plenty of stupid ones.'

There was silence for the rest of the drive back to the rue du Colisée.

She paid in silence. I gave her change in silence. She got out under the street lamp. Then she came back and leaned in through the cab, and again I smelled her faint fragrance and saw the smoothness of her skin. This time she looked straight into my eyes, and said, with disarming frankness,

'I hope I didn't say the wrong thing. I'm still just figuring things out.'

I nodded, with my lips still clamped tight. Even if the humbleness of that last comment had surprised me, I wasn't going to let my guard down again.

She didn't go away. She continued, 'And I want to ask – could I employ you to help me for a few days?' Her voice was all breathy with hope, but I wasn't going to soften. I waited to hear her job offer. 'So that I can track down the Zhenya my grandmother was thinking of?' she stammered. I could tell in advance that she was about to say, tremulously, that, because she couldn't speak Russian and didn't understand enough about the Russian world in Paris to know where to look for this Zhenya, she'd like a fellow detective – or a Sherpa, paid, humiliatingly, by the day. I cut her off.

'It's a fool's errand,' I said. Why should I care if she knew I'd eavesdropped like a servant? Wasn't it time at least one smug, frivolous, rich girl got a taste of reality? 'Madame Sabline was right. There are thousands of Zhenyas in Paris. You'd be wasting your money.'

I put my foot on the pedal. The engine raced. 'And I'm fully employed,' I added.

'It wouldn't take long,' she stammered, sounding stung. She didn't let go of the window. After another moment's thought, she added, 'Well, can I at least show you her letters? Her apartment's full of letters in Russian. I can't read them.'

I shrugged. 'There's a bar I stop off at every night at about four in the morning, next to the station you'll have arrived at,' and I reeled off the address. It was a real place, and I really did park up nearby every night, and stop in it for an hour or so before going to pick up clients arriving on the early morning train. But I knew in advance that she'd never go near a cheap bar like that. It wasn't in a part of town that her rich sort ever went to. It would be invisible to her.

Looking defeated, she did, at last, step back from my window. Taking out her keys, she went up to the door of number 29. Her shoulders were drooping. I was already feeling angry with myself for having been too angry, but some Dostoyevskian impulse to cut off my own nose to spite my face was still pushing me to go further: offer her one last taunt I knew I would regret at leisure later. While she was still struggling with the front-door lock, I called out softly, 'Look.'

I saw hope in her eyes as she turned.

I pointed at the brass plate on the door, next to the bottom bell. 'Do you see what that says?' I asked. I knew without looking that it said *Miller/ROVS*.

'It's my father's office. It means General Miller of ROVS – the White Russian military headquarters. I come every evening and take him home, you see. I don't like him wandering around Paris unprotected. Because, futile though his work might be – all their work – it's risky all the same. The Bolsheviks do watch them, just in case; and, every now and then, they've managed to pick off a ROVS boss . . .'

In the monochrome light of the street lamp, her face was a black-and-white picture of bewilderment.

'And do you know why I'm telling you all this?' I added, realizing, now it was too late to stop, how bitter and spiteful I must sound, and what a fool I was making of myself. She shook her head.

'Because', I finished, not savouring this hollow triumph half as much as I'd expected, 'his first name is Yevgeny, too. My point is, if you multiplied the two of us that you've found in a few minutes in this street alone by all the other streets in Paris, and all the other Yevgenys, it might give you some idea of just how idiotic it would be to go round trying to find the one Yevgeny your grandmother thought might need her help.'

And then, unable to bear my shame, I revved up again and drove off to park.

It was a night for hearing things through open windows.

Once I'd parked the taxi, down the road, and was walking back up to number 29 to pick up Father – I wasn't going to brook any argument from him this time – I caught a snatch of him in conversation with his number two, General Skoblin, behind the closed shutter which was all that separated them from the pavement.

It was something to think about to take away the taste of my own bad behaviour with that girl. (I was both relieved, and sorry at the same time, to find she'd disappeared inside already.) Again, I found myself listening.

Skoblin was more talkative than usual. 'There'll be two of them, old man, arriving any day now,' he was saying encouragingly. 'And once we've got the agreement sorted out, there'll be money, intelligence, everything. It will make all the difference. Think how helpful that sort of back-up would have been that time in Poland . . .'

'Or with the man in Switzerland,' Father replied, sounding much more like himself.

'They know they need us with a war coming,' I heard

Skoblin add, and when Father laughed, and agreed, 'Our moment has come,' I could hear real pleasure in his voice.

I rang the front-door bell. 'That'll be my son,' I heard Father say behind the shutter. He sounded relieved. I realized with a soft pang of tenderness that he must have been looking forward to my arrival. 'It's late. We'll talk tomorrow, dear colleague.'

17

Evie

When I'd let myself in last night, there'd been no trace of the wake. The apartment was spotlessly clean and dauntingly quiet. After taking a bite of the cold meat Marie-Thérèse had left in the kitchen, I flung myself straight to bed, barely pausing long enough to pull off my clothes. I'd wanted nothing more than to let sleep blot out all the events – and discouragements – of my long day. Especially that last conversation.

Even now, after a heavy sleep, with coffee and a croissant beside me, Marie-Thérèse audible in the kitchen, clattering pans and the sun pouring through the long windows, I didn't really feel better.

It was futile to try and make sense of Grandmother's note, I could see. I'd never find her Zhenya.

The taxi driver had been right.

The other people I'd come across here who understood Russian, and whom I'd thought might help, weren't quite the noble souls I'd expected from Tolstoy. Some were turning out to be full of flattery and charm, but too clearly on the make to trust (the artists and Plevitskaya). Some had been plain rude (that woman last night, Madame Sabline). The officers downstairs seemed far too busy with their mysterious military planning.

The only person I'd met who, every instinct had told me, would be trustworthy, had been the driver last night, Jean. There'd been something in the sadness of his eyes that I'd felt at one with as soon as we'd started talking.

While he'd been talking so articulately about exile, I'd felt I almost understood his predicament. I'd been wondering, too, whether Grandmother had been attracted to people living with the sense of loss he was describing because of the private sadness I knew she must also have felt at being cast out from her past world? I'd even been thinking that maybe I'd one day be able to ask him what he thought of that idea, and that maybe it was something he'd understand. And then, suddenly, all the warmth of the conversation had switched off, just like that.

Of course, it was only because it had been late, and there'd been so many other disappointments in the day, that I'd felt tears springing as he'd driven off. But still, that sudden coldness had hurt.

Hughie would probably have been able to explain it away and make me laugh, I thought, and for a moment, as I recalled his voice, saying of a Russian that he 'couldn't stop telling us all the usual stories: about how grand he'd been before the Revolution, and how tragic his life had become since', I felt just a little nostalgic for home. Yes, Hughie would have said something amusing about the Slav soul that would have taken the sting out of last night.

But, as it was, I was on my own. And when I called to mind the hostility I'd last seen in the driver's surprisingly beautiful pale-blue eyes, the closed look on his chiselled face and the harshness that seemed to have come into his voice in those last few minutes, I couldn't help, even in this morning's sunlight, but feel downcast.

I looked around the room I'd woken up in, and suddenly I didn't know what I was doing here, camping in this stranger's life, halfway across the world from everything I'd ever known.

Pull yourself together, I told myself, trying to be robust, but it made no difference to the cold, lost feeling inside.

I tried to reason with myself. I had somewhere to live, money to live on, and I was in the City of Lights. Even if I accepted that none of the things I'd imagined doing here were going to happen – that Grandmother was gone and with her the flickering idea I'd had that, through getting to know her, I would learn something important about myself – it would be insane to walk out on Paris without even trying to have an adventure. Imagine what Eliza and Winthrop and Bill would say. Surely I could just substitute another kind of adventure for the one I'd wanted? Surely I could find the other Americans here, for a few days or weeks at least? I could go to Shakespeare and Company, the bookshop, where all the young writers went hoping to be recognized. I could join some of the young men writing modern books in very short sentences. Or I could go and pay homage to the weirder young Frenchmen writing surreal poetry. Hadn't I been thinking I might try my own hand at writing, just a few days ago on the train on the way here? And even if I couldn't do any of this, surely, surely I could just go dancing in nightclubs and have affairs? There were plenty of girls here doing that.

I sighed. I didn't have the remotest interest in doing any of those things. The kind of meaning I'd wanted to find on this journey had been so different. But, if I didn't want to do those things, and the thing I did want to do was, as Jean had so brutally said, impossible, well, then . . .

When I got out of bed, I thought gloomily, it might make sense to pack. Then I should tell Marie-Thérèse I'd go home soon . . . And then I should go to the shipping office and get myself a ticket.

All that I could imagine. It was the part that came next that I couldn't bear even to contemplate: sliding back through the front door into my old life.

Wrapping a robe around my nightdress, I went into Grandmother's room. It was empty of her presence now to the extent that the bed had been stripped, the drapes and windows and shutters opened, and the sickroom accoutrements taken away from the bedside tables. But it still had a clutter of her belongings on the surface of the other furniture: the scent I'd borrowed yesterday, a few bracelets. Marie-Thérèse, I saw, had put some crates neatly in a corner. Grandmother's clothes would need clearing.

I didn't want to think about that. I turned my eyes away from the boxes to the scatter of small things above the fireplace that suggested she might reappear at any moment. Next to a small string of amber beads (Heavens, were they the huge ones I remembered her wearing, long ago?) was, I saw, a cracked, faded photograph propped against the glass. It showed two young people in a rowing boat, on a river, with more people on the shore to one side in the background. It was summer. A corner of a picnic table was visible. There must have been someone on the river bank

– one of the picnickers – with a camera and a tripod.

I couldn't help but be fascinated. I took it over to the window.

My sense of being utterly alone lifted a little when I recognized, in the young black-haired woman with the mutton-chop sleeves sitting in the boat, the same younger version of Grandmother I'd already seen pictured in that photograph in Mother's room. The girl was in profile this time, and her looped-up hair was messier and wispier than in that other studio shot, as if she'd got the breeze in it. She looked happier, too, as if she'd spent the whole day smiling. I smiled too, to see that familiar face; for a moment, it felt almost as though I were greeting an old friend.

Then I turned to the young man opposite her, with oars in his hand. I was expecting to see the same thin, dark, related-looking person who'd been in Mother's picture – my grandfather, Eddie. But, however long I looked, I couldn't make this image resolve itself into that remembered one.

This young man was tall and thin, too, but much fairer, with thick nearly blond hair under a peaked military cap and a tunic buttoned up to the neck. The uniform was unfamiliar. It didn't look like anything from the American military that I'd ever seen. The young man's face remained equally, stubbornly unfamiliar, however much I stared. Still, I liked the look of him; he had the same carefree air as Grandmother. Who was he? Perhaps a boatman, or her driver – a servant? (Though that uniform looked very smart for a servant.) I turned the picture over. There was a Russian scribble on the back. Nothing more.

My misery returned. I'd never know. I should leave all this alone, I told myself, not quite understanding the darkness that settled on me as I put the picture back. But it was pointless wondering, and wishing I understood and could piece together the bits of Grandmother's past. It was gone: dust to dust, ashes to ashes. I was only torturing myself by trying.

And then, through the window, I saw a taxi draw up at the kerb outside, and the same driver – the Russian Jean – get out, with swift, beautiful economy of movement. He held open the door. He was smiling tenderly at his client. He drew out the same elderly gentleman I'd seen on my first evening here, the one with the splendid military uniform.

As I stared – well, it didn't matter if I stared now, did it? They couldn't see me up here – the memory of that first evening filled my mind. It must have been Jean who'd given me that furious scowl, but been so affectionate to his customer, out in the street. And the portly man with whiskers must be his father, General Miller.

Then something else struck me. I hadn't recognized the father yesterday without that eye-catching jacket, festooned with gold frogging, and with his hair damped and combed into submission. But now I was looking at him again, it was obvious. It had been General Miller who'd come, in shirtsleeves, into the church at the beginning of Grandmother's funeral, and whom I'd seen, later on, sitting by her grave. It had almost certainly been General Miller who'd left that romantic scatter of carnations, too.

General Miller, whose office was only a few feet from Grandmother's apartment; General Miller, whose name, Jean had told me last night, was Yevgeny . . .

The world shifted a little, as pieces of the puzzle seemed to lock into shape.

All at once, I thought I could see, in this slightly unlikely assemblage of corpulence and elaborate facial hair and bulk and Ruritanian frogging, the man who not only brought out the gentle side of the moody son I'd so warmed to last night, but whom my chic grandmother must have known, and maybe loved, and wanted me to make amends to.

Suddenly I was full of hope again. I couldn't stop myself. I was already running downstairs.

'You're General Miller, aren't you?' I said quickly, emerging through the front door into the sunshine. He looked uncertain, but I took his hands in mine and rushed on, 'I recognize you from yesterday, because didn't I see you at my grandmother's funeral? Thank you, if so. Thank you for coming.' He bowed his head.

'And thank you for the flowers, too, because it was you who left those, wasn't it? The carnations . . .' I said, but I was already faltering over the last words of my burst of bravery, because I didn't understand his reaction. He wasn't hugging me, or bursting into tears, or starting to tell me how he'd loved Grandmother, or any of the novelish things I'd been half hoping for from a Russian gentleman – reactions that would have shown Jean, who was standing so close but whom I couldn't bring myself to look at, that I wasn't just on a fool's errand.

Instead, before the General had lowered his head in that bow, he'd looked terribly embarrassed. He'd shut his eyes, too, and they were still shut now. His head was still down, as if fearing what he'd see if they were open.

What had I done wrong? Perhaps the Russian gentry didn't come hurtling out of doors, blurting. Perhaps I should have waited to thank him till after we'd drunk a glass of tea from a samovar, and sat in silence together under an icon.

A bit bewildered, I let go of his hands.

As I stepped back, humiliatingly aware of how wrong my attempt to start up a conversation with the General had gone, I couldn't help but see Jean's face.

He looked furious. Again. Ignoring me, just as I'd ignored him, he turned towards his father and began questioning him in Russian. I couldn't understand a word, of course, but I could see the old man flinch and hang his head. '*Stydno!*' I heard Jean mutter. He shook his head before, still without looking at me, he ushered his father inside.

And then the door clicked shut, and I was alone on the sunny pavement.

18

Jean

'Are you insane? Sneaking out on your own like that, running all kinds of risks, and for what?'

Father was at his desk with his head in his hands. He looked like a child who hasn't been able to resist doing wrong: shamed to have been caught, but still defiant.

I stopped. I took a deep breath. I was right to be angry. I loved this man. I had no one else. He shouldn't have been hiding from his security men and going off alone. But it wasn't doing any good raging at him. He appeared . . . well, I took a more careful look . . . just exhausted, maybe, but greyer and more wrinkled somehow, too. Old.

'She was a neighbour,' was all he said. 'I owed her that respect, *sharik*. I can't stop being a human being altogether, just for the sake of politics.'

He looked up cautiously. I knew, from the use of that childhood pet name, 'little ball' – I'd been fat, apparently, as a toddler – as well as from his timid glance, that he'd sensed I might soften and was trying to appeal to my affection. He wanted me to shrug and smile and say, Oh, well, let's put it down to experience.

'Did you at least leave a note, like I always tell you to?' I said, less harshly, but still not letting go of my anger altogether. 'Like Kutyopov's, only with proper information?'

When General Kutyopov had disappeared, the police detectives had only had one clue to follow. There'd been a note in the diary in his desk, saying he was worried about the secret agent whom Skoblin had him down to visit that morning. But Kutyopov had written no more about where the meeting was supposed to be, or who the agent was. And Skoblin then told the police that the man, who, he said, must have been a double agent, had disappeared, leaving no trace. No wonder the investigation had got nowhere.

When Father took over the job, he'd made it the organization's policy that he and all future White military leaders should be properly guarded. Much more reluctantly, he'd also made me a private promise: that, if he *were* ever to go out alone, in some emergency, he would leave a detailed note of where he was going, whom he was meeting, and why. He didn't like the idea. He wasn't a detail man. But I'd insisted, and he'd given in.

Or had he? Looking at him now – at the lowered eyes, and the tired skin – I could see, without waiting for his answer, that, no, he *hadn't* left any notes yesterday.

'Father,' I said reproachfully as he shook his head.

'Look, nothing bad happened,' he muttered, letting his head droop on to his arm. 'I was a fool. I took five minutes of freedom. I won't do it again. There's no need for distress.'

But when I let my footsteps take me round to his side of the desk, and put an arm round his shoulder, I could see his cheeks glistening.

'I'm sorry,' he said, indistinctly. 'I'm just tired. All those celebrations, earlier this week. They take their toll.'

Awkwardly, I gave him a sideways Cossack embrace. I could hear this was more than just tiredness. He'd never said anything that suggested discontent with his life the way 'five minutes of freedom' had sounded, just now. I'd never seen tears in his eyes before.

This first glimmer of understanding that Father might, just possibly, also feel trapped in the role Fate had picked for him to play was baffling, because he was completely absorbed by his life at ROVS – wasn't he? He didn't have time for friendships outside this apartment – did he?

But if he was so happy, why had he wanted to go to the funeral of the American woman upstairs?

I squeezed his shoulder harder. 'I don't want you kidnapped,' I said.

The next thought that came to me displaced Father's cigar smell altogether. Another scent came into my nostrils instead: the elusive half-flower, half-innocent perfume of the American grand-daughter, with her lovely face, her painful naïveté and her foolish quest for a man called Yevgeny. Maybe, I was thinking, she hadn't been so wrong. And I'd been rude. Maybe – the idea surprised me, but wasn't displeasing – I should apologize.

I tried the girl's door, one floor up, before leaving. But the housekeeper said Mademoiselle had just popped out in the car.

That evening, after I'd woken up, and the old nurse had brought me a cup of tea and a rusk on my divan, and got me to wheel poor Katerina Ivan'na – which is what she went on respectfully calling Father's wife, even now, when the poor woman was long past recognizing any of us, or appreciating her respect – out on to the balcony for some fresh air, I went to pick Father up. But first I tried the girl's bell again.

Her new-world enthusiasm had jarred on me, but maybe that said as much about me as it did about her? I'd wanted to think of her as a spoiled American heiress, refusing to take no for an answer, but she was better than that. She was just trying to carry out the last wish of an elderly person whom she'd loved and wished to know better. She was trying to show respect. And what was wrong with that?

I rang three times. There was no answer.

After I'd waited a long time, and not much liked the thoughts crowding into my head – pictures of her out dancing with smug Americans in the smoke and jazz and crush of Zelli's – I pressed Father's bell instead, and drove him home.

When I'd left him on the balcony, next to Katerina Ivan'na, I went out for the night in the taxi, but as I did so I looked back up. There they were, on the balcony. He had an arm around her shoulder, and he was staring at the sky. His cheeks were wet.

She'd been gone for years. She couldn't walk or talk. She couldn't die, either. Poor Katerina Ivan'na. Poor Father too, I thought. He looked after her so carefully. Why had I never thought how lonely he must be?

He could so easily have been close to the American woman, I thought. I couldn't help hoping, suddenly, that he *had* found love up those few stone steps from his office, on the first floor.

It was nonsense, of course, what that girl had been saying about her grandmother thinking that Father might need protecting. After all, he had me. But how I wished now that I'd agreed to read the letters she'd talked about – because it now seemed possible that they might show me whether, if there really *were* some flesh-and-blood Zhenya in the American woman's life, it was Father.

I'd try her bell again in the morning, I thought, as I opened the taxi door.

19

I drove around all night with the unfamiliar feeling that, for once, my misery was of my own making.

I'd messed everything up with my savage tongue and my quick temper. I always did.

But when I got to the rough café where I always stopped in the pre-dawn hours, already full of loathing for everything I would find in it – for it was many years since I'd found any tragic charm in the dark poetry of human perdition – the American girl I'd been thinking about for so many hours was sitting at the bar.

It seemed so unbelievable that she would be here that, for a moment, I blinked, in case she just vanished. Rich girls didn't come to places like this. Everyone (except me) stayed in their own fixed orbit. I knew that. I'd known it for years.

But nothing changed when I opened my eyes again. Her golden curls were still bobbing above the heads of Monsieur Martini, completely drunk by now and only an hour or so away from being ejected on to the street, and of Suzanne, with her rough white-blond hairdo and gold teeth, having a night off, perhaps, from the *maison de passe* where she'd recently found grander employment, and of the middle-aged woman with grey hair sitting quietly with that familiar big oilskin shopping bag, waiting for her clients, and of the cloth-capped heads of the other drivers playing cards while they waited for the dawn train. There was a glass of milk in front of her.

There'd been so many times when I'd taken each of these people to task for the way they were ruining their lives. Monsieur Martini, for instance, who taught classics and lived out of town with his wife and six children: I'd once told him he shouldn't be sitting here once a week spending his two hundred francs on so many drinks that they put him in the gutter at dawn, but he'd only laughed and reproached me for my bourgeois mentality. 'For heaven's sake, don't you understand that you'll end up in a hospital bed with DTs?' I remembered bawling as he downed another Martini. But all he said back was:

'You don't understand the essence of Gallic philosophy.'

'What?' I replied, astonished.

'Yes,' he repeated, filling his pipe. 'Life is given to us for pleasure.'

I'd also outraged the old lady who owned the café, the one now chatting with Evie, who had accumulated a substantial fortune long ago, but couldn't stop working. Yet how indignant she'd been when I'd told her that, however much she prided herself on her industriousness, the truth was that her life was as pointless as Monsieur Martini's; how furiously she'd bawled back at me, 'How can you compare me to that alcoholic?'

Perhaps I'd been fully corrupted since then. But, at any rate, I felt no desire at all to protest at any of my bar acquaintances' depravity tonight as I passed between them, heading straight for the long stretch of zinc and Evie.

She only turned when I was almost touching her. There was a cautious look on her face.

'There. Just as I told you, see? Regular as clockwork, he is,' the café owner told her calmly. She was looking more like a benign witch than ever. She plunked down another glass of milk at the counter for me. Turning to me, she said, more kindly than I'd have expected, 'I gave her what you have, milk.'

Then she removed herself a metre or so down the bar, and started polishing glasses, though of course I knew she was listening. They all were.

I picked up my milk and examined it carefully. The mere fact that Evie had left her rich Paris where she must feel at home to enter this other world had impressed the hell out of me. And there were so many other reasons why I wanted to be different, and gentler, with her, now, too. But I wasn't quite sure how to begin, with all those eyes on us. 'I really never thought', I said, quietly, so the café owner would at least know not to join in, 'that you'd come *here*.'

Another line from Tolstoy came beating through my head: 'He knew she was there by the joy and terror that took possession of his heart . . . Everything was lit up by her. She was the smile that brightened everything around.'

Evie's slow, relieved smile filled the room. With a pang of mortification, I realized that she'd expected me to be angry again.

Without my meaning it to happen, my face softened into a smile, too.

'I've been thinking,' I heard myself saying, with

something strangely like the joyful innocence I'd thought, until then, only happened in films, or dreams, or other people's lives. She raised an encouraging eyebrow. 'I've been hasty . . . and I'd like to . . . I mean, it seems to me that you might be right, and the Zhenya you were talking about might be my father . . .' She leaned closer. I took a deep breath and started again. 'You need help with those letters, don't you?'

20

I didn't expect her to blush. But her cheeks stained red instantly and she lowered her head.

'Well,' she stammered, and picked up her own milk glass again, looking suddenly so embarrassed that the sentimental film music playing in my head went discordant and jangly. 'Yes, but . . .'

I waited, baffled.

'Maybe it would be better if you would help me find someone else . . .'

'Why?' I said, astonished. 'I wouldn't want money for it, you know.'

She just shook her head, hastily, as if to say: Oh, *that*, I realized right away that it was a mistake to offer to pay you; let's not even talk about *that*.

'Well, then, what?' I said.

She looked at me imploringly from under her lashes. 'Because if your father *is* the Zhenya she was talking about,' she said at last, 'then their . . . friendship . . . must have been a secret between them. And if the letters she's kept are from him, then I'd be showing you his secrets if you read them. And if they're secrets that would upset you, or maybe your mother, and cause a problem in your family, it would distress him. And that would be the last thing I'd want.'

She gulped in air. 'I should have thought more carefully,' she continued after a moment. 'I've been sitting here realizing how crass it would be. Because I wouldn't want to make you see your father differently, or embarrass you . . .'

It nearly knocked the breath out of me, her explanation. She wasn't angry; she was just trying to protect me. I couldn't remember anyone taking my possible feelings into this kind of consideration for a long time.

'You know, we aren't', I said cautiously, 'really that kind of family. It wouldn't matter.'

Her eyes came up questingly, looking straight into mine. She'd gone pink again. I could see she didn't find asking straight questions easy.

'Not', I added, 'really a family at all . . . in your sense of the word. I mean, my father does have a wife, but . . .'

I paused. I couldn't think how to describe Katerina Ivan'na.

'He married her after we'd left Russia . . . in a refugee camp.' But even this didn't convey anything of the pity of it; of *her*. Even when she'd first met Father, in that forlorn barrack outside Constantinople after the retreat, Katerina Ivan'na had been so down on her luck: a widow with drooping hair scraped back in an apologetic bun, whose daughter had died on the way out of Russia; the kind of friendless, influenceless person who was never going to get papers and never going to get away. She earned her crust in the camp by looking after the officers' paperwork. But she was always quietly weeping into it, until any paper that came out of the cabinets looked blue-streaked and salt-stained. I think Father just felt sorry for her. He never told me he'd married her out of kindness. He just said one day that they'd gone to the priest, and that when we moved on she'd be my mother. And then, when we did get out – was that to Bucharest or Belgrade first? I could barely remember – we all moved in together. Had they ever even lived as man and wife? I doubted it.

'She's an invalid,' I added. She was lost in transit, I thought. She didn't know what to do with herself in all those new places. The night we reached Paris, she told Father that she had pins and needles. And then she went to bed, and didn't get up. We didn't even realize she was seriously ill, at first. For longer than we should have, we just thought she'd given up. 'She's been sick for years. She's in a wheelchair, and he looks after her. He feeds her; he does everything.'

Evie nodded sympathetically. 'She's not your mother?' she asked softly.

I shook my head. I'd tried calling Katerina Ivan'na 'Mother'; still did sometimes. I'd been – what? – eight, nine, ten, not far off her dead daughter's age, when we started living together, but she'd never mothered me. I'd never expected her to.

'So . . . what happened to your real mother?' Evie whispered. Her voice was careful, as if she was afraid the memory would make me weep.

'No idea,' I said baldly, and I was surprised how much pleasure I was suddenly taking in talking about myself. I never usually told people this, or, in fact, anything much about my family. 'Because *he's* not my real father either. I was an orphan, in a little place with a difficult Russian name you won't be able to pronounce, and even I can't remember properly, with lots of Zs – near Kursk – and hungry; we all were. We spent our days out in the woods looking for food, and his regiment was there. So I became what Russians call a "son of the regiment" – haunted their encampment, ran errands, blacked the soldiers' boots, smoked their cigarettes to make them laugh – anything for a kopek or a bit of potato. When they left I followed. I loved being one of the strong men, not the victims. And when we got to Constantinople, my father told the camp authorities I was his son, which meant I got papers. God knows what would have become of me otherwise. He educated me and everything, too, along the way. He's a good man. Kindness', I added, taking strength from the thought, 'is his besetting sin.'

'How old were you?' Evie asked faintly.

'Oh, five or so, at the beginning, when I was running wild in the woods,' I said, rather enjoying her shock. 'Though by the time we got to Paris I was eleven. There are a lot of Russian "families" like us, you know. That's just how things are, when you get survivors clinging to the wreckage. You can't choose who else is holding on to the same spar.'

She nodded.

'So you see,' I finished, 'it wouldn't upset me in the least if those letters showed my father was close to your grandmother. A White officer taking on a wolf-boy from the woods: I already know he's always been good at finding love in unexpected places. I'd be happy for him.'

She looked at me for a moment longer, then nodded again.

I thought she was going to praise Father's charitable instincts and loving nature. I hoped she was. I was all ready to nod and smile bashfully – another new departure.

But all she said was, 'Well, he made a good investment in you, I'd say.' That startled me. 'Because you're so loyal to him, I mean,' she added hastily. 'Loving son. Breadwinner. Bodyguard. You do it all – much more than anyone else I know does for their family, and certainly a hell of a lot more than I do for mine. Where would he be without you?'

It was possible she'd blushed. I couldn't tell. I'd gone too hot and red in the face myself at the frank admiration in her voice to be able to look properly for a moment. I picked up my milk glass – there was no point in turning into an alcoholic like everyone else in here – and drained it. At my side, I heard her doing the same.

It was a while before I heard her put her glass down. Her voice was muffled. 'So, about the letters: if you really mean it, when do we begin?'

The sky was lightening, and there were pink streaks on the horizon as I drove her home, and, in the quiet streets, the first scrapings and bangings of deliverymen trundling the day's barrels and boxes into doorways.

'Where did you live before the soldiers came?' she asked, companionably, in the taxi. She sounded muffled by now, as though she were fighting sleep. Unlike me, she wasn't used to being up all night. For the first time in years, I found myself wondering what it would be like to be awake by day.

'In an orphanage. Well, a kind of orphanage. A nunnery, really.'

She made a little sound of enquiry.

'It wasn't bad,' I said. 'Well, it wouldn't have been if it hadn't been for the war, and being hungry all the time. The nuns weren't unkind. I was lucky. They'd kept me after they found me in the woods when the other war was still on, the one with the Germans. And the Germans had left them pretty much alone. I was just a little kid when they found me, they said – so young that I couldn't even walk properly yet. They kept me a few years before I went off with Father and the regiment. They called me sharik. It means "little ball" – Father still calls me that, when he wants to get in my good books. Apparently I'd had a knitted ball tied to my wrist when they found me – a toy that must have been a nice light colour once, they told me; but it was so encrusted with dirt by the time they found me that they just cut it off and threw it away. Mothers tied toys to their children all the time: there was less chance of losing the toys if you had to pick the child up and run. But the nuns used to have a joke about how I'd really been given that nickname because I'd been such a fat toddler . . .'

'Mmm,' she said drowsily.

The pink on the horizon was tinged with gold. The birds were singing.

'I knew it must be a joke,' I went on, 'even then, because I was so thin. We all were. Like skeletons. All I ever thought about was eating.'

There was silence from the passenger seat. I glanced around. She was breathing very softly, and asleep.

It didn't matter. We could read the letters later. The important thing was that we'd agreed.

I touched her arm. She stirred. 'You're home,' I said

gently. 'Get some rest now. You're tired. I'll come before work, this afternoon. I could stay an hour . . .'

She nodded, dazedly. Long after she'd gone in and I was on the road again, to pick up Father, I was still treasuring the look of trust I'd surprised in her eyes. I was astonished, too, that I'd had the presence of mind to resist that overpowering urge that had come over me, just for a moment when I'd watched her sleeping, to kiss her.

21

Evie

I woke up at midday, panic driving me to my feet. Good God, I was still in yesterday's clothes, I realized blearily. I must have just lain down on my bed when I'd come in at dawn and passed out straight away.

How had I slept so late? He'd be back in a few hours.

There were so many things to do first. I should set out the letters on the desk, make sure there were chairs, and that Marie-Thérèse knew to put out something for him to eat and drink, and find a book to write translations of the letters into, and pens, and ink . . .

But what I found myself rushing to do, instead of all that, was to bathe and wash my hair. Marie-Thérèse was doing the washing today, and nothing would be ironed and ready in time. Thank God I still had one clean dress left: the plain beige linen one with the short sleeves. I thought it too severe, but it would have to do.

Once the dress was on, and Marie-Thérèse had promised to leave out some cold cuts and the fruit tart she was already stoning apricots for, I went tiptoeing back into Grandmother's room. I was intending to borrow her big modern black-and-white bangles, to wear for luck. But when I tried them they kept banging against my wrists. I knew I'd never be able to write with them on.

In the end, I put on the amber necklace I thought I might recall Grandmother having worn long ago instead. On me, it had none of the wildness I remembered, but the beads gleamed discreetly against the pale linen of my dress, and took away its severity, at least.

I also opened Grandmother's square, faceted, black-edged, glass-stoppered bottle of scent and dabbed it at wrists and neck, as I'd done yesterday. The perfume aroused no memories of her in me, but I liked the mysteriousness of it. It made me feel more worldly. I patted down my curls, so they would dry flat. The face in the glass looked white but, I thought, feeling a little reassured, far more composed than I felt.

For luck, I picked up the picture of young Grandmother, and took it with me when I left her room. I put it above my own bedroom fireplace, and went on looking at it. But, inside, I was half thinking, even as I looked at it, of another face.

It was the sudden tenderness I thought I'd seen in Jean's pale-blue eyes, leaning over me in the cab, which had unsettled me.

I'd so hated his coldness earlier. His dismissal had seemed unjust enough to be worth fighting, because, I thought, what he'd been turning away from wasn't *me* but the smugness that he must think went with whatever he assumed was my place in life. I knew I wasn't that girl. I might not have been expelled from my past in quite the same way as he and his father had – or Grandmother, come to that; I might not worry about money, either. But, all the same, I knew what it was to feel an outsider.

How strange, I thought, that, after always feeling so detached from all those other young men – the Winthrops and Bills, with their sense of fun and their interesting clothes and their certainties; or Cousin Theo in his midnight-blue dinner suit and his (different) certainties – I should suddenly mind so much what this one, in this shadowland city filled with ghosts and regrets, might think of me.

As I carried the letters along the corridor to the study, where I'd decided to sit with Jean – it got the late sun – a line from Grandmother's poetry book flitted through my head.

> I have dreamed so much of you
>   that my arms, accustomed
> while embracing your shadow to cross themselves over
>   my chest would maybe
> not fold around the contours of your body.
>   And that, faced with the actual appearance of
>   what has haunted and
> governed me for days and years,
> It might be I who became a shadow.
> O sentimental scales.

'Wish me luck, Grandmother,' I said, out loud. My hands were trembling.

22

Jean

I almost laughed when Evie showed me the desk where she'd set out her treasure trove. Why, this was a classic love-story cliché: a whole bundle of yellowed letters, faded ribbons, the smell of lavender – you could see, even before reading them, what flowery phrases these letters must be full of. I imagined Father downstairs at his desk, being careful not to breathe too hard in his tight jacket in case he popped the straining buttons over his gut as he sat penning these sentimental billets-doux to the thin woman I remembered living up here. Why, the old rogue, I nearly said, and even though I bit back the jocular phrase, I could feel the corners of my mouth turn up. She'd had long limbs, the American woman, I recalled, and at least as much grace and dash as you could have expected of a woman of her age. She'd worn expensively tailored clothes under the kind of straight boyish blackish haircut that had been fashionable a decade ago, and big modern jewellery. But she was old. Wrinkles at the eyes. Wrinkles at the neck. And he was too.

If you'd asked me how he'd be in love, I'd have guessed at something a bit more worldly than these old-fashioned, lavender-scented outpourings. He wasn't an unsophisticated man, for God's sake. Why hadn't he just picked up the telephone, or walked upstairs?

As I sat down at the desk chair Evie was gesturing me to, with one side of my body as intensely aware of her slipping into the chair beside it as if our bodies had become magnetized, something else occurred to me. The size of the bundles alone suggested that this *sekretny roman* must have gone on for some time. Many dozens of letters had been preserved, and this was only one side of their correspondence. Could those two already have been in correspondence as far back as, say, three years ago, when the Stavisky fraud had brought down the government (and nearly got all us Russians thrown out of the country)? Or five years ago, when the lunatic Gorgulov had somehow got through the President's guards and shot him dead at a book fair (and also nearly got us all thrown out of the country)? Could it possibly have been part of his life as long as seven years ago, when poor Kutyopov had been kidnapped? I couldn't believe I'd had no idea at all when, all that time, I'd been driving him to and from work every day, thinking he had nothing more significant on his mind than clipping articles from the Soviet press that suggested possible weak points in the enemy's defences, and setting up more evening classes and retirement homes around Europe for failed fighters, and moving pins around on his maps . . .

Father must, I couldn't help thinking, feeling a mixture of reluctant admiration and – though I didn't like to admit this to myself – hurt, be far better at keeping secrets than I'd thought.

I shook out one of the packets. Letters fell in a scatter

on to the desk. I opened the top one up for a proper look. Then I stopped.

With the letter still in my hand, I turned to her.

She was sitting almost timidly at my side. She'd opened a big leather-bound book of thick creamy sheets and was smoothing down the first page. I noticed that pen and ink were set out at her side. 'I thought you could translate,' she said encouragingly, as if her plan of work needed explaining, 'into French, and I could jot down as much as I can, in English. That way I'll be better able to keep track . . .' Her voice died away.

I said, 'Have you seen the dates?' and pointed.

She couldn't read the Russian letters, but she could understand numbers. The piece of paper in my hand, covered in brownish ink, bore the date 20 September 1893.

Her eyes widened. 'You mean they're *old* letters,' she whispered, doubtfully. 'From nearly a lifetime ago . . .?'

Then her fingers started scrabbling at the other brittle sheets. Mine too. The letters were in two sheaves. Those in the fatter one were all from 1893, the other contained letters sent in 1894 and 1895. Both lots were more than forty years old.

I could see Evie's head drooping as, with her hands still twitching at the confetti of old paper now covering the desk, she turned her suddenly sad face to me.

'So does that mean that they're not . . .' she said in a small voice, 'not what I thought? Not letters from your father to my grandmother at all?'

I turned one over.

'I don't know,' I said, and hope made my voice suddenly bold. 'They still might be, you know – if you think it's at all

possible that they could have got to know each other first years ago, much further back than we thought, when they were still young in St Petersburg?'

I pointed at the scribbled single-letter signature at the bottom: a 'Ж' – 'Zhe' in Latin letters. 'Because this one's signed "Zhe".'

We read chronologically. The letters described a life that, though relatively recent, was already so utterly vanished that it was as alien to me, in everything but language, as to Evie. We were both explorers in a foreign country.

The first letters were punctilious. Correct. Distant, almost. They were addressed to 'Worthy Madame Vanderhorst' – Evie's name now, it turned out, and her grandmother's then, she said, as the mother had married a cousin, so at least we could be sure who one of the people in the correspondence was.

But, after just a few moments, the whole question of 'who' almost stopped mattering. As I read them out loud, I was quickly so entranced by the courtly, carefree, young people's world of waltzes and quadrilles and concerts and parades and dressing-up and cheerful gossip that I was entering that I just let myself get carried away by the story. Usually I would have shut my eyes and ears to any reminiscences about this past that wasn't – never would be – quite mine. Usually such reminiscences had a nasty colouring of self-pity and loss. But these letters had none of that, because it hadn't all been lost yet. These people were just enjoying themselves, living. Perhaps part of my willingness to enjoy their story was because Evie was at my side, with her writing arm working so fast, and her other carelessly on the desk, so close to mine that for once I didn't feel alienated by the thought of that other life, but almost as if I were actually there myself, in the thick of it with the writer.

The letters started as no more than polite thank yous for an embassy reception here, an outing to a concert there. Monsieur Vanderhorst was also thanked, in the third person. The writing was clear and simply phrased. The writer was doing his best to be comprehensible for a foreigner.

After a while, however, compliments on the standard of Madame Vanderhorst's Russian became a dominant theme, along with the discussion of articles in that week's press, the loan of books and recommendations for more reading, as the writer, 'Zhe', became Madame Vanderhorst's guide to St Petersburg culture. 'I am so thrilled', he wrote, 'that you enjoyed *First Love*. Turgenev has always been among my favourite writers . . .'

There was a period of intense artistic discussion: a planned trip to the opera to see *Prince Igor*, with observations about the ethical superiority of the disciplined Russians over the sensual Asiatic Polovtsians – proof, as one rather sententious comment had it, that the Mighty Five group of composers had not, after all, been too rebellious for their times and that they'd fully understood the need for patriotism and support for the great imperial idea.

'I think of my grandmother as having always known a lot about art – but she didn't, back then, did she?' Evie said doubtfully when, accidentally brushing against my forearm for a moment, she put down the pen and shook a hand that must be aching from all the writing she was doing.

She'd filled several pages in her book already. 'She was still learning; and he was her teacher . . .'

'Let's just see what happens next,' I said, not wanting to stop, or dwell on my own dawning realization of how very different Father's youth among all that glitter must have been from mine, and how much more of an adjustment he'd have been compelled to make from that busy life at the heart of a civilized metropolis to the aimlessness of our exile now . . . We couldn't even be sure, yet, that this young letter-writer *was* Father. But I was rooting for him to have had this happy interlude, long ago.

Gradually the tone changed. Sometimes there were two or three notes in a single day, all glowing with absorption and interest, the tone getting steadily more relaxed and chatty. The pair were clearly having a wonderful time getting to know each other, even though the subject matter went on being so innocent.

All 'Zhe' was really talking about, still, was military parades, and poker nights at barracks. There was nothing furtive about the month of planning the almost impossible task of getting tickets for the premiere of Tchaikovsky's Sixth Symphony at the Assembly of Nobility (until 'joy of joys!', 'Zhe' managed to get a pair of seats after all, from his colonel-in-chief). There was nothing underhand about the passing on of enjoyable bits of art gossip, including the snippet that Grand Duke Konstantin Konstantinovich, the royal poet, had heard the *Pathétique* in rehearsal, and was said to have wept at its beauty and called it 'a requiem' for the age.

It was my turn to pause and feel doubt. I still couldn't be sure that this was a younger Father writing. Even though it was a young officer from Father's regiment, signing his letters with Father's initial, I didn't quite recognize Father in 'Zhe'. This young man had loved music and dancing and talked quite knowledgeably about the artists of his day, while the older man I knew never talked, or as far as I knew, about anything artistic. I'd always thought of him as a military man through and through – a bit of a Philistine, in many ways. I certainly couldn't imagine him writing 'joy of joys!' at the idea of a Tchaikovsky concert, though it was true he did sometimes vent his frustration at some Paris reverse by putting a recording of the 1812 Overture on the gramophone and banging along to the 'God Save the Tsar' bits, and the bells and cannon, with glasses and spoons.

But perhaps in those days, before life had shaped him in the particular way it eventually did, he'd still had the capacity to be enchanted by art? Perhaps he *had* known enough, back then, to teach a young foreign lady the essence of Russian court culture? And perhaps, if he hadn't spent those years and years fighting, and losing, and planning his return – and being diminished in the process – he'd have come out a different kind of man . . .

We ploughed on. But, however much we wanted just to reminisce with 'Zhe' and his reader over all their small pleasures, we couldn't help sitting closer and letting our arms cross (till they touched and we pulled hastily back) as we pointed out one thing or another, or asked each other questions. We couldn't help noticing, either, that, before the year was out, they'd got closer. There was no more 'Worthy Madame Vanderhorst' (she'd been just 'K' – the letter 'Ka', which is what the Russian version of the name 'Constance' would have been abbreviated to – for months) and there was precious little mention of Monsieur Vanderhorst either.

It was hints, at first. A line saying, 'Perhaps all the uproar about Tchaikovsky's death will make your Eddie hear his music with different ears?' suggested that Monsieur Vanderhorst wasn't, perhaps, developing his St Petersburg artistic tastes in the same way his wife was. And then, when 'Zhe' was sent away to the provinces with his regiment that winter, he started writing nostalgically about how he missed playing the dandy along Nevsky Prospekt, stopping at fashionable restaurants and dance halls, theatres and bachelor parties. The last letter in the packet ended with the wistful line, 'I admit I do have a great weakness for the capital. What can I do? Everything that is dear to my heart is in Petersburg, and life without it is positively impossible for me.'

That line was underscored in pencil, as if the reader, Evie's grandmother, had been struck by it, and sat reading it over and over again, pondering its meaning.

'Poor "Zhe" . . . Do you think', Evie said with compassion when, having written down my translation in her book, she held out her left hand for the letter, to see the underlining for herself, 'that this is the moment they first really knew they were in love?'

Then she eyed the second pile of correspondence. Like me, she'd clearly noticed that the pile of letters to come was much thinner. Something must have changed, soon after that rather melancholy note had been written – something we'd soon discover, I supposed, when we started on it.

The dusk in the room had thickened to the point that Evie switched on one of the two desk lamps. 'He'll be waiting,' I said, rising. 'I'm late. He'll be wondering where I am.' But I couldn't be sure whether I was talking about the same 'he'. My doubt must have shown.

'If only we knew for sure', Evie said, 'that this really was him. If only there was proof.'

Father was very quiet as I drove him home, staring fixedly at the road ahead. So was I. I felt awkwardly that I'd spent hours prying through what I was almost sure were his secrets, while, at the same time, feeling frustrated that I had no idea whether I actually had been, or was any closer to knowing whether he'd had a relationship with Evie's grandmother.

'Someone was talking to me today about Tchaikovsky's last symphony, the *Pateticheskaya*,' I said as I slowed the car in front of our building.

His eyes were clouded. He nodded dully, but I didn't think he was listening.

'It premiered very shortly before his death,' I nudged. 'In St Petersburg, when you were there . . .'

'I'm tired,' he said, and got out.

But when I picked him up in the morning – freshly pomaded and brushed and in new linen, while I was yawning and crumpled after my night at the wheel – he said, as soon as he got in beside me, 'Such sad music usually makes everyone weep, but – contradictory, what! – it always made *me* feel happy.'

'What?' I said, blearily.

'The symphony you were talking about last night,' he explained. 'Couldn't get it out of my head, after you'd gone. Spent the evening humming it.'

'Oh,' I said, slowly catching on. I added: 'Happy memories, then?'

He paused. 'Just youth,' he said; then very shortly: 'All long gone now.'

Maybe I'd just imagined that catch in his voice. But there was nothing imaginary about the way he'd started staring fiercely at the road ahead. I could see the conversation was over. He didn't even say 'thank you' when, after I'd settled him at his desk, I brought him coffee from the ROVS kitchen. He just got out a letter from his drawer and put it on the table and stared at it as though it were the most important thing in the world. Important enough, clearly, for him to work on a Sunday, but then he often worked weekends. The secretaries came in every day of the week to watch over him anyway, so it felt normal.

'Well, goodbye,' I said, feeling disappointed. He didn't look up. Just waved a dismissive hand.

I could see that the letter he was gazing at so sternly was written in thick black Gothic script. German. That was unusual – so unusual that I wondered whether he wanted me to ask about it. But something in me recoiled from doing so. I knew they all dreamed, down here in this office, of getting military support from Germany for their cause. But then they didn't have the half-mocking, half-fearful, always scornful commentary of my friend Sirin ringing in their ears as I did – Sirin, who'd left Berlin for Paris because of the rise of the little man with the little moustache, full of crass proletarian menace, because of Kristallnacht and the Night of the Long Knives, because of his Jewish wife. There were things about Father's work in this office – compromises I sensed they'd all willingly make, if they could only have a chance of getting home to Russia – that I preferred not to ask about, and, usually, he preferred not to tell.

Instead, not quite able to leave, I went to the fireplace and picked up the picture: Father young and happy, in a boat, with summer people all around. I stared at it, trying to read into that sepia smile a cultured youthful love for Turgenev and Tchaikovsky that maybe only defeat and exile had beaten out of him.

Sighing, I shook my head. I'd let myself believe I could achieve something, for once, by helping that girl read those letters, but the reality was that I was as helpless as ever.

Suddenly desperate to sleep, I let myself out.

That afternoon's letter-reading session with Evie – muted in sleeveless light grey today after a day walking around the city – went just as badly.

She started by saying, sounding forlorn, that her housekeeper had told her Father used to come up for lunch with her grandmother about once a week. I read disappointment in her eyes that there'd been no hint of gossip of anything less innocent. For my part, I swallowed my separate disquiet that Father had never mentioned those lunches, innocent or not. (Why should they have been a secret? the worried voice in my head was saying. What other secrets might he have?)

Nodding without comment, I sat down at the small second pile of letters.

I read out a series of uninformative short notes, each one from a regimental barracks somewhere new in the provinces, and each saying something very brief about the gift that must have come with it – a cigarette case, one time ('I will imagine you in a cloud of scented Turkish tobacco smoke, smiling mysteriously'), a bracelet in another case ('sapphire for your eyes'). Those were expensive-sounding gifts to my envious ears, and, I commented, probably the kind she'd have wanted to keep private from her husband.

'Oh, I don't know,' Evie said, looking up at the mention of the gifts with a kind of dazed wonder that I didn't understand but which made her dazzlingly pretty. 'Maybe in those days no one thought anything of giving expensive gifts.' Then she gave me a nervous look and bit her lip. Perhaps she thought I'd be angry at the idea of money not mattering.

'So,' I summed up, 'we still don't really know what was between them.' Evie shook her head.

The next note was different – a scrawl. 'My God,' it said, 'I've just heard the tragic news. I'm going to the station. I'll be in town tomorrow. Wait for me.'

' "Wait for me . . ." ' I repeated. Evie was still scribbling furiously. I was so close that I could see fine golden hairs on her tanned arms.

She said, eyes on her page, 'Eighteen ninety-five. So that will be when my grandfather died; he was somewhere in the provinces himself, after the old Tsar died, and there was a Nihilist bomb.'

I could see she thought this was where everything would be revealed. She looked expectantly up, waiting for whatever was to come next.

I opened the final letter. There was only a single sheet, though there must have been more, once. It was as blotched as any of Katerina Ivan'na's wept-on military documents.

' "Please put all thoughts of my army career out of your head. It means nothing to me, compared with you, and the army will do very well without me," ' it began.' "Your family will come to terms with the change, too, in time. A colleague in the regiment has promised me his house in Paris for a year. So I beg you to put all these futile considerations you're torturing yourself with out of your head, and simply make up your mind to leave here with me, and settle there. Don't punish yourself, or me. I implore you to at least . . ." '

The page ended. The writer's tormented stream of thought stopped. I stopped too. We might guess that they'd been lovers – the odd snatched meeting here and there, maybe, when the husband was away and 'Zhe' was in town. But we couldn't know. And we could sort of piece together that, after her husband's death, he'd wanted to take her overseas; maybe that he'd wanted to marry her; but that she'd resisted, either because she didn't want to cut short his army career, or possibly, if they had been lovers, because she felt guilty.

But there was no more to read. No real connection between past and present, 'Zhe' and Father. Just fragments.

I could see the hope fade from Evie's eyes. 'Is that it?' she asked.

Evie

I wanted to cry. The letters I'd put so much faith in had led nowhere. I hadn't found out what I'd wanted, or become able to do what I'd promised Grandmother. I'd failed her.

Jean would get up and leave in a minute.

And, once he'd gone, there'd be no more reason for me to stay, either; not in this room, not in this city. If I couldn't find Grandmother's Yevgeny, there'd be no reason not to give up, pack up, and go home.

Jean got up.

I couldn't bear it. I shut my eyes, willing something to come into my head that would stop him leaving.

Jean
She just stepped into my arms.

For a moment, looking at her upturned face from so close, I was aware of eyelashes and her parted lips. I was too giddy with desire to be able to speak. I mustn't, I heard a voice inside myself say. But my body wasn't listening. And then, for much longer, there was nothing but breath and the feel of skin under linen and the thump of blood.

23

Jean

By the time I was able to think again, we were on a rumpled bed in a room full of rough canvases. For a moment, it was the pictures that caught my eye. There were plump naked women daubed across them in blue paint, running away from something. They looked like a call girl's scared memories of a police raid on a *maison de passe*. I almost laughed.

And then I didn't. Because here I was on a blue counterpane myself, with a naked woman's cheek against mine, and her body stretched out under me.

Her eyes were shut, I saw in trepidation.

I thought she'd be horrified by what we'd just done. But when, eventually, she shifted her head, and then shifted sideways, so we were side by side, she didn't leap out of the bed and run away, trailing draperies. She didn't move more than a finger's length. Her arms and legs stayed entwined with mine. She was breathless but smiling a heavy-lidded smile. 'I never imagined it would be like that,' she murmured. 'Though I don't know what I *did* think . . .' She didn't finish that thought, but I could feel her hands on my back.

'Zhe . . .' she whispered, a long while later, keeping her body's length against mine, with her head turning slightly towards my ear, so I could feel warm breath on my neck. Then she kissed me below the ear and added, with a trembling hint of voice, '*My* Zhe . . .'

It took all that for me to really believe she *wasn't* angry. Overcome with relief, and the beginning of confidence, I kissed her eyebrow, the nearest place, and held her tighter.

I didn't want to think beyond this moment. It might not mean anything. It might be just a clinging in the darkness, after we'd failed to find the meaning we'd been looking for.

But, for now, she was here. And the miraculous unlikeliness of that made me feel suddenly reckless and dizzy with – at least temporary – happiness.

'It's "zhi", not "zhe",' I whispered back, playfully.

She opened her eyes wider. 'What?'

'The name of the first letter of the French name "Jean" is "Zhi", not "Zhe",' I said, stroking her hair.

She nodded, and burrowed closer, still clinging to me. I could feel that she didn't want to end this embrace any more than I did; that she, like I, had no idea what might come next.

I lay still, savouring the feel of skin on skin, trying not to think. ' "If you want to be happy, be," ' I reminded myself. I shut my eyes. I opened them and looked unseeingly around the room and its strange pictures. But I couldn't stop my mind racing.

If she went away now, what would I have left?

Wasn't that what had happened to the 'Zhe' of the letters and the American woman?

What had he done afterwards?

I hadn't ever thought about why Father would have stayed unmarried until, years later, he'd taken pity on Katerina Ivan'na. Might that be why?

And then my eye fixed on a picture on the mantel. I sat up.

Evie

'What's that?' Jean shouted.

He looked as though he might be going to have a heart attack. My heart was pounding too. He'd dislodged me when he sat up so suddenly, so I got up and wrapped a blanket round myself and went and got the picture for him.

His eyes opened wider and wider when I handed it over. Then he smiled – a huge, relieved, still-astonished grin. I didn't understand why. He hadn't even read the Russian scribbles on the back.

'Has this really been up here all the time?' he asked, half laughing.

I nodded, bewildered. After all the intensity of everything that had happened between us in the past hour, that sudden laughter was incredibly endearing. Transforming, too. It turned him, instantly, from cinema detective to screen idol. But what was so funny about the picture?

Jean was pointing at the fair-haired young man in the boat. 'It's just – this is him,' he said. 'My father. Can't you see? He keeps the same picture in his office downstairs. If only I'd looked . . .'

I sat down beside him again, trying to concentrate on the picture and not on the feel of his thigh against mine or the heat of his skin. I couldn't quite believe it, even when

I gave the young man in the boat my full attention. What, that thin lad – the portly general downstairs?

'And that', I said, pointing at the ringleted girl in the same boat, aware that I was suddenly smiling as radiantly back at him as he was at me, 'is *her.*'

We stayed like that, poised on the brink of discovery, for a long, swaying moment before I even thought to ask, 'And what does the writing on the back mean?'

Jean turned it over, and peered at it for what seemed forever.

When he did, eventually, speak, I saw, to my astonishment, that there were tears in his eyes.

' "He could not be mistaken," ' Jean translated, very quietly. I could hear at once, from the reverent way he formed those words, that it was the beginning of a quotation. ' "There were no other eyes like those in the world. There was only one creature in the world who could concentrate for him all the brightness and meaning of life . . ." '

And suddenly I knew, and tears filled my eyes too, because – of course! – it was the great love passage from Tolstoy's *Anna Karenina*, when the philosopher-hero, Levin, trying to devote himself to the simple life and be a good master to his peasants, unexpectedly catches sight of the woman whom he thought he'd lost, years before, and realizes that he has always loved her, that nothing else matters, and that he must go to her.

Taking Jean's free hand in mine, I began speaking with him. ' "It was she," ' we both said, completing the quotation in unison. ' "It was Kitty." '

And then our own eyes met, and then our lips.

After a while, we parted, and Jean held the photo out

again. 'He put a date; April three years ago,' he whispered. 'I know his writing. It's much worse these days than in those letters from before. I suppose he must have made her this copy of the two of them, from back there, when they met again, here. And, look, he's written one more line from *Anna Karenina*: "Only with her could he find the solution of the riddle of his life, which had weighed so agonizingly upon him of late." '

'So it *is* him,' I started to say, interrupting Jean who was also murmuring, pensively, 'So they *did* find each other again, in the end.' (And so had I! I was telling myself privately. Marie-Thérèse's hunch had been right all along! I'd actually found Grandmother's Zhenya! He was real! And now I could go and talk to him and tell him her last wish.)

We stared at each other for a moment, letting the triumph sink in.

'They'd become so different from each other, by the time they got here and met again,' Jean said, and I saw his smile fade as he tussled with his thought. 'She with her wild avant-garde artists, while *he* . . . with his cause—' His voice broke off, and, although his slight frown told me that he was thinking something about his father that made him unhappy, he didn't hint what.

'It didn't matter, maybe,' I said, wanting to take the shadow off his face, 'because finding each other again here, when they were older, let them go back to being who they'd been when they'd first met, and start again. And they weren't so different, back then, at the start; just young, and maybe both lonely? Maybe, back then, getting to know each other helped each of them feel less trapped by their

214

backgrounds? Maybe that's what they loved? Because who can say where people will find love? Or feel free?'

Jean was looking so intently at me that I nearly lowered my own eyes. It took courage to keep my gaze meeting his.

'How sad, though,' I went on, trying to keep my voice steady, 'that, even here, when they met again, they still weren't really free. That this time he was married—'

'What good luck,' Jean said, abruptly, and his voice was strong, 'that they somehow *did* manage to meet again, against the odds, and took what happiness they could.' And then we were kissing again.

24

Jean

The time . . .

'Oh God, I've done it again, look, it's half dark and he'll be expecting me . . . I must go,' I said, sounding, as even I could hear, shamefully inept. But neither of us moved.

'Can I come too?' she whispered.

I was so startled by that that I did let go of her.

'Why?' I said.

'To talk to him, of course. To explain what we know, and ask him to tell me all about Grandmother.' She sounded a little impatient, as if it were obvious. And, of course, it was.

But I also knew that it was a nonsense. Because her bit of paper didn't represent her grandmother's last wishes, and Father wouldn't for a moment take seriously her notion that she was on a quest to carry them out. And anyway, if he'd never talked about his relationship with her grandmother, even with someone as close to him as me, why would he open his heart to her?

When I looked down at Evie's expectant face, and into her eyes – which, I thought, with a new kind of foreboding, must have that moonlight look because she expected to be able to just walk downstairs and find herself in conversation with some handsome young cavalry officer, all courtly manners and Tsarist mystique – I realized that I didn't even want her to try.

I didn't want her to talk to Father as he was now, or find out how different he'd become from that young cavalry officer of her grandmother's letters.

She might think she'd like their funny little world in the office downstairs, but that was only because she probably imagined it as a realm of ghostly charm, and thought they just went round bowing very formally at each other in their threadbare uniforms under dusty chandeliers, and calling each other 'Your Excellency', and quoting Tolstoy together . . . But what would a girl who'd so recently spouted that naive bit of know-nothing socialism at me – 'how good it must be to live and work among simple, honest people' – make of Father today: too fat for his jacket, staring at that letter with the black Gothic print that I'd seen him with this morning, dreaming whatever terrible dreams he must be dreaming of marching back to Moscow at the head of a fascist army?

I knew the White cause wasn't romantic any more. It hadn't been for a long time. Sirin had taught me that, once and for all. After his only visit to ROVS, during which he'd maintained an ironic politeness as Father poured him brandy and plied him with his best *zakuski* and talked excitedly about the state of the world, Sirin had taken me aside for a private, laconic word. It was no wonder, he'd said, that Hitler's view of history was so distorted when so many of my father's men, the very Whites in question, also spent so much of their time ranting in this way against the

Bolshevik murder squads bumping off everyone who didn't bow to what they called the Jewish–Bolshevik dictatorship.

I'd cringed, thinking of Sirin's Jewish wife. That *was* exactly the sort of way Father talked. And I hadn't even seen, until I'd been shown it through his outsider's eyes.

I hadn't wanted to take anyone to ROVS since then. I didn't want to take Evie now.

I tightened my grip on her shoulders. 'But will he talk?' I said, shaking my head so that she'd understand the answer would be 'no', hoping she'd be acquiescent enough to accept my judgement.

There was a mutinous look in the eyes gazing back at me. I could see she didn't agree.

Trying harder to be persuasive, I went on, 'Whatever their reason was for keeping their relationship secret – whether it was his having a wife, or her having a whole separate life sponsoring all those young artists (because he won't have appreciated them, you know; he doesn't follow art today), or even if it was just that she wasn't Russian (because they like to make a big thing of preserving their Russianness, you know, and try to keep themselves and their children as much apart from foreigners as possible) – it will still hold. He really won't want to talk to you.'

She shook her head. 'But, Jean,' she said insistently, 'talking to him was the whole point.'

'He'll have some old-fashioned notion of honour,' I said, a bit louder, overriding her voice. 'People's dignity is important, too – their privacy. Sometimes people don't have anything else,' I added sternly.

I could feel her thinking. After a moment, she looked up again.

'But Grandmother wanted me to make amends to him,' she said. ' "Protect" and "Make amends".'

She still sounded so determined, so American.

'Look, let me think about it a bit more,' I said finally, wanting somehow to find a way to make all these incompatible wishes come true, but lost as to how. 'I'll see if I can think of a way to approach the subject with him. But you think too, meanwhile, because you should be aware that telling him all this won't change anything, for you – it won't bring your grandmother back – any more than it will improve things for him. And it might distress him more if you turn up, raking over all his memories . . . because he's grieving, you know. He's been quiet and irritable for days. Isn't it enough for you just to *know* about him and your grandmother?'

At last, at that, her eyes softened – a bit. 'Can we talk about it again tomorrow, at least?' she said. Her hand brushed against mine – the softest of touches, but one that sent a powerful current running up my arm.

'Same time?' I agreed, moving towards the door, more relieved than I had words for, both that she was letting herself be talked out of confronting Father, and that, even though the letters were now all read, she still seemed to want to see me again.

25

Evie

I put on a robe and sat at the desk without switching on a lamp until it was quite dark, and the photo in my hands had faded to no more than grey-and-yellow smudges, remembering Jean.

So he'd come back tomorrow. I could already picture his eyes lighting up as they met mine, and feel the heat and tremble of his body once he was holding me in his arms.

My thoughts went round in a rapturous circle: from lovers in the photograph in my hands, forever in their boat, on another summer's day, long ago, to the miraculous-seeming way they'd been hiding here, all along, just waiting to be found, to the flesh-and-blood touch of *his* lips on mine this evening.

I didn't want to let my mind focus on the other, much more unresolved question: why Jean was so against my going to talk to his father, the General, and how I was going to persuade him tomorrow that it would be all right.

But it was there, nagging away, because of course I couldn't just sit here. I'd been on the point of telling him, 'But, you see, I've got the gifts he gave Grandmother,' and,

'Grandmother wanted me to share her jewels – all those little gifts he wrote about – and her pictures, with her Zhenya.' And then caution had stopped me. Because that was a conversation that might so easily have gone wrong with someone as touchy as Jean. I could so easily have made a mistake, and insulted him. He could have asked, 'But why didn't you say?' And then I'd have had to explain that Marie-Thérèse told me not to tell anyone, and he wouldn't have been altogether wrong to think she'd suspected Russians, as well as the taxman, of being after Grandmother's money. Or I could have done something even worse, and said, 'The jewels look valuable. He'll want them back,' and he might, again not altogether wrongly, have heard, 'He's poor now; he might want to sell them.' So I was glad I hadn't taken the risk of insisting further tonight, when there was so much to absorb, and so much else to be glad for.

I went to bed, still pondering. Every time I went round that loop of thought, it seemed clearer that Jean must be wrong. I couldn't believe that someone who'd loved Grandmother for as long as his father had wouldn't want to have someone to talk about her with. I wanted that, too, but, now I knew he must be her Zhenya, I also *had* to talk to him, and offer him whichever jewels and pictures he wanted. Finally, there was a newer reason for wanting to stick to the plan in my head. It was one so new, at this fluid moment when nothing was yet certain, that I could barely articulate it to myself. I certainly wouldn't be able to explain it to Jean. But I knew it, without needing much in the way of words, to be important. I wanted to befriend the man who was Jean's father.

Maybe all I needed was a night's sleep to find the right

words, I thought sleepily. And then the memory of Jean's lips came into my head again, and I floated away.

'I'll be back at four; I'm off to the Louvre,' I called back, shutting the apartment door. When I'd woken up, my first coherent thought as I came out of a warm, relaxed sleep-memory of an embrace was that it might never have happened, and there might have been no Jean in my life, if it hadn't been for Grandmother. My first grateful whisper, half letting myself believe for a moment that she was up there, somewhere, watching over me, had been, 'Thank you, Grandmother.'

It was another glorious morning, with a breeze rustling the sticky leaves outside. I had six hours to kill before Jean came back, and Paris to visit. I had my Baedeker in my hand. But as I clattered down the stairs, enjoying feeling so strangely happy and heading for the building's main door, I saw first a head, then a large body in shirtsleeves, in the courtyard. It was General Miller, moodily smoking a cigar.

It was irresistible.

'Good morning,' I called breezily, telling myself it would be rude not to.

He straightened with automatic courtesy and sketched a bow. He had very light, wide-set eyes above his beard and moustache, I noticed – you'd have thought them beautiful if he hadn't been so bulkily masculine that the idea seemed absurd – and there was a pleasing frankness in them. How dignified he looked.

I walked out into the courtyard, with my hand outstretched. 'General Miller.'

Why, I could sort everything out before Jean even came

back, I'd started telling myself, elated that Fate had put this opportunity my way. The General and I might be firm friends by teatime.

And then he realized who I was, and his face became still and guarded.

That was less encouraging, but now I was there I couldn't just run away. Still smiling, I let my hand drop away – for he was showing no sign of taking it – and said, 'I just wanted to say again how grateful I was for the flowers you brought my grandmother . . .' Trying, rather desperately, to charm him into a laugh, however reluctant, I added, '. . . and I'm sorry if I got you into trouble with your son, too.'

He just nodded, watchfully.

Good grief, I'd never even heard his voice, I thought. Opting, on the spur of the moment, for strong-man tactics instead, I went on, 'And, now that I've started going through my grandmother's papers, I'm beginning to understand what very old friends you were . . .'

There was a flash of alarm in his eyes at that. But at least he engaged. His voice, when he did speak, had the deep, measured, sorrowful bass of the Volga boatmen, but his manner was poised. I could see at once that he was much more a man of the world than his son, for, rather to my surprise, he was as quick as someone like Hughie might have been to respond with what looked like ease, even charm. He wasn't a panicker.

'May I offer my condolences on your loss, miss?' he said in slow, excellent English with a faint American accent (but why be surprised at that? He'd have spent a lot of time talking to Grandmother, after all). 'And invite you to step into my office, if you'd like to talk?'

Without another word, he led me through a French window off the courtyard into his office – a sombre, mannish sort of room, with just a huge desk, a hard chair on either side of it, a map of Europe above the fireplace and, in the corner, a shabby divan. The chandelier was so high up that you were only vaguely aware of the cobwebs.

Even if he hadn't wanted to talk in the open, I still hoped he'd become confiding now he felt private in his own office. I waited till he'd settled me in the visitor's chair. Then I went on, more uncertainly, '. . . whereas I didn't know her at all. There was an estrangement in the family. Perhaps you knew? But she'd started writing to me, and I'd been hoping we'd become close. And then I got here, and she died . . .'

He kept his eyes on me as he walked around the desk. He didn't flinch at the mention of her death. I couldn't help admiring that old-Europe soldierly steadiness.

I drew a deep breath and squared my shoulders. 'And I was hoping you might tell me more about her,' I finished bravely, looking straight at him. 'Because I'd like to know – oh, what she talked about, what she laughed about, what she was like . . .'

He nodded, settling himself into the other chair, behind that long sweep of scuffed mahogany. How straight he sat: a cavalryman's stance. He wasn't going to be hurried.

'Whom she loved . . .'

'You're very like her,' he said, brushing that last foolhardy phrase away. He wasn't going to answer any of my other questions, either, I realized with a sinking heart – or at least not properly. He looked at his hands. They were extremely clean, with neatly squared nails. He looked back up. 'I don't mean to look at. She is – was – so dark. I mean that you're very sure of yourself.'

But I was feeling more and more like a child, caught being naughty before a superbly self-possessed grown-up – worse still, before one whose assurance made me want to impress him with mine. Now, *this* man – unlike Jean – I could so easily imagine at ease in the chandeliered salons I'd read about in Tolstoy's novels, rubbing shoulders with the Karenins, or dancing a perfectly executed waltz, or galloping down the Field of Mars with his regiment, sabre in hand. I could, equally, imagine him talking with Hughie and my mother, and all of them feeling quite at home.

He steepled his hands on the desk. With awful certainty, I saw that he was preparing, if not a polite lie, then at least the most minimal version of the truth. I'd seen Hughie do this too often not to know the signs. 'It's absolutely true that the Countess Sabline and I were acquainted, a very long time ago, in our youth,' he said smoothly. 'She was a diplomat's wife at the American embassy in St Petersburg, and I'd been seconded from my military academy to brief her husband at the time on Russia's position on the Balkans. As you will know, he – your grandfather' – and here he looked at me and gave me what seemed, but wasn't, quite, an almost avuncular half-smile – 'was the US military attaché. The three of us got on well. Your grandparents were good enough to make me several invitations.'

'And then he was killed,' I blurted, full of disappointment that he wasn't, after all, going to confide in me. He clearly regarded me as no more than a young stranger to be politely got rid of. It was an effort to call to mind the blurry, pleading letter this man had written, after that death, begging my recently widowed grandmother to let him leave the army and take her away from Russia (had it been her tears that had wet that page, or his?). It felt crass to intrude the ugly fact of my grandfather's sudden death into this calm narrative. Yet I so wanted to provoke him into at least a reference to what Jean and I had read yesterday in that correspondence that I couldn't resist. 'What happened next?'

But he wasn't going to be rattled. He only spread his hands, and shook his head with a public speaker's practised regret. 'She went back to America, to her family,' he said mellifluously. 'We didn't see each other for many years. And then, one summer's day a few years ago, I was playing chess under the lilacs in the Luxembourg Gardens with my deputy; I felt a tap on my shoulder; and there she was . . .' He nodded, with just the right amount of reminiscence on his face. 'A widow again, and a Russian by marriage by now, but quite unchanged otherwise. After that, naturally we met, occasionally, for lunch. Our lives had taken quite different paths. But it's always a pleasure to renew an old acquaintance.'

He smiled. I could see he was waiting for me to go. His performance was complete. And it was a good one. It told a bland public version of his relationship with Grandmother, and, feeling myself turning back into the quiet, don't-rock-the-boat child I'd once been, I realized I had no idea how to challenge him.

'You'll appreciate in time how one treasures former acquaintances, I expect, when you're as old as me,' he added when I didn't get up. There was a note of finality in his voice, as though, if I didn't take the hint and go, he might start looking at his watch and getting papers out of his desk drawer.

His beautiful dark voice wasn't unkind, exactly. But it was enough to rattle me. Clear though everything had seemed while Jean and I had been reading those letters the evening before, my mind now went blank as to what we'd found out. I could barely remember why we'd felt so certain that Grandmother and the General were so close.

Dumbly, I scraped my chair and stood up, holding my Baedeker.

And then, after all, I did find words.

'It must have been a surprise, after you'd met by chance in the Luxembourg Gardens, to find she'd been living one floor up from your office all along?' I said.

For a moment, I saw his eyes flicker. 'That came later,' he said, after a pause.

And then, after another pause, he added: 'I knew it was vacant, and she was looking for somewhere to live. I wanted to do her a service.'

Even though, by now, he was doing his best to give me that superb ambassadorial smile again, we both knew he'd just explained a little too much.

And then I saw it, leaning against the map of Europe, in the gloom: his framed copy of that same picture of young lovers in a boat that I had upstairs. With relief, all our discoveries of yesterday came flooding back to me – because this was his copy! That was proof in itself, wasn't it?

'Oh look – I recognize your lovely picture,' I said. 'The one Grandmother also kept, upstairs. How beautiful that you both went on treasuring it all your lives.'

For a moment, as I watched him look up at the picture, then bite his lip, I felt triumphant.

And then, as he turned back to me, all hope faded. With his now cold eyes on me, I saw I'd taken quite the wrong approach – much too frank, too New World, too hectoring. He didn't want to be shown to be evading the truth. He was feeling bullied. The last thing he was going to do was level with me.

It was new for me to have had such a strong negative effect on anyone. Most men of his age, if they noticed me at all, did so with avuncular, or what they liked to call avuncular, affection; no one at college or elsewhere had ever responded with hostility, or felt threatened if I asked questions. It must be a sign, I thought, of how vulnerable this man felt below the grandeur of his carapace, and I was suddenly sorry.

'Alas,' he said, and his nostrils flared to white points. He was speaking very slowly and clearly, so as to make his point absolutely comprehensible. 'I have few mementos. Few possessions of any sort. Like all my fellow officers, I left Russia with what I stood up in. I'm afraid mine is a life devoted to public duty, miss. I spend my days looking after the needs of my fellow countrymen in exile, and, when I'm not on duty, I spend my evenings looking after the needs of my wife and son. I have little time for other friendships.'

'I understand . . . I understand. But please just hear me out,' I said. I fixed pleading eyes on him. 'You see, there's something I think Grandmother might have wanted me to do for you . . .' and I explained about how her last wish had been for me to find a person called Zhenya.

'Last wish?' he said faintly. He blinked, once or twice.

Yes, I rushed on, hoping I'd found the right note at last,

she had some things she wanted me to share with this Zhenya. There were the pictures she'd been buying – lots of them, in every room. And there were her jewels – not just the very big jagged modern ones she'd worn in recent years but also, I was careful to mention, some little Russian trinkets. A marble ostrich egg with a troika on top. A cigarette case. A sapphire bracelet. Things that she'd kept in a box for most of her life, and that must have meant a lot to her.

I'd have given anything for just one little twitch of a muscle somewhere, especially when I told him about the Fabergé ornaments he'd once given her. Even if he wasn't going to share his memories with me, I so wanted him to at least look touched, for a moment.

But he didn't look touched. He just looked down, so I couldn't see what he was thinking. Then he steepled his fingers again.

'Ah . . . and, since my name is also Yevgeny, you thought she might have been referring to me?'

Putting out of my mind what Jean and Madame Sabline had told me about how common the name was, I said, 'Yes.'

He crossed the steepled fingers, making his hands into a clasped double fist on which he rested his chin. Then he looked at me. 'In point of fact,' he said, 'what your grandmother always called me was "Miller". Or, occasionally' – and he did, for a moment, look genuinely sad about the eyes as he said this – '*chubchik*. A name from a song. It means forelock – and my hair has a tendency to fall forward at the front. It used to get me into trouble on parade.' He blinked again. 'So, while I appreciate your generosity in seeking me out, miss, I fear I'm not the Zhenya you have in mind.'

'But that wasn't all,' I gabbled, 'because there was

something else, too. She wanted me to look after this Zhenya and do what she called "making amends" . . .'

A flicker of what I thought was distaste crossed his face. 'She told you that, did she?' he asked. One eyebrow went up. 'On her deathbed?'

'Well, not exactly,' I stumbled. 'She wrote it down . . .'

'In a letter?' he said sceptically. There was a challenge in his eye.

Miserably, I shook my head, and explained.

'I see. Blotting paper,' he repeated. 'Notes from her delirium.' He stood up. 'My dear young lady,' he said, and he began his weighty walk to my side of the desk. 'Surely you can see I'm not the man you're looking for. Your grandmother could have no possible reason to want to "make amends" to me. We were old friends.'

He smiled, but I no longer thought it was a charming smile.

He was right beside me now. Breathing audibly, he put a hand on my arm, as if I were already moving towards the door and he were helping me. I let myself be propelled into motion.

'Besides, those awful daubs . . .' He was shaking his head beside me. His voice rose a notch. 'By all those terrible young men, the delinquents of every degenerate race in Europe: Romanians, Catalans, Jews; Bolsheviks, one and all . . . I always told her she was a fool to spend so much time with them. I was perfectly frank about it. She wasn't in any doubt about my views, I can assure you. She'd *never* have thought I'd want to be left any of their filthy nonsense.'

I was shocked at how different he'd suddenly sounded. It was enough to erase the feeling I'd started out with,

that this man would have fitted in beautifully with my family – because now I could see he wouldn't, not at all. After all, the way they talked never sounded like the vicious shouting I'd sometimes heard rebroadcast from Germany, denouncing entire races as degenerate. Even if Aunt Mildred did occasionally also say things about Jews that went against what I'd found out for myself at college, even if I knew that our college mixed-race summer-school programme had been wildly radical, and not something to be talked about overmuch with my family (for these things were delicate, and moved forward only a little at a time, and evolution was better than revolution), why, even Aunt Mildred could also be relied on to say that everyone knew that those people – the ones in power in Germany now – were no better than thugs.

Or perhaps it was really me he was so angry with, even if it was the degenerate peoples of Europe and their decadent daubs that he was barking so furiously about?

Perhaps he also regretted having allowed himself that burst of rage, because, after a quick glance at me, he went on, in a more neutral, explanatory tone, with some of the charm I'd been impressed by earlier returning to his manner, 'We became very different from each other, with time, your grandmother and I.' He opened the door. 'People do change, as they grow older. But at least, when we met again in Paris, we were both old and wise enough to know how different we were, and accept the limited ways we could still be friends, given what life had made of each of us.'

I was outside now, in the corridor. 'Well,' I said, 'thank you for your time.' I bobbed my head, feeling choked, and turned stumblingly away. I couldn't bear to look at him.

26

It was only when I pushed open the door at the end of the corridor that I realized I'd gone the wrong way. I wasn't in the courtyard I'd come in from. I'd reached the big front office of ROVS. At four big desks, three solid young men in elaborate uniform (though with patches at the elbow) were clacking away at typewriters. In one of the two armchairs in the window, which had stuffing coming out of the armrests, a man in late middle age was reading a newspaper and underlining bits with a red pen.

I thought, quite wrongly, that if I just tiptoed past they might not even notice me.

But of course I wasn't as inconspicuous as I hoped. They all turned round and stared.

Then the older man, the one in the armchair, rose to his feet, clicked heels, and said, in quiet good French, *'Mademoiselle?'*

How different this man was from General Miller, and not only because he had a normal civilian suit, slightly worn, on his slender, average-height frame. This man stooped slightly, and his hair was thinning on top. He was the kind you'd always know would listen to what you said.

He had attentive eyes, the kind that took you in carefully as you were speaking. As soon as he'd heard enough of my mumbled explanation – about staying upstairs, being Grandmother's relative, having called on General Miller to pay my respects, and got lost on my way out – this man bowed deeper, smiled and, after the usual formalities, said, as affably as anything, in his quiet, amused voice, 'So, poor old General Miller got confused about showing you the right way out, did he?' laughed a little, just long enough for one or two of the secretaries to join in, in a way that made it perfectly clear their laughter was at General Miller's expense, not mine. 'Let *me* show you out. I'm his number two, General Skoblin. And *I* can be relied on to know the way to the front door.' And, with a smile, he held it open, and handed me out into the ROVS front lobby.

Feeling much better now, I let him slip courteously ahead of me towards the next door, too, which I could see would open into the apartment building's main hall, and I'd be back on the stone stairs up to Grandmother's apartment one floor up.

I glanced around. This was exactly the front lobby you'd expect of a hard-up organization: a black-and-white tiled floor, a hat stand, coat hooks, and a table containing lots of piles of leaflets in Russian, on cheap flimsy paper. A bookshelf behind the table contained tired-looking books, perhaps available on loan to callers, as there was an exercise book and a pen on top. And there was a pile of newspapers, too, with a mug containing change beside it. The newspaper's title was the only bit of all this reading material that I could read, since it was given on the masthead in French as well as Russian: *La Pensée russe* or *Russian Thought.*

Finally, on the back of the door that the quiet number-two general was fumbling with, was the little room's one note of colour: a poster, also in Russian, but in vivid reds and yellows this time, with big, swirly lettering.

I couldn't help smiling when I saw that the poster was of Grandmother's singer friend. 'Plevitskaya!' I said in recognition.

General Skoblin turned around. He looked extremely surprised. Pleased, too. 'You're reading what's on this poster? You speak Russian?' he asked eagerly.

'Oh! No, I just recognized her picture. She's terribly famous, isn't she? The Tsar's Nightingale. I heard her sing once, in New York. And I believe she was my grandmother's friend, too . . .'

The effect of my vague compliments was startling. Thank God, this time at least I'd clearly said something much more right than I'd known, for his quiet bureaucrat's face was positively lit up with pleasure.

'Yes, she's a wonderful singer,' he agreed warmly. Then, with pride, giving me a little conspiratorial look, as if he wondered how I'd take the news, 'And she's my wife, also . . .'

That did surprise me. He looked much too quiet and correct and upper-class for the blowsy, self-willed female I'd met. I couldn't imagine them together.

But you couldn't ever quite tell with foreigners, I reflected, so I opened my eyes wide and congratulated him effusively on his showbiz-star wife, and enjoyed the way we bowed and bobbed politely at each other for several minutes more.

'Do', he said eventually, straightening himself, 'call on

us if you get a moment. My wife would be delighted.' He dug behind some of his Ruritanian braiding for a card and handed it to me. 'We live out of town, but we would be delighted to welcome you if you could arrange a visit to our home,' he continued. Then, as if the thought had just struck him: 'Or she will be singing here in Paris twice this week. Tonight, in fact, and tomorrow. You would be most welcome if you were able to join us there . . .' Taking back the card for a moment, he scribbled a restaurant name on the back, and a couple of dates.

I couldn't refuse, and anyway, I didn't want to. After the awful failure of my attempt to make friends with General Miller, I wanted at least to walk out of this office having made *some* sort of step forward. And this was what I had.

I hadn't thought much about Plevitskaya, except to notice that she was probably a fraud in claiming Grandmother's friendship the first time, and, the second time, that she was definitely drunk on Grandmother's brandy. But perhaps I'd been wrong to write her off completely. If she had a serious husband, she couldn't, surely, be quite as dubious as I'd found her. Perhaps she had really been friends with Grandmother. Perhaps, if I could talk to her properly, preferably when she was sober, and maybe in French rather than in her terrible English, she'd tell me more.

Nodding more thanks to the charming second general, I slipped away.

27

Jean

When I parked on the rue du Colisée at four o'clock, I saw Evie walking along the road back to number 29. She was carrying a travel guide-book in her hand and wore a thoughtful, faraway expression. The sun had brought out a few freckles on her nose.

They'd laughed at me at the station café at dawn, all the tarts and drunks, for looking so happy. I hadn't minded their lewdness, for once, their tawdry gestures and filthy words. It was kindly meant. I'd hardly slept all day for thinking of her. And even this first glimpse of the woman who now meant everything to me, tall and fair and swaying, with no idea how beautiful she was, was making me smile and catch my breath. I could almost smell that scent, which she'd told me was Chanel. I was already imagining the next kiss, not so far away, once we were upstairs and alone again: her breasts against my chest, the slow slide of hands over rumpled cloth and then skin, the sinuous twining of legs . . .

I whistled like an Apache through the cab window. Looking offended, she spun round, but when she saw it was only me grinning at her, her face softened, and when I growled, Apache-style, 'Carry your book, lady?' she laughed out loud.

I could do nothing but smile back, like a fool, wondering at her eyes and those freckles on her nose. Everything I'd always known about the world I was permanently shut out from had stopped applying. There was just this moment, this afternoon gold, this smile, and two of us inside the same magic bubble, full of the same wonderful uncertainty.

'It's early,' she said, hastily. 'Marie-Thérèse will still be in the kitchen . . .'

And then she blushed, deliciously wordless, and we both looked at each other, knowing.

Impossible though it seemed that she could feel like this about me, too, there was no other explanation for that blush.

'Apéritif?'

And so we went to the café at the end of the road, me carrying her book. Our hands had brushed as she passed it to me. Even that touch of skin took my breath away.

The café was empty but for two men on the *terrasse*, both with cheap suits, bad skins and pudding-bowl haircuts, hunched over a chessboard, muttering. I could see they weren't French. They had a faintly Slavic look about them; big cheekbones and short noses, pale eyes. But I barely glanced at them. I had no eyes for anyone but her.

We sat at the next table. When I ordered milk, so did she.

The waiter returned with our drinks and two beers for the neighbouring table. I was half aware that the men at it hadn't been talking about their chess game but about a cargo at Le Havre. Now they fell silent and reached for their drinks.

When I laughed at the white moustache on her upper lip, she giggled and licked it off with a pink tongue.

'You don't think you've got one too?' she laughed at me. There were golden flecks in her eyes. I could smell Chanel . . . I put a hand on her knee, under the table. I couldn't resist. She drew in a small, astonished breath, and looked at me in a way I couldn't quite read. She didn't move my hand.

But, a moment later, she did glance sideways, and I saw that, without my having even noticed, there was another man sitting down right next to us with the chess players: a market trader wearing an apron. He gave me an expressionless glance out of pale eyes. Then he and the chess players nodded at each other and mumbled greetings. Evie's nose wrinkled. 'Let's go,' she said. 'I smell crab. Not good with milk.'

When we got up, she put her hand in mine for a moment, as if it went there naturally.

We walked out, and back along the pavement towards the building. 'Were they from your father's office?' she asked. It was only then that I realized the men had been talking Russian.

'No one I knew,' I said, and reached for her hand, rejoicing in the feel of her skin against mine.

We'd read all the Russian correspondence from Father to her grandmother, so there was no real need, any more, to go to her apartment. There was no point, either, in hoping to be alone there, since her housekeeper wouldn't go away for at least an hour, until after I was supposed to pick up Father and take him home before I started work.

But I had no idea what else to propose. Going anywhere that took us away from the relationship between our relatives – which had been secret, maybe, but at least between equals – would put the social differences between the two of us in sharp relief. I couldn't try entering her world and taking her somewhere grand. I didn't have the money. Should I take her to a movie? Or to eat in some dive in Montparnasse, where the artists were? Or out dancing?

'Would you like', she said, and the pressure of her hand on mine grew pleasurably stronger, 'to go with me to a Russian restaurant called Tsarkaya Okhota?'

I laughed out of sheer relief.

I squeezed her hand back. I turned sideways and, overcoming the inexplicable shyness that my desire had shackled me with, almost dared meet her gaze.

She was laughing back at me from under her eyelashes, as pleased as I was to have solved the problem.

In the car, on the way, grateful now for the need to look at the road, I said, 'How did you even know that restaurant existed?'

'There's a singer who's going to perform there tonight . . . Someone I saw in New York, who told me she was Grandmother's friend. I thought you and I could eat together . . . and then, after you've gone to work, I could stay and listen to her, and maybe have a proper chat with her . . .'

'Skoblin's wife,' I guessed, enjoying making the unlikely connection and feeling our worlds join up by another small silver thread. 'Nadezhda Plevitskaya.'

I felt her nod beside me. I could almost hear the shimmering of hair. 'The Tsar's Nightingale . . .' she agreed. Then the unnerving, if exciting, silence fell again.

I parked within sight of the soaring cathédrale Saint-Alexandre-Nevsky, of the glittering mosaic and the three spires, each topped by a small gold dome, and the front porch topped by another small gold dome, and on top of each gold dome, another delicate Orthodox cross. You didn't have to be a patriot to feel a sudden rush of pride in your Russianness.

'The little *restoranchiki* are all up the side, look,' I said proprietorially. 'And if the place I took you the other night was a province of Little Russia, this is the heartland . . . look, Tsarskaya Okhota is the third one up.' I took her hand. 'How did you know Plevitskaya would be singing tonight?' I asked.

There was no response; no words, no squeeze of the hand. With my lover's antennae, I felt her withdraw, and didn't know why. I glanced at her. She looked uncomfortable.

'There was a poster,' she said in the end, biting her lip.

There was a poster for these shows at ROVS. I'd seen it myself, on the lobby door. But it was in Russian. She'd never have been able to understand it.

'It was in Russian . . . I didn't understand it, but I recognized her picture. General Skoblin explained and wrote it all down for me,' she added. 'It was his idea.'

Having never much liked Skoblin, I wasn't too sure I wanted him to be involved in this idea.

'You've met General Skoblin, too, then, have you?'

I was about to ask, 'Well, where?' when she came to a decision. She turned around to face me, took both my hands in hers, and said, in a breathy rush, 'Look, I met him this morning at ROVS. We got chatting. And, before you ask, I was there because I went to try to talk to your father.

240

I just saw him, having a smoke in the courtyard. I couldn't resist. And I know you didn't want me to do that and told me not to try. And I'm sorry.'

She was staring up at me as though she'd committed some dreadful crime; as though she thought I'd just walk away. She was so beautiful, with that imploring look in her eyes.

'You were quite right,' she went on. 'He didn't want to talk to me at all. I started wishing I hadn't started trying about half a minute after I did start trying. But it was too late by then. I had to go through with it. I'm sorry. Really I am.'

She'd understood, then. She'd realized the futility of approaching him. Nothing terrible had happened. I could stop worrying about her and Father.

I kissed her, right there and then, in the street. I couldn't not.

'Ach, you won't help grief with tears,' I whispered through the thump of blood as we came up for air. Smiling forgivingly down, swept away on my wave of desire, for nothing mattered except this, surely, and whatever difficult little exchange they'd had would get forgotten soon enough . . .

She laughed a little, and raised her mouth to mine again.

The next time she pulled back, she was laughing more, and flushed, with pupils dilated at the astonishing wantonness of this public kiss. 'People will be looking,' she whispered, though something in her breathy voice suggested she didn't altogether mind. I'd never been part of the sexual frenzy of night-time Paris before, never thought of it without the most extreme disapproval, and it wasn't even night-time now, for God's sake, but I was almost ready to suggest just forgetting Plevitskaya and going back to Evie's apartment right there and then when, in something much more like her ordinary voice, Evie added, 'Shouldn't we go to the restaurant?'

I nodded, slightly shocked by the ease with which I'd let myself be carried away.

We separated. I ran my hands through my hair and composed myself. We walked up the side of the cathedral.

'I'm so relieved you aren't angry,' she said, slipping an arm through mine so I could feel the whole length of one side of her pressed against me, and the whole tumult started again. 'I thought you might . . .'

I turned towards her, but she laughed and drew her head back, out of reach of the kiss I'd intended.

'. . . be furious,' she finished, slightly teasingly.

That she could say that fearlessly, and that I could smile back without anger, felt like a new kind of intimacy. We were on unknown territory. But we were there together, growing in confidence.

We stopped in the doorway.

She was wearing a light fawn coat. I drew it off her. Every touch was a delicious torture, and every breath deeply felt.

She laughed up at me, dazzling with relief. 'Because, my God, your father was so shockingly right-wing when he got angry, and I'm afraid I did make him angry, though it was the last thing I meant to do, I promise,' I heard her saying. 'He started calling all Grandmother's poor young artists degenerates and delinquents from the dustbins of Europe . . . and Bolsheviks, and Jews.'

The coat was off, and in my hands. And, now we weren't

touching any more, I did hear the next thing she said, loud and clear. She giggled, a bit miserably. 'He got really quite Herr Schickelgruberesque, you know?' she said, and did a little mocking Hitler salute-and-moustache gesture with her hands.

It struck me like a blow, her mockery of Father. It was unbearable. After all, the thing I'd wanted to avoid had happened. She'd seen just what I hadn't wanted her to see in him. And she was laughing about it.

Worse. She wanted me to laugh with her.

The darkness came rushing in, a wave of rage that felt terrifyingly like tears about to pour down my cheeks. If it had been earlier in our relationship, or if she'd been someone else, I might easily have howled, 'Don't dare call my father a fascist!'

But I couldn't, now, with her. I didn't know what I could do.

I thrust the coat into her hands. 'I have to go,' I said. And I ran.

PART FOUR

The Red Russians

PART FOUR

The Red Russians

28

Skoblin was smiling sympathetically as he drove through the summer night in the Cadillac and listened to his wife in the passenger seat complaining about the lack of audience at that evening's restaurant show.

Things were going so well, suddenly, with his own career that, for once, he was able to feel genuinely sorry for his poor Nightingale.

In two days' time, if everything went according to plan, he'd be the head of ROVS.

As he cruised forward, feeling the restrained power of the engine, enjoying the polished walnut and the comforting smell of soft, expensive leather and car fumes, he felt, expansively, that he wanted his wife to have something to be happy about, too.

'I think you'll be surprised by someone in your audience tomorrow,' he said.

She eyed him. 'What do you mean?' she said. 'Who?'

'The American girl who's moved in upstairs,' he said, and even if he couldn't make his quiet voice ring out it still vibrated with the pleasure of a conjuror pulling a rabbit from a hat. 'Constance Sabline's grand-daughter. She came into the office today. We had a chat. I sang your praises. She promised she'd come and hear you, either tonight or tomorrow.'

He could sense Nadya's interest. That made him feel so unexpectedly tender towards her that, when he spoke again, he further softened her formal first name, Nadezhda, into a still more affectionate diminutive.

'She was very friendly, you know, Nadyen'ka. It seems she's taking the business of winding up Constance's affairs very seriously. She's not leaving Paris yet. She said she'd asked the servants to stay on till Christmas. Well, all Americans love Paris. So, if we get a proper chance to talk to her, I think we should explain about the recording Constance was doing for you, and see if she would want to finish it off in her grandmother's place? It would be a shame to let all your work go to waste.'

'Oh!' he heard, and in her voice was the sound of hope returning. 'Ask her home,' he said. 'If you can. Light the samovar, give her *zakuski*, sing her sad songs. Do what you have to do. Persuade her.'

It was an entirely selfless impulse, his wish to get the American girl to take her grandmother's place in paying to promote Nadya's career, he told himself as he negotiated the turning towards Ozoir-la-Ferrière, and their little house with the Russian birch trees his wife had planted in the yard. He was feeling rather proud of his altruism.

He no longer had any personal reason to need recording equipment and engineers in the apartment above ROVS. Just one week of listening in to what went on in that office had proved to the visitors from Moscow that it was he, Skoblin, who really organized everything down there.

They'd soon seen that he'd been right all along to say that Miller was a useless, lazy old buffoon, always sneaking off for lunches or shutting himself away for long, long solitary strategy sessions – which everyone knew were just naps, really. Even the secretaries laughed at their boss, behind his back. The men from Moscow had heard all they wanted even before Constance Sabline had so unexpectedly keeled over, forcing the sudden withdrawal of the editing equipment from her flat.

All the same, he genuinely hoped the girl would now step in and pay up. If she did, he could surely find a way to get the recording machinery back and have some other engineers edit it, in the weeks to come. Nadya deserved a bit of hope.

His wife had been good about agreeing to help him with this career plan. Even though she hadn't looked shocked, she must have been scared when he'd first explained as she packed for her New York trip. But she hadn't backed out, even when the thing got closer and the men from Moscow, once here, had (after listening to what went on inside the ROVS office for themselves) definitely decided to back him. In fact, she'd gone out of her way to help his cause and charm them. She'd even managed to look and sound convincingly enthusiastic about the crazy job the Muscovites were now assigning to her – the job of providing him, Skoblin, with the kind of far-fetched, truth-is-stranger-than-fiction alibi that those proletarian-intellectual spooks from Moscow were so keen on. Privately he'd thought the whole idea quite crazy, and it had showed. In fact, if it hadn't been for Nadya's acting ability, he might have slipped up and lost their favour. Yes, she was actually putting herself out for him, for once, his Nightingale. And he was feeling kindly disposed towards her, and wanted to reciprocate, so would help her carry on with her singing.

His wish to be head of ROVS had been growing inside him for many, many years. It was an emotion, more than anything else: the remnants of his long-ago, boyish hero-worship of General Vrangel', that long, straight, utterly noble man, who, before he'd had to cut his losses and organize what they still called Vrangel''s Fleet to get the last hundred thousand White soldiers away from the Bolsheviks, had raised him, Skoblin, to be the White Army's youngest general. He had wanted to inherit that mantle ever since. He wanted to become the incarnation of that charisma. He wanted to be the man who conferred blessings, to stand in the Alexander Nevsky Cathedral in front of the massed ranks of men in uniform and take their salutes. He wanted to wear, not Miller's absurd opera-general uniform – which was for the cavalry snobs of the Preobrazhensky Regiment only – but the sombre Circassian coat the first, nobler, ROVS leader had preferred. It consumed him, that longing.

He should have got the job seven years ago, when Kutyopov had disappeared. As Nadya had always loyally said, it was only cruel fate – in the shape of that whispering campaign in the Paris Russian press – that had robbed him of it, and made that pompous, stodgy fool Miller seem a safer candidate. Skoblin had insisted on the rumours being put before a ROVS court of honour, which had eventually exonerated him, because the case against him was, when it came down to it, only hearsay; but what comfort was that when the damn-fool judgement had come too late? The job had been Miller's by then, even if the old buffoon had given him the number-two post and, magnanimously, allowed him to do all the real work. To this day, Skoblin couldn't bear to pick up the *Posledniye novosti* newspaper, which had accused him, so stridently and repeatedly, of being a Soviet agent.

But he didn't rage any more. He just smiled, and kept his thoughts to himself. They'd accused him of being a Red; well, then, they only had themselves to blame if he'd secretly become one. Now he was about to have the last laugh.

Skoblin's chance of revenge had come right in the middle of his despair. No one – not even Nadya – knew that, a few years back, when the storm was still raging around him, a quiet, polite man called Kovalsky had visited Paris from Moscow. He'd invited Skoblin out to an expensive restaurant and, over cigars and brandy, had listened sympathetically. With an uncharacteristic frankness born of misery and one too many liqueurs, Skoblin had explained the wrong direction ROVS had taken by appointing Miller, and the man had nodded with understanding. He'd been understanding, too, when Skoblin had complained about his wife's decreasing earnings and reckless spending. And he'd sympathetically shaken his head and ordered more brandy when Skoblin had told him about the little farm he'd brought outside town in the hope of becoming a wine-grower if all else failed, though this was losing money, too.

And then he'd given Skoblin a letter, and sat, gently smiling, while Skoblin read it.

Everything about that letter had been astonishing. For one thing, Skoblin had had no idea that his mop-headed little brother, Petya, who'd stayed at school in Moscow years ago, had later gone into the Communist secret service. In fact, he'd had no idea that Petya, or anyone else in his family, was even still alive. And, for another, there was a salary attached to the offer Petya, or rather Moscow, was making: a lump sum of five thousand francs, and a monthly stipend big enough for him to stop worrying – almost – about Nadya's spending.

And so, for the past few years, Skoblin had done two jobs. As ROVS security chief, he'd sought out secret contacts within the Deuxième Bureau, the Wehrmacht, the Gestapo, and the Sicherheitsdienst. And, in his other role, he'd used those contacts to provide dossiers needed by the Soviet NKVD.

Sometimes, too, he'd passed Moscow information about the rare acts of sabotage Miller got round to organizing. Miller himself barely seemed to notice that none of these acts worked, or that the agents he sent out were – always – arrested.

And Skoblin hardened his heart. He'd earned his car, all right (no one had ever even asked how he afforded his beloved banana-lemon Cadillac; he supposed they thought the Nightingale's concerts paid for everything.) Lovingly, he patted the wheel. But now there was more in store.

Play your cards right, the gentle Kovalsky had said, all those years ago, and, who knows? One day, Miller might go the same way his predecessor did . . .

And now, finally, it was about to happen.

Moscow's men were primed and ready. Their arrival was his reward for the last damning 'red dossier' he'd managed to get the Germans to put together, on Tukhachevsky, just before the Soviet Marshal's high-profile trial and execution in Moscow in June. Or, maybe, the reason for their arrival was that the new big man in the Lubyanka, Yezhov, was preparing for war in Europe, and wanted to be sure there would be no surprises from the little White Russian organization in the West.

Skoblin frankly didn't care why. He was just happy they were here, and in such numbers. Even so, they were keeping things simple. The Muscovites called him Farmer. He called them Duplus (the crab salesman), Finn and Swede (the pair organizing transport in and out of Paris, and surveillance) and Alexander and Veletsky. These were the men who would be waiting behind the green door, in two days' time, with the chloroform pad and the ropes . . .

Duplus had selected the anonymous-looking house attached to the green door, which was owned by the Soviet embassy, and which was located as far as possible from anywhere the White Russians ever went to in Paris. He'd told Skoblin to get Miller there, the plan being that they would first meet on foot, a good hour's walk away, at a very different sort of rendezvous in the lovely, leafy, shop-free, traffic-free, café-free calm of Passy.

For the Muscovites couldn't do their job alone. Miller was too canny – or lazy – ever to leave the ROVS chancellery without his taciturn son or some other guard. The Muscovites needed Skoblin to winkle their target out.

Of course, Miller trusted Skoblin, and would probably have gone with him willingly enough if he had simply asked him out for a walk. That, in fact, was what Duplus was expecting. But Skoblin had already had enough questions asked about his loyalty to last him a lifetime. This second disappearance would cause more fuss than even the kidnapping of Kutyopov. If he were to take over Miller's job, this time he'd have to be seen to be above reproach.

So he'd taken the trouble to dream up the idea of a phony letter from the Abwehr – a nice touch, that; Miller's dream come true – and got Duplus (who he knew was in reality State Security Major Semyon Spiegel-Glazer, of Jewish–German extraction, who was pretty good at German, since it was his first language) to write the letter.

He'd told Miller to destroy the letter, but he knew Miller wouldn't. The man was a sentimentalist with no tradecraft, and the smug way he kept patting the right-hand pocket of his jacket showed he'd kept the letter on him ever since he'd first received it. Skoblin would make sure, when the time was right, that that letter got dropped. And, when the police found it, the trail would lead everywhere but to Skoblin or the Muscovites.

When Miller stepped out with him on Wednesday morning to meet the Abwehr men, he'd be worriedly running over his best German phrases in his mind. And then, ba-boom! Skoblin nearly laughed at the shock the boss he so resented would get.

Skoblin knew, in some buried place inside himself, that these thoughts would have shocked Vrangel', had his hero the general come back from the dead and learned of them. But, he told himself, truculently, times change.

These days, when he looked at the careworn reflection he saw in the mirror, Skoblin found he didn't much care whether the price of running the White Russian army was betraying it, in private, to the Reds he was supposed to be fighting.

All he wanted was to stand at the front of his men, in the cathedral, wearing Vrangel''s uniform, bowing as he received the archpriest's blessing on the White Army's behalf and leading the bass voices in praising God. He just wanted to drive, in a proper car (already paid for using his second salary) to a proper apartment (which would be the next bonus he would offer himself, once he was boss) and know that everything depended on him – the same set of banal, normal desires that, he now knew, also motivated most of the supposed Jewish–Bolshevik enemies in Moscow, including his own brother Petya.

He just wanted to see admiration in the eyes of his wife.

29

Nadya Plevitskaya looked anxiously at her husband.

He was mumbling to himself, as he did increasingly often these days. Any minute now, he'd start wagging his finger reprovingly at the dashboard of his car. She'd caught him at that several times in the past few days.

He'd always been quiet, but she'd liked it better before he'd started this odd, wordless, grunty *swelling* he did now, all the time – as if all the pent-up things he'd never quite said, but spent years thinking, were about to come pouring out. It made him look a bit mad, she thought.

Partly just to stop him, she touched his hand. He jumped, and then he turned and smiled at her. A great, big, absent-minded smile, as if he had more important things in mind.

'On Wednesday,' she said, and she couldn't stop the slight shake in her voice.

'Do you remember it all?' he asked. He sounded sharp, like a schoolteacher talking to a lazy pupil. 'It's very important.'

She gave him a devil-may-care grin, hoping to reassure him. 'Ach, all that: of course I remember. I create your alibi, by acting. He's right – it will be easy for a woman like me.'

'Tell me again,' he insisted. 'Just in case.'

She knew every step, of course. But she humoured him and ticked them off anyway.

'Early morning: pick up the nasty little Peugeot – less conspicuous than the Cadillac – in case something goes wrong and we need to make a getaway. Then drive to the corner café on rue du Colisée.

'At nine o'clock, have breakfast together, for an hour, and talk noisily, in the most visible place we can find on the *terrasse*, greeting anyone we know and saying we are having a day off together.

'Soon after ten o'clock, drive on to Monsieur Epstein's boutique. We both say hello to him. You have a newspaper in your hand. You look a little impatient, and say you're going to sit outside in the car and read the paper while I try on some new stage clothes. "Men!" I say, and roll my eyes. Monsieur Epstein laughs. We get going. No one sees that you aren't really sitting outside reading the paper. You've driven away . . .'

She didn't mention where her husband would have gone, or what he would be doing by then. She didn't want to think about that part. She was happier concentrating on her role.

'Meanwhile, I'm still at Monsieur Epstein's, trying on every expensive dress in the shop. Sometimes I walk outside, and say I want to show one to you. I talk, loudly, out there, so they can hear me through the window. "Darling," I say, "do you like me in gold?" or, "*Chéri*, do you think this one is too *décolleté*?" and then, "Oh, really? I'll ask Monsieur Epstein what *he* thinks then." Of course Monsieur Epstein thinks you're still there. And I spend the rest of the morning there, going in and out, "talking" to you.

'Then, not before one o'clock, I finally choose two dresses, for a combined value not exceeding three thousand francs, and sign for them myself and ask for them to be delivered to me at Ozoir. The cost will be reimbursed, on production of an appropriate receipt, by . . .'

She paused, suddenly imagining herself buying a gold Epstein dress on a Soviet expense account, then wearing it on stage while her admirers cheered.

'Kolya . . . Kolyen'ka, I will actually get to wear those dresses, won't I?' she asked wheedlingly. 'Afterwards?'

Skoblin nodded. As if that mattered, she could see him thinking. But then, he never had understood anything about performing.

'And then you come and pick me up, at quarter past one, and we go together to the railway station to join the rest of the delegation seeing off General Kutyopov's daughter to Brussels,' she finished quickly. 'As far as anyone knows, we've been together all day.'

He nodded. He looked reassured, for now, but she knew it wouldn't last. He'd ask her to go through it all again several more times before bed.

'That wasn't what I was going to ask, actually,' she said, pouting. The house was coming into view now – over the fence, a graceful tracery of birch twigs and small fluttering leaves. (He kept talking about leaving it and moving into a flat in town, once he was boss. He never asked whether *she* wanted to leave her little courtyard behind.)

He raised an eyebrow. 'What, then?'

'I wanted to know, what happens if it all goes wrong?' she asked as the car slowed. 'No one talks about that.'

He glided to a halt. Without emotion, he answered, 'We

go to the Soviet embassy. We ask for the crab salesman. They take us back to Moscow.'

Plevitskaya hadn't expected the idea of Moscow to surge into her mind with so much nostalgic force. The fresh smell of cucumbers and snow filled her nostrils, and her head swam with visions of little lopsided yellow-stucco houses piled up around churches with golden cupolas up and down the seven hills; of bright snow under a blue sky; of the faint cries of children skating on the Clean Ponds or squabbling happily over creamy round *vatrushka* cheese-cakes or climbing on the Pushkin statue, and the jingle of harness, and the bells ringing . . .

'God forbid,' he continued, just as calmly.

He would say that, Plevitskaya thought, without rancour. He hadn't been interested in anything but Paris for a long time.

But she wouldn't be sorry to see Moscow again.

Sometimes, still, all these years later, she dreamed of Russia. Not of Moscow, as it happens, and not of any of the sleigh-bells-in-the-snow, storks-on-the-rooftops daydreams she filled her music with, either. This was a real dream – always in the same place, in the same forest, in that first war, the one against the Germans, in that somewhere on the south-western front that was tattooed into her brain, where the leaves were just beginning to drop from the trees overhead and there was a rumble of death somewhere up ahead. Milling back and forward from the front line were people going off or on duty, or to hospital, and trucks and carts grinding back and forth. Her husband – the long-ago husband of those days, whose face these days, after years of her later marriage to Skoblin, she barely recalled – was up there, in the fighting. He came back, once every couple of days, exhausted, stinking, sunken-eyed, to sleep. She'd cancelled her singing engagements – for she had singing engagements, even with a young child, in wartime – to be with that man. She wasn't going anywhere unless it was with him. Why would she? They were a family. She didn't think it was foolhardy staying near the front, whatever anyone said. She knew enough about life to know you clung to the happiness that came your way, and stayed near your man. There was food, for the moment. And she was sure that she and the child were safe here in the rear, anxious though everything might always be . . .

Until the moment the dream starts, that is. Until the day they're not safe. Until the morning the greenish twilight of the woods explodes into strange, streaming, roaring, red-white hellfire, and everywhere she turns there are crackles and hisses and branches breaking off and fire. She can hear Yevdokia the housekeeper whimpering somewhere behind, with men shouting and jeering in foreign tongues. There's only one thing on her own mind – getting herself and the little one away. So she's running across the yard, panting – how is her breath so loud? – to snatch the child. The child's in the outhouse. Or he was. But now there's no outhouse any more, just a roiling midden where the log cabin used to be, and broken logs scattered everywhere, and, much later, a noise to break your head apart. And then she's just running, running, running, in and out of trees and over roots, and there's nothing else except that blood-rhythm, going on forever, and the tree-trunks: not her, not the child, just the thud of her feet on the pine-needly forest floor, heels, toes, heels, toes, and her breath. She doesn't know where the child has gone. Even when they creep back, much later, there's just a burning house, beyond saving. Yevdokia's mauled body. The splinters of the outhouse. The thickset stink of the uncovered shit pit, buzzing with flies. But no little boy. No trace.

All these years later, she'd still wake up whimpering from that dream, feeling for his little lost body, as bereft each subsequent time as she had been in that first naked moment as, in one awful dawn after another, she reunderstood her child's absence.

It was brutal, this pain: always had been, always would be; although over time she'd managed to banish it, mostly, to the realm of sleep. It was an entirely different order of feeling from the soft, fuzzy, faint nostalgia she still sometimes also experienced, remembering the husband of those faraway days, who'd had soft blue eyes (or had they been grey?) and who'd been sent off to a different camp by his commanding officer with no time to grieve, then killed in the war soon afterwards. Once both son and husband had gone, her rage against the monstrous lack of feeling of the commanding officers, mixed up with her grief, had pushed her, in the war that came immediately after the one against the Germans, to go defiantly out singing for the rebellious Reds. The Reds all had their grudges against the power that had abused them, those righteously angry men, just as she did. Why not go out and cheer them along with her voice? She'd been so wild with fury and loss, back then, and had nothing to lose. She was alone. Sometimes she'd almost hoped an enemy bullet would carry her off.

But there'd been no merciful oblivion. She'd been

captured, not killed. And, in the White camp where she'd been held, she'd been astonished to find herself fêted as the exotic darling of the camp, adored by the very type of officer she'd blamed for her tragedy, because, as it turned out, for them, she and her voice and her fame added up to a symbol of the old glory days they were vainly fighting for. And slowly, agonizingly slowly, she'd finally wept for her loss in the arms of her White jailor, Skoblin, who'd become her last husband and life companion. Fate had ended up carrying them both, with their separate griefs for all that had gone, along with all the other survivors – each of them mourning one private lost thing or another that no one could either share or escape – away to this place of exile in Paris.

But time and happenstance hadn't stopped her remembering her real home in Russia.

If she could only go back to Russia, she sometimes thought, she could follow the trails that had been impossible in wartime, scour the orphanages, trawl the schools, interrogate the priests; and somehow, miraculously, she might find herself running towards him, her child turned handsome young man, a man whom she'd recognize at once, with her arms out, rapturously smiling, racing into that embrace she held perpetually in mind.

Just being back in Russia – and Moscow, even if it hadn't ever been quite home, was the jumping-off point of Russia, the place where power now was and where her friends in high places would be found – might be the start of making it all come true. Even now, all these years later, when she was fifty-three. Her husband beside her was consumed by his ambition; she understood this. She understood it not because she wanted her singing career back, though that

would be nice, but because of her own secret but consuming ambition to do the impossible: turn back time, go home, and find her lost son.

30

Evie

I was late for Plevitskaya's lunchtime performance. I stood near the front of the restaurant, still dazzled by the bright light from outside, watching sunspots fade from my eyes while, in the near-dark of inside, she finished her last number. According to the list at the entrance, it was called, 'You're Buried in Snow, Russia'. She was standing crushed into the one tiny table-free space at the back of the hall, in constant danger of bumping into the accompanist squashed beside her at an upright piano. As she drew the song out to its sentimental end, she drooped lower and lower, as if truly heartbroken.

There was the usual thin applause when the last note died away. The red-shaded table lamps went on again. An elderly couple – the woman in black with jet beads, the man in uniform – were revealed stolidly eating meatballs and buckwheat porridge close to the music. An older man still, with a red nose and tears slipping unnoticed down his cheeks, was nursing a drink not far from me. There wasn't anyone else. They could have made her more space, I thought, clapping extra

loudly. They could have cleared another table.

I waved. Her gloomy face lit up. I'd ordered two glasses of champagne before she'd even got to the table where I was sitting. Although she was smiling now as she approached, bosom heaving under her shawl, I saw that she had real tears in her eyes.

'That was beautiful,' I said, surprised by those tears, and moved, too. She sat down heavily. After finding her so erratic in English, I was trying French, and it seemed to be working. She ducked her own head, with dignity, and replied, in rather good French, maybe by way of apology for her glistening eyes:

'Ach . . . how hard it feels, sometimes, to go on living with one's ghosts.' She sniffed, smiled and shook her head all at once. 'That is the saddest song in my repertoire,' she went on, and started reciting:

'No paths left, no tracks through the plains,
Through the storm and endless snow;
No way back to the sacred homeplace,
To the dear voices I once knew . . .'

The champagne came. Unobtrusively, as she lifted her coupe to her mouth, she wiped the eye furthest from me. Then she drained it and furtively wiped her other eye. 'It is not always so hard,' she added more robustly, putting the empty glass down on the table.

'I would have come last night—' I began.

'Ahhh . . . Last night was *wonderful*,' she said, loudly and stagily, capping my voice with her surge of theatrical enthusiasm. '*Many* more people. Why didn't you?'

'Oh,' I said uncertainly, remembering that, from the doorway, last night, which was as close as I'd got before Jean vanished and everything changed, there hadn't seemed to be many more people inside this restaurant than there were today. 'Something came up.'

Plevitskaya looked harder at me and spoke with a kindness so unexpected that it almost made me well up, too. 'You look a bit pale. I hope you weren't unwell?'

I shook my head. It had been so bewildering when Jean left. Even when I'd started looking around for him in earnest, I hadn't been able to believe for several minutes that he really wasn't there. There'd been other people in the street, and as he took my coat I'd been looking at them, and at the people going towards the church, and peeping into the dusty interiors of the little restaurants. I'd actually been feeling relieved, I could remember, that he hadn't been angry.

And then, when he'd suddenly pushed my coat back into my hands and rushed off, I'd gone on standing, dithering, looking around, thinking – hoping – that maybe he'd just run back to the taxi for something, or wanted to buy cigarettes or a newspaper. But I'd had a sense of all not being well, too. I'd felt my heart constrict with every examined head and body that turned out not to be his as the moments went by.

It had only been when I'd finally thought to look and see whether he was now walking back from the parked taxi, with the missing wallet or whatever it might be in his hand, and gone a bit of the way down the road towards the taxi myself, that I'd noticed it wasn't there any more either. He must have driven off in it.

It had taken what seemed a long, quiet, strange time (in

which the rest of the world had gone on just as usual, the late-afternoon sun shining, people walking along the kerb) before I finally believed he wasn't coming back. Not in a minute. Not in ten. Not at all.

There were little jumbled scraps of thoughts in my head: that by now perhaps he was already home, wherever that was, or that he was picking up a book, whose letters were too alien to me to even guess at what was in it, or heading for a café where he'd meet the other writers he'd talked about . . .

But it didn't matter where he was. He'd gone where I couldn't follow.

Maybe I should have been angry, or cried. His disappearance was too strange for me to know what I felt, beyond a bit shaky and unreal.

Maybe I should have shrugged it off and gone to hear Plevitskaya and to talk to her, as I'd planned. But I couldn't somehow face brazening that out on my own, either.

So I'd just walked home, feeling shamed, in a quiet, quiet way, as though I'd done something wrong. Faintly, I was remembering reading in the preface to some translation of Dostoyevsky that the Russian language, whose sensitivity to insult and injury had, the book said, resulted in a vast and subtle vocabulary for every possible shade of humiliation, even had a special single word for 'a slap in the face', a word Dostoyevsky was fond of using. Well, I felt as though I'd been given one of those one-word face-slaps, even though I didn't know why.

He hadn't been angry that I'd gone to see his father. He'd said so. It hadn't seemed to matter. But as soon as I'd started telling him some of the detail of our conversation, he'd gone – and before I'd even had time to ask him whether we might have drawn the wrong conclusions.

Because we might, mightn't we? I'd been thinking about that possibility all afternoon. Because, after all – whatever we'd learned from reading the letters, whatever we now knew about Grandmother and the General having loved each other, and however certain I might be that the General's first name was indeed Yevgeny – there was some sense in what the General had told me. Why would Grandmother ever have thought that he would have wanted to share those pictures, if she knew he hated them? If what he'd said was true – that she'd never even called him 'Zhenya' but the much more bracing-sounding 'Miller' – was it possible that Marie-Thérèse and I had somehow got everything muddled up, and that there was some other explanation?

I wouldn't be able to talk this over with Jean now – which didn't matter, as I kept telling myself stoutly, not at all. I didn't need Jean. I'd be able to work it out for myself – except maybe not right now, since I didn't even know what should be in my own head when, for the whole of the immediate past, it had been so full of Jean. So I'd let myself back into Grandmother's apartment and – full of lonely defiance at the unwanted memory of Jean's milk-drinking – poured myself a brandy to watch the stars come prickling out by, and then another. But I hadn't let myself go completely. Even if, in the middle of the night, when I'd woken up, I'd said to Grandmother's photo, which I'd taken unsteadily to bed with me, 'Well, *you* didn't mind having no place back home, because you found a new home here among all the poor outcasts from Russia – but even *they* don't seem to want me much,' my self-pity hadn't made me cry. Even if I'd got up this morning feeling fuzzy, disappointed and empty, I'd had my plan. I'd looked at the diary, whose key I hadn't yet found, and been tempted for a moment just to break it open and read the rest of what Grandmother had left me. But then I'd remembered that I didn't want to rush my time here. I'd told Marie-Thérèse to stay on, with Gaston, until the end of the year. And I thought, No, I'll wait; it's better to find the right key to the diary, and the right answer, in the right time . . .

So I'd bathed and dressed and come back to talk to Plevitskaya, as I'd planned.

'No,' I said, more firmly now, feeling proud that I was able to put aside the darkness of the night but be grateful for her concern all the same. 'I'm not unwell.'

The last thing I expected was that, a moment later, tears would have overwhelmed me, or that I'd be mumbling about Jean through chaotic sobs, or that she would be murmuring soothing little bird-noises, or hugging me, and wiping my face with a corner of her shawl, and murmuring, '*T'en fais pas, ma petite; t'en fais pas. Tout se guérit dans la vie, même les coeurs brisés.*' ('Don't fret, little one. Don't fret. Everything heals, even broken hearts.') I'd never thought, not for a moment, that I could be so weak, or she so kind.

After a while, when my tears had subsided a bit, and we'd found a napkin to replace the damp corner of the Nightingale's shawl, and she'd run through the things people say about heartbreakers – 'The boy must be a fool to want to break *your* heart' and 'Not that I know General Miller's family, but everyone knows that boy has always been a loner; maybe he's just not the type for love, or not ready' – she added, very gently and sweetly, 'And it's more than just a broken heart with you, I know, because you are in grief, too . . .'

There was a near-sob in her voice at that. 'That is no surprise. Your grandmother was a wonderful woman; her death so unexpected. Even *I* find it hard to believe, I, who have seen so much suffering, when dear Constance was so full of life just a week ago. I am sorry she's gone.' She squeezed my hands in hers.

Our glasses were empty. She picked hers up and waved at the waiter. I sniffed acquiescence.

'Please tell me more about her,' I asked, trying, with only partial success, to dry my eyes. 'I so want to know.'

She remembered Grandmother all right. She said they'd sat up all night talking, in New York when they'd first met – an instant rapport. 'Kind, glamorous, beautiful, Constance,' she reminisced with lyrical enthusiasm, applying herself to the second glass. 'She was wearing a silver fox wrap, and I recognised it *at once* as one of Ours . . . a Russian fur. And so naturally we started to talk in Russian – she spoke wonderful Russian, you know – and before we knew it we found we shared the most important possible common interest, she and I . . .' She sighed again.

'Because she loved your husband's boss, you mean? General Miller?' I asked.

She gave me an odd look – startled, I thought, for a moment, as her wide-open eyes met mine. But amused disdain quickly took over. '*Vryad li,*' she said firmly, bringing down her eyelids and wrinkling her nose. 'Surely not. What, that big dough-ball of a general and my elegant Constance, with her beautiful soul? Constance, who loved *art*? No, no. Unimaginable.'

She sounded so utterly certain – and looked so appalled, too, by the idea of the General as Grandmother's lover – that despite myself I nearly laughed. Instead I did a little half-shrug, half-bow, to signify my apologies for interrupting, and she swept on.

'No, no,' she breathed tragically, 'it was nothing as banal as *that*. No. What bound me and Constance together, from the first, was *this* . . .' She leaned closer, over the table, and her breasts, squashed against the tabletop, billowed out alarmingly. 'We had both lost a beloved child,' she whispered. 'The strongest bond of all . . .'

A tear cut a shining line through her make-up. Her shoulders were shaking. It didn't look like the hammy overacting I remembered. My fingers squeezed hers.

'I'd never had anyone I could talk with about my little boy,' she muttered. Small individual circles of wet were landing on the table. Helplessly I squeezed harder. 'I met my present husband later, you see. It wasn't his child, and it was wartime, and there was so much grief, and nothing got better afterwards. And we Russians, well, these days, we each have our separate crosses to bear, and we suffer in silence. There was no one who wanted to hear my sorrow. But *she* understood, because she'd lost her daughter, too. She knew how grief felt . . .'

She looked up. Her wide lips were trembling and their lipstick was smeared. But she'd forgotten her appearance.

'She used to say, "Oh, Nadya, I know the pain you feel, the helplessness." She was so sympathetic to me. It wasn't quite the same for her, of course, because there was no death in her story, while my little boy almost certainly died, lost and alone, with no one to bury him. Still, her daughter was lost to her, as surely as my son to me, and the daughter had shut her out of the next generation, too. There are many kinds of exile . . .'

She fixed those woeful eyes on me. I could see she'd forgotten, in her tale about herself and her friend, that she was also talking about my family and me. But I didn't mind. Around the edges of her story, I was privately seeing the faint outline of another story: Grandmother holding Plevitskaya's hands and thinking about me.

'But we found a shared home in our suffering, at least. And she understood, oh, no one better, how much I went on dreaming of going back to Russia somehow, to find my child, alive or dead . . .' Plevitskaya's face became more animated at this prospect, but then she sighed. 'But of course I couldn't – can't – because here we are in France, and there's no way back, never will be. I know that. But how I appreciated Constance's kindness, all the same. A good, good friend . . .'

How magnetic Plevitskaya was. By now I'd forgotten to ask what Grandmother had said about me because I was realizing how very small my concerns were – my heartbreak for a man I hadn't known a month ago; my nostalgia for a woman I'd only known as a child – next to Plevitskaya's all-enveloping tragedy. Her pain, I could see now, was on a different scale.

'What was he called?' I asked softly, holding tight on to her hand. 'Your little boy?'

She looked straight at me. My eyes were used to the red-lit darkness by now. I could see her lips moving, as if in prayer.

'Zhenya.'

*

I felt myself go very still.

A brief flicker of hope stirred in me. Could that possibly mean . . . Could it possibly be *your* child Grandmother wanted me to look after and make amends to? I asked her from somewhere deep inside my head. But I didn't say anything, and, a moment later, when Plevitskaya began talking again, I was glad I'd waited.

'Yes, Constance did me nothing but good, all the time I knew her,' she said, and though I could still hear anguish in her voice, I thought I could also hear something steelier. She sat up, drawing back the billowing breasts. 'God bless her.

'But her tragic death has interrupted the last wonderful thing she did for me,' she went on, and something smooth and prepared in what followed set me on my guard. 'Maybe I have already mentioned that she was funding a gramophone recording of my voice? I hoped it would be a new lease of life for my career. Move with the times, she told me, and she paid for the use of a wonderful German Magnetophon. How happy she was to help me, and how happy I was to receive this wonderful help from my dear friend . . .'

She eyed me. 'But now it might never happen.'

I stayed still and kept my face uncomprehending. I still so wanted her to be, for another few minutes at least, that comforting maternal presence, wiping away my tears. And I wanted to go away and think, in my own time, about her lost son being called Zhenya, and what that might mean. I didn't want her to shake me down for money for her recording. But I could see it coming.

She sighed. 'When she died, I think the company took away the equipment from her apartment, and anyway the last payments have still to be made before the edit can be completed. I saw nothing at the apartment at her funeral.'

She took my hands. Any minute now, I thought, feeling manipulated and claustrophobic at her touch, yet ungrateful too, she'll just ask me straight out to complete the payments.

Quickly, loosening her grip on my hands, I got up. I knew I probably would end up paying for that recording, but I didn't want to be railroaded into agreeing to it now. I didn't want to agree as a result of the warmth I'd felt from her while she was wiping away my tears. I wanted it to be a sound decision, taken calmly.

'So that's something you'd like me to look into,' I said – smiling, but with infinitely more distance than a few minutes before, 'while I'm going through Grandmother's papers? Of course I will. And now . . .' I bowed my head again, trying to hide my disappointment behind at least a brittle imitation of politeness. 'Thank you . . . but I must run.'

But I happened to meet her eyes as I turned away, and was stricken by the panicky look of loss in them. Even if she was just manipulating my emotions to get me to pay for something, I could see she was also genuinely frightened of what lay ahead for her without that recording. And how kind – more than kind – she'd been.

I patted her shoulder as I passed. I didn't want to commit myself. But I didn't want to leave her without hope. 'Leave it with me,' I said. 'I'll try and work something out.'

31

General Miller was tweaking the points of his moustaches. How tiresome the boy could be: dogged and repetitive, with that angry look in his eye.

'So are you absolutely sure there are no secrets you should be telling me?'

Miller patted the air down under his hands at waist height, as if smoothing down his son's feelings and massaging them away. That had been all that was needed, once. For a moment, remembering, he felt nostalgia for the great simplicity of that time in the woods, when Jean had still been a skinny dark-haired urchin, soaking up that gesture with his great, burning, trusting eyes, pale as water, wanting nothing more than to believe everything Miller told him.

'No, don't do that,' Jean said now. 'Just answer me.'

Wondering rather uneasily if there were any way Jean could possibly have got wind of anything about his relationship with poor Constance, or even about the awkward visit yesterday from that girl, Constance's American relative – but no, that would be quite impossible, surely – Miller twirled his moustaches and smiled his blandest smile.

'I do wish, dear boy,' he said, 'that I could at least offer you a drink.'

Because, if he *were* to tell the other news, the news his professional mind was concentrating on, which was keeping at bay everything he might otherwise have allowed himself to feel about Constance's death, they'd want to raise a toast to the future, wouldn't they? And a proper toast, too, not a damn glass of milk.

'Father,' Jean said warningly. 'I can see in your eyes there's something. Come on.'

And so, in the end, he broadened his smile and began, 'Perceptive of you, dear boy, because, as a matter of fact, I *do* have some rather exciting news . . .' and he'd told him the whole story of the letter from Canaris, head of the Abwehr, offering German support to ROVS. The Germans behind us! Skoblin's hard work repaid! All we have to do is satisfy the two agents who are on their way to Paris, right now, that we've thought everything through; there'll be secret talks in the next few days and then an alliance against the Bolsheviks in time for the coming war – and, soon, Victory! The Future!

He couldn't say those phrases himself without skipping through the whole necessary-evil phase of war – planning, advances and all the rest of it – and straight on to imagining himself watching a vast, familiar, yearned-for panorama fade into twilight, and the tremendous satisfaction of smelling the moss and melancholy of a summer nightfall, where he belonged. The scent of the pines. A great hurrah.

But he couldn't say the phrases to Jean without a twinge of nervousness, either, because the boy had his own bookish views, learned from all those night courses he'd been on, no doubt, and those writers he was currently following around, which no doubt he'd grow out of in time – it was all a question of age and maturity, surely. But still, the boy and he didn't always see eye to eye on the really important questions, and the last thing he wanted, with something as important as this, was some foolish quarrel.

So he was already shaking his head and smiling warningly even before Jean began to speak, while his young eyes were still threatening and his fists clenching and unclenching, before he'd even got out that first ill-considered yelp: 'What – you don't really mean you're going to make a deal with the Nazis?'

Because, really, what could a boy know of high politics?

Jean

So *this* was the secret. Not a love affair, or not only. *This* was what Father and Skoblin had been muttering about the other night. I shouldn't be half this shocked. I should have guessed. They'd been angling for some sort of support from Germany for years. I'd just never thought for a moment that they had a hope in Hell. I should have been paying more attention.

For one appalled moment, I told myself that what Father was saying, with that foolish don't-oppose-me-dear-boy smile clamped on his face, must surely have been Skoblin's idea – or anyone's, anyone's, except his.

And then, before I could stop it, a mental picture of Evie imitating Father with a Hitler salute and the mocking words 'Herr Schickelgruber' flashed into my mind. She'd been right, then. Odious, vile, smug . . . but right. The thought made me hot with rage and cold with humiliation all at once; and, at the same time, filled me with a new protectiveness towards Father, who shouldn't be mocked like that; who, though misguided, was a good man, deep down.

With an effort, I put her out of my mind, knowing I could never speak to her again.

Or I tried. Because she was still lingering there, like an unquiet ghost, which meant that for a moment I actually thought of arguing against Father's plan on principle.

But then the hopelessness of it struck me. It would mean nothing to Father that I found the notion of that German alliance morally repulsive. He simply wouldn't hear if I started telling him what my friends, just out of Berlin, had been telling me – which, in my mind, I'd coalesced down to two or three images. Triumphant yobs in uniform picking out their victims; a bowed old man going down under their fists here; a window smashing into a thousand pieces there . . . Or Schickelgruber himself, spitting and howling at a crowd of fools under a giant swastika, turning that gentle land of music and philosophers and students into a brute wilderness where the bully-boy was king.

What was the point of trying? Father would just start going on about boys not understanding high politics, or talking lyrically about the power he saw in those displays of brutality: the number of tanks, the number of feet marching . . . I couldn't believe that was the heart of it, for him – not really – because I also knew that his real motivation – the strength of his yearning for that long-ago peacetime home I'd never known – was, genuinely, something I couldn't understand. I could only imagine how strong it was, because of what he was prepared to do to get it back. For

me, as an exile, imagining how Father felt about home was all working backwards – as if by seeing a shadow I could draw a picture of the object that had cast it. But, since I was tied to ROVS out of love for this stubborn old fool, I'd just have to try to understand his point of view, and tailor my counter-arguments accordingly.

So, when I said, 'Don't do it,' I tried to put my horror and anger aside, and keep things simple. I told him all the practical reasons I was frightened. I tried to appeal to his love.

I asked him: didn't he worry about all the rumours that Skoblin had a hand in the last kidnapping? I asked: what if his number two was a double agent for the Bolsheviks? And I said: what if this was a Red ambush?

But when I saw the coldness in Father's eyes, I saw that this was hopeless, too, and stopped, because he'd started again. If I can't persuade my son to work with me, I must have faith in my other friends, he was saying. Skoblin is a good man. Skoblin is much maligned. We are old, old comrades, together since Constantinople and the camps. It's dishonourable to think he might betray me in the way you suggest. I trust him absolutely.

There was no point in arguing. I knew from past experience that neither of us would change our minds. I let it wash over me. I'd heard it all before.

But it seemed worse today, our obstinate non-agreement – much more claustrophobic and depressing than usual. I didn't let myself think of Evie – or not exactly, not more than I needed to resolve that I wasn't going to betray Father like that again or expose him to her ridicule. But I was aware that what seemed so much worse was that, for the past few days, I'd believed there might be something else for me beyond the loneliness of living at one remove from all this. And now that was all closed off again, and there was just this, again, like prison gates clanging shut.

'I mean,' I said dispiritedly, 'don't do it *without telling me,* at least. Please.'

For some reason, that seemed to reach him. I could see his eyes smile. Perhaps, for once, he'd heard the unspoken declaration of love that was always in my voice. At any rate, he nodded and touched me briefly on the shoulder with his big hand.

'Do you know yet when the meeting will be? And where?' I went on. 'Can I take you?'

But no, he was already shaking his head, smiling that confident smile. I could see he didn't want me involved.

'As for the date, well, it all depends on when our German colleagues arrive, of course,' he said, and he couldn't keep the excitement out of his voice. 'All I know is that, when the time comes, Skoblin and I will slip off to meet them somewhere quiet . . . Passy . . . Auteuil . . . you know.'

The smartest bits of residential Paris, beyond the Trocadéro: retired ministers, countesses walking Pekes, big spreading trees, the rudest taxi clients. Everywhere was somewhere quiet in those secluded streets. 'Where?' I said.

'I don't know exactly where myself, dear boy,' Father said, and again I heard an unfamiliar note of weariness in his voice, as well as caginess. 'I think he might have said rue Jasmin, or rue Raffet, but I'm not really sure. I'm everyone's prisoner, as you know. That's all in Skoblin's hands. But now – I'm in yours. Will you take me home?'

I wanted to say something loving; something that

would dispel the fatigue in his voice, and show that, even if I detested the idea of the alliance he wanted to make, I supported *him* with every fibre of my being. Always had. Always would.

But I didn't know how, any more than I had words for the helpless, childish rage locked away inside me that he could be so indifferent to what I felt or wanted for him. Even if he was the family I'd chosen, the family I'd always choose, that was just how things were. There was no point in quibbling. So I nodded and picked up his briefcase.

My taxi-driving knowledge told me that there wasn't even a café on the rue Jasmin or the rue Raffet, which met each other between Passy and Auteuil: just old money and conventional good taste behind the shutters for as far as the eye could see in every direction. But, I was thinking, if I could find out when the planned meeting would take place, perhaps I could at least sit outside, in my cab, and keep watch till Father came out.

It was the last thing I wanted to be doing with my life. But I needed to keep busy. I needed not to think.

32

Evie

There was something a bit furtive in the way Marie-Thérèse looked up from the dish she was prodding with a skewer. A very large meaty object secured in a net was bubbling in a pan on top of the stove, in a broth seasoned with vegetables, parsley, peppercorns and salt. There was far too much of it for just me. But then I'd worked out, by now, that her cooking fed not only me, her and her husband, but also assorted other out-of-work family members: all those cousins and nephews who couldn't find jobs in the Billancourt car factories. I saw the casseroles in the pantry, lids tied on with string, waiting to be delivered, and sometimes I saw Gaston taking them out to the car or, of a morning, bringing back empties. Well, that was fine by me. I'd learned that the cuts of meat she chose for these cookathons were economical ones. I didn't particularly want to eat a whole calf's head myself anyway. And I knew these were hard times for many.

'Mm,' I said politely. 'That smells good.' I wanted to put her at her ease. But there was uncertainty in her answering nod.

'It won't be ready until dinner time,' she said, averting

her eyes. 'You need to boil it for at least five hours to be sure it's cooked.'

'Oh, I'm not hungry now,' I said quickly. Heavens, I'd only just had breakfast.

I wanted to ask her a quite different question. Something Plevitskaya had said yesterday about Grandmother had been coming back into my head all morning: '. . . her death so unexpected . . . when dear Constance was so full of life just a week ago.'

It had made me wonder: had Grandmother's stroke been brought on by a sudden shock?

For a while that morning, that thought, gloomy though it was, had at least been a distraction from the emptiness that not thinking about Jean kept leaving me with. But then an awful new thought had struck me – had the shock perhaps been the prospect of my arrival?

'I've been wondering,' I went on casually, 'what you think made Madame la Comtesse take ill so very suddenly . . . when, as everyone says, she was so full of life just before?'

Looking relieved, and suddenly interested, too, Marie-Thérèse put down the meat skewer. 'It *was* very sudden,' she said. 'I've wondered that myself. As if something had happened to bring it on. But, you know, mademoiselle, there was nothing . . .'

Leaning against the cooker, she added reflectively, 'She was in the study that evening, where the young men had been working with that machine. *Ah, cette musique!* Playing the same tune over and over again, far too loud – enough to make anyone ill, you'd think; *my* head was certainly aching from it. But *she* was fine; she didn't seem to mind it in the least. Then, that last evening, after they'd gone, she took her apéritif in there – well, it's the best place to watch the sunset from. She was right as rain when I took it in – even asked me to make up a bed for you and get Gaston to meet your train, nice as anything. But then, just a few minutes afterwards, she came staggering out, calling for me. I could hear at once that her voice wasn't right. I rushed out from your room, where I was making up your bed. But she'd already collapsed, right there in the doorway, before I'd got halfway down the corridor.'

She nodded, not without gloomy satisfaction. 'So you see,' she finished, 'there can't have been a reason. It just happened, from one moment to the next; the will of the Lord.'

I nodded back, feeling fractionally reassured that Marie-Thérèse had at least said Grandmother had sounded calm when she'd told her I was arriving in Paris.

'But of course it was those men coming back the next morning that finished her off,' Marie-Thérèse added crossly. 'The Russian thieves.'

Well, I thought dispiritedly, not wanting to argue, it did look as though, this time at least, she must be right. Those men *had* just taken their chance and pinched the machine.

It was painful for me to remember that morning's commotion – the shouting and barging, and Marie-Thérèse's hiss of '*Sacrés Russes!*' as the door slammed behind them. I'd never forget it, because that was also the moment when, behind the bedroom door, Grandmother had woken up, and had her second, fatal attack. I was never going to be able to banish the horror in her face, the hand flapping, her agonized 'MMMM!' and the pandemonium that had followed, or the way I'd failed to listen; the way I'd run away.

But right now the person I felt sorriest for was Plevitskaya

– because the only real loser from that morning's theft was her and her recording, which had vanished with the machine. She must have thought, when we'd last spoken, that I could get the recording back and have it finished. She must think I had the machine. But I didn't. It had gone with the engineer thieves. She'd never have her disc.

I sighed. On second thoughts, the person I felt sorriest for now was myself.

Leaving Marie-Thérèse to her pots, I wandered back to my bedroom, taking stock.

There was no Grandmother in Paris, no cosy friendship with the General, no cosy friendship with Plevitskaya either (she'd really only been so nice to me to get her recording finished, I could see now), and no Jean – nothing but dead ends.

What I should have said to Marie-Thérèse when I went into the kitchen just now was that I was giving her and Gaston notice. (Details were running through my head at a great pace. I'd give them wages until Christmas; she could have Grandmother's fur coat; would it be absurd to give Gaston the car?) Only cowardice had stopped me, or inertia – the same inertia that had stopped me even thinking of wiring the family news of Grandmother's death (which I now saw, in a sudden, separate agony of self-reproach, had been terribly wrong, because however estranged Mother had been from her, she'd surely have wanted to be told that her own mother had died. Anyone would). Now was the time to face up to these things, because, whatever anyone said when I got home, and however much I might be dreading my return, I had to accept that there was nothing left to do here but get ready to leave.

33

It didn't take long. Even with Grandmother's box, and the photo, and the book I'd written my scrappy translations of those letters into, I didn't have much.

When my box was closed, I pulled it into the study. What I should do soon, I knew, was to sit down and write to Mother to set her mind at rest about me and tell her about Grandmother. Not just a wire; a proper letter. But I couldn't quite face that yet. So I was relieved when I realized I could keep busy, for now, by making a list of the pictures Grandmother had left me. I'd get a piece of paper from the desk, number them, give the list to Marie-Thérèse, and ask her to get them crated up and shipped after me.

Organizing the actual shipping of the pictures wasn't something I needed to do myself. But I'd go out in a minute and ask Gaston to take me to the shipping office to pay for everything, and for my ticket. I could probably be on the train to Le Havre tonight.

For a moment, I stood looking round, wishing all this had ended differently.

I walked over to the big expanse of desk. It was spotless, with two chairs drawn up against it.

I tried to imagine it covered in a clutter of whirring machinery, with those two men I'd heard sitting at these chairs wearing big headphones. I could still see the socket on the wall which they must have plugged the equipment into, because the electric cable from the nearer desk lamp, which would normally be plugged in there, was still trailing uselessly along the floor. Marie-Thérèse must have forgotten to put it back.

Kneeling down myself I plugged it into the wall.

It was only when I was down on my knees, on the parquet floor, that I saw the other wire. It had been pushed along the small gap between floor and skirting board. Only the end was sticking out.

At first I just thought it was an uncharacteristic piece of mess in the otherwise immaculate room. Gingerly – what if it was still connected to something? What if it gave me an electric shock? – I pulled. Several feet of cable came out from the wall: enough, I could see, without even trying, to stretch comfortably to the desk.

At the wall end, this dark-coloured cable, which you could hardly see against the brown of the parquet, went right into the floor, a few inches below the electric socket in the skirting board.

I shuffled closer to the wall, intrigued despite myself. From here I could see that the two oblongs of parquet next to the wall were no longer properly glued down to the floor. They were just lying there, held by the other pieces around them, like loose bits in a jigsaw puzzle. Turning to reach for a paper knife from the desk, I ran the blade round one of them. It flipped up easily.

A small square had been cut in the floorboard

underneath, and the dark-brown wire ran down through that square into the ceiling of the room one floor below.

I knew what that room was. I'd been in it. It was General Miller's private office.

I hadn't taken seriously those stories Jean had told me about the Soviet agents circling his father's office, waiting to attack. But now I sat back on my haunches, with the piece of parquet still in one hand and the paper knife in the other, looking slowly from the end of the wire that disappeared downwards, then back to the end that would reach so easily to the desk.

Then, feeling increasingly uneasy, I got up, put down the things in my hand, picked up the other end of the wire and walked with it to the desk. When I sat down at the desk with it still in my hand, I could see that it really was a perfect length to come just to about *here* . . . the exact place where a machine might have been placed on the mahogany surface. There were even dents in the cable at the end of the desk and at the floor, indicating exactly how it had lain.

But there was no way of seeing how the wire would have plugged into anything. Not any more. The end of the cable in my hand had no fitting. It had been cut – one neat, quick knife stroke. The men who'd taken the machinery away had been in a hurry, all right.

I felt suddenly sick. Whether those young Russian men with the recording equipment had been editing a recording of Plevitskaya's voice at all now seemed in doubt. The only thing that this wire showed for sure was that they'd definitely been doing something else, too – using Grandmother's study to spy on the General's office downstairs.

It made a whole different, and more sinister, kind of sense

of the way the two men had just grabbed their stuff and rushed off with it so hastily as soon as Marie-Thérèse tried to shut them out of the apartment, saying Grandmother was ill. If they were spies, they would have wanted to clear their equipment out. They'd say: better safe than sorry; and make off.

Other thoughts came pounding into my mind.

Had Grandmother sat in here, on that evening, looking at this wire, and putting two and two together just as I was now doing? Was it this discovery that had brought on her *crise*?

And had it been the return of those two men, the next morning, which had brought on her second, fatal seizure? When she'd started trying to speak, buzzing with the sound she couldn't quite get out, and I'd rushed out of the room to fetch the housekeeper, mustn't she have wanted me, *someone*, to stay with her, and listen, and understand?

I couldn't feel sorry for Plevitskaya any more either – not at all. She'd got this equipment in here, in the first place, playing on Grandmother's pity and affection – so she must have been involved, mustn't she?

And then everything became clear. I got up.

It didn't matter what Plevitskaya's role had been. I didn't have time to worry about her.

The only real point was General Miller. Someone was spying on him. I didn't have to work out who it was. But I did have to hurry.

I realized, with something like relief, that all I needed to do was to find Jean and, whether or not he wanted to speak to me, tell him what I knew – that his father was in danger.

It might also have been, I thought, remembering her urgent moan of 'MMMM . . .' ('Miller?'), what Grandmother had wanted to tell me.

34

Nadya Plevitskaya had got up early to curl her hair. She was wearing a ruched dress with red flowers on a black background and, under her chic Wallis Simpson hat, big gold hoop earrings. It was hot enough, even by the end of breakfast, to make her rather regret the black linen jacket she'd added to the ensemble. But she'd put a big red chrysanthemum in the buttonhole, which looked festive, and the jacket did, at least, cover up the bulges at either end of her corset.

Throughout the long-drawn-out breakfast on the sunny *terrasse* of the rue du Colisée café, she flirted cheerfully with the proprietor and various fellow clients. After commenting that her husband was not fond of too much talk this early in the day, even on a holiday like this, when they were off to select stage outfits for her from no less a personage than Monsieur Epstein of Chez Caroline, she sent out a waiter for a newspaper for him to read while she talked and breakfasted. When the young man returned with *Le Figaro*, she looked at it in playful horror before saying that she couldn't possibly let her husband read the thoughts of a perfume manufacturer – and, to gales of sycophantic laughter from the proprietor, sent the waiter breathlessly back out again for *La Croix*.

'That's women for you, eh, Jacquot!' the proprietor chuckled, slapping his nephew on the shoulders, the second time back. She was doing a magnificent job, she thought, and holding half the street's attention: teeth flashing, laughter pealing out – unlike her uncharismatic husband, who was barely even trying. The only time anyone could have told that *he* wasn't actually dead was when he'd held out a hand for the paper.

She drank three bowls of chocolate. She dipped a *tartine* with strawberry jam into her first milky drink (until she caught her husband's glance up from *La Croix*, at least). Then (to hell with her figure, and her husband) she ate two more croissants.

The sun rose. She was damp under her black jacket. She waved her hands around flamboyantly enough that, from time to time, without seeming to be looking, she caught a glimpse of the time. How slowly the hands on her watch seemed to be moving.

'*Bozhe*,' she cried when, eventually, they said ten o'clock. 'Is that the time already?' And she rose, without waiting for her husband, and sailed off down the street towards the waiting car.

The last thing she expected was for the American girl – who, as she only noticed too late, had been running in her direction – to cannon into her in the street.

Not by accident, either. The girl, who was a good six inches taller than she was, grabbed her by both shoulders.

She had none of yesterday's forlorn, crossed-in-love charm. She was panting and indignant. Good God, Plevitskaya thought, disconcerted, she's making straight for me; and she looks as though she's about to *shake* me . . .

She glanced quickly behind. Her husband – never there when you wanted him – was still on the *terrasse*, folding up the paper and waiting for his change.

'I found the wires,' the girl was stammering, so angry she could hardly get the words out. Plevitskaya didn't know what she was talking about. Politely, she tried to wriggle herself free. But the girl was clutching on to her shoulder pads for grim death.

Then, practically spitting into her face, the girl went on furiously: 'Wires down through the floor to the General's room. Was your recording – the one you wanted me to pay for – something to do with spying on ROVS?'

'No!' Plevitskaya said. 'Of course not!'

And, in the breathy silence that followed, she took advantage of the girl's look of doubt – and weakened grip – to shake herself loose.

Well, really, she was telling herself – feeling indignant, too – recording or no recording, whoever did this girl think she was? Why, she'd never been manhandled like that in her life . . .

And then, just as she was puffing herself up into a fluff of hurt pride and shock, she realized what the American girl must mean. Wires – from the recording equipment.

She stopped. Blackness flooded through her: a depth of cold rage such as she'd never known.

Was *that* the real reason why her husband had been so helpful about persuading Constance to have the recording edited at her home? Just so he could bug Miller for the Moscow team, before the kidnapping?

When she glanced around again and saw him, newspaper folded under his arm, finally sauntering up the street towards her, smiling as if butter wouldn't melt in his mouth, she was appalled at the certainty she suddenly felt.

Of course it was. Moscow wouldn't have invested all this effort and money in her husband just on trust. They'd have wanted him to lead from the front. They'd have wanted him to prove he was ready to betray Miller himself.

Which meant that the recording that she'd invested so much hope in, but he'd dreamed up, had just been a ploy – a Trojan horse, to get wires into Constance's apartment.

He hadn't given a hoot about her career. He'd been playing dirty tricks on her, all along, as surely as he had on that fat old fool Miller. And here she was, helping him out.

Suddenly all she wanted was to walk away, and for the whole thing to fail. Why should she care? If it all went wrong today, she'd end up in Moscow. And she'd a million times rather be there, looking for her son, than propping up her snake of a husband here.

She gazed back at the American girl, with her mouth half-open, listening to those unhurried footsteps coming up behind her, bursting with words – but too painfully full of all the contradictory things she wanted to say to be able to manage a single one.

And then she sighed, and the words all went away, because it was too late. She thought of the crab salesman, and knew she was afraid. She'd have to go through with it after all.

'Mademoiselle,' her husband said, with a formal bow and smile to the stunned-looking American girl (who didn't challenge *him*, she noticed). She felt his arm slip through hers. With dreamlike dignity, she nodded, too.

As they moved slowly off, she heard herself saying almost apologetically to the American girl in whom she'd so nearly, for that one moment of insanity, confided, 'You see, I have an appointment at the dressmaker's.'

35

Evie

I hadn't meant to go rushing up to Plevitskaya. But when she appeared, right in front of me, I saw red. All that sweetness, yesterday; all that concern . . . I could still remember how comforted I'd felt by her embrace. And all the time she was part of something so unspeakably awful as spying on General Miller. I couldn't help myself.

But it felt like a dream, my moment of anger, because nothing came of it. She and her husband just went smoothly off, with their arms linked, leaving me standing there.

Except . . .

Except, now that I came to think of it, that when I'd first mentioned the wire she'd looked, for a moment, as shocked as I'd felt when I'd first seen it. And then she'd turned and glanced at Skoblin coming up behind, with his meek little half-smile and his paper.

And when she'd turned back to me, her face had changed. Could she have been scared?

I was standing in the street with the sun beating down on me. But, when I now called to mind the face of Skoblin – the neatly combed, thinnish hair, its once-black colour turning to iron; the small moustache and quiet eyes – I suddenly felt cold.

Perhaps it had been *his* presence that had frozen me. He knew ROVS. He knew spying. And she, after all, had had every reason to want the recording completed. Wasn't *he* likelier than his wife to have wanted to do this, and known how?

I couldn't make it out. But I had a vague sense, even then, out there in the innocence of the hot Paris morning, that just beyond my inner fog of incomprehension, a new landscape of unimaginable deceit might be about to loom into view.

I was still standing, transfixed, when I heard the sound I'd been waiting for.

A taxi drew up in front of Grandmother's building. I saw Jean get out and go to the passenger door.

'Jean!' I called, rushing towards him. 'General Miller!'

I was a good hundred feet away. As I ran, I saw the General rise above the chassis, look in my direction and then, with irritation and embarrassment plain on his face as he saw who was calling out, hasten off towards the front door. 'Wait!' I called, frantically waving. 'Please!' But he was fiddling with his key, and looking away.

The door clicked shut behind him just as I reached the taxi.

I would have let myself into the building behind him and banged on the door of ROVS until they answered, but Jean stepped in front of me and barred my way.

'Please,' I panted, hardly daring to look into those blue eyes. I had my hands on the tensed muscles of his upper arms. He was so close that I could smell soap and

the cigarettes of the station café on him. 'We need—'

'Just leave him alone,' he interrupted with cold anger. 'Let him get on with his work.'

I let go of him. 'You don't understand,' I said desperately. 'Please don't go.'

He looked at me then. He stopped. Waited.

'It's not about me, I promise,' I went on, trying to make my voice steady and persuasive. 'It's about *him*. He's being bugged.'

Jean rolled his eyes to the heavens and turned on his heel.

'No!' I cried. 'I've found a wire.'

He'd already opened his car door by the time what I'd said sank in.

Then he stopped.

'What wire?'

It took what seemed forever to persuade him to come up and see for himself. I was all fingers and thumbs with the keys and locks and handles.

But when I did finally get him into the study, and pulled out the wire, and held it so he could see how it had been cut through the floorboards and fed down into his father's study ceiling, he stopped scowling and looking sceptical.

Instead he went very quiet.

Then he came over to where I was standing, and – quite gently – took the wire out of my hands. He tugged a little. But it was attached to something under the floor. It didn't come loose.

'I thought', I whispered, 'that it must have been connected with the recording they were editing up here; you know, of Plevitskaya's voice.'

He took no notice of me. He just stared at the wire.

'Because,' I went stammering on, feeling foolish, 'even if the other end has been cut, you can see it was just the right length to have reached the machine . . .'

He looked up, straight at me. I knew this wasn't the moment for personal feelings, but I still couldn't help a pang of joyful relief when I saw that he wasn't angry any more – at least not with me. His eyes said, as clearly as anything, 'I now see that you're not just meddling.' But some other emotion had overwhelmed him. He was searching for words.

'The meeting's a trap,' he said. I stared back, lost. He didn't explain – not, that is, unless a quick, appalled headshake and a mutter of 'Skoblin' counted as an explanation.

'Skoblin,' I repeated, wishing he hadn't looked away again. 'Because it's his wife's recording? Yes, that's what *I* thought, too . . .' But Jean was shaking his head and looking sick.

He threw down the wire, grabbed my hand and started pulling me towards the door. In spite of everything, I was grateful to feel his skin against mine.

'I'll explain,' he said breathlessly. By then we were clattering downstairs and into the ROVS office. 'I've got to talk to Father.'

We charged in through the front door, hand in hand, barging past the bewildered man who'd opened the door, and through the room full of uniformed secretaries typing at their desks – who all stopped and stared – and down the short corridor to the General's room.

No one bothered with translating. '*Gdye Ghe-nye-RAL?*'

Jean called loudly over his shoulder, or that's what it sounded like; and – though it was a shock to hear him speaking Russian – even I could more or less understand when the young men, pointing towards their boss's office, started rising to their feet with the beginning of alarm. I could hear their footsteps, following ours.

But as soon as we opened the door it was clear we were too late.

The French windows at the back of his office – the ones opening on to the courtyard, from which you could sneak out of the service door into the back alley – were open, and the dingy muslin drapes were blowing in the wind. We stepped in with the young men following us. But the room was empty. General Miller had left.

It was only in the aftermath – once Jean started yelling in panicky Russian, and the young men started shouting, too, and then two of them chased out through the courtyard to see if they couldn't stop the General somewhere further down the street, if he hadn't gone far, while a third rushed to the phone and began calling, all with interruptions and orders from Jean – that, at last, he started explaining. It was only then that I heard what Jean was suddenly so frantic with anxiety about.

First, Skoblin had been planning a meeting between his master and two German agents. It had been supposed to be so hush-hush that none of the secretaries knew. Jean had pestered the secret out of him, as well as a vague sort of address. He had sensed his father was still holding back on him, but thought that was only because they both knew *he* so disapproved of the whole notion of the alliance with the Nazis that his father so wanted. ('And not just me – I was imagining what *you* would say, too,' he added, shaking his head. He didn't quite look at me.)

Now that Jean had seen that someone, and it must be Skoblin, was also behind the clandestine bugging of the General's office, this planned rendezvous – which was about the only thing, except Grandmother's funeral, that would have lured his father out of the safety of his office – was taking on a still more sinister colouring. This one extra piece of knowledge made it seem all too likely that the talk of a secret meeting had, all along, been just a ploy to get the General out of his office. Skoblin might have other masters, maybe even Soviet Moscow.

The two young men soon came back, looking frightened. It was obvious they hadn't found the General. I'd had no time to form an opinion of the General's startling intention of forming a pact with the Nazi government before hearing the equally startling information that the plan had probably never existed outside his own head, and Skoblin's.

I sank down on to one of the leather armchairs in the secretaries' room, to keep out of the way of all the pacing and scurrying. The returning young men rushed to their phones, too. They picked them up, but even I could see they didn't know whom to call. They waited, with the earpieces up and hands poised, mutely asking for instruction. They were underlings, I could see, and there was no fight in them, now there was no one left to give commands.

'Jean,' I said, putting a hand on his arm.

He raised his head a fraction and looked at me with blank, appalled eyes.

'Do you remember the address your father told you?' I asked.

He nodded, and his eyes quickened with relief. Perhaps he was tired, I thought. This was when he'd normally go to sleep, after his night-long job driving. But I could see his purpose returning.

'Go there,' I said. 'Now. Go in the taxi. See if you can get there in time to stop them.'

He stood up. 'Will you come?'

It was a request. His voice was humble. I could hear he wanted me with him.

'No,' I said, because I could still hear Plevitskaya's voice saying, 'I have an appointment at the dressmaker's.' 'I'm going to find Nadya Plevitskaya. She knows about this, I'm sure.'

36

I knew where Plevitskaya and her husband had had breakfast. And I knew she was a talker. So, as soon as I'd found out from the café owner which couturier she'd been boasting of visiting, I jumped in a taxi myself, and followed.

Of course it was a long shot. But I couldn't believe that the woman who had embraced me so tenderly yesterday, who'd briefly been so full of sorrow and understanding – whom I'd so wanted to trust – could have been plotting something so evil. And what I was counting on was that fleeting look of shock and uncertainty that I'd surprised on her face earlier: the possibility it seemed to hold out that, if she *were* involved in all this, she might in some way be willing to talk to me.

All mixed up in my tumult of feeling, as I slammed the door of the cab and sat, perched on the edge of my seat, willing the driver forward, was the flickering possibility of a rage more intense than anything I'd ever experienced – because if Plevitskaya *had* been sitting at the restaurant with me, drying my tears, holding my hand, hugging me, reminiscing, talking about her pain at losing a child she loved and ordering up champagne, when all along she was

302

planning to steal the man Jean loved so much . . . why then, it was betrayal of the most unforgivable kind.

My knuckles tightened to white points as I clutched the car seat.

Chez Caroline turned out to be on one of the twelve opulent avenues that radiate out from the place de l'Étoile. As we turned off from the Arc de Triomphe, I recalled the pride in Jean's voice when he'd told me, on an earlier drive along the Champs-Élysées to this central tourist point, about its Russian connections with the past. The great white arch had been commissioned by Napoleon in 1806 to celebrate winning the Battle of Austerlitz, but had then been abandoned, half-finished, for many years, because soon afterwards Napoleon had been forced into retreat and defeat after trying to conquer Russia in 1812. My heart wrenched with pity at the memory.

My taxi drove quite a long way down the broad, tree-lined avenue Victor-Hugo towards Passy; I should have gone with Jean after all, I was thinking as we got caught up in a slow-moving crowd of honking taxis, between towering *hôtels particuliers* in grey-white stone with delicate wrought-iron balconies. Then, on a suddenly empty stretch of road with no cars parked for several yards in either direction, my driver stopped and let me out.

I'd been half expecting pink fur bears, dresses with trompe-l'oeil drawers for pockets, necklines trimmed with lobsters – the alarmingly avant-garde Surrealist Paris fashion scene that New York magazines were always writing about. But instead I found myself in front of a small, expensive-looking but respectable store, just right for this neighbourhood. It was the kind of place I could imagine my mother enjoying. Under an awning on which the word 'CAROLINE' was written in dignified capitals, its window contained a single slender dummy kitted out in quite conventional evening glitter: a black ball gown with an ugly, over-sequinned halter neck, and a glistening mink wrap above. Still, my heart was pounding as I rang the bell.

An intimidatingly groomed and very tall young woman answered.

I took one look at her supercilious expression, recognized her type, and decided not to rush in with any explanations about wanting to have a frank and perhaps unpleasant conversation with one of her clients whom I thought might be inside.

'*Bonjour, mademoiselle,*' I began instead, stepping smartly forward as I started on my alternative story about the imaginary party for which I had no dress, and how struck I'd been by the *chic* of the pre-assembled *ensemble* in the window, which would go so splendidly with my diamond earrings. Even if I had no appointment, did she think I might, just possibly, try that dress and mink stole on?

I kept my accent almost laughably American throughout on the assumption – correct, as it turned out – that, however haughty the shop assistant might appear, the thought of the mighty greenback I represented would persuade her to let me in.

Finally, after careful examination of the quality of my shoes, bag and dress – I'd never been so grateful for that understated dress Mother had bought me – she nodded, sweetened visibly and led me up to the first floor. We entered a high-ceilinged, chandeliered salon that took up the entire space. Its walls were done out in pale-grey velvet panels, with knick-knacks and armchairs everywhere, in the manner of a luxurious private home. I could hear conversation from two remote corners of the room, each screened off by a small fence of Chinese lacquer-work.

After moving another Chinese screen around the armchair she'd arranged me in and taking a few tape-measurements, she wafted off, now all flirtatious smiles and come-hitherishness, promising to have a glass of champagne sent to me while she found the clothes I wanted to see modelled.

Knowing I'd have a good five or ten minutes before she reappeared before me, wearing the dress herself, no doubt with elbow-length evening gloves and possibly a cigarette holder, I applied myself to listening as hard as I could to the conversations coming from behind the other screens. There were two stages to this buying process: first the sales model sashaying around, looking magnificently bored yet perfect in a long, slim version of the chosen outfit; then the customer trying a wider, shorter model. The screens were intended to spare everyone's blushes if the effect, at that second stage, was less alluring than the designer had intended.

I needed to establish where Plevitskaya was, but, for the moment, all I could hear was everyday sales patter – 'The line, you see, so fluid . . .' and 'The stuff, *chère madame*, so fine . . .' – which didn't give the slightest clue as to the identity of the customer.

And then, suddenly, I intuited which was the right conversation. Not because Plevitskaya herself had spoken – her deep Russian rumble would have been an unmistakeable giveaway – but just because of the excessively sycophantic tone the entourage was taking. '*Ça, c'est magnifique!*' a man's voice was cooing, delightedly, while lesser female voices echoed, '*Ah oui! Épatant, madame!*' and '*Ça alors!*'

What that told me was that Plevitskaya must be on the second, try-it-yourself stage, and require theatrical adulation. Quietly I got to my feet and sneaked out round the edge of my lacquer screen.

I peeped through the slit between the two panels and, sure enough, there was Plevitskaya, pirouetting in front of a mirror in a long gold dress whose intended slinky line was so interrupted by the billows of flesh in her centre that it was hard to tell how it had originally been meant to hang. She was absorbed in contemplation of herself.

I could see from her expression in the glass that she was enjoying the praise from her audience. Infuriatingly, and quite against my will, I found myself warming to her childlike showing-off. I could see, too, that she was red-faced and almost unable to breathe for holding her tummy in, and – from the dissatisfied sideways glances she kept giving her reflection – uncomfortably aware of the way the surplus flesh on her exposed upper arms was drooping and quivering.

'There! The stole, just a *little* lower, madame,' the perfumed salesman sang, tweaking the near-transparent white silk oblong she had round her neck down over her arms. Plevitskaya noticeably relaxed as the offending portion of blancmange-like flesh, now modestly covered, disappeared from view.

'Maybe', she said flirtatiously, after another long consideration of herself, and a further chorus of praise from all around, 'I should step outside and show this to my husband, too. What do you think, Monsieur Epstein?'

There! I told myself. We must be wrong! Skoblin must be somewhere here, after all.

The relief was tremendous. I'd go back to ROVS, and the General would be sitting with Jean, and there'd be laughter everywhere and—

I was actually looking around, as though I'd suddenly see Skoblin hidden behind a newspaper on one of these genteel chaises longues, when I heard the salesman's reedy laugh. 'Poor man, waiting in the car all this time,' he was saying. 'Your husband is a patient man, madame – but the husbands of beautiful women have to learn patience.'

The sheer outrageousness of that piece of flattery brought my attention sharply back to the group behind the screen, because I had a clear memory that there had been no one waiting outside in a car, and definitely no Skoblin. The street had been empty.

If Plevitskaya was making out that her husband was here, just outside, then she was lying.

The hurt, angry rage I'd felt earlier came closer.

I needed to catch her in this lie. And I needed to do it right now, because I was also uncomfortably aware of the sound, approaching me from behind, of a pair of high heels clacking over the parquet. It was my saleswoman with my glass of champagne. There was no time to lose.

Boldly, I put my head round the screen.

'Aha, so it *is* you – I *thought* that was your voice!' I said brightly, and moved forward to kiss Plevitskaya on both cheeks to establish, in the eyes of our audience, that we were friends.

There was, however, no trace of the faintly friendly hesitation I'd sensed earlier in her; none of yesterday's tearful fondness either. It was obvious she just didn't want me here.

When I went on, still brightly but with determination, the others all began to look a bit worried, too. 'General Miller's vanished, did you know?' I said, keeping my eyes on her, aware of the awkward movements all around as the sales staff – now joined by a new six-foot beauty with a brimming champagne glass on a tray – started registering how uncomfortable this newcomer was making their client. 'His men are all out looking for him. His son Jean's gone to the rue Jasmin, not far from here. He thinks your husband was taking him there to meet some men from Germany.'

Plevitskaya stuck out her chin as I eyeballed her. I could see she was going to fight. 'Germany? No!' she said, shaking her head vigorously but also giving me the sort of defiant smirk that someone always does give when they see a way of saying something that isn't – quite – a lie.

Something clicked inside me and the world went light and hot and red. I'd never dared openly confront a woman of my mother's age before. But now I had the General in mind, with his whiskers and beard and pot belly – a flesh-and-blood elderly man under that fancy uniform, with many weaknesses and blind spots, for sure, but someone Jean loved, and Grandmother had, too. He was probably bleeding in a sack somewhere, while Plevitskaya blithely

tried on gold dresses. It was overwhelming, how angry I suddenly was. I'd do anything to force her to tell me the truth.

Plevitskaya, though, was giving her Monsieur Epstein a look that said, perfectly clearly: Please get rid of this annoying interloper. Throwing out one arm in a magnificent (if quivering) gesture, she told me, with a smile that now seemed utterly false, 'My husband is *here*, as it happens; he is just outside in the car, waiting . . .'

'No he isn't,' I said. 'The street is empty.'

And I pulled back the linen at the window to make my point.

Plevitskaya stayed right where she was. But Monsieur Epstein looked down. So did the women. So did the girl with the champagne glass. They let their eyes follow my arm, pointing dramatically down to the empty kerb.

For a long, embarrassed moment, Monsieur Epstein just wriggled like a butterfly stuck on a pin.

'Ah, well, Monsieur Skoblin will no doubt have finished his paper and gone to buy another,' he finally said with a nervous giggle. Given what he'd just told Plevitskaya about the husbands of beautiful women having to learn patience, he could hardly suggest, without insulting his client's appearance, that her husband had simply got bored and gone off. Clearly trying to get his bearings again in this confusing conversation, he turned to his client and put a hand on her arm. 'I suppose we *have* been a long time, you and I, *chère madame* . . .'

I could see he was about to have me thrown out for upsetting his client, who was so close to buying that hideous gold dress. There was definite hostility in his eyes when he turned back to me. In all their eyes, in fact: the saleswomen looked as though they'd happily stick hatpins in me to make me disappear. For a cowardly moment, I almost let myself be distracted by the idea of these lovely creatures manhandling me out.

Then, catching myself losing my resolve, I forced myself to be braver and look straight into Plevitskaya's face. I read guilt in her eyes, but also a defiance that made plain she didn't intend to tell me anything.

Catching her other arm, and trying to stop my voice trembling, I pleaded, 'If you know anything, I beg you to help. Jean is beside himself. He thinks the General's been kidnapped by Soviet agents – that good man, who's been so like a father to him.'

Plevitskaya snorted, and – another proof of guilt, I felt – ignored the key word 'Soviet', which had made the rest of the audience catch each other's eyes. 'Ah, I can see you don't know any of the people you're talking about very well, mademoiselle – because our General *is* the father of the young man you're talking about.'

'No, he's not,' I angrily corrected her. 'He adopted him in the war, which is why I think Jean loves him *more* than most people love their fathers – because he *saved* Jean, back then, in some army camp in the forest in Russia. And so Jean would be distraught if anything happened to him. Surely you can understand this?'

I paused, aware that the shop assistants were looking in puzzlement from one to the other of us. They didn't know whom to believe. Be braver, I told myself. Be simpler. There's nothing she can do to you, after all. Stop saying 'Jean's upset' and tell them what *you* think.

'*I* also believe your husband is part of a kidnap plot,' I said loudly, 'and I think you know about it.'

Even Plevitskaya was gazing straight back at me now, with wide, shocked eyes.

'Adopted him where?' she asked.

'I think near Kursk?' I replied stupidly, before realizing this was just another diversion. She was trying to change the subject again. I shook my head, and tightened my grip on her, feeling the soft material of her dress crease under my hands.

'That's why I'm asking, please, Madame Plevitskaya,' and I could hear now how imploring my voice had got, 'to stop General Miller being kidnapped. If there's anything you know, anything at all, then *please . . .*'

I gulped. I wasn't acting at all. That half-sob had just come out.

'Zyzyrovka,' Plevitskaya said into the lengthening silence. Her voice was flat. Then her eyes flickered, and she looked away.

'I must find my husband,' she said suddenly, as if she'd made a decision. 'Monsieur Epstein, please.'

Hastily, he undid the pins, and she went behind the screen. None of us could look at each other any more. The couture-house people weren't going to help me, I could see – well, it had been naive to hope they might step in and clap handcuffs on her. I knew that, really.

A few moments later, she emerged in a black-and-red flowery dress, doing it up as she walked past us, without a word to or a look at anyone. Her shoes were in her hand.

It was only when she'd reached the door that I realized she was off, without even her jacket.

'Hey!' I called. The door slammed. I ran after her. But by the time I reached the street, she was already getting into a taxi. As luck would have it, there were no others at the rank. 'Rue de Grenelle,' I heard her say, swinging herself inside. 'Number 79.'

There was nothing I could do but stand in the midday sun and watch the taxi head into town.

When, a few minutes later, another taxi drew up, the first thing I asked was, 'What's at 79 rue de Grenelle?' I had decided to follow her there, and catch her with Skoblin.

It was only when the driver answered, with a scratch of the head, 'The Soviet embassy, mademoiselle; is that where you want to go?' that I finally gave up.

'No,' I said, 'I need to go home.'

37

Plevitskaya sat very still in the taxi until, after it had crossed the pont de l'Alma and turned along the Left Bank, down the tree-dappled quai d'Orsay, she bent down and put on her painful shoes.

She wasn't watching the traffic, or the glitter on the Seine, or the fishermen on the banks, or the *bateaux-mouches*.

If it all goes wrong, go to the Soviet embassy and ask for the crab salesman, she was repeating to herself, inside her head.

Well, now that the American girl's interference had prevented her from establishing her husband's alibi, it *had* all gone wrong.

But still, this taxi journey was the last one in the world she wanted to be making.

She shut her eyes, feeling sick, when she thought of the crab salesman. No, it was unbearable to think of *his* reaction . . .

She could hardly bear to think of her husband, either, who wasn't even aware yet of how wrong it had all gone, so would be turning up at the gare du Nord in an hour, as planned, as part of the group waving General Kutyopov's daughter off on a train ride. She winced as she imagined how he'd be expecting her to join him there, so they could go on making a show in front of the others of having been enjoying a jolly day out together all the while, and talking loudly about their purchases from Monsieur Epstein.

It would only be when everyone started asking, 'But where is your wife, Nikolasha?' that he'd begin to guess. Then he'd have to get in his own taxi, and head with all haste towards embassy-land and, later, she supposed, the hold of the freight ship *Maria Ulyanova*. But even this was in doubt, because what if someone had already had the wit to get the police out to the gare du Nord to arrest him?

She felt sicker still when pictures of the inside of the *Maria Ulyanova*, chugging through grey waters to Leningrad, started crowding into her mind. Would they have to see Miller again, in there? Would he look at them, from above his gag and bound hands, with eyes full of hurt and hate? Or, and now she began to feel really sick, might they all end up gagged and bound, she and her husband just as tightly as Miller, and all being delivered, at the other end, in the same van marked 'bread' or 'milk' to the Lubyanka? When she called to mind the crab salesman's quiet eyes, anything seemed possible.

That she could ever have hoped for today's project to fail now seemed unimaginable. That she could ever have wanted to be sent back to Moscow felt insane.

She laced the fingers of her hands together, and squeezed them tight to stave off panic.

She'd thought she might search for her son if she got home to Russia, hadn't she? But what if he'd been gone for years, just as she had? What if he'd emigrated?

It had never occurred to her, until today, that he might have left too. Never, until that damn girl had started talking about Miller, and about his son – whom she was so clearly in love with – and Plevitskaya had remembered Zyzyrovka, where she'd lost *her* son . . .

'What's that you say, madame?' the taxi driver asked.

It was only then that Plevitskaya realized she must, without intending to, have muttered the place name out loud.

'Nothing,' she said. And then, 'No! I meant, I was saying, let me out here. I've changed my mind. I'm not going on.'

A moment later, she was standing alone on the pont Alexandre III, with its exuberant art nouveau lamps, cherubs, nymphs and winged horses, with its foundation stone somewhere far below the waters which had been laid by the last Tsar, long before he'd known he'd be murdered. She watched the taxi she'd just been sitting in dwindle and disappear, too, into the distant heat haze beyond the shining glass of the Grand Palais, and wondered what to do with the freedom she was taking, and which tomorrow to choose.

38

Evie

I failed, I told Jean, as soon as I arrived back at ROVS. She knows. I found her. But she got away.

I failed, too, he told me.

All he'd found had been a piece of paper skewered on a railing in the rue Jasmin – a torn-off bit of the German letter his father had been carrying around for days.

The entire Russian community was now mobilizing. But this didn't help a bit.

There were a lot of people already in the ROVS front office, and every hour brought more. The growing cast of characters wouldn't have been out of place in a Chekhov play. Men in uniforms, both the absurd imperial kind and the blue salopettes of Parisian workers, or in sombre suits; women in darned black European clothes or peasant headscarves, young, old, older, ancient . . . It was uproar. There were people rushing in and out, crying or shouting, some muttering darkly to whoever was next to them, some striking their heads in gestures of elaborate despair, some covering their eyes, some phoning (though it was beginning to seem to me that the entire Russian community of Paris was already here). Yet none of them were achieving a darn thing. It was true I couldn't understand what they were saying, and might be missing a nuance here or there. But I didn't need to. I'd never seen such a parade of uselessness.

In the small back room, which had been Skoblin's office, a particular type of despair was being addressed with vodka. Thank God, I thought – numbly watching mournful old men troop through the main room, one by one, on their way to the bathroom – that Jean never drinks.

Jean had got the secretaries ringing around every single place any White Russian had ever been to in Paris and beyond, in case, by some chance, General Miller had shown up there.

But no helpful information had come back from the Russian aristocratic estates – from Kovalyovsky's house at Meudon and Prince Troubetskoi's at Clamart, and even Petrovka, down near Marseilles, home of the Tian-shansky family – or, for that matter, from Madame Sabline's old people's home in the château which I'd once visited with Jean, or the host of other places with connections to Russia. Jean called the newsrooms of *Latest News* and *Renaissance*, the two biggest Russian-language papers, but they hadn't heard anything either.

No one had seen the General.

It was only when the delegation that had been seeing someone important off at the station thronged in, too, that one fragment of news about Skoblin filtered into the room. He'd briefly appeared on the station platform, looked dazedly around the group for a moment, said his wife was feeling unwell and he had to go to tend to her at the nearby café where he'd left her, then walked straight off towards the taxi rank. No one had seen him since, either.

The only result of all the telephone calls was that, one by one, people from all the various Russian organizations showed up at ROVS.

Jean and I sat, watching them mill about, in the dusk. Finally he lowered his forehead on to his hand.

'I should be doing something,' Jean said. He was pale. Well, he hadn't slept in twenty-four hours. But his voice was oddly bright and conversational. 'Not just sitting here helplessly, watching events unfold. But I have no idea what.'

'Call the police,' I whispered. 'You've got to.'

Jean shook his head. 'It wouldn't help,' he said. 'The French police can't understand foreigners – unless they're very definite ones, maybe, like Americans.' He looked at me. 'But we Russians, well, we're just ghosts to them. They can't pronounce our long names. We don't even have proper passports. And they know what an unlucky lot we are. Of course they steer clear. We're no good for cops who want flesh-and-blood people, with beginnings, middles and ends – people who leave evidence.'

'Well, change your luck! Don't give up! *Get* them some evidence, now!' I hissed. 'We need to talk all these idiots round! Show them the evidence and make them agree you can call the police, because there still might be time to get your father help – but only if you hurry.'

He looked at me. I could see he didn't know what I was talking about.

'Didn't you say you were always on at him to leave a note in his desk, saying where he'd gone?' I asked.

He nodded, looking utterly forlorn. 'But he didn't,' he said.

That wasn't what I wanted to hear. I shook my head.

'Perhaps you just didn't look properly,' I whispered determinedly. 'Perhaps you missed it. Which would be a pity, because *if* you had a note in your hand, signed by him – saying he was heading to the rue Jasmin with Skoblin to meet men he'd been told were German agents, but suspected it might be an ambush and Skoblin might be in cahoots with Moscow; and *if* it also told the reader to call out the police if he didn't come back by afternoon – well, then, the police would *have* to do something, wouldn't they?'

I opened my bag, pulled out a notebook and a pen and passed them over.

After a moment, he took them, and began to write.

It was a few more minutes before he slipped off to search his father's room again.

When he came back in, to what by now was the almost complete darkness of the front room, he announced his return by switching on the electric light.

The hubbub stopped. They all turned to stare.

Holding up a note, he began to speak to them in a voice that carried through the apartment, deeper and stronger with every word.

How I wished I understood. But, in a way, I *could* understand the really important part.

It was only after a surprisingly short crowd discussion, which ended with everyone muttering agreement, and after one of the secretaries had picked up the phone and was asking to be put through to the police, that Jean looked over at me, and nodded. There was a ghost of a smile on his face.

But the French police search was no more successful than the Russian hunt had been.

The second half of the General's letter was picked up before dawn, several miles away, in a quiet street not far from the market and slums of Les Halles. He must have dropped it. A baker's apprentice walking to work in the dark unscrewed the ball of thick, expensive paper, hoping for a banknote inside. When he saw official-looking German writing, then realized that the crumpled-up letter was lying outside an empty building whose green street door had been left gaping open, he reported a burglary in the hope of a reward.

Skoblin must have given the General a rendezvous at one end of Paris, then delivered him right across town to another address, and to his kidnappers, we worked out later.

The General must have had enough presence of mind to leave the letter, in pieces, as a trail. In due course it became known that the building with the green door belonged to the Soviet embassy. And it was immediately clear that he hadn't left it peacefully. Behind the green door the police found rags, rope and a used bottle of chloroform. An unknown van parked on the street for an hour at the end of the previous morning had blocked the traffic.

There were no more clues.

For a day or two, France's ports and borders were closed.

For a day or two, a public furore convulsed Paris.

Word got about that the kidnappers, who had

disappeared as completely as their victim, must be hiding in the Soviet embassy, where General Miller was probably also a prisoner. A crowd several thousand strong besieged the pretty mansion on the rue de Grenelle – not just White Russians, but reporters, police and ordinary Parisians like Gaston, too. They booed and roared and threw things when Monsieur Suritz, the ambassador, with his little Trotsky beard, came out to announce that the French police had no right to target Soviet territory, that he would not allow a search of his premises, and that anyway General Miller would not be found. But they could do no more than shout. The law was with the Soviets.

Thousands of scandalized words were published in the next day's papers about the kidnapping, the exotic murder habits of Russians, and the police investigation.

I spent those days, scratchy-eyed with exhaustion, imagining a truck trundling towards the ports of the north French coast, carrying a box which occasionally emitted bangs and groans. I imagined men in the cab, sweating and smoking cigarettes. Maybe one would have Skoblin's eyes, under a beret. I pictured the dread on their faces as the police flagged down their car – and then the smirks as they waved them on.

It was almost a relief once the crowds thinned and the newspapers found something new to write about, because our sense of failure was so crushing. I don't remember properly sleeping or eating in those few days. We sat in ROVS while people came and went. We dozed on armchairs. Occasionally I went upstairs for a change of clothes or a bath. Sometimes I slept for a few hours upstairs. Jean looked exhausted, with shadowed eyes. I don't know if he slept at all. If he did, he must have fallen asleep at the desk or on the sofa, at ROVS. Sometimes the police were at ROVS. Sometimes we were at the police station. There was a lot of talk. Nothing much mattered.

Jean was lost in a Russian world, barely speaking except in his native tongue. I could see that, by being there, and helping the ROVS people come to terms with what was happening to them – with what I could see was dignity – he was trying to be worthy of his father. As a true foreigner for the first time, someone who didn't speak the language everyone around me was talking, I understood so little of what went on that I was of no practical use. But I knew he wanted me there. He touched me, blindly, from time to time; reached for my hand, hugged me close. I knew from that alone how lost he felt. I couldn't leave him. Not for a moment.

But we couldn't talk, either. The only subject would have been the General, and his kidnappers, and the tragedy enveloping him, and this was too painful. I couldn't even think of the two people who'd destroyed him – for Skoblin and his wife had both vanished, and must both be equally guilty – though I heard their names come up all the time in the puzzled, angry, defeated (and otherwise incomprehensible) conversations in Russian all around me. Between ourselves, Jean and I certainly couldn't share out loud our private questions about where the General now was – if he was still alive at all: how long it took to reach Moscow by ship; whether he'd have survived until he met the interrogators waiting for him at journey's end; and the awful, formless terror of what might happen next. And I'd never now be able to ask Jean why he'd always done so much for, and been so loyal to, a man I thought so flawed. All I could do was respect his anguish, and observe the silence.

I knew too that home, for me, was now where Jean was. My search for Grandmother, which had started from some flickering memory of a past love of her, had maybe not led me to her Zhenya, as I'd hoped, but it had at least led me to find meaning in loving this man, here, now. Grandmother had shown me *my* Zhenya. I had to stay.

Still, I treasured the few moments when the gloom briefly lifted. Marie-Thérèse redirected her food packages downstairs, for all comers.

'You don't mind, mademoiselle? They're respectable, serious people, those ones,' she said to me in an undertone, putting down a giant tureen of soup on one of the secretaries' desks, talking as if she'd been trying to persuade me for some time that not all Russians were bad lots. 'Army officers. Hard-working family men. Educated. Not dirty thieves like that other lot – the Soviets.'

I nodded, almost relieved when she explained the other reason for her change of heart, sending a soft glance in the direction of Jean, who was talking to a policeman in a corner of the room.

'He's nearly as French as I am, that one, wherever his family came from,' she said approvingly from the doorway. 'A good lad. He doesn't deserve this.'

It was maybe the third or fourth evening, when all the light had leached out of the sky and there was hardly anyone left at ROVS, that our vigil ended. Jean woke me from my doze in a ROVS armchair. 'Can we sleep?' he said dully. 'I need to sleep.'

Arm in arm, we walked through the downstairs lobby, not stopping to look at the two policemen snoozing at either side of the door of the ROVS office. Slowly, we climbed the stairs.

Jean inclined his head questioningly towards the salon. But when I thought of all the spindly, uncomfortable chairs behind that door, I walked past it, leading him instead to my room.

To hell with what Marie-Thérèse might think. I didn't think she'd mind, anyway.

Nothing seemed to matter any more. I didn't believe there'd be a happy ending, or even any ending. I'd spent all those days listening to words I didn't understand, until I was stuck in the same dark fog as Jean had lived in for so long. Like him, I was by now just being swept helplessly along in the darkness.

We both collapsed heavily on to the bed. I barely had time to drop my shoes to the floor before sleep overcame me. We'd lost the General. He wasn't coming back.

39

Jean

I looked at her for a moment. It was nearly midnight, and Evie was asleep. She seemed so young, arm thrown across the bed, hair rumpled, with innocence in the flush of her cheek; so beautiful. Then I got up and went to the salon and sat down on the nearest lumpy chaise longue. I'd never felt more alone.

Before my father and I had reached Paris, while we were still living our nomadic existence and I still had hope, I'd been used to everything changing: a constant flux of cities, countries and conditions. Back then, I remembered, I'd thought that there was a meaning of some sort in this endless shifting, and that, one day, I'd come to understand it. Back in those days, I think I may even have believed that I would, could, stop my journey myself when I found myself in a place lovely enough that I no longer wished to move on. But all that actually happened was that we ended up in France, and couldn't keep travelling, and the infinite world in which I'd lived so many distant and miraculous lives dwindled to nothing more than endless driving round and round a cage of streets. That was when I realized I'd always been helpless to change my fate, and always would be.

But it had never occurred to me that things could get worse, or that I could lose more.

Now I had. These last couple of strange echoing days walking through Father's office, knowing he was gone yet always expecting to see him behind every door – how they hurt. Every moment I spent down there was fresh proof that, with him gone, I'd lost my past. I'd never understood, I realized now, how unmoored he and his comrades must always have felt with their past swept away. I hadn't understood, either, how unmoored I'd feel if it happened to me. And now here I was, at last, immersing myself in the ROVS environment that I'd always kept myself so aloof from, listening to the endless, aimless discussion about how to, or whether to, elect a replacement for Father, or just to accept defeat and disband ROVS altogether. Disbanding it was what I'd always wanted, wasn't it? Let the past go, I'd said, more times than I could remember. Stop hanging on to what's lost. Accept reality.

But now it was I who didn't want to let it go, or at least didn't want to let Father go. It was I who kept saying to the ancient colonels and generals and the young secretaries, 'But how sad he would be to hear . . .' and 'Surely you owe it to him to press on . . .' as if, by rallying the faltering troops, I might somehow bring Father back to pat me on the head and look proud and pin a medal on my chest.

He'd gone, and would never look at me again. There were so many other things I might also have thought about. But it was the way he'd always looked at me that I clung on to, inside my head. It was the one memory that was a comfort as well as a torment.

When I was just a kid in the forest, long ago, he'd found me crying once. I was in the camp boot room because I'd persuaded a bigger kid called Lyosha to let me help with the blacking. But Lyosha had been called off to do something else and I was on my own. I was a novice. My hands were all black and I'd smeared black on the wall. A nail in one of the boots had cut my hand. I was bleeding a bit from it. I suppose I was crying, without really knowing I was – scared kid's tears – when the big man came in and saw me. My first shamed instinct was to run off but he picked me up, right there in that little room. He didn't seem to notice that I was expecting a beating; he just looked very seriously at me out of his pale, wide-set eyes and then said, like a judgement, 'The full man doesn't understand the hungry man' – a proverb; he liked folksy proverbs. 'Let's get you something to eat, eh, little man.' I expect he got me some bread or soup next, though that's not the part I remember. What stayed with me was just that serious, slow, light-eyed look; the feeling it gave me that, probably for the first time, someone was really seeing me and my troubles for what they were.

That look had given me hope, and changed everything. That's what I'd lost. That's what I realized, now he was gone. Though of course he hadn't looked at me like that in a while. For the last few years, it had felt like me looking after him more than the other way round: handing him into the taxi and out; running errands. Maybe he'd been hurt that, in spite of all I owed him, I hadn't wanted to follow in his footsteps. Maybe he'd just got old, and weary, and preoccupied with his own business – with his military plotting, or his secret loves. Maybe there'd never even been quite as much promise in that look as I'd seen. He hadn't shared *his* private concerns with me, after all. Never. And recently I hadn't talked to him about . . . well, so many things; though what hurt most right now was that I'd never mentioned my friendship with Evie. He hadn't known, and this suddenly seemed one of the saddest things of all.

I wasn't going to think of where he might be now: of the boat, the box, the truck, the chloroform, the ropes. I wasn't going to think he might already be dead. He'd given me the capacity to hope, and I was going to hold on to it.

Even so, I was beginning to behave as though he might not reappear. For instance, earlier yesterday I'd taken an hour to make arrangements to have Katerina Ivan'na cared for at Madame Sabline's home, with her nurse – an insurance policy taken out by my father would, I'd discovered, cover the cost – so I could move to a room, alone.

Now, as I sat on the chaise longue in the salon, I resolved to tell Evie to go home to America. I was, I realized, more trapped in France than ever before. And watching her struggle with my reality was one of the worst parts of this new awfulness. I was dragging her down to my level of poverty and despair, and had no right to expect her to live in the swinish way I always had and always would. She deserved better.

Evie
I was woken by knocking at the apartment door, a quiet but insistent tattoo. It was past midnight, I saw, turning on the

lamp and glancing at the clock. Who'd come calling at this hour but the police?

Jean wasn't there. I got up, hunting for my shoes, and went out into the corridor. The lamp was on in the salon. I heard heavy breathing from the chaise longue. He'd fallen asleep there, with his legs and arms hanging uncomfortably off, I saw, looking with compassion at his face, careworn even in sleep. I didn't want to wake him unless I had to. I was hoping that, even if it was the police, I could deal with them myself.

'*Qui est là?*' I called quietly, with my hand on the lock. But no one answered. The quick knocking just went on, until it became more of a scrabbling of nails. It was clear now that it wasn't the police. I thought I could hear someone stifling sobs behind the door. I could feel the knot tighten in my stomach. I had to force myself to open up.

When I did, the door burst open on me. The person outside must have been leaning on it, because a large shape practically fell inside, half knocking me over.

Righting myself, I stared.

The last person I expected to see was Plevitskaya. She didn't look the same. She was tear-stained, wild-haired and still in the dress I'd last seen her in days earlier. She looked ten years older. And she was crumpled and smelly enough to have been sleeping rough. But it was Plevitskaya all right, and she was staring right back at me. She still looked defiant, but she looked so pitiful too.

For an instant I let myself wonder if she'd come to lead us to the General. But nothing in her ravaged face gave grounds for hope.

'I need to talk to Jean,' she said in a strangulated voice.

There was so much to say to this woman, who, in the past few days, had become such a monster in my mind, that I couldn't think what words to begin with. I started angrily shaking my head, but she just looked at me as though anything I might say would be superfluous, and marched on into the salon where the lamp glowed.

'No!' I called, thinking she was going to weep out some sort of terrible confession to him. I would have preferred her to tell *me* whatever it was, so I could do something to prepare him. 'For God's sake, leave him be!'

But I was too late. She'd hurled herself tremulously across the room and was on her knees beside him, shaking his arm. '*Sharik*,' she muttered, urgently, '*sharik . . .*'

And then, once she'd got him to open his eyes, and he was looking at her in rumpled, sleep-dazed horror, she grabbed him into a fierce embrace. '*Moi sharik . . .*' she cried, and then a whole lot more hysterical Russian with tears coursing down her face.

He sat up, trying to shake her off, but she went on clinging round his neck, sobbing. 'What the hell?' he half shouted, and I was surprised to hear that, even in his half-waking confusion, it was loud French that came out of his mouth, and not Russian. 'What are you doing here?'

I remembered that *sharik* meant 'little ball', and it was what the nuns had called Jean, because he'd come to them so fat. But what was *she* doing here, howling that word at him?

This wasn't at all what I'd thought I'd hear. I'd expected a torrent of incomprehensible words, sure enough, but also repentance, and shame, and a cowed demeanour. Not this ferocious embrace. Not this outpouring. Why, she hardly knew Jean, did she? She hadn't even known he wasn't the General's real son, the other day.

And then, suddenly, I thought I made out the word 'Zyzyrovka' in the torrent of words, and when she turned and pointed towards me, as if explaining something, a wild surmise filled me. Because hadn't she said that same word to me, recently, in the dressmaker's, when I'd started telling her about Jean being an orphan?

And hadn't she lost a little boy herself?

For a horrible moment, Jean froze in her embrace, looking suddenly ill, and then he started to struggle in earnest. He caught her arms and, pinioning her by the wrists, pushed her off him and held her as far away as possible.

'Zhenya!' she howled imploringly, and her elbow banged against a pile of my belongings – books and papers – that Marie-Thérèse had got out of my box. It all went flying. '*Zhenya!*'

I glanced down. There was a scatter of papers on the floor. Grandmother's letters, her diary, with its lock now broken open, the photo – but I couldn't move.

'Don't call me that,' he said in French. 'I'm not your Zhenya. You've got it all wrong.'

Still weeping, she said in thickly accented French, 'You had a little knitted ball on a string, round your wrist, a red one. So it wouldn't get lost.'

I looked from her tousled dark head to his, and waited. It sounded so very like what Jean had told me about how he'd been found.

'No,' he said, after another long pause, and his eyes were full of rage. 'I'm not your son. The father I love is the man you just helped kidnap. The man you and your husband betrayed. The one whose blood will be on your hands if he's gone for good.'

The energy went out of her. She stopped struggling. She drooped.

Over her head, Jean gave a wild, wolfish smile I'd never seen before. 'Evie,' he said, 'call the police. Call them now.'

40

Jean

Evie ran for the police while the woman I hated went on wailing. I shut my eyes and ears and heart. Even holding her at arm's length, I was still touching her, repelled by her damp skin and plump wrists under my hands. Her bones felt frail under my grip. I was aware of a murderous desire to squeeze tighter . . .

The police separated us in the end and took her away.

I wouldn't look. I was determined not to give her a single memory to pick over in her cell.

But when the door had shut behind them, and Evie had come to me, I shifted myself so I could see out of the window on to the street before I opened my arms to accept the comfort she was offering.

I didn't intend to, but when they led that woman out into the car outside, I couldn't resist looking down over the top of Evie's head at Plevitskaya's, just for a moment.

She couldn't be right, that woman. Even the thought of what she'd said made me feel unclean. It simply must be an insane fantasy that I could be her son, the flesh of her flesh.

And yet, as I looked down, my gorge rose at the realization that her hair was as dark as mine.

She couldn't be right. But, then again, perhaps she could – because perhaps the lost past she'd entered into was a place where any dream could come true, and any nightmare too.

If only I remembered something about the mother who'd lost me: eyes, a voice, a song – anything. But there was nothing I could cling on to as a defence against the horrible, invasive doubt that woman had left me with. All I could remember was the fantasy mothers I'd imagined for myself, years ago – young, pretty, attentive mothers out of books, girls out of Tolstoy, girls like Kitty Shcherbatskaya, with pink cheeks and shyly sparkling eyes and an infinite capacity for kindness and little hands in muffs (mothers whom I'd then stopped imagining, because they were part of the absurdity of fantasizing about the lost past, and I didn't approve of that).

Shutting my eyes again, I tried to remember *those* other hands and arms, the ones I'd so recently had in mine and wanted to crush. Were they, could they be, like mine? Recognizably related? But all I could recall was the way my own flesh had crept at the feel of hers.

But Plevitskaya hadn't always been old, I told myself. She hadn't always looked the way she did now. And I knew she'd only met Skoblin later, during the retreat, when she'd been arrested by the Whites and ended up marrying her jailor, so there was no point in calling *his* hated face to mind; it would be an earlier husband who'd fathered me. The dark way I looked, so different from the fair man I called Father – colours, yet also the line of toenail and fingernail

334

and shoulder, all those biological codes that meant nothing but everything – might as easily be an inheritance from that possible unknown father, as from her. If she was right. Which she couldn't be.

Outside, the car door slammed. The engine started. Evie stirred and raised worried eyes to mine.

'Was there really a Zyzyrovka . . .?' Evie began. But when she saw my expression she quickly looked down. The car roared away. 'Of course not,' she went on in a whisper.

The horrifying thing was that I thought there might really have been a village with a name something like that, not all that far away from the nunnery. I vaguely remembered the signboard on the road, under the pines – a whitewashed board, rotting softly away, with the last letters missing in a fringe of splinters. I was almost sure there had been a 'Z' at the beginning of that board.

'She's wrong . . . or crazy,' Evie whispered, her face hidden against my chest. 'You know that, don't you?'

But I didn't know. In any case, I couldn't do anything right then but sway on my feet, because, all at once, I'd been assailed by a mental picture of Father as he might be now. He was in torn and crumpled clothes, with grey stubble on his chin, backing away towards a damp wall from men I couldn't see who meant him harm. He wasn't the reassuring, all-knowing hero any more. He was a terrified wreck. And when I imagined him like that I, too, found myself melting into the kind of hot, childish panic that might once have turned into tears.

I wasn't going to weep. He'd brought me up to be strong. If there was one thing I *could* cling to in all this, it was the conviction that I had to be worthy. I was an officer's son, or I'd been raised as one.

'We'll talk tomorrow,' I said brusquely. I let go, ignoring the hurt look on Evie's face. 'I'm going down to the office now. I need to be alone. I need to think.'

I needed to be down in the messy darkness of the office because the poster of Plevitskaya was still in the lobby. She wasn't young in it, or thin, but she was younger and thinner. I pulled it off the wall, and took it into Father's office, which still smelled of him. 'I'm sorry to bring her in here, Father,' I muttered. 'But I have to know.'

I stood by the cloudy mirror in the uncertain lamplight, looking at her face, then mine. Her hair was as dark as mine, but it was so greased down that you couldn't tell whether it could ever be wild like mine. Her eyes were dark while mine were light, but was there something similar in the cast of them? She was much shorter than me. Hands, legs . . . I couldn't know.

I looked all night, and I thought all night about Father, and his fearful eyes against that concrete wall. I thought of all I owed him. I thought about blood and family, duty and honour.

And as I thought I opened his bottle. I drank one draught. It went down like fire. Then I drank another, with nothing to eat between gulps that might have soaked up the alcohol. And then another.

I was still thinking about Father, and still looking at myself in the glass and then at the ripped-off poster of Plevitskaya when, at dawn, the police inspector came in. He was a thin man whom I'd heard talk to his subordinates in rough Parisian *argot*, with a fag hanging out of his mouth, but who spoke to me in elaborate sentences full of complicated tenses and arcane bureaucratese.

The inspector nodded when he saw the poster. He wanted to tell me about what that woman had said during her preliminary interrogation. She'd informed him that Father was bound for Leningrad on board a Soviet freight ship. Madame Plevitskaya was being further interrogated, he said, and might be lying to mask some other reality, and the ship was out of contact, and might be innocent; but, at least, it was a clue.

I heard Evie's footsteps, padding down the stairs and into the secretaries' room where she waited. I was glad she wasn't in the room with us to see me struggle to maintain composure. The inspector, grinding out his cigarette end, was so excited with his clue that he couldn't stop grinning as he left. Tact was not his forte. What struck me was that Father was as good as dead if he was a prisoner being taken to Soviet Russia – that he might as well be cowering against a crumbling wall as the brutes in my dream approached, because that was how he'd end up, sooner or later.

'I'm going to Russia to find him,' I told Evie when, in her nightdress, she brought me tea on the bone-hard sofa. 'I have no choice. I have to try to get him out.'

I made my voice hard. I didn't want to sound weak. I couldn't sound weak if I was going to Russia.

By now, dawn was breaking and the sun was turning the Parisian sky rosy pink. Even as I spoke, and looked out of the window at the horrible loveliness of a new day, I knew it was impossible for me to go to Russia. What would I do, after all, without documents? Steal a passport? Stow away on another Soviet freighter? Drive my rented taxi to Poland and walk east? Go and ask the Soviet ambassador in Paris to give me a visa and help me find a hotel in Moscow?

That wasn't the point. That wasn't the point. There was only one point.

If Nadezhda Plevitskaya really was my mother – which meant my own flesh and blood being to blame for Father's destruction – I had a debt of honour. Truculently, I told myself if Evie respected me she'd understand.

Evie took my hand in hers. She looked very sad. But she nodded. I should have been grateful, I knew, that she didn't say a word.

'I owe it to him,' I said, knowing it was stupid to half wish she'd argue. 'I must put things right.'

She tightened her grip. 'Yes.' She bowed her head. 'I love you,' she said simply. 'I understand how terrible this is for you.'

For a moment, I felt sorry for both myself and this girl, as all the happiness I'd imagined coming to the two of us, in a shared future that would not now exist, flowed away. What had been between the two of us felt distant, now, as if I was only seeing our illusory might-have-been, this last time, from behind thick, thick glass. I was with Father already, in that cell; we were facing our tormentors together.

Perhaps Evie didn't understand how little chance there was I'd come back? Didn't she see that I was going, willingly, to an almost certain death? The thought of my heroism brought to my eyes tears that – even in that moment – I knew to be cheap and sentimental. Vodka tears.

My death would be the only way to avenge his, I told myself. My sacrifice for him would be the only way to show the Nightingale how completely I denied whatever blood tie linked me to her, and how fully I chose instead the man who'd raised me, as the parent I would shed my own blood for. I had to die to expiate that woman's sin.

'I'm sorry,' I said stiffly, wondering why my tongue felt so thick in my mouth. I was tired, mortally tired. I could barely get words out. My voice was slurring. My limbs were heavy. The room was going round. 'Sorry . . . about *us*. But you must see . . . this comes first.'

'Yes,' she said. 'I do see.' She looked at me – a serious, calm, careful look that showed me, even in my lurching drunkenness, that she really could see my worries. For a moment, as the stuffy room lurched like a ship's cabin, I felt – just a little – comforted.

'But first you must sleep,' she said.

I shook my head. 'Got to go now.'

'Just lie on the sofa. We'll talk again when it's a bit lighter. I'll get dressed. I'll help you make a plan. I promise I will.'

I was swaying on my feet. She found the blanket in the cupboard.

I let her tuck it round me on the divan. She took away the bottle and the glass and closed the shutters.

I'd never sleep, I knew that. Never. But I shut my eyes.

41

Jean

It was evening when I woke up, the quiet golden hour when the air is honey. She was sitting at the desk reading, and had a plateful of rye-bread *buterbrody* with pickled herring waiting at her elbow.

My head was pounding, my tongue cleaving to the dry roof of my mouth.

This was why I never drank, and why I despised drinkers: *this* – the sick shame that came after that vain hunt for courage at the bottom of a bottle. I shook my head at the hangover cures on that plate that some knowing Russian must have assembled.

She smiled, and passed me a glass of milk. How beautiful she was. How calm she looked – happy almost – as though nothing could dent her tranquillity.

I couldn't quite yet remember anything beyond how bad I felt, except how good it was that she was here. In a moment, I knew, some awful reality would explode over me. But I wanted to stay here for a little longer, in the fragile peace of her presence, before I let myself call it to mind. I wanted to be in her world, in that still calm.

'We've all been talking about it out there,' she said. 'About Plevitskaya believing that she was your mother.' She paused. 'The secretaries,' she went on, very softly, as if worried that her voice might crack open my head. 'The colonels.'

The knowledge of what had happened to my father was beginning to return now, and the fear of who my mother might have been. I groaned, and put my hands to my clanging head. The memory of what I now had to do was coming back as well, and so was the darkness that went with it.

'And the colours are wrong,' she added. 'Have you noticed?'

I could feel helpless tears start up. They were real tears, these, and it was the kindness in her voice that had made them prickle into life. I closed my eyes. In a minute I'd have to go, set off on my impossible journey, or I'd be completely unmanned.

But for now I just lay there and listened to the echo of her words in my head.

'Your eyes are blue, and hers are dark. You don't get blue-eyed children from dark-eyed parents. And the toy on your wrist, the little ball, was white, not red.'

The sickness was still swimming around my body. I didn't remember telling her the toy on my wrist had been white, just light-coloured (though I probably hadn't told her, either, that by the time the nuns saw it they said it stank too badly of shit to be saved; there was so much that would always be beyond words). And now everything was too confusing, and I didn't remember. But something was lightening inside me.

'But . . .' I said, or maybe I didn't say anything, because perhaps it had been white.

'None of them believes a word of it,' she said. 'Every colonel and general in the office says they remember a village called "Zi" something or "Zna" something near every town in the war from Poland to Siberia. The village name means nothing. She just so wanted to find the son she loved, and the past she'd lost, that she let herself believe it was you.'

Evie looked towards the window. There was sadness in her eyes.

'Poor Plevitskaya,' she murmured, almost to herself. 'She thought she was giving herself up for love. She thought she'd found her long-lost child, and she wanted to prove to you that, whatever she'd done, she wasn't as bad as she knew you'd think her. And now they'll execute her, or give her twenty years' hard labour – but she gave herself up for nothing. You're not her son. It was all a delusion; maybe looking for the past always is.'

'I still have to . . .' I started weakly, but the combination of my uncertain insides and the tears pouring down my cheeks stopped me. Anyway, I didn't need to finish the sentence. She knew what I'd been going to say. She had the answer.

'You won't find your father if you try to go back to Russia.' She still sounded faraway and a little sad. But she turned her gentle gaze back on me. 'You'll just meet the awful end he spent half his life trying to save you from, twenty years late,' she said. 'It would be the worst thing he could imagine, that you'd do that – give yourself up. It would make you like her. And it would make his life meaningless.'

I couldn't sit up. But I did, gratefully, stretch out my hand to touch hers.

And, there in that room, at that time of complete failure, something changed. When the woman who meant everything to me looked into my eyes with that quiet depth of understanding, and saw me truly, she absolved me from my past and set me free.

I didn't understand that at the time. All I knew was that she squeezed my hand back, and said, 'He wanted you to live. So live. Stay with me.'

My father was never found. People said, afterwards, that they thought the Reds might have got him all the way to Moscow, like Kutyopov before him, to have secrets tortured out of him (if he knew any secrets). We never found out how he died.

Skoblin disappeared forever too. Rumour had it that he was smuggled out of France by the Soviets via the Spanish war, and was killed there.

The past was shutting down on all sides. ROVS was closed. The office apartment was sold. The proceeds went to fund Madame Sabline's old people's home.

It was late autumn before Plevitskaya's trial opened.

In the dock she was full of artifice. Every inch the show-woman, she wore black. She pleaded tearfully that she knew nothing, and was just a simple woman duped by her disappearing husband. We were in the gallery. We could see people – other women mostly – nod and sigh sympathetically. And then the code books that had been found in the cat baskets at her home were brought into the courtroom, and the experts who knew what the strings of

343

numbers meant, and it turned out she'd been in it up to the hilt. But she didn't turn a hair. She was no coward. You could see she was going to go down fighting. 'Yes, my husband liked to write numbers in those books,' she said, and her voice trembled helplessly. 'But *I – I* am a woman. I have *never* understood numbers. I have *no idea* what he was writing.' And the women leaning over the gallery sighed and tutted again.

I still hated Plevitskaya. Of course I did. There was no doubt she'd helped destroy my father. She wasn't even repentant. But it wasn't the same, now I knew she wasn't my blood. I looked at her from the back row of the gallery (I didn't want to be near, or have her see me), and felt distant from her, and all the strange, sad workings of the past that had drawn her and her fellow conspirators into their wickedness.

The start of the trial didn't bring the emotional release I'd hoped for either. At the end of the first day I got up feeling oddly empty and unsatisfied. When Plevitskaya was led back to her cell, Evie turned to me and said, 'It will go on for weeks more, you know.'

She looked as uncertain as I felt.

'She's nothing to us any more, is she?' Evie said as we walked out into the evening, all wind and bluster and the last of the falling leaves, smelling of decay. 'Let's not torment ourselves going over the whole thing again. It won't change anything. Let's go away.'

I knew she missed home. She'd been writing long letters to her mother and stepfather and an aunt and to friends in New York while we waited for the trial.

'We can't,' I said.

'Why not?' She linked her arm in mine and looked up at me.

We walked on.

It was true, in a sense, I realized. There was nothing holding me back any more. It had never occurred to me that freedom might come so easily – might sneak in through the back door without my even noticing. Even when she said, 'Because I want to take you home with me to New York,' I just went on shaking my head, half in negation, half simply in surprise.

'But I can hardly speak English,' I said.

'You'll learn,' she replied. 'I'll teach you more words on the boat.'

'I'm not going to live on your money,' I said.

'You can't,' she agreed. 'I've got some, but not enough to support us both in style forever. We'll have to do something. We can open a bookshop.'

'I'd be like your orphan, in New York, without friends; I don't want to be anyone else's orphan,' I said.

'Ach, you won't,' she said. 'You're a great adapter, and anyway you won't depend on me for long. Your writer buddies will all be leaving here too as soon as they get papers, won't they? They'll want someone who's already settled over there. You'll have plenty of old friends round you soon enough. And there'll be new ones too. I think you'll like mine.'

When I ran out of objections but still looked doubtful, she smiled. 'There's no past where I'm from, Jean,' she said. 'Just the future. Take a chance.'

And I nodded, because – setting my pride aside – of course I didn't want to be an émigré any more. I never had.

345

I wanted to arrive somewhere for good and have a real life.

But then I caught my breath, because she was looking up at me in that determined way I'd come to love so dearly. 'But we'd have to marry for you to get a visa, and you haven't asked,' she said, and her smile was a challenge.

'But I don't want you to think I want to marry you just for papers,' I said anxiously.

She took no notice of that, except that her smile broadened.

Then she stopped walking. I could tell she was waiting.

We'd walked all the way to the rue du Colisée by then. We were outside number 29, that familiar building with the shuttered ground-floor windows where Father had once been. There was litter swirling in the wind, and a round white street lamp cast imitation moonlight on Evie's upturned face. Her eyes shone brightly with its glow.

'We choose our families, and I choose you,' I said, finally knowing that what I was about to do was good, and right, and that Father would have approved. 'Will you marry me?'

EPILOGUE

The American Boy

Jean

And so here I was in a new city, on a dark December afternoon, with eddies of snow swirling around me and a brutal wind that wouldn't have been out of place in Siberia, looking at the black East River as we walked along a road with a number – E 58, E 59? – towards Evie's family's house.

I was nervous about meeting them. I'd spent the time since I'd got here being gawped at like a zoo animal. There was a clumsy kindness in all her friends' eyes. A whole crowd of bright-eyed innocents had been coming by at all hours to stare at me since we had arrived, two or three days before, in the big but crowded bare-boards apartment above a bakery, somewhere far away in a less intimidatingly rich part of town, where we were staying. (Two girls lived there, Eliza and Dorothy. There was no furniture to speak of, only boxes for tables and a few broken-down chairs and mattresses on the floors. The room they'd put us in was speckled with paint; Evie's grandmother's paintings, when they arrived, were going to fit right in.)

For tonight, Evie had taken me shopping for a Brooks

Brothers suit. The shirt had a stiff collar that rubbed. She'd insisted it was proper to wear the astonishingly colourful argyle socks I couldn't feel sure about. If anything, the dressing up had made me feel even more like an exotic pet animal. I was aware that the family I was about to meet would find my broken English as comical as Evie's friends clearly did, and might think me a fortune-hunter too. But I was keeping my reservations in check, because, after hearing so much about these people, I was curious.

It was Evie who looked most nervous, swinging that big bag she insisted on carrying herself, biting her lip.

Evie

We were sitting in the familiar bower of orchids and gardenias, on the yellow silk cushions, watching Mother pour out pale tea into near-transparent cups. I'd almost forgotten how big this room was, and how immaculate Florence always kept everything. It didn't feel half as fussy and suffocating as I'd remembered. It just felt a pleasure to be back, breathing in air scented by those colourless but exotic flowers.

There was a more robust and cheerful smell in the air today, too, of roasting pumpkin and poultry, reminding me how, after whisking in here with the tray and the petits fours, a shiny-faced Florence had stared approvingly at Jean, grinned at me, and rushed back to the kitchen to go on masterminding the Thanksgiving cooking. Hughie would be along to join us in an hour; the cousins would start appearing later for dinner.

Meanwhile, here we were, the three of us. So far Mother was coping well with meeting my Russian husband. Perhaps it was just that she knew we'd had to marry for him to get into the country, but to my relief there'd been none of the pursed lips, averted eyes and chill I'd rather feared – not even when I said that his job, for now, would be translating for an émigré association, but that we were looking for a premises in the Village to set up a small bookshop with a Russian section.

'Welcome, welcome,' Mother kept saying, smiling and smiling and fussing over the cup with her sugar tongs and slivers of lemon before passing it to Jean. His English was still uncertain, so he wasn't saying much in reply. But he looked back at her, suddenly, with a tenderness I hadn't expected, and, to be honest, didn't really like either.

She glanced up at Jean from under her long eyelashes. She took the second cup of tea for herself. The third stood steaming but forgotten on the tray. It would have been absurd for me to spoil the moment by asking for it to be passed to me.

Of course I should just have been pleased that Jean and she were getting on so well. But, for a moment, all I did feel was a familiar helpless disappointment. For a moment, I felt too tall, and awkward, and not half pretty enough, again – as much the overgrown child no one quite knew what to do with as I'd ever been.

But only for a moment. Because once Jean had finished smiling back at her, he turned to me, and gave me a crinkly-eyed half-smile and a faint, but very encouraging, nod, and passed me his cup.

He didn't withdraw his hand, either, once I'd taken the tea. He put it lightly on my elbow. And he moved his chair, so he was just a bit closer, and facing just a little more towards me. Relief flooded through me. It felt as transforming as if he'd shouted, 'I see!' and 'I'm here!' and 'Don't forget you'll always have me!'

Mother looked briefly puzzled. Then she laughed gaily and said, to him, in her sweetest voice, 'Oh my! Do please forgive my absentmindedness, I forgot all about the tea; I'm so hopeless these days . . .' and passed Jean the neglected third cup.

She still had eyes only for him. But, with his hand on my arm, it suddenly didn't matter.

I leaned forward and kissed her cheek. I suddenly wanted to show her that I'd stopped being the kind of thoughtless young girl who'd just take off overseas on a whim, leaving a provokingly uninformative note on my pillow (though Mother had been surprisingly forgiving about that when I'd first called, as soon as we'd docked, and rather nervously apologized. 'We did worry, darling; but we hoped – well, we were sure – that you'd know you could tell us if you needed help,' was all she'd said, in a careful voice, as if she'd taken the trouble beforehand to think out an answer that would absolve me of blame and then committed it to memory. I was grateful at this proof that she'd been trying to understand how we could get on now I was an adult; I wanted to try too). It felt a shock when, from close up, her eyes met mine. 'It's lovely to be back, Mother,' I said. 'I missed you.' I thought I saw all kinds of emotions flit across her face – relief, surprise, maybe, and maybe a note of shyness, too. Or perhaps that was just what I was feeling.

There was so much we'd never be able to say to each other, she and I. I could see that too. Even if she hadn't found my bookishness and travel whims odd and threateningly unconventional, she was too much of a man's woman ever to feel entirely comfortable with another female in the room. But we'd get by.

I got out the box from the bag I'd put at my feet. It was a capacious old one of Grandmother's, and the sight of it reminded me of all the other things of Grandmother's I'd left behind in Paris. I'd given her car and fur coat to Gaston and Marie-Thérèse, and – in private – also got Marie-Thérèse to choose one of the Fabergé trinkets as a keepsake. (I'd been rather relieved when, looking overwhelmed and close to tears, the one the housekeeper had picked out had been the reddish jewelled dog I liked least.)

My heart started beating faster.

After the police had taken Plevitskaya away, I'd picked up the broken remains of Grandmother's now-opened diary. By then, my quest to know her hadn't seemed that important, compared with everything else happening around us. But I still wanted to know what was in it. Of course, there was nothing much except inconsequential nonsense – recent lists of scrappy pros and cons that we couldn't understand, often headed, 'Tell M?' ('She must have been very indecisive,' Jean said drily later, when I showed him.) But there was one more old letter that we hadn't read, one which must have been tucked inside. Grandmother had clearly never sent it. It was from her, soon after her husband had been killed, addressed to the lover she'd left. She must have written it while on her way home, halfway across the world, from Russia. I could see why she hadn't sent it, of course. It was too full of pain – a tearful mess of bleak, hopeless phrases from 'I can't live without you' to 'I'm expecting a baby'.

Now I caught Jean noticing the little furrowing of Mother's brow above her wide-set pale eyes – an expression that, I could see, reminded him of his father – and nodding slightly.

I'd never be able to tell Mother about Jean's thoughtful voice, saying, 'Of course, Zhenya is also a girl's name . . . Yevgeniya. As you'd say in English, Eugenie.' Or my small reply: 'Or Jeannie, for short. My mother's name.'

For a moment, after that conversation on a gusty afternoon on deck, I'd forgotten Jean altogether. No wonder Grandmother had been unable to settle at home on her return from Russia, I thought, or love her newborn daughter. It must have felt too painful to bear, to look every day at a small face so like the adult one she couldn't be with, and to know she'd never be able to tell her secret to the familiar people around her back home. No wonder she'd left the European clinic where they'd sent her to convalesce, and gone off to hide until it was too late, and she'd been locked out forever. But Aunt Mildred hadn't been altogether wrong to keep her away, either, because her sister's flightiness and pain must have been very visibly damaging the child she'd left behind. Look at how Mother had grown up, so anxious to lead the conventional life, still playing the cosseted, manipulative, little-girl darling of an older husband. Poor Mother, too – because who wouldn't do anything to be loved, after being abandoned like that? And then I'd come back down to earth, and put all those thoughts aside, and smiled up at my new husband, who was smiling rather quizzically back at me.

He was right. I'd never be quite sure enough that I'd understood the past right. There was no way of checking.

I couldn't know for sure which Zhenya Grandmother had had in mind when she scribbled the name on a piece of blotting paper. I could only be grateful that, in Paris, I'd found my future with Jean.

At least I could, now, see more clearly why Grandmother had loved that poem about the unknown woman. I'd warmed to the yearning of those lines, because I'd thought she might have been thinking about me. But it was just as likely, wasn't it, that, all along, she'd been thinking of the child she'd run away from and lost?

So tonight I'd brought along the box of gifts sent to Grandmother, long ago, by her lover. I couldn't say who Zhenya was. But I wanted Mother to hear that her mother had been thinking of her at the last. I wanted Mother to have her mother's jewels.

Author's Note

Far-fetched though it might seem, the Russianized Paris of the twenties and thirties was very much as I have described it here – plots, kidnappings and all.

Nearly two hundred thousand White Russians who escaped from Russia after the 1917 Revolution came to live in France. By the late twenties, Paris was the cultural and political centre of the diaspora.

Paris had Russian-language newspapers, a literary scene, a theatre, schools, night classes, orphanages, an old people's home or two, a cathedral and many restaurants. Many émigrés were gentlemen ex-officers who'd fought the Reds. Most were now broke. It became a cliché that Paris in the twenties and thirties was full of former grand dukes working as doormen or waiters or in car and yoghurt factories, princesses sewing or modelling for the rag trade and city taxis driven by former White officers. The Union of Russian Cab Drivers had three thousand members just before World War II.

Paris Russians lived mostly around rue Vaugirard (in the 15th arrondissement), around place des Ternes, rue Daru, rue Pierre-le-Grand, and rue de la Néva (in the 8th and

the 17th), and in outlying areas like Issy-les-Moulineaux,
Vincennes and Boulogne-Billancourt.

The exiles had expected (and been expected) to return
to Russia when the Bolshevik revolt faded. But, when it
didn't, visible European and American support for the
Whites' plans to overthrow the Reds became covert and
then vanished.

Because the Bolshevik government had stripped the
exiles of their citizenship shortly after taking power, the
White Russians became stateless persons as soon as France
recognized the USSR in 1924. An international commission
was formed to give them travel documents called Nansen
passports – usually known as 'nonsense passports'.

At first the Russians at least got French sympathy. But
by the time the Thirties and the Depression came, and
there weren't enough jobs to go around, they'd outstayed
their welcome. The sense of loss every Russian lived with
festered, in a few, as a hatred of communism so virulent
that the opposite extreme of fascism – then taking shape
in Germany and Italy and Spain – exerted a pull. For a
few, this rage translated into violence. In 1932, a Russian
immigrant called Pavel Gorgulev assassinated the French
President, Paul Doumer, who, he said, hadn't done enough
for the White Russians.

In their turn, the Bolsheviks infiltrated White Russian
organizations and compromised every political opposition
movement. The Russian expatriate community was riven
by suspicion and double-dealing. It was impossible to tell
who was with you and who was in the pay of the Soviet
secret agents from the Cheka, later known as the NKVD
(and later still as the KGB). Many figures were lured back

into Russia where they were arrested and executed.

In 1930 a kidnap team from Soviet Moscow snatched and 'disappeared' the head of what was left of the White Army, General Kutyopov. He was never seen again.

His replacement at the White Army successor body, known as ROVS or the Russian General Military Union, was General Yevgeny Karlovich Miller, a White Russian officer of German ancestry.

On 22 September 1937, ROVS's intelligence chief Nikolai Skoblin led General Miller to a Paris safe house, where he was to meet with two German Abwehr agents. The agents were not who they appeared to be. They were in fact officers of the Soviet NKVD disguised as Germans. They drugged Miller, placed him in a steamer trunk and smuggled him aboard a Soviet ship in Le Havre.

However, Miller left behind a note to be opened if he failed to return from the meeting. In it he detailed his suspicions about Skoblin.

French police launched a massive manhunt, but Skoblin could not be found. However, Skoblin's wife, the gypsy singer Nadezhda Plevitskaya, was arrested, convicted and sentenced by a French court to twenty years in prison. She died behind bars just a couple of years later.

We now know that Skoblin fled to the Soviet embassy in Paris and was eventually smuggled to Barcelona, where the Second Spanish Republic refused to extradite him to France. After that the trail goes dead.

We have also learned since the Soviet Union collapsed in 1991 that the NKVD successfully smuggled General Miller back to Moscow, where he was tortured and summarily shot nineteen months after the kidnapping, on 11 May

1939. According to General Pavel Sudoplatov, who proudly described the whole kidnap plot on Russian TV decades later, 'His kidnapping was a cause célèbre. Eliminating him disrupted his organization of Tsarist officers and effectively prevented them from collaborating with the Germans against us.' Copies of letters written by Miller while he was imprisoned in Moscow are in the Dimitri Volkogonov papers at America's Library of Congress.

I've always been fascinated by this wistful, desperate, shifting, duplicitous world-within-a-world (which more or less vanished soon after the time of my book, as the Second World War prompted many Paris Russians to carry on west to the USA).

Of course, as a student of Russian, I read about these waifs and strays in the literature they wrote. Famously, Vladimir Nabokov's novel *Lolita* features a Colonel Taxovich, a stocky, platitudinous White Russian who's been reduced – of course – to driving a taxi and has become infatuated with the narrator Humbert Humbert's first wife.

Nabokov himself lived in Paris from 1931, after Berlin, where he had initially taken refuge in the wake of the Revolution, became too dangerous for him and his Jewish wife. He is a rich source of amusing stories about émigré life (I reference his pen name, Sirin, in my story, as a bit of an *hommage*. The first short story Nabokov ever wrote in the English language was a mocking feuilleton about the General Miller of this book).

Less well known today is another wonderful Paris Russian writer, Gaito Gazdanov. It's his work that has really shaped how I see the White Russians of Paris – especially his novel *Night Roads*, which gives an autobiographical account of what it was to be an angry young man from the Russian diaspora driving a taxi by night and struggling to become a writer. That was my starting point for imagining my male lead, Jean.

My interest isn't only from books. My first Russian teacher, Nina Wilsdon, *née* Brodyanskaya (another name that crops up in this story), was from one of these Paris émigré families. And, while learning Russian at university, I had a taste of the life myself when I spent five months in a White Russian school-turned-monastery-turned-language centre at Meudon, just outside Paris.

So perhaps my fascination grew out of the stories I heard in all these classrooms, too.

At any rate, I still can't think of anything braver than the sheer cussedness of those early twentieth-century exiles, people so brutally expelled from their past and so incredibly down on their luck, who just wouldn't give up trying to find a future.